Fire and Ivy

Todd W. Hiller

Halo
PUBLISHING
INTERNATIONAL

ISBN: 978-1-61244-834-3
Library of Congress Control Number: 2020906780

Printed in the United States of America

Halo Publishing International
8000 W Interstate 10
Suite 600
San Antonio, Texas 78230
www.halopublishing.com
contact@halopublishing.com

For my family and friends.
Thank you for believing in me.

Contents

Prologue

"Claiborne Area Dispatch. What's your emergency?"

"Help…"

"Hello, sir, what is your emergency? Sir, are you all right? Is anyone there?"

"Dispatch to forty-five, respond to sixty-three Rudley Street for a nine-one-one call. Caller said something I couldn't understand and, I believe, disconnected. Could be a possible eighty-one, but respond code two."

The dispatcher heard a sound on the other end of the emergency line. The caller hadn't hung up. She closed her eyes and listened. She heard crackles, like someone walking on broken glass. It sounded fast and alive. It sounded like fire. She practically shouted into her headset. "Sir! Sir, can you hear me? Is there a fire at your location? Where in your house are you?"

Nothing.

"Dispatch to forty-five and forty-seven, I've got a possible building fire at sixty-three Rudley Street. Respond code one. Dispatch to engine two, ladder four, rescue seven, Ambulance eighty-one, battalion one, respond to sixty-three Rudley Street for a possible building fire. Time out, four twenty-seven."

She listened into her headset and tried getting a response from the caller. Each time she got no answer. All she heard was what sounded like a train heading through a subway tunnel. Fire. Growing, living, breathing fire. Louder and faster, the sound was like an open-mouthed scream growing louder and louder and louder. And then, silence.

"Forty-five to dispatch, I'm on scene. Heavy smoke showing. Vehicles in the driveway. Given the early morning hour, I'm going to assume we've got people inside."

"Roger, forty-five. Heavy smoke showing. Occupants believed to be inside the dwelling, four thirty."

"Forty-five to dispatch, fire is getting bad pretty quickly. Trying to see inside the structure."

She held her breath. Being a dispatcher was a job that always required you to keep your cool, but she felt her throat tightening every time she tried to speak into her headset microphone. Her hands were cold, and she felt them start to ache. She realized they were clenched in tight fists.

"Battalion one to dispatch, I'm on scene. Engine two, ladder four also on scene. Heavy smoke from the A side. I'll be out investigating."

"Roger, battalion one, engine two, ladder four on scene, four thirty-two."

She wondered if the smoke had gotten heavier or if the flames had broken through the smoke. Her pulse quickened.

"Rescue seven to dispatch, on scene."

"Roger, rescue seven on scene, four thirty-three."

She stared at the screen of her computer, waiting. It seemed to be getting closer and smaller. She could feel her pulse getting heavy in her forehead, and her eyes began to strain. As she sat there, the seconds felt like an eternity. Just as she began to reach for her mic, she heard a heavy-breathing battalion chief huff into the radio.

"Battalion one to dispatch, heavy fire from the C side. We've got a working basement fire. Neighbor reports occupants in the building. I repeat, occupants in the building. I need another alarm. Engine six, ladder twelve, rescue nine. Full response."

She blinked quickly, trying to come out of the trance she had almost fallen into.

"Roger, battalion one." Her hands flew over the keyboard. "Dispatch to engine six, ladder twelve, rescue nine, respond to sixty-three Rudley Street for a building fire. Reported by battalion one to be a working basement fire. Your time out, four thirty-eight."

"Battalion one to engine six, when you get here, grab the hydrant on the corner of Wyatt and lay into the scene. Get a line stretched and charged to the A side door. Engine two's crew is finishing the primary search on the first floor. Ladder twelve, head to the B side, bravo side, and park on Dexter Street. I want ladders to the A side second-floor windows. Let's see if we can get on the roof in the C-D corner to vent some of that smoke on the first floor."

"Engine six copies."

"Ladder twelve, roger."

Sweat beads collected on her forehead and on the tiny hairs on the back of her neck as she waited for her radio to crackle to life.

"Ladder twelve to battalion one, we've got ladders up. We're headed to the roof to vent."

"Battalion one copies. Call engine six's crew before you vent. They just headed in with a line to attack the fire as best they can."

"Ladder twelve, roger."

"Engine six to ladder twelve, we've got no access to the basement. The stairwell is fully engulfed. I repeat, no access to the basement. We're gonna back out to the A side door. Go ahead and open that roof. If we get the roof open, ladder four should be able to get that master stream into the stairwell once everyone is out."

"Ladder twelve copies."

A series of long moments passed as the firefighters went to work putting the fire out. After the flames were quelled, and the smoke was mostly dissipated, a young lieutenant walked from room to room in the basement. He stopped in the first room and froze. After a minute of stunned silence, he crossed to the room opposite him. Again, he stood motionless, his eyes the only thing moving as they drank in the scene. He began to speak into his radio, then stopped. He had been to dozens of basement fires during his time with the department, and he had seen a lot of things. What he saw now, however, had him thoroughly baffled and slightly unnerved. He grabbed his radio microphone and tried again.

"Uhh, Chief?"

"Go ahead," the chief responded into the small microphone clipped to his lapel.

"You should probably call the Major Crimes Unit. And O.F.I."

The chief paused, then clicked his microphone and spoke. "We need Claiborne PD Major Crimes *and* the Office of Fire Investigation?"

"Uh, yeah. Ten-four, Chief. They're gonna want to see this."

Chapter 1

Amanda Killingly was a pretty normal twenty-something. She lived with her boyfriend, Brian Whiting, on the outskirts of the city of Claiborne. It was a quiet city for the most part, with small businesses still speckled amongst the busy landscape of conglomerate coffee shops and super-stores. You could still walk downtown on a Sunday afternoon and enjoy the parks and fountains. Brian was the lieutenant of the B-shift on Claiborne's ladder four. His schedule rotated from twenty-four hours on to seventy-two hours off. The schedule was decent but kept him away from Amanda more than he liked. Amanda was an emergency dispatcher and worked twelve-hour shifts three days a week. The only downfall of having a three-day work week was that the three days she was working all day always seemed to be the three days that Brian was home. She made the most of it, though. They always took a trip in January to somewhere warm and tropical, and they always took a long weekend to her father's farm out in the country in the late summer or early fall. Plus, they always had dinner together at least once a month. For the most part, Amanda's life was pretty normal, or at least as normal as she could make it.

When she was twenty-one, Amanda had taken a job tending bar at the local pub. Her dad had known the owner for years. It wasn't great, but it paid the bills. She had regulars who came in every day. There were younger guys who were incessant flirts and older ones who knew her father. The younger men were never shy about telling Amanda that her five-foot-six, one-hundred-and-twenty-pound self was the perfect fit for a bartender. They would tell her she had striking green eyes, flawless skin, a perfect ass. Some of them even proposed after a few drinks. Despite the sometimes-crude compliments, they were harmless. They even walked her to her car most nights. It was usually more of a stumble for some, but they were at least present for her walk through the dark lot.

There was one giant light on the front of the building that cast a hazy, yellow glow across the first quarter of the parking lot. The single light above the side door did little to help illuminate anything more than the doorknob. The parking lot was incredibly dark. Her customers joked with her about carrying a flashlight but jested that her usual fare of pink mini-skirts and white crop tops left very few places for her to keep one.

One night she had a guy point to her very ample, pushed up, tightly-packaged cleavage and offer in a hazy slur, "I bet we could get something in there to make you feel safe." Some girls would have slapped him and had him thrown out, but he was a regular, and Amanda liked her tips, so

she giggled while she looked down at herself and adjusted her bra. One of her usual customers told her he could make a loop of rope to hold a flashlight and that she could tie it around her wrist. Amanda threw her foot up on the bar and suggested it go through one of the holes in the fishnet stockings she was wearing. She laughed and told him she would wear it, but only if he would tie it around her thigh for her. The old man managed a quiet smile but was both mortified by her comment and worried about her naïve tendencies when it came to men.

He and a few of the other older customers had taken to calling her young lady, and they couldn't help but tell her how much she looked like her mother. Amanda loved to hear their stories. Her favorite stories were the ones about her mother and father as a young, head-over-heels in love couple set out to change the world. Amanda wished her mother had had the chance. Her mother had died when Amanda was only six years old, and she had few memories of her. She never imagined that at age twenty-one she would be working as a bartender, listening to her mother's old friends tell stories about how young and full of life she had been. But then again, she also never imagined that at age twenty-one she would be kidnapped, raped, and left for dead.

She had gotten off of work at 2:00 AM. She helped the owner, Dave, close down the bar. The glasses were clean and reset in the glass racks. Dave counted the evening's cash and handed Amanda a handful of twenty-dollar bills.

"Here, kiddo. They tip you better than anyone else."

Amanda smiled. "Thanks, Dave. Dad says that's because I've got his charm."

"And your mother's looks, thankfully," Dave added with a grin. "See you tomorrow."

"Night."

As she walked to the parking lot, Amanda noticed how unseasonably warm it was. It was mid-September, but the air was still warm, and the breeze didn't have the slightest bit of chill. The crowd of people that was usually loitering around the parking lot after the bar closed was drastically smaller than it typically was. As a matter of fact, there were only three people. Two younger men about her age leaned up against a white pickup truck. One smoked a cigarette while the other drank slowly from a beer bottle. The one with the beer bottle was tall and muscular. The one with the cigarette stood a little shorter. Tattoos lined the arms of the taller man, and there was even a tattoo on the side of his neck. They smiled at her through crooked and yellowing teeth. The man with the cigarette turned to throw it on the ground. As he ground it out with the tip of his boot, he turned, revealing a long scar that ran from the side of his eye all the way down to his neck, then disappeared into the collar of his shirt. A man of about forty-five sat behind the wheel, also smoking a cigarette. His face was weathered, and his eyes were deeply sunken and dark. Bony cheeks made their way down to a gaunt, drawn mouth. His thin, cracked lips pulled at the cigarette, the end glowing bright orange in the dim light, and his greasy hair was thick, wavy, and starting to gray.

"Hiya, sweet-cheeks," the driver called out. Amanda shifted her gaze to the ground and began to walk a bit faster. She fumbled in her purse in an attempt to retrieve her keys.

"What's the rush, baby?" the man growled. "I like your mini-skirt. Looks more like a belt than a skirt, but that's all the better for me to watch those tight little ass cheeks of yours bounce while you hurry away."

The man with the beer bottle downed the last of it and threw it at her. It hit a nearby car and shattered, sending shards of glass everywhere. She froze in fear for a brief second and then continued her now almost-run toward her car. A deep sense of panic started to stir in Amanda. The shorter man with the scar whistled and flicked his tongue at her.

"Come back here and let me see what you taste like. You've been working all night, but I bet that little hole is still as fresh as a new peach pie."

Their sobriety long gone, both men laughed and slapped each other on the back.

"Stop hurrying and come over here," the taller one said. There was an almost matter-of-fact tone to his voice. That tone quickly disappeared as he continued, "Come on, bitch. Let us get a look at that little snatch of yours. I bet its shaved bald and smooth. I shave, too. Wanna see?" He grabbed himself and thrust his hips at her. His companion laughed and spit a large chunk of thick saliva in her direction.

Her pace quickened, and she was still trying to get her keys out of the tiny clutch purse she carried. She couldn't think straight. She had nothing to defend herself with. No mace or pepper spray. No knife. Not even a whistle like some of her college friends carried. She was helpless and, at this point, just hoped she could make it to her car. Amanda had never worried about walking to her car. Her group of regulars was always in the parking lot when she left. Drunk and loud, yes, but she felt comforted when they were there because, if nothing else, they were people she knew. She had never seen the three men with the truck before. She walked quickly to her car. Faster and faster she stepped, until she was almost running. Keys in hand, she glanced over her shoulder to the three men by the truck. They hadn't moved. She was relieved that they hadn't come any closer. She unlocked her car with the keyless remote and took out her cell phone to call Dave inside the bar. She paused for a fraction of a second to dial, and someone grabbed her from behind and threw her phone to the ground. Her keys fell onto the asphalt parking lot. Amanda tried to scream, but her attempt was muffled by a gloved hand. He picked her up, and she saw that the two men by the truck had moved. One was sitting in the back seat, and the other was dragging her toward the truck. The man in the back seat opened the back door. Inside she saw a piece of rope and handcuffs. She tasted leather as she opened her mouth to scream, and the gloved hand pushed farther into her mouth. They threw her on the back seat, and she heard the man driving crow, "Buckle up, sweetie. You're in for a rough ride."

The man sitting next to her put the rope around Amanda's neck while the other one handcuffed her hands behind her back. She kicked hard at him, and he slapped her face and jabbed his tongue in her ear. Amanda cringed and struggled. She tried to turn her head away. He slapped her face again and grabbed her by the belt buckle, his grimy fingers rubbing on the waistband of her panties. He shoved his other hand under her skirt and tried to force a finger inside her.

"Hey, knock it off. The boss says he goes inside her first. Once he's done, we can have her for as long as we want."

"How the hell is he gonna know I shoved my fingers in her? His dick gonna tell him?"

He pushed his fingers against her panties and forced his finger, and her panties, up inside her. She winced and jerked back as much as she could. She continued her struggle, and she felt the rope tighten around her neck. One of them grabbed her by the throat and slapped her, hard. Again, he hit her across the face. He moved his hand from her throat to her chest, grabbing barbarically at her breasts. He squeezed and wrapped his other hand around her hair. Amanda felt helpless. She was handcuffed like a prisoner, with a rope around her neck like an animal being led to slaughter. The man with the scar on his face continued his attempt to keep his fingers inside her. He had moved her panties aside now and was trying to force three fingers in. She kicked and turned as much as she could, which made his attempts mostly unsuccessful. He pulled his hand out from under her skirt and smelled it.

"Ahhhh, you've got one fresh pussy, girl. Gonna be a sloppy mess when we all get done with you, but it sure smells good now." He thrust his fingers under his partner's nose. "Smell that, fucking young and sweet." He shoved his fingers in Amanda's face. "Take a whiff of yourself, bitch. It'll be the last time that little hole smells good. You'll be as loose and sore as an old whore by the time we finish filling you up."

Amanda turned her head away from his fingers and tried to look at her attackers. She kicked at one again and made contact with something that cracked when her foot smashed into it. He let out a brief growl of pain and slapped her again and again. She turned her head with each impact. After the fourth or fifth slap, her gaze landed on his arm. She could see a tattoo of an ivy vine crawling up his forearm. There were words underneath it, but she couldn't make them out through the tears in her eyes. She braced both feet against the door and pushed back, trying to break free.

"When are you gonna fucking learn to stop struggling?" His hot, alcohol-soaked breath blasted her as he screamed inches from her face. He slowly wrapped his long fingers around her throat again and spit in her face. Amanda closed her eyes and turned her head against the restraint of the rope. They blindfolded her and began running their hands all over her body. One of them bit her neck, hard, and Amanda felt a warm, thin line of blood slide down her neck. For a moment Amanda thought they would kill her. And then, she hoped they would kill her. At least then it would be over quickly. She didn't know how far they had driven, but suddenly, they stopped. They carried her out of the truck and threw her onto what felt like a mattress.

"Here she is, boss. We didn't fuck her or anything. Just like you asked."

"Good. Now get her clothes off and tie her arms and legs to the bed so I can get as deep inside her as I possibly can."

They stripped her naked, ripping at her clothes fast and forcefully, like frantic hyenas desperate to tear the last hunks of meat off a dying zebra. Once she was naked, they tied her legs to the bed posts. Spread wide, and bound with coarse, taught ropes, she couldn't move her legs no matter how hard she struggled. She screamed as they yanked her hands above her head. Her hands still handcuffed together, they stretched her arms out straight above her head and tied them to the head board. She was absolutely helpless. She felt him climb on, his hands grabbing her nipples as he forcefully thrust up inside her. She screamed as his hard, dry thrust forced its way into her equally dry skin. His hot, wet breath covered her face and ears as he lay on top of her. He moaned and breathed into her ear as he scrambled to get deeper inside of her. His entire weight smashed against her, as he had stopped holding himself up with his arms, and now he reached underneath her and pulled her apart. His rough, coarse fingers groped and tore at her. He shoved them inside her anywhere he could. His pace quickened until his pelvis was smashing into hers at a violent and furious pace. After an especially forceful thrust, she felt him pull out of her quickly. It burned, and she gasped and winced at the abrupt exit as he yanked himself out of her.

"Our turn, boss?" one of them asked eagerly.

"Not even close. Flip her over and tie her up again."

She had no energy to struggle, but she tried anyway. Her efforts were useless. The men untied her, threw her onto her stomach, and bound her legs wide open again. This time they tied the rope around her neck to the headboard, too. She felt a searing pain run down her leg as one of them spanked her brutally. Slap after slap after slap landed on her helpless body. The next round felt like punches, and then came the biting. She screamed in agony as they tore pieces of her flesh off with their teeth. Someone reached underneath her and pulled at one of her nipples. He bit it, and she screamed in agonized horror, as it felt like he had bitten it off. The punches and slaps continued for what felt like an eternity. Once they stopped, she felt a back-breaking thrust into her that caused her to inhale so fast she felt like she was suffocating. Thrust after demoralizing thrust. She felt as if he was ripping her to pieces and destroying her womb. She wished she would just die. He pulled her apart with his fat fingers as he buried himself as deep as he could inside her. After several minutes of torturous rape, she heard him howl as he yanked her head back by the hair. She felt his wet, warm, disgusting seed run out of her and onto her thighs. He yanked himself out of her once again, and there was a brief sound of feet moving. She tried to see, but the blindfold was still tight. She tried to move, but she was still bound and unable to budge. She screamed for help, knowing full well that it was a futile attempt. Even if someone had been around to hear her, her voice was hoarse from screaming and came out as a choked whisper.

"I don't care who goes next, but let me know when you're done. I need to cum in her one more time before you kill her. I need a minute to recover. I'm not as young as I used to be."

One after the other, the two men who had beaten her in the back of the truck and the raspy-voiced driver did as they pleased with her. They were rough and eager, like dogs fighting over a piece of meat that had been dropped off a serving plate. They started pulling each other off of her so they could take another turn, until one of them eventually called out, "Stop your fighting. She's got three holes."

She screamed until she was hoarse, and her voice fell silent. She cried until her tears dried up as crusty lines on her cheeks and neck. She had no more will to live, no more voice to scream with, and not one shred of dignity left anywhere inside or outside of her body. After she felt more of the hot, stinking liquid run out of her body, she felt some of it spray across her back and onto her thighs. Some landed on her neck and hit the side of her face. She heaved and tasted hot bile but somehow forced the mouthful back down. After a moment of quiet snickers, she felt one of them climb on the bed and kick her in the head. Again, then again. He kicked her in the side of her temple as hard as he could. She remembered praying for death, begging to just pass out and never wake up. She remembered pain. Blinding, searing pain. She remembered the driver's voice rumble, "Fucking whore." And then Amanda blacked out.

Chapter 2

When she woke up, she found the rope around her neck tied to the bed frame, but Amanda noticed the blindfold was off. She opened her eyes, and the light hurt almost as much as the kicks to the head. Amanda looked down at her bruised body. Empty beer bottles littered the floor. Her clothes were in a crumpled heap on a blue arm chair that sat in the corner of the room closest to the bed. She tried to move, but the pain stopped her. Every single inch of her entire being hurt. Her breasts were bruised and bitten. Her thighs held fingerprints outlined in reddish-purple tones. Her spine hurt from top to bottom.

Amanda took a ragged breath and tried again to move. Her legs felt like lead. Her head was pounding. She thought about crying out but thought better of it. Not that she thought she could. Her throat felt like she had swallowed sand laced with shards of glass. Her lips were cracked and streaked with dried blood. She didn't know if it was a result of the attack or if she was dehydrated. Probably both. Suddenly, Amanda wondered where she was. And she wondered if the men were gone or just resting up for another round of torture. She managed to slide her legs together and get them to the edge of the bed. The rope around her neck was tight but had slack in it where it was tied to the headboard. She inched her feet over the edge of the bed and tried to sit up. Her body wouldn't move. She tried again and again until tears began forming in her eyes.

Her abdominal muscles burning, she began to slowly sit up. She got into a sitting position and felt the rope begin to tighten around her neck. She was tired and broken and felt helpless against the rope's restraint. She wanted to give up. To lie down and hope to die. But the thought of the men coming back and finding her still alive terrified her. Amanda moved her arms. Even her fingers burned with pain. She was able to get her fingers between the front of her neck and the rope. She pushed them down as far as they would reach. Slowly, and painfully, she began to slide the rope up her neck. It was tight on her throat, and the thick hemp was rubbing her skin raw. She moved and pushed and pulled with everything she had and slowly managed to get the rope to her chin. The muscles in her forearms burned.

She thought she heard a noise outside the door. Her heart raced, and she froze. She strained her ears to listen. She didn't hear it again, so she went back to the rope. After more tears and more pain, she finally had the rope off of her neck. Amanda slid herself to the edge of the bed. For the first time, she looked at her surroundings. She wasn't in an abandoned warehouse or in some run-down, vacant apartment. Amanda was in a bedroom. Art hung on the wall, and a mirror stood in the corner. There was carpet on the floor. Next to the door was a small table. On it was a pack of cigarettes, a small handful of beer bottle caps, and the handcuffs she had been shackled with. Every time she moved, she felt as if someone was stabbing her with a hundred tiny knives. Amanda took a few weary steps and somehow bent down to retrieve her clothes. Her skirt was intact, and so was her bra. She cringed as she slipped them on, remembering them being so violently pulled off her. Her tank top was in shreds. She left it. Her denim jacket lay on the chair by the door. She picked it up and put it on over her bra, buttoning every button.

Barefoot, bruised, half dressed, and feeling dead inside and out, Amanda walked toward the door. She turned slowly to look at the room where she had been held captive. It was a modern bedroom, with tapestries and dressers. It had tan carpet and only one window close to the ceiling. It was a basement judging by the window placement. She started remembering the noise she had heard. If it had been a person, they were probably watching the door. She didn't care; she had to get out of there, or at least try. Amanda turned the doorknob slowly. The door creaked, and she froze. She didn't hear anything, so she pushed the door farther. She got it open enough to slip into a hallway. She winced. It hurt terribly to walk. She took slow steps toward a door that she hoped led to a staircase. She opened the door slowly and found white carpeted stairs. It was excruciating to climb them. Her leg muscles ached, her head was pounding, and everything female about her felt as if it had been put through several invasive surgeries without any anesthetic. She kept climbing. She had to keep going before whoever it was that did this to her came back and noticed she was gone. She got to the last step. Another door. She began to tremble. Amanda pressed her ear to the door and listened. She heard nothing in the room beyond the door. She closed her eyes and took three deep breaths. After the third breath, she quickly turned the knob and pushed through the door.

Once on the other side, Amanda saw no one. She was so relieved she could have cried. She stared into the room before her. She was standing in a kitchen. Amanda looked around in amazement. She was in someone's house. What kind of sick freaks would bring her to an actual house? She began to walk toward the door. She started slowly, as her muscles hurt, and she was being cautious to be quiet. Soon fear and instinct took over, and her pace increased. Her body burned with pain. Without hesitation, she opened the door. She walked outside into blinding sunlight and stepped onto a small stone porch with concrete steps, a paved driveway below. She was certain she looked out of place. A half-dressed girl wandering down the driveway of a house she had never even seen before. Barefoot, bruised, and bleeding.

She made it to the street and began walking. She hadn't gotten very far when a woman stopped alongside her in a minivan. Amanda froze.

"Are you okay, sugar?" the woman called out in a warm, southern drawl. "You look just awful. Do you need a ride?"

Amanda's stomach turned when she started to think of the last ride she had been taken on. She decided that it may not be the best choice to ride with her, but walking in the neighborhood where she was assaulted was no better.

"Okay," Amanda hesitantly said as she climbed in the minivan. "I live on Wentworth. Is that far from here?"

"No, not too far at all. Do you need to go to the hospital or the police station?"

Amanda hesitated. In her present state, it was obvious she should go to the police. She needed to report the crime. But she felt so dirty. Amanda cleared her throat.

"I just want to go home," she managed. "I had a nasty fight with some girl at the bar last night."

"Some kind of girl fight by the looks of you, sugar. But if you wanna go home, that's where I'll take you."

"Y-yes, please," Amanda sighed. "Wentworth. Four-twelve Wentworth. Thank you."

"Okay, sugar."

"What...what day is it?" Amanda inhaled.

"Monday, sugar. You *sure* you're okay?"

Amanda's mind raced. She had left work on a Saturday night. It was *Monday*? She had been gone for almost two days. How many times had she been violated? Did the men come Sunday and abuse her again? People must have been looking for her. Her mind went a thousand directions as she tried to answer countless questions.

"I..." Amanda started. "How did..." She trailed off again. "Monday?" Amanda's head pounded.

She had wanted to ask so many questions, but she was in pieces. Before she could finish her sentence, Amanda passed out.

She woke with a start at the sound of the woman's voice.

"We're here, sugar. Four-twelve Wentworth. You sure you're okay?" Amanda nodded. "You live here all alone?" the woman questioned.

Amanda didn't answer. She did live alone. It was a house her father owned before he moved to the farm full-time. She was staying there until she found steady work and another place to live, and while her Dad made arrangements to sell it. That was far too much to explain in her current condition, so Amanda tried to smile and just said "Thank you." She took a ragged breath and climbed out of the car, walking up to her front door. She realized she didn't have her purse, which meant she didn't have her keys. She lifted the old-fashioned milk jug on the front step and slid the spare key hidden there out from under it. Thank God she had a spare. She opened the door and began to walk inside.

"Take care of yourself, sugar," the woman in the minivan yelled.

Amanda waved. She didn't have the energy to yell back. She crawled in the house and locked the door behind her. She dragged herself upstairs and locked every window. Amanda turned the shower on as hot as she could stand and climbed in. She could barely stand up, so she supported herself on the small shower seat in the corner. She stayed in the shower until the water ran cold. She went through a bottle of shampoo and two bottles of body wash, but she still felt disgustingly dirty. When she climbed out, her body still ached, but the hot water had felt good while she was in the shower. Amanda checked every window and door again to make sure they were locked. She took the shotgun her father had always kept in the closet and set it at the foot of the bed. She donned clean sweatpants, a t-shirt, and a hooded sweatshirt. She sat down on her bed. Amanda tried to formulate a plan to begin getting her life back on track. She needed to go to the police, get her car, call her father, and try to make sense of the past two days.

Her dad had had the house phone disconnected when he moved out, so her only contact with the outside world was her cell phone and her laptop. Her phone fell in the parking lot when she was abducted. Her laptop was in her car. Amanda hugged her pillow, and before she could answer any of her own questions, she fell asleep.

A loud knock rattled the door and woke her.

"Ms. Killingly? Are you home?"

Amanda tried to sit up. Her body was still a wreck. Her head throbbed.

"Amanda? This is Officer Glen. I'm here with Officer Mason and your father."

Amanda felt suspicious and sick to her stomach. Why hadn't her father come in if it was really him? Her head swirled as she remembered she had taken the spare key. She inched over to the window and peered at the sidewalk below. She wasn't sure she could even face her father. She limped down the stairs and called out, "Daddy?"

"Amanda!" her father shouted. "Honey, are you okay? Let us in. Where have you been?" Amanda opened the door. Her father grabbed her in a hug, and Amanda winced and cried out. He stopped and backed away slowly. He looked at her and gasped, covering his mouth.

"Amanda." He paused. "What happened to your face? Your neck? You're bruised and...Oh my God. Are those teeth marks?"

Amanda started to cry harder. It was her first real cry since everything had happened. She fell against her father's chest and sank to the floor. He knelt with her. She sobbed and sobbed. She felt claustrophobic when he hugged her and didn't want to be touched, but she was too exhausted to pick herself back up at the moment. Her muscles were still sore, now even more so from crying. Her father held her while she wept. One of the officers radioed for an ambulance.

"Amanda." Her father gently lifted her chin up to look at him. "You need to tell us what happened. Dave reported you missing yesterday when he found your keys and cell phone in the parking lot. The police just got a phone call from a woman who said she dropped off a young girl at this address who had been severely beaten. Honey, what in the world is going on?"

Amanda took three deep breaths and tried to find some way to tell her father what had happened. She had no idea where to begin, but she tried anyway. She managed to get out one full sentence, and then she froze, unable to speak for the lump that was again rising in her throat. The tears dripped off her cheeks. Her father sat on the floor with her in silence. With tears in his eyes and his jaw clenched, he held his daughter's hands tenderly. He asked her again what had happened, but she just shook her head and sobbed.

When the ambulance arrived, the two police officers informed John that they would follow the ambulance to the hospital, where they would hand off the case to two detectives. Amanda was very thankful that two female paramedics had shown up with the ambulance. They asked her so many questions, but she had so few answers. She didn't know what her injuries could be; she had blacked out from the kicks to the head. The other questions were far too painful to answer. She couldn't bring herself to describe the gruesome details of being bound, beaten, and brutally raped over and over. It wasn't that she didn't remember; it was that the last thing she wanted to do was relive it by telling the paramedics. She told them about the kicks to the head. Those, she remembered well, and she figured it would give them something to focus on, and maybe that meant the other questions would stop.

Once in her hospital bed, it seemed like an endless stream of doctors came in and asked her more questions. Her first doctor was a tall but kind looking guy who appeared to be a little older than her. She had a hard time talking to him. She felt grotesque and disgusting, like she would never be clean, and she didn't want to tell a strange man about what had happened. Someone must have noticed her hesitation, or maybe it was a shift change, or maybe it was just common practice for rape victims, but from then on, Amanda found herself with female doctors for the rest of her stay in the hospital.

After the doctors had gotten her checked over and started their series of tests, two detectives knocked lightly on the door. One was a very muscular guy of average height who looked to be about thirty. With him was a tall, well-toned, and very attractive blonde woman. She was dressed in plain clothes but looked both professional and quite pretty. When Amanda motioned for them to come in, the tall blonde walked toward her slowly, her partner staying close to the door and quietly taking out a small pad.

"Hi, Amanda, I'm Detective Walsh." She gestured over her shoulder to the man at the door. "That's my partner, Detective Collins." She took out a badge as she spoke to Amanda and showed it to her. After Amanda had looked at it for a brief moment, she turned it over and revealed a photo ID with the woman's picture and the words "Claiborne PD-Detective Walsh" on it.

"Amanda, I know telling your story isn't pleasant, but I have a few more questions for you. It will help us catch whoever did this to you. Take your time answering; there is no rush. I can stay as long as you'd like."

The questions started out simple enough. Where she was the night she was abducted, what she was doing, what she was wearing. She asked if she had gotten a look at the pickup truck or any of the men inside it. After that, the questions grew far more difficult, and Amanda found herself stopping after each question to stop her tears, wipe her face, and take a few deep breaths before attempting to answer. The detectives stayed for what seemed like hours. As they were leaving, another doctor rapped lightly on the door frame and entered without waiting for a response. She was tall and slender, with raven-black hair that was tied up in a neat bun. Her eyeliner and mascara were light around her eyes, and the rest of her skin seemed flawless even without makeup. She wore a pencil skirt, black high heels, and a purple blouse with a ruffled collar, with a neckline slightly lower than any doctor Amanda had ever seen.

"Hi, Amanda, I'm Doctor Fairchild." She walked over and sat delicately on the edge of the bed. "I'm one of the hospital administrators. I have a quick question, and I'm sorry, but it's a difficult one. We have a lot of tests to run, and they do take some time. In all the samples we took, though, we couldn't find any DNA from your attackers on you. We typically find hair, fibers, or fluids on the victim. Did you shower before you came to the hospital?"

Amanda lowered her head. She knew instantly that while she felt her exceptionally long shower was desperately needed, it had also washed away any and all evidence that her attackers had undoubtedly left behind.

"I'm so sorry. I had to," was all she whispered before she started to sob quietly.

"It's okay, Amanda. It's not your fault. Not at all. You get some rest, and we'll keep checking on you."

"Doctor Fairchild?" Amanda said before the doctor reached the door.

"Yes?"

"Was one of the tests a pregnancy test?"

"Yes, it was. Unfortunately, it takes a handful of days for your hormone levels to change enough for us to see on a blood test. We will let you know as soon as we have the results."

"Thank you."

"You're welcome. I did notice that your medication list contained birth control. It's not a perfect drug, but I'd be willing to say it drastically reduces your chances of pregnancy, even in this situation. Try to get some rest."

"Okay. Thank you again."

Amanda rolled over and pressed her tear-streaked face against the cool pillow. She wept quietly, until her battered body fell into a deep sleep once again.

Doctor Fairchild crossed into a nearby supply closet and took out her cell phone. She dialed quickly and spoke just as fast. "She showered. No DNA left behind whatsoever. You got lucky." She hung up, opened the closet door, and left without another word to anyone.

Amanda slept off and on for days. Sometimes she slept all night and spent her days reading or mindlessly watching television. Other times she slept the day away and stared at the ceiling until long after midnight, when a nurse would come in to check on her and would find her crying quietly. One morning, when she awoke, her father was not in his usual armchair in the corner of the room. She asked a nurse who was checking her vitals what day it was. She had been in the hospital a week. Her memory of her stay was a blur, save for a few conversations she had with nurses, and she remembered that she had ice cream a few times. Television shows all rolled together into an endless loop of binge watching. On the days that she left the television off, she read a variety of books that her father had brought her, along with a few magazines and even a self-help book that one of the nurses had brought her. Finally, on her eighth day, her nurse greeted her with, "Good news, Amanda. I'm pretty sure you get to go home today."

Amanda wasn't sure how she felt about that. The hospital, albeit a foreign place, provided a sense of security and comfort that she couldn't explain. Nevertheless, she managed a small smile and said, "That's good."

Amanda's father came into the room, although she wasn't sure when he had left. Most of her blurry memories had him sitting quietly in the chair in her room, reading a book. He had told her he would talk to her about anything she wanted or he would stay quiet and let her rest. He was there for whatever she needed.

"The doctor says we can go home, kiddo."

"I heard," she said, trying to smile.

He helped her to her feet, and she headed to the bathroom. She got dressed slowly. Her body still ached, but the aches were at least becoming dull and distant. The sharp and stabbing pain of being brutalized had faded only slightly. The skin on her neck was pale where a mouth-shaped scar had formed. She pulled her hair over her neck, took a deep breath, and opened the bathroom door. She walked out of the bathroom to find her father standing with a wheelchair.

"I can walk, Dad."

A voice called from the doorway, "Standard procedure, girly." It was her nurse. She had grown to like her nurse a lot, so she didn't protest the wheelchair ride. They made their way down the hallway and outside. Her father opened the door of his truck for her. Amanda stared at the passenger seat. It took everything she had not to cry. Her father cast a glance at her while he returned the wheelchair to the doorway of the hospital. As he walked back, he was about to ask her what was wrong but stopped himself. She hadn't told him much, but one detail he did get was that she was kidnapped in a pickup truck. He slowed his stride in an effort to have a moment to think. He had no idea if it would help or not, but he decided he'd ask her to drive. Maybe that would give her a sense of control and make her feel a little better. He walked to her side of the truck.

"Hey, kiddo, wanna do me a favor?"

Amanda turned to face him. "A favor? Okay, Dad, what's the favor?"

"My back is bugging me from sleeping in that hospital chair, so I need to sit kind of sideways. Can you drive? I hate to ask, as you're still recovering and all, but this old man has a sore back."

Amanda gave him a relieved look. She realized this was her father's way of trying to help her with her obvious hesitation to get into the truck.

"I get to drive this giant thing? And pick the music?" She managed another half-smile. "Deal."

"Let's not get carried away with the music," he said with the slightest of smiles.

Amanda climbed into the driver's seat slowly. She adjusted the seat, and they drove home in silence. When they arrived, Dave was in the driveway.

"Why is Dave here?" She asked, her voice shaky. Amanda's father explained that he had called him and asked if he could bring her car home. She got out of the truck and passed Dave without a word. She gave him a small wave as she hurried past him and into the house. Amanda's father helped her upstairs and gave her the pain medication they had prescribed. He offered to sit with her, but she said she was okay. When he had left, she quietly locked the door and fell asleep.

Her father trudged down the stairs with his head in his hands, rubbing his face.

"It isn't your fault, John," Dave said as he held up a cup.

"I made us some coffee."

"How did this happen, Dave?"

Dave took a long sip of his coffee and stared out the window. After a long silence, he said, "It's my fault."

John stared blankly. "*Your* fault? How in the hell is this your fault?"

"I should have walked her to her car. I should have never let her walk out alone. It's just that the bar crowd is usually outside, and they all talk to her. It's people she knows, ya know? I mean, usually I didn't worry. I just... I should have gone. I mean, Goddamnit, John, I should have walked her to her car."

John drew in a long breath and let it out through pursed lips. "It isn't your fault, Dave. Like you said, usually there were people outside that she knew.

"I guess so." Dave sighed. "I still can't help but feel responsible."

"Do you have any idea who the bastards are?" John asked.

"I've got a few of the guys from the bar asking around and keeping their ears open. I'll let you know if I hear anything. In the meantime, maybe the cops will find something."

"Yeah." John paused. "Let's hope they do."

Chapter 3

The next few months were a blur for Amanda. She saw a few more doctors and got a few more test results. She was not pregnant and was negative for HIV, Hepatitis B and C, and the rest of the things they had tested her for. She was relieved that the tests were negative, but every doctor she saw and every test result they called her with were a stark reminder of what she had been through. Dave had told her to take as much time off as she needed. Amanda thanked him out of politeness, but she didn't bother to tell him she was never going to set foot in his bar again.

As she tried to pick up the pieces of her life, her days were filled with a lot of idle time, which was both good and bad. Most days she showered, cleaned the house a little, showered again, read some, watched TV, usually showered a third and fourth time, and then went to bed. She ate sporadically. She felt constantly hollow, and it didn't take her long to realize that is wasn't food her body was searching for. Her soul was empty, not her stomach. Her spirit was present, but it wasn't really alive. She felt alone, empty, helpless, and hopeless. She went silent on social media, stopped checking her email, and, for the most part, never even picked up her cell phone or opened her laptop. As much as she tried to hide it, and as hard as it was to admit, she was a burned-out husk of her former self.

She had reverted back to sleeping with a stuffed raccoon that her mother had given her as a toddler. She found an old picture of her mother and taped it to the mirror in her room. On one day among the many, Amanda found herself talking to the picture of her mother. She was apologizing for being a disappointment. Tears streaming down her cheeks, she sobbed as she apologized to the closest thing she had to a mom. She wasn't sure if she was crying more about feeling responsible for her attack or more because the only version of a mother she had was an old, creased and weathered picture of the one woman she wished so desperately to talk to.

On another occasion, Amanda experimented with drinking. She figured being drunk might make everything easier to deal with. That phase ended quickly. Alcohol reminded her of the bar, which reminded her of the attack. And she remembered, shortly after starting, how much she despised being drunk. Add to that the sobering reality of creating an even more helpless and unable version of herself, Amanda's drinking stage was over shortly after it began.

Her pain meds were an ever-tempting way to become numb to it all. She figured if she took enough, they may even kill her. She flirted with the idea of taking six or seven instead of her recommended one pill but could never quite convince herself to. There were so many hard days, though, that one day she opened the bottle, dumped out most of its contents onto her bed, and stared at it. The large, oblong pills lay scattered in a small pile. Amanda picked up an entire handful and studied them. Death, she thought, would be the end to all her negative thoughts and horrible nightmares. If she were dead, she wouldn't remember the brutal attack, the pain that radiated over her entire body, or the feeling of the sticky, disgusting liquid running down her bare, bound thighs.

She shoved the handful of pills into her mouth. Some pressed against her lips but fell onto the bed with a small, silent bounce. She picked up a glass of water from her nightstand and put it to her lips. Her hands trembling, she tried to tip the cup back, but something inside stopped her. Tears began to slide down her hot cheeks, and she tried again to drink but didn't. Her mouth was filling with saliva, and the pills were starting to stick to the inside of her mouth and press against her cheeks.

She stood up and stared in the mirror on her wall. Her hair was limp and flat from so many showers. Her clothes hung off her body from having no consistent food intake. Her eyes were hollow and dark. The laughter and light behind them had grown so dim she could barely recognize herself. She couldn't die. Not like this. She had been stripped of all her dignity by filthy men she had never met. She was not about to kill herself and remove any chance of regaining that dignity. She spewed the pills out of her mouth and into her hand. The once oblong and hard pills had started to dissolve into smaller shapes with a layer of mush on top of the heap in her hand. Not knowing how much of the drug had actually gotten into her system from so many pills starting to dissolve, Amanda reached for her water. She drank the entire cup in a few quick gulps and immediately ran to the bathroom to fill it again. She drank three more full cups of water, until she felt like she would throw up if she tried to drink anymore. She fell onto the bathroom floor, the mushy mound of pills still in her left hand. She sank against the wall and threw the handful of gooey narcotics into the toilet. She wiped her hand on a nearby towel, leaned back, and sobbed uncontrollably. After that, her days and weeks passed painstakingly slowly. Amanda trudged on, hoping that someday she'd find her old self buried not too deeply down inside the abyss she had become.

As Amanda lay awake in bed one night, hoping not to dream, she had a thought. The men that did this to her were still out there. Amanda wanted to do something to change that. She wanted to do her part to make sure what happened to her never happened to anyone else. She didn't know who they were, where they lived, or what their names were. She remembered the man behind the wheel of the white truck. She remembered his ugly face, his yellow teeth, and his stinking cigarette. She remembered his voice. That ugly, nicotine-soaked voice that spoke to her. Other than that, she didn't remember much. Were the two men standing by the truck that night tall or short? Were they close in height? What color hair did they even have? She didn't know. One thing she was sure of was that she wouldn't rest well until she had some form of closure. She started reading books written by women who had been through abuse and rape. They were written for women who needed to feel connected to something. The books helped some, but they mostly reminded Amanda of what happened to her. She certainly didn't think she would ever be completely over it, but she hoped that one day she would be recovered enough to go about her life in a somewhat normal fashion. She lay awake until her drowsiness got the best of her, and finally, she fell asleep.

When Amanda woke, she could smell her father cooking bacon. Not a healthy choice, but her father was always one to cook what he considered a good, hearty breakfast. Healthy breakfasts were always optional in her father's mind. She reached for her sweatpants and hesitated. She picked them up and set them in a drawer. Amanda decided that it was time to wear normal clothes. She pulled on a pair of jeans and a cowl-neck sweater. She washed her face and put on a little bit of make-up, then pulled her hair into a ponytail. She donned a pair of flats and headed down to check on her father's bacon. The days that she wore sweatpants all day made Amanda feel like she was slowly giving up on herself. It was a feeling she resented.

"Something smells good."

"Bacon and eggs. Your favorite."

"Actually, my favorite is raspberry yogurt and granola."

"Bacon has been the foundation of a good breakfast since the Civil War." John Killingly chuckled softly. "You want me to find you some yogurt?"

"No, bacon and eggs are fine, thank you." She kissed her father on the cheek, something she hadn't done since before her attack. She hadn't really meant to, but it seemed to happen out of second nature, and even though it was her father, she still felt her stomach tighten and flip a little when she made contact with another person. It was a small glimmer of normalcy in her otherwise upside-down world. She sat down and started in on breakfast. As much as she didn't want to admit it, the bacon and eggs tasted wonderful. Her father always had the ability to make whatever he was doing for her seem perfect. They sat together and ate, not saying much. After a few quiet moments, Amanda broke the silence. "Thanks for cooking," she said.

"You got it." John lowered his head. After a long pause, he looked up.

"Amanda..." he started but trailed off. "Have you ever thought about maybe moving away from here?"

Amanda knit her eyebrows. "I guess I hadn't thought about it much," she answered.

"Maybe a little closer to me?" her father added. "Or somewhere a little farther from here?"

"I don't know, Dad." Amanda took a deep breath. "Lately, I've just sort of been..." She searched for a word.

"I know, kiddo. I'd just like to be able to look in on you more often."

"I'll think about it." Amanda nodded. "You cooked. I'll do dishes," she said in an attempt to change the subject.

Amanda picked up the dishes from the table and set them in the sink. As she began to scrub them, she looked over her shoulder.

"You know, Dave told me stories about you and Mom when we'd close the bar."

John raised his eyebrows. "If they were Dave's stories, they couldn't have been good."

46

"They were great, Dad." Amanda managed a small smile. "It was nice to hear about Mom. I don't have that many memories of her. I remember her reading to me and you guys taking me to the zoo and to the beach. But I never got to know what kind of person she was."

"Well, when you get a chance," her father said, smiling, "look in the mirror. You get to be more like her every day."

Amanda smiled. "Thanks, Dad." She set the dishes in the drainer and told her father she was going to go read for a little while. She thanked him again for breakfast and headed upstairs.

In her room Amanda sat at her desk and picked up one of her books. She read a line aloud.

"It is never your fault, and it can always get better." The author had made a point of reiterating the phrase over and over again throughout the entire text of the narrative. Amanda wondered if it could get any better. She had started eating again and had begun talking to her father and Dave whenever they came to see her. It was still difficult to talk to Dave. Every time she saw him, she started to think about his bar and her dreadful last night of work there. She managed to make some small talk, though. She was sleeping a bit better at night. Her bruises were fading, and her cuts didn't sting as much when she took a shower. Her physical well-being was getting better with time, but her mental and emotional self was still battered and broken. She did her best not to show her father how disrupted her spirit still was. But he was very good at sensing when she didn't want to talk about things and never asked too many questions.

As she read, she couldn't help but get distracted by the thoughts she had about the men who attacked her. They had the time and ability to kidnap her, drive her to a house somewhere, rape and torture her for almost two days, and not get caught. Her stomach churned, and she felt grotesque and hollow as soon as she thought of them. Her frustration grew as she wondered how they could seemingly disappear after doing such awful things to her. She wanted nothing more than to know that they would never do what they did to her to anyone else, but how could she know that if they were still walking around as if nothing had happened? Her mind drifted to a dream of the police finding them and putting them in jail for the rest of their miserable lives. Her frustration continued to grow with the thought that the police hadn't immediately caught her attackers. A college kid with a computer and some basic coding skills could find almost anyone with a cell phone, tablet, or social media account, so why couldn't the police find ruthless criminals in broad daylight? *That was their Goddamned job*, she thought to herself.

After some angry brooding and curses under her breath, she was able to form a somewhat rational mindset and realized they didn't have much to go on. Although she had told them everything she remembered the men saying and had given the best descriptions she could, she hadn't provided them with much. Her memories were blurred, and she hadn't see very much since she had been blindfolded. She had never seen them in the bar before, and she had no idea where they had taken her. Her anger with the police subsided slightly as she kept thinking. She had a friend in high school who had always wanted to be a police officer. Maybe she could call him and see if he had ever made it. Maybe he could do something about it. The thought of talking to a man she hadn't seen in several years made her want to throw up.

She swallowed hard and opened her book again. Amanda forced herself to read and tried to get her mind off the awful thoughts she had, but every line she read seemed to have a word in it that triggered a deep, emotional response. Every time she saw the word 'attacked,' she remembered the slaps and punches, the brutal kicks to the head, the bites, the hands ripping at her thighs and pulling her apart. The word 'recovery' made her depressed and angry because she was still trying to figure out how to recover, and that brought on a helpless feeling that things would never be better. 'Family' was a stiff jab to her gut and then an uppercut to her chin, as it brought about the realization that she had been relying on her father for everything. It made her long to see her mother again, or it sometimes made her want to have a sister who could hug her, cry with her, and help her find pieces of herself to cobble back together. The more she read, the more she found her thoughts drifting to the night of her attack. Her book told her that the longer women wait, the harder it is for them to remember details. Amanda had told the police what had happened, but she wondered if, in her state of shock, she had told them everything. They asked her questions that were difficult to answer, so she probably hadn't offered any of the horrific details unless they asked for specifics. Had they?

Amanda closed her book. She picked up a pen and a piece of paper and began to write.

THINGS TO DO:

1-Go to police. Ask for any progress.

2-Call Matt M.-Cop?

3-Find out names of attackers. Details. Who/Where/Why?

She began to circle the word 'why.' Faster and faster, she circled the word feverishly. She kept writing, and with every word, Amanda wrote more quickly. She felt herself start to subconsciously scribble on the page. An angry scrawl of her suppressed feelings. She longed to feel happy and normal again, but instead she felt like an empty bottle washed ashore, the cap stuck on from its voyage across a dark, massive, salty sea. Stuck on so tight that nothing could get in or out. She was mad at the world for letting this happen to her. Memories flooded back to her, and she wrote them down. Things that gnawed at her insides and burned a hole in her so deeply that she worried she would never fill it in. Amanda found herself starting to pound her hand on the desk as she wrote. Harder and harder, she slammed her fist against the paper. Tears ran down her cheeks as she threw the notebook across the room. She slid from her chair and onto the floor, gathering her knees against her chest. She squeezed her knees tightly and took a few more breaths, each one becoming slower and more controlled. She wiped her cheeks and sat on the floor in silence. After several minutes, Amanda stood up. She flattened the wrinkles in her sweater and took a deep breath. She decided it was time to go to the police station. She wanted to ask them if they had any details about her case. The more she thought about it, though, the more it scared her. She didn't want to be reminded of what happened, or talk about it, but she had to. She had to know if the police were doing something to find the men who did those terrible things to her. Before she could talk herself out of it, Amanda grabbed her coat and her purse and headed downstairs. She got to the door and opened it.

Amanda headed to her car. She got in, locked her doors, and headed to the police station.

At the front desk of the police department, there was a girl that Amanda recognized. She had been in the bar a few times. She had blond hair, longer than Amanda's. Her blue eyes were bright and friendly. She was well-dressed and very pretty. Amanda was glad the first person she saw was female.

"Hi." Amanda said. The girl glanced up from her papers.

"Hello. How can I..." The girl paused. She stared blankly and then suddenly managed, "Hi, Ms. Killingly. How are you? I mean... I...what are you..." She stopped and took a breath. "How can I help you?"

"You don't have to call me Ms. Killingly," Amanda started.

The girl looked down. "I'm so sorry about what happened to you. I don't know everything... I mean, well, it isn't like I'm nosey or anything... it's just, working here, you know... I hear what's going on sometimes."

Amanda looked at her. "You work at the police station. I'm sure you would have found out eventually."

"Right," said the girl. She took a deliberate breath. "How can I help you?"

Amanda took a step forward. "I'm just wondering if there has been any progress in finding the..." Amanda stopped and took a breath herself. "People," she started again. "Any progress in finding the people who attacked me."

The girl behind the desk nodded. "Hang on," she said as she picked up her phone and dialed an extension. "Sergeant, could you come to the front, please. Amanda Killingly is here." She hung up the phone. A moment later the door next to the desk opened, and Sergeant Harding stepped into the lobby of the station. He stood and extended his hand.

"Hello, Ms. Killingly. I'm Sergeant Bill Harding."

"Hi." Amanda instinctively took a half step backwards. She stared at his extended hand. Bill Harding was an average-sized man, but he seemed to take up the entire room. He had short, neatly-cut hair and sharp cheekbones. His steely eyes were a bluish-gray, but they were at least kind when they looked at her. She wasn't sure she could reach out to shake his hand. She had enough trouble learning to hug her father again, let alone shake the hand of a strange man she had only known for a few seconds.

The sergeant caught on to her hesitation and lowered his hand. "How do you do, Ms. Killingly?"

"Okay, thanks," she said, feeling herself turning her body slightly away from him. "I was just wondering if there were any leads in the case involving the people who attacked me?" She felt like that sentence took all the energy she had to put together.

"We have our best officers on it, Ms. Killingly. They are doing everything they can to make sure justice is served."

She glanced past him and saw a young officer come to the desk and ask the girl sitting there a few questions. His name badge said "McPherson." *Matt*, Amanda thought to herself. The boy from high school. Truly, Amanda hadn't been friends with Matt; it was more that they had simply known each other's names and knew enough about each other to make small talk. Nonetheless, Amanda saw it as an opportunity to gain as much information as she could. Not wanting to ignore Sergeant Harding but not wanting to continue talking to a strange man much longer, she turned slightly toward him and managed a quiet smile.

"Thank you, sergeant," she said. "Thanks for everything."

"Yes, ma'am. You're welcome, Ms. Killingly. You have a good day." With that, he walked back behind the desk. Starting to leave and absolutely unsure if she could even talk to another person in her current state, she hesitated before calling out to the young officer. An uneasy feeling started to wash over her. Before it could get the best of her, she called to him.

"Matt?"

He turned to face her and, after a brief pause, said, "Amanda, hey." He stared for a moment, not sure of what to say next.

"Hi," she offered.

"Time flies. Long time, no see." He took a few steps in her direction. "Do you need help with something?" he asked politely.

She took a half step back when he advanced. "Yes. I hope you can help. A while ago I was..." Amanda paused and looked at her feet. "Well, attacked."

"I heard one of the officers on the case talking about it. I'm sorry you had to go through that."

"Thanks." She managed a fraction of a polite smile. "I didn't know if you had any way of knowing if there was any progress in finding my attackers."

"Oh, right. Um, well, I wasn't assigned to the case. I hear the other guys—I mean, officers—talking about the cases they are working, but I don't typically ask for details."

"Right." Amanda lowered her gaze. "Not your case, not your problem. Thanks anyway." She turned to walk away, but he called after her.

"Wait." He crossed in front of her. She met his eyes and then immediately looked down.

"Yeah?" She looked back up into his eyes and realized it was the first time she was able to look someone she was not familiar with in the eye for any length of time. As soon as she realized it, she broke eye contact again.

"The officer on the case is a good friend of mine. He trained me when I first got hired. I'll ask if he has any new information, and if he does, I'll have him contact you."

The thought of another strange man talking to her about being brutally beaten and raped made her nauseous. "Can you contact me instead?" she asked before she realized she even had something to say.

"Um, I'm not sure. I'll have to ask the officer assigned to your case. I don't want to disclose anything I'm not supposed to."

"Like who the hell attacked me?" Amanda felt a surge of anxiety throughout her whole body as soon as she said it. It wasn't like her to blurt something out like that. "Sorry. I didn't mean to…"

"It's okay." He stopped her. "You've been through a lot. No one can blame you for wanting answers. I'll see what I can find out and let you know."

Amanda let out a sigh. "Thank you."

"You're welcome. It was nice to see you. I've got to head out." With that, he turned and disappeared through a door labeled "Employees Only."

54

She hadn't exactly gotten much information, and although it had been slightly terrifying, Amanda felt satisfied with her visit. She had let the sergeant know that she wanted more information and had gotten to talk to Matt and let him in on her questions. Amanda thanked the girl at the front desk again and headed for her car. She got in and locked her doors, a habit she had formed since the attack. She started her car and put it in gear. She was about to drive away when a police cruiser pulled up next to her. Matt got out and approached her window.

"Hey," she said, trying her best to look at him.

Matt smiled. "Hey."

"What's up?" Amanda asked.

"I wanted to give you my card, in case you need anything or have questions. I know sometimes it seems like the cops aren't doing anything to help, but there are good people working on your case. But in the meantime, if you need anything..." He pulled a card from his uniform shirt pocket. "Feel free to call."

"Thank you," Amanda said as she took the card and put it in her purse.

"You're welcome. Drive safely." With that, he smiled, pulled his sunglasses down from the top of his head, and walked back to his cruiser.

Amanda brushed a stray piece of hair behind her left ear, exposing her neck. She glanced in her rearview mirror at the scar and felt a chill run down her spine as she began to drive away. She glanced in the mirror one more time and pulled her hair back over her neck. She headed home, determined to find out who was responsible for the long, jagged line that would forever brand her neck.

Chapter 4

In the months that followed, Amanda did her best to work toward a sense of normalcy. Every book and article she had read said that establishing a routine was a crucial part of moving on and getting back on track. "Set your alarm, find a hobby, cook hot meals, read new books, wear your best clothes." They made it seem like waking up at six in the morning, starting a rock collection, and making chicken parmesan for dinner would solve all the problems a rape victim could ever have. It sounded like such an easy transition on paper, except that it was anything but easy. Sometimes she wondered if the authors had really been through something as terrible as she had. In some books the writing seemed so superficial, like the author was trying to recover from having her ass fondled in the grocery store line. Long, wordy paragraphs filled endless pages with buzz words like progress, self-betterment, and journey. She didn't mean to downplay any type of abuse or rape, but given what she had been through, those types of books were of little help. Despite the somewhat insincere tone of some of the books, she read them anyway.

There were a select few of them that she just couldn't stand, and they found themselves in the donation bin. Others were more genuine, and so she did her best to follow their suggestions in an effort to regain her former self. It wasn't until she'd had some very dark days, however, that she finally got to some better ones. She still didn't like talking to people, male or female, really. She didn't leave the house for days at a time, so much so that she seemed to lose track of what day it was. The only reason she knew when the week was drawing to a close was because the newspaper only got delivered Thursday through Sunday. She had tried lots of things to get her mind off her attack, but one was no more effective than the others.

She started a journal in an attempt to help herself heal. It didn't work as well as she had thought. Instead, it always seemed to set her up for failure, as the more often she opened the little purple and white book, the more often her mind pulled up thoughts of her attack. She saw a psychologist a few times via the internet. Going out in public was too much to handle. Her father had done his best to keep his distance, but he was worried about her. He had tried, several times, to get her to go out with him to the grocery store or to put gas in his truck. They were subtle requests at first, and then he grew a little more serious with his requests. He wasn't stern, but he quit the subtle tactics and simply told her she needed to stop lying in bed day in and day out. Amanda was upset at first and then slightly annoyed. She felt as if her father was being pushy and didn't realize how much of a mess she still was. In his mind, though, John was doing whatever he could to help her heal. He believed she needed to get out of the house and actually do something. He understood that she wouldn't want to go alone, so he kept asking her to go with him. Eventually, she just stopped answering, and he stopped asking.

After the minor falling out with her father, she fell into a deep depression. John was growing more upset by the day. From the outside he could see how she was literally turning herself into a prisoner in her own house. In her mind Amanda would never be able to be a normal member of society again. She was slowly letting the dark, cold grip of depression get the best of her.

She still showered with water so hot it just about scalded her skin. She still read her books but felt that they weren't going to help her. Apathy was slowly taking control as her most dominant emotion. Some days she felt like eating; other days she felt like hiding under her covers for the entire day. Some days she felt like dying. She often wondered why it was that she didn't die. They beat her almost to death, but why had she survived? For what purpose? She often thought it was cruel that she survived. That she would now walk forever with the heavy weight of being a victim hanging around her neck like an anchor, dragging her to the very bottom of herself. The old Amanda that she knew and loved was certainly long dead.

She had lost weight from not eating. She was a slender and attractive young woman before the attack, but her ribs now showed through a tank top. Her face was drawn, and her cheeks were sunken. She was literally becoming skin and bones. Her face looked tired. She wondered if she could starve to death or if her body would have some basic instinct to eat and survive. She didn't care if she lived or died anymore. In her mind she was mostly dead as it was.

In the beginning she did nothing to reverse it. But every –so often she'd drag herself back up from the limitless abyss that was her sadness and depression and search for a small glimmer of hope and normalcy. She tried keeping herself emotionally afloat by calling the police twice a week to ask for new information. They assured her they were still working on it. After a while of the same phone call with the same result, she lost a bit of hope and only called them once a week, and then once a month. She spoke to Matt a few times, but after a while he had told her that, unfortunately, as much as the police investigated, they had no leads. The men who attacked her seemed to be normal citizens hiding in plain sight. Eventually, she stopped calling the police altogether. She slowly put away the books she had bought about dealing with her attack. She kept out one that was more of a guide to self-betterment.

One afternoon, while packing up some of her books and rearranging clothes in her drawers, Amanda found a small, brown and white, stuffed owl buried in her closet. Its giant, glossy eyes were happy and blue. A small orange beak sat just above what looked like a little smile on its face. In a somewhat childish moment of vulnerability, Amanda began speaking to it. "Where'd you come from, birdie?" she said, running her fingers over the bird's soft, fuzzy stomach. She set in on the bed, and in a continued state of child-like playfulness, she began to address it as if the fluffy little brown and white bird were a board-certified physician, clinical psychologist, and FBI detective.

"Do you think I'm getting better?" she asked the motionless bird. "I don't know if I am. Or if I ever will. Does the scar on my neck look like it will fade more?" she asked, lifting her hair out of the way to reveal the half-moon scar on her neck. "And what about the pain medication? I haven't taken much lately. I don't want to take any medication anymore. I have those anti-depressant pills, too. But to tell you the truth, I think they make me feel worse. Is that possible?"

She looked at the bird and paused. She wasn't sure if she was slowly going crazy or if she was simply talking out loud because she hadn't talked to anyone in a very long time. "So, where do people like the ones who attacked me hide? I mean, how on earth have the police not been able to catch any of them or do anything to help? Do you think they are still around here? Or do you think they are in a different state, or maybe Mexico?"

She stopped folding the sweater in her hands and stared at the stuffed animal. "Are you going to say anything, or am I doing all the talking?" She set the sweater on the bed and picked up another. "That's part of your plan, isn't it? You sit quietly and listen, and I talk and it makes me feel better? Shouldn't I be on a couch for this type of thing?" The bird remained motionless. She picked it up and stroked its head. "Well, if that's your plan, I guess it's working." She set the owl back on her dresser and twisted her mouth in a sideways half smile. "I'm definitely losing it." she said aloud.

She realized, however, that despite being somewhat juvenile, talking to the owl helped. She imagined talking to anyone would help, but in her current state the only one she felt like talking to was the little toy. In addition to helping Amanda get her feelings out to an audience with absolutely no judgement, her conversations with her little stuffed bird provided a series of self-help checks about her progress through the dark and seemingly endless tunnel that had become her life. That, and it allowed her to actually talk out loud. She barely spoke throughout the course of a day, and even when she did, it was usually to herself. She didn't use the phone, she didn't have visitors, and she didn't leave the house. Little by little, Amanda was forgetting what she even sounded like. One of her books had sternly prompted, "Never lose your voice. Be loud, be in the moment, be heard." A nice sentiment for the reader of the book, maybe. But Amanda wasn't a loud and in-your-face kind of person before the attack, and she certainly wasn't about to become one now. Much to the point of the book's author, however, by not talking to anyone, Amanda was slowly losing her voice. Until she found the box with the little stuffed bird. She named the owl Marsha and made her a permanent spot on the nightstand in her room. Childish or not, Marsha was staying put. For now.

Days turned into weeks, and weeks into months. Amanda kept moving forward as best as she could. Her father dropped by on weekends to visit when he could. His visits were seldom, but they were a nice treat that Amanda looked forward to. As time passed, his trips grew less frequent, until one day they stopped all together. She had become silent and seemingly hollow. He would bring in groceries, vacuum, fix a loose door knob, change out a light switch. Things that didn't really need to be done, but he did it to pass the time and be present in case she wanted to talk to him. And though she never said much, she needed those visits more than she could explain. Her life was dull, depressing, and provided little hope of ever being normal.

She loved her father's visits. And once they stopped, her days grew longer and longer.

At first her father sent her money. Every Saturday he would mail her a check with enough money to get her through the week. She always felt guilty taking the money, but she wasn't sure what else she could do. Finally, Amanda decided she needed to start making it on her own. People couldn't feel sorry for her forever. She called her father one Saturday morning and asked him to stop sending her money.

"Hey, kiddo. I'm so glad you called. How are you doing?" John asked in an attempt to not sound like he was concerned something was wrong.

"Hey, Dad. I'm okay. But I need a favor."

"Name it, kiddo."

"Please stop sending me money."

There was a brief pause while John tried to figure out the reason for the request.

"I'm happy to send it, honey."

"I know, Dad. And I appreciate it more than I can even say. But I'm never going to get better if people coddle me and do everything for me. If I need money, I'll ask. I promise."

"Okay, sweetie. If you say so."

"Thank you. Have a good day."

John wanted to keep talking to her, but her telling him to have a good day was a clear hint that she was done talking.

"You, too, honey. I love you very much."

"Love you, too, Dad. See you."

Two days passed, and in her mailbox, she found the usual envelope from her father. He had enclosed a note that said he had already written the check and was on the way to the post office when she had called.

"Easier to just mail it rather than void it and waste the paper," she found written in her father's somewhat scratchy but very organized handwriting. She smiled as she read it. With her last check in her hand, she stuck to her usual routine. She wrote 'For deposit only' neatly on the signature line on the back. She got a fresh envelope, enclosed a deposit slip along with the check, stamped and addressed it, and put it back in the mailbox for the outgoing mail the next morning. With one final check to be deposited, she needed a way to sustain somewhat of an income. She didn't eat much, and her father insisted she would never, ever pay rent in any house he owned, but she needed to survive.

She researched online and found several dead-ends. Most of them required her to leave the house. One very odd ad seemed to suggest than a woman would drop her children off for her to watch. The ad continued that the woman would be gone for "an indiscriminate and varying amount of time." This made Amanda feel as if some woman was looking for a place to dump her screaming children while she ran off with her boyfriend or joined the circus. After more than an hour, she found something that seemed like it could be promising. She found an anonymous, online tutoring service that was run through the high school. She found the link to this service right on the home page of the local high school's website. The school knew which children were in need of tutoring and only had limited time and resources in-house to help them. They required only a username and password for you to log into their online tutoring site. Since there was no personal information exchanged between student and tutor, the login credentials were enough to track the time and amount of work Amanda put into tutoring the students. The fairly limited details were also enough to convince her it was okay to do.

She still wasn't comfortable with people, but she had always loved to read, and she was fairly proficient at editing written work. At first she worked a day or so a week, and rather sparsely throughout the day. Once she established a routine, however, she worked more and more often. After a few weeks, she had increased her work load to four days a week. Working as an English Literature tutor for high school students helped her stay focused on something other than being so depressed. Good, bad, or indifferent, Amanda gave feedback day after day to students she would never meet. She liked helping people, and earning money also drove down the feeling of helplessness that had crept in while her father was paying for her to lie in bed for days at a time. Tutoring wasn't going to make her a millionaire, but it was enough to cover the few expenses that she had. It was rewarding in a way she couldn't explain. Slowly, very slowly, and in no particular amount of time, Amanda felt herself starting to heal. Her physical wounds had been better for a while, but she still needed to put herself back together emotionally. Tutoring may not have picked up all the pieces, but it at least helped Amanda find them all.

"Listen, Marsha," Amanda began one day, rubbing the little owl's fuzzy stomach. "I'm down to two showers per day. This is real progress," she said firmly to the round-eyed little fluff ball. "And I eat one meal, lunch, consistently. That's better than eating one meal every two or three days. I wear normal clothes and go outside at least twice a day. Once to get the mail and once to check on my flowers. And my career as a professional paper-fixer-upper is really taking off. I mean, these kids have never met me, and probably never will, but I'm helping them. They are working hard and doing the things I suggest. Their work shows it. And that makes me very happy. Or as happy as someone like me can get, I suppose." Some conversations with Marsha weren't so positive. Some days they were about how it felt to be beaten, how sometimes she could still feel the pain of being raped, and even some philosophical thoughts about what it would feel like to commit suicide, or how it feels to die. The little owl passed no judgment and simply stared at her with its shiny, over-sized glossy blue eyes. Childish, maybe. But little by little, and week by week, she talked to the owl less and less.

Chapter 5

It had been more than a year since the attack. Her father still called her quite often to check on her. Dave sent her flowers every week for the first few months as an apology for what happened, but Amanda never worked at Dave's bar again. She had told her father countless times to tell Dave that she didn't blame him for what happened. One Tuesday afternoon Amanda's phone rang. She realized that she had not had much contact with anyone other than her father in quite some time. She stared at it as it rang and decided it was safe to pick it up.

"Hello?"

"Ms. Killingly?" a voice said.

Amanda paused. "Who is calling, please?"

"This is Sergeant Harding from the police department."

"Oh. Hi, Sergeant. Sorry, I wasn't expecting a call. It has been a while."

"Yes, ma'am, it has. I'm very sorry it has been such a long time. But I have good news, of sorts.

"Okay..." Amanda didn't know what to say. She had done her best to put her attack behind her, to move on with her life. She hadn't bothered to call the police and ask for progress in ages. The last thing she expected was for them to find new information. Her heart raced. She wasn't quite sure how to feel, how to react. New information introduced the possibility of her having to retell and relive the details of her attack. Amanda blinked hard. "That's, uh, great, isn't it?"

"Well, it is if you can help us."

"I don't understand." Amanda inhaled quickly. "I told you everything that I remembered." She could feel her pulse increasing.

"I know, and you did great with that information. We have some pictures that we hoped you could look at and tell us if you recognize any of the men in them."

Amanda was flooded with emotions. She was terrified at the thought of possibly looking at one of the men who did this to her. *Now or never*, she thought to herself.

"Okay, Sergeant. When should I come to the police station?" Amanda said slowly.

"Could you come today? I will be here until eight or so tonight."

"Can I come right now?" Amanda asked hurriedly, as the thought of being out after dark made her feel cold and afraid.

"Right now?" Bill Harding paused. "Yes, ma'am, right now is just fine."

"Thank you. Bye." Amanda hung up the phone and stared in the mirror. Her mouth felt dry. She could feel her pulse pounding in her temples. She told herself to relax and stay calm. It was easier said than done, though. She finally pushed herself to leave and headed out the door. As she drove, she couldn't help but feel nervous, anxious, and slightly afraid. The books she had read talked a lot about facing your attacker. Unlike most of the women in the stories she had read, however, Amanda was fairly certain she had never even *seen* her attackers before. She took several deep breaths as she pulled into the parking lot of the police station. She got out of her car, made sure it was locked, and then all but ran to the front door. As she walked in, the same girl she had talked with months ago sat behind the desk.

"Hi, Ms. Killingly." She smiled.

"Hi." Amanda managed a slight smile. "Is Sergeant Harding here?"

"Yes, he is. He's expecting you. If you want to take a seat, he will be out in just a minute."

A moment later a figure appeared in the doorway.

"Hi, Ms. Killingly."

"Hi, Sergeant."

"Please, call me Bill."

"Okay. Hi, Bill." Amanda smiled as much as she could.

"Much better. Thank you for coming on such short notice. Sometimes these things are very time sensitive. The longer people wait, the more they think about what they *should* say or what they *should* remember. Don't psych yourself up for anything."

He set a line of pictures on a long, wooden table. Amanda looked at them uneasily. She looked from picture to picture, but nothing seemed to stand out. As she studied the photos, Amanda remembered the man's tattoo. The ivy vine creeping up the forearm of the son of a bitch who raped her. She looked at the arms in the pictures. Some were only visible from the elbow up due to the proximity of the camera. Her gaze fell on one of the arms visible almost to his wrist. Her spine tingled as she studied the long, green vine that wrapped around his forearm. Silent tears fell onto the table as she glanced up at Sergeant Harding.

She pointed. "Him." It was all she could say without breaking down and sobbing. The memories were smashing through the barrier she had put up in her subconscious.

He looked at her understandingly. "You're sure?"

"Positive."

Harding gathered up the pictures and reached for a box of tissues on a nearby desk. He handed them to Amanda.

"Did I do it all right?" she asked, wiping her eyes.

"You did great. I'll show you to the lobby."

As they walked, Amanda wanted to ask him what happened next. She had hoped that with her positive identification they could just arrest him and send him to death row. She was certain that was not the case, but it would make her feel better. As they reached the lobby, Sergeant Harding smiled.

"Thanks again for coming down, Amanda. I'll let you know how things progress. You sure you're okay?"

"I'm sure. Thanks."

With that, he turned and walked to the back of the station. Sam, the girl at the front desk, smiled at Amanda.

"How'd it go?"

"Good," Amanda replied. "I hope."

"It must be so scary. I mean, to look at all those guys and think that one of them, well…" Her voice trailed off in an attempt to avoid an awkward and uncomfortable moment.

"Yup." Amanda said quickly. "Have a good day. I guess I'll see you around."

"Bye." Sam smiled.

As Amanda walked to her car, she looked around the parking lot for any sign of Matt. She was staring at a parked police cruiser in the upper parking lot as she walked. She became so focused on trying to see who was sitting behind the tinted glass that she ran right into someone walking toward the front door of the station.

"Oh my gosh. I'm so sorry." Amanda looked around and realized that when they collided, the papers the other person had been carrying had gone everywhere. She bent down to help pick them up. She was gathering them all in as neat of a stack as she could manage in her post-collision, somewhat blurry vision. As she stood up, she rubbed her head with her free hand. She extended the other hand, full of papers, toward the person opposite her.

"I'm so sorry about that," she said as she finally looked at who she had run into.

"Not a problem. You weren't texting and walking, were you? They have signs warning people about that now, ya know."

Amanda smiled. Her first real smile in quite a while. And as quickly as it had come, it faded.

"I wasn't texting. I was just looking for someone."

"Must be someone pretty important."

"Yeah...kind of..." Amanda trailed off as she studied the man she was standing across from. He was wearing a Claiborne Fire Department uniform shirt and navy-blue pants, and he had a radio slung across his chest with some kind of leather strap. His silver name badge read "Lt. Brian Whiting."

"So, you're a fireman?" Amanda said, realizing how foolish it sounded.

"No, ma'am. Actually, I'm getting a really good head start on my Halloween costume."

Amanda looked down and didn't respond. He was going to continue the joke, but he must have felt bad embarrassing someone he had just met.

"Yes, ma'am. I am a firefighter for the city of Claiborne. They ask us not to say 'fireman,' as we have a few females in the department who don't especially care for the 'man' at the end of their job title."

"I see," said Amanda, shifting uncomfortably. "If you're a firefighter, what are you doing at the police station? Too many unpaid parking tickets in the firetruck?" Amanda forced a smile and tried to ignore the uneasy feeling she got from talking to a stranger.

"Actually, we pay those online now. We never even have to leave the firehouse. It's very convenient."

"Sorry I ran into you." She tried a smile again but stopped herself. After what she had been through, any type of contact with men other than her father and the police had been difficult.

"I should let you get inside. Sorry I bumped into you."

"I'm not."

With that, he smiled and continued into the police station.

When she arrived home, Amanda sat in her car in her driveway. She had shut it off but was still sitting behind the wheel. She felt stunted and stuck, like the days of her life were falling off the calendar and lying in a lifeless pile on the floor. She ran her fingers through her hair and looked at herself in the mirror. It had taken her some time, but the feeling of true anger had finally arrived. She decided not to let the anger consume her. It was time to start living again. What happened to her was disgusting and brutal, but after all she had been through, however broken she may feel, she was still alive. It was time to start acting like it.

She turned the key, and as soon as the car started, she put it in gear. She let her foot off the brake but applied it again and paused, unaware of where exactly she was going. She apparently hadn't decided where to go, just that she needed to go somewhere or do something to keep her life from growing more and more stagnant.

Chapter 6

W hen Amanda pulled back into the driveway, it was late afternoon. She parked and opened the trunk of her car and started to unload the things she'd bought while she was out. New sheets, new curtains, and throw pillows for the couch that actually matched the living room. (She loved her father dearly, but he was a terrible decorator). A few groceries, a new coffee pot, and a stack of job applications. After her last trip to the car, Amanda stood silently at her front door, looking at the street. She realized that for the first time in a long time she had had a somewhat normal day. There was still the uneasy feeling every time she passed a strange man in the store or parking lot. She checked over her shoulder constantly no matter where she was, and she parked as close to the buildings as possible.

She stood quietly and looked around her neighborhood. She only knew one neighbor named June, and she didn't know much at all about her except that she knew Amanda's father. In a further attempt to put herself back on the list of functional human beings, Amanda stepped down from her front step and headed to the house across the street. She reached the front door and drew in a deep breath, then let it out slowly. She knocked a quick two raps on the door. She decided it was a bad idea and turned immediately to leave, but before she could take a step, the door opened.

"Amanda? How are you?" the woman said brightly.

"Hi," Amanda said in what had become her typical, flat tone.

"Hi, dear, how are you? Come in, come in."

"Oh, I just stopped over to say hello. I don't need…"

Before Amanda could finish her sentence, June opened the door farther and put her hand behind Amanda's shoulders to guide her in the door. As Amanda walked in, she couldn't help but notice how good it smelled inside the house. The décor was bright and very well matched. The curtains nicely complemented the color of the walls. She noticed the way the furniture was laid out and how neat the shelves of books and pictures were. It made it seem like she had just walked into a magazine.

"You have a beautiful home," Amanda managed.

"Oh, thank you, honey. I've lived here for quite a while now and try to keep things looking as nice as I can."

"You do a great job." Amanda felt herself running out of things to say already.

"You're too sweet. So, what brings you over here? It's so nice to see you. How is your Dad? What have you been up to?"

Amanda realized that June had enough questions to keep her from running out of things to say for quite a while.

"Dad is good. I just wanted to stop by and say hello. I know you and my Dad have been friends for quite some time, and I realized that I had never visited you."

"Well, I'm certainly glad you did," June said happily.

Amanda hadn't realized it, but during their short conversation they had somehow managed to end up in June's kitchen. Amanda looked around. Even the kitchen was perfect. Pots and pans hung on a rack above the island. The counters were clean and shined as if they had never seen food and had instead been polished daily. The stainless-steel appliances sat quietly and neatly, nestled snugly in their nooks between the kitchen cabinets. Amanda was looking at the beautiful flower arrangement on the kitchen table when she heard June say, "Lemon, honey, or both?" Amanda turned to see June holding up a large teacup with a sunflower on it. She smiled to herself at the irony that it looked just like the one she had thrown at the wall.

"Oh." Amanda glanced at the jar of honey on the counter. "Both, if that's okay?"

"Of course it's okay." June set the mug down and spooned in some honey. She squeezed a fresh lemon wedge in and looked at Amanda. She didn't need to say anything. Amanda knew what she was about to ask.

"You can put the lemon in there. That's fine. Thanks."

Amanda managed a smile as she took the mug from her.

"To the living room we go," June said as she motioned for Amanda to walk in front of her.

"Your home really is just beautiful," Amanda added as she walked. "I should have you come over and redecorate my house. It feels so…" Amanda searched for the right word. Before she could say anything, June smiled and said, "John Killingly-ish?"

Amanda actually laughed a little.

"Yes. It is *definitely* way too John Killingly-ish." Amanda smiled as she sat in a beautiful tan armchair.

"Well, anytime you need a visitor, friend, or redecorator, you just let me know." June laughed.

"Sounds great." Amanda smiled.

Amanda took a sip of her tea and sat back in the chair. It felt like the chair was hugging her. It was incredibly comfortable.

"In all seriousness," June added, "if you want to shop for some new house décor, please call me. I would love to shop with you and help decorate."

"Yeah?" Amanda raised her eyebrows.

"Absolutely," June said happily.

"I'd like that," Amanda said. "I haven't really been out with anyone since…" Amanda felt herself starting to not know what to say. She continued as seamlessly as possible. "Since Dad stopped visiting so often. He's a busy man."

June set her tea cup on the end table. "Amanda, honey," June said and then paused. "I know what happened. And you can talk about it if you ever need to, or you can never talk about it at all. Just please know I am always here to listen. And if you don't want me to listen, I'm here to get a manicure with you and gossip about the locals or shop and pick out the most expensive shoes we can find and call your father and have him pay for them," June said, smiling.

Amanda managed a weak smile. "I'd like that," she offered. "Maybe Dad should pay for more than just the shoes." She laughed. Amanda was nowhere near ready to tell June what happened, but she was thankful that she had decided to stop by and say hello. She felt slightly less isolated than when she had woken up that morning. They chatted for a little while longer. Enough for Amanda to learn that June had been quite close with her parents before her mother had passed away. June had been in their wedding, attended the same church, and frequently went on vacation with them and her late husband Phillip.

"Oh, we were just kids back then," June said, finishing a story. She looked nostalgically at Amanda. Her eyes glistened. "I'd give anything to go back to those days. We were so young and energetic. Your dad and Phillip had the answers to all the world's problems, and your Mom and I figured we could keep ourselves busy for the next hundred years keeping those two out of trouble."

"I hear so many people say that Mom was so vibrant when she was younger."

"Oh, sweetheart, she absolutely was. Your mother could power a locomotive with an idea and stop one with her smile. She was tremendous."

Amanda felt her eyes start to sting. She had lost her mother at such a young age that she hadn't thought about missing her in quite some time. She thought about how nice it would be to have a mom during this time in her life. Another female, someone she could tell everything to. She wondered if it would help ease the pain. Not wanting to ruin the positive mood that had been set by June's stories, Amanda took a quick breath and raised her eyes to June's.

"Thank you for talking about her. I never get to hear stories much anymore. I have heard dozens from Dad and Dave and some other friends, but they didn't seem to know all the fun details that you do." Amanda gave a quiet smile.

"Oh, I have so many stories, my dear. I kept a journal that is around this house somewhere. Quick little stories about your Mom and I, quotes from your Dad and Phillip, places we visited, stamps from the states we drove through on road trips. I may even have your Mom's wedding vows in there. Oh, she was just so nervous she must have written about a dozen drafts." June took a deep breath and let out a happy sigh. "That was a wonderful time in my life. So many things to look back on. Your mother started every day like a shot out of a gun. No slow starts. She had momentum from the moment she woke up. Some days I think your poor father felt like he was strapped to the passenger seat while she blasted through life at change-the-world speed." June smiled at the happy memories.

A picture formed in Amanda's mind of her parents, but it was pushed aside by another image.

"Gun and passenger seat." Amanda said.

"What's that, dear?"

"Gun *in* the passenger seat." Amanda furrowed her brow.

"Oh, I just meant that as a colorful analogy, love," June said.

"No, I mean..." She stopped and thought for a moment. "The men that attacked me. One of them had a gun in the passenger seat of the truck. It wasn't like anything I'd seen. It almost looked gold, and it had something on the handle, a symbol, a circle." Amanda pressed her hand to her temples. "What was it? An eagle. It was an eagle!" Amanda took a deep breath and looked up at June. "I need to talk to the police." She must have looked more panicked and upset than she thought given the look on June's face.

"Do you need to sit down for a minute?" June reached for her arm.

Amanda stood up and pulled her keys from her pocket.

"I'm okay. I just need to tell them before I forget."

"Okay," June said with a gentle smile. "Good luck."

Chapter 7

Amanda barely remembered driving to the police station. She hurried to the door with her keys and cell phone in hand. When she reached the front lobby area, Sam looked up and smiled. Before she could say anything, Amanda started speaking rapidly. "Is Sergeant Harding here? I need to see him. Or Matt. Or the other guy working on my case. What's his name? McWilliams? Officer McWilliams. Where is he?" Amanda felt herself rambling and forced herself to take a breath. Sam looked up at her.

"Hi, Amanda. Are you okay? Sergeant Harding isn't here at the moment, but I think Officer McWilliams is. Would you like me to get him for you?"

"Yes," Amanda said abruptly. "Yes, please."

Amanda stood, fidgeting at the front desk.

"Amanda, you can sit if—"

"I'm fine," Amanda answered before Sam could finish.

"Okay, I'll find him." Sam picked up her phone, and Amanda heard her murmuring quietly. A few minutes later the door behind Sam's desk opened, and Officer McWilliams appeared. He was older than Amanda, but not by much. He was of average build, but he was much taller than Amanda. He leaned in to greet her.

"Hi, Ms. Killingly. Sam said you seemed like you were in a hurry. Is everything okay?"

"I remember something else about the night I was attacked." Amanda remembered how hard it was to say that phrase when she first went to the police. Now, sadly, it seemed so ordinary and commonplace. Attacked. Raped. Words she never thought would be easy to say seemed far too normal.

"A gun," she started. "I remember seeing a gun. It wasn't really normal looking. It was shiny and chrome, or maybe gold. And it had an eagle on the handle. Almost like an emblem or a seal of some kind. That helps, right? I mean, not just anyone would have a gun that looked like that."

"That's a start, for sure. Where do you remember seeing the gun?"

"It was setting on the seat of the truck. I couldn't see much that night. I could only see the seats and the floor, and their arms and legs."

"Okay. So, there was a gun on the truck seat. It was shiny and had an eagle on the handle?"

"Yes," Amanda said. "It was either gold or chrome. Maybe both?"

"Okay, gold and chrome and an eagle on the handle. Anything else?"

"No. Nothing else. Is that enough? I mean, it seemed like a lot of information. Like it was fairly specific. I'm sorry. It's helpful, right? Please, I haven't heard anything from the police in months. I was hoping it would help."

Officer McWilliams put his hands together and looked at Amanda. "I will make sure I talk to some people about the gun. I'll see if it turns up anything. Gold, chrome, and an eagle on the handle."

"Yes, thank you." Amanda looked down. She felt like what she had thought was a valuable piece of information had lost its importance now that some time had passed. "Sorry if it isn't valuable information," she added as she started to turn to leave.

"It's great information to have Amanda. Thank you. I'll walk you out." He opened the door for Amanda and gestured for her to walk out first. Amanda waved to Sam. Sam waved back and mouthed, "Bye". He opened her car door for her. Amanda climbed in and closed it behind her.

"Thanks again," she offered.

"You're welcome, Ms. Killingly. Drive safely."

As Amanda pulled out of the parking lot, she turned the radio up and tried to calm her mind. She was only a few minutes from home when she rounded a corner and saw a road full of flashing lights. A man in a bright green vest stood near the edge of the road with his hand up. Amanda slowly came to a stop. The man called out to her, "It will just be a minute, ma'am. They're packing up now."

"Oh, okay," Amanda called back. "Thank you." As Amanda waited, she found herself trying to see what was going on. It looked like there had been a car accident. She could just see the back end of a severely damaged car on a flatbed wrecker. As the wrecker started to pull away, she caught a glimpse of the back of a firefighter's coat. "Lt. Whiting" was written at the bottom of the coat in bright green letters. Whiting. Brian Whiting. The firefighter that she had run into, literally, at the police station that day. She felt a slight eagerness to wave to him. The eagerness mixed with a slight feeling of nausea.

After a handful of minutes, the man in the vest called out, "Okay, ma'am." Amanda looked up and saw the man waving his hand and motioning for her to pull forward. She pulled ahead slowly, and he said, "Go ahead. There should be room. Just go slow, please."

"Okay," Amanda answered as she pulled forward. As she got closer, she could see Brian standing next to the firetruck.

Amanda slowed down and rolled her window down. She wasn't sure why she rolled it down, and she hadn't intended to say anything, but before she could second-guess herself, she found herself starting to speak.

"You know, you really shouldn't obstruct traffic." Brian turned and immediately smiled when he saw her.

"Well, if you members of the traveling public went a little slower, we wouldn't have to interrupt your trip to get coffee."

Amanda looked down. She was doing her best to be normal, but she was still so unsure of how to talk to people. "So what happened? Was there a car accident?"

Amanda regretted the question a little as soon as the words left her mouth. She knew it was a silly question. What had happened was rather obvious. She raised her eyes to look at Brian, embarrassed and feeling foolish.

"Actually, we had a call for two elephants and a giraffe running up and down the road. We just happened to find that smashed up car when we got here."

Amanda was relieved that he chose to play along and not embarrass her.

"Oh, well, I hope you find them. I'd be worried sick if my elephants and giraffe got out of the house."

"Well, who wouldn't be? I mean, two elephants and a giraffe... they're practically helpless." Brian leaned down just slightly so he could see Amanda's face a little better. He patted the door of her car and said, "Drive safely, please, Ms. Killingly."

Amanda smiled. He had remembered her name. She drove past the parked firetruck, leaving her window down to enjoy the air.

When she pulled into her driveway, she saw that June's door open and that June was standing just inside it, washing the glass on the sidelight windows of the front door. Amanda shut her car off and headed across the street. Before she could say anything, June called out to her. "Oh, thank goodness. I've been worried sick about you. You rushed off so abruptly before that I didn't even have a chance to check to see if you were all right."

"I'm fine, thank you, June. I just...I felt like I needed to tell someone about what I remembered, because if I didn't tell someone, I might have forgotten. I guess a phone call to the police would have been less dramatic. I'm sorry if I worried you."

"Oh, it's okay, dear. I'm glad you're okay. Did you want more tea?"

"Actually," Amanda started, "if you're interested, I'd like to have you come over for pizza. My treat."

June's face lit up. Amanda could tell she tried to downplay her excitement a little.

"Oh, well, I think I could do that. Are you sure you don't mind, honey?"

"Positive," Amanda said happily. She wasn't sure if she could manage a dinner date with Brian, but she was okay with the idea of having pizza with June. "Meet me at my house at six?"

"Wonderful." June smiled. "I'll see you soon."

Chapter 8

T he phone on Officer McWilliams's desk began to ring. His shift was ending soon, and he would rather not have to answer it now if he could help it. After the third ring, however, he decided it might be someone returning a call about the gun Amanda had described to him. And so he answered. "Claiborne Police. McWilliams. Yes, that's me. Okay. Okay, sure, let me get a pen. Sounds great, thank you. And that's the address on the registration form for the gun or the address of where it was sold? Okay, great. Thanks very much." Officer McWilliams hung up the phone and typed the address into his computer. He pulled out Amanda's case file and looked at his computer screen. He picked up his pen and wrote a note on the paper. He picked up the phone and made another call to the same person he had just hung up with. It was a short conversation, but he wanted to double check the address.

"You're sure that's it? Not a different zip code or something that's throwing it off? Okay, appreciate it. See ya."

Officer McWilliams stared at the paper and then looked up to his computer screen. He thumbed through the case file and made a few more notes. Finally, he stood up and crossed over to a map hanging on the wall of the office. He pushed a red thumb tack into the board that the map hung on. He picked up a second tack, green this time, and pushed it in the map below the red one. He studied the map and looked at the papers in his hand. His brow furrowed as he read the address over and over and looked back to the report about Amanda's case. After a few moments, he closed the case file and walked toward Sergeant Harding's desk. Harding looked up when he heard the brief knock on his open door.

"What's up, kid?"

"I got a return call about the gun Amanda Killingly described. Sounds like we'll be able to track down the owner. Here's the address the registry office gave me from the firearm registration form."

Officer McWilliams set a piece of paper on Sergeant Harding's desk. Harding looked at the paper. He stared for a few seconds and took off his glasses. He looked up at McWilliams.

"I'll be a son of a bitch."

"Yeah."

"You're sure?"

"Positive. I didn't think it was right, so I called the firearms unit back. That's the address. So now what?"

"We cover all our bases. There has to be some kind of connection, but I don't think it's the obvious one. We play it smart, and we play it slow. Gather information quietly without raising any red flags."

"Okay, got it," McWilliams said as he walked toward the door.

"And, kid..." Officer McWilliams stopped and turned to face Harding. "If it really is his gun and he really is behind this, you tell me and no one else. We clear?"

McWilliams's brow furrowed with a mixture of hesitation and concern. He pressed his lips together as if he were about to speak but instead held the breath for a beat, then let it out silently before relaxing again. He drew in another breath, nodded slowly, and said, "Yes, sir."

Chapter 9

Amanda heard a knock at her door, something that still bothered her a bit. She looked out the side window and saw June standing on her front step. She had done her hair and makeup just enough to highlight her bright green eyes. Amanda opened the door and smiled. "Okay," she started, "now remember, this is the house that had Dad as a decorator. Please don't judge."

June laughed and stepped inside. As she looked around, she said, "Oh, honey, it looks wonderful. You made it sound so terrible, but it's a beautiful home." June glanced at the pile of bags on the kitchen table. "Been shopping a little already, have we?"

"Well..." Amanda pressed her lips together in a subtle smile and then looked at June and let out a quiet laugh. "I bought a few things just to make the place feel a bit more like home."

"Well, I'd be more than happy to help you set them up while we wait for the pizza to be ready. Or did you want to go out for pizza?"

Amanda heard her question and realized she hadn't been out to eat in quite a while. She had gone out with her dad a few times quite a while ago. One of the times, she panicked and asked her Dad to get the food to go, and they left. Not wanting to delay her response much longer, Amanda made a quick decision and hoped she wouldn't regret it.

"The bags can wait. Let's go out to eat, if that's okay."

"Of course it's okay. I can go get my car."

"June, you're not very good at this whole *my* treat thing, are you?" Amanda said.

"Well, honey, I guess not. It's been quite some time since someone took me out. Is this an official pizza date?" Both of them laughed a little as they walked out of Amanda's front door. They climbed into Amanda's car, and she did her best to be discreet about her habitual vehicle check. She looked in the front and the back, checked her mirrors several times, and looked under her seats. She opened her glove compartment and console, scanned each of them, and closed them quietly. June understood what she was doing and didn't say a word. Grateful, Amanda shot June a shy and somewhat embarrassed smile, then headed out.

"Okay, June, since it's our first date, it's your choice as to where we get pizza," Amanda said, smiling. It felt good to smile. She had experienced a whole host of emotions in the past several months, but smiling was certainly not something she had done much of.

"Antonio's. Could we go there?"

"Of course," Amanda said.

Amanda was so happy to have found someone to talk to. Conversation was something that she missed so much. She had always been a talkative person, but since her attack, she had become quite the opposite. Amanda remembered being so nervous only hours before that she and June would quickly run out of conversation. She was thankful that was not the case. Their topics changed from Amanda's father to June's house to her former job as a roller skate-clad-waitress when she was much younger. Amanda was grinning as she pulled into the parking lot of the restaurant. "A bright red curly-haired wig, a denim skirt, and *roller skates*? Tell me there are pictures." June's eyes watered from laughing.

"Ohhhh, Amanda, I haven't laughed like this in years. Thank you so much."

"Don't thank me yet," Amanda kidded. "I'll find pictures of you in that outfit somewhere and make sure I get them in the newspaper somehow." Their laughter turned to sporadic giggles as Amanda shut off her car. They walked up the steps and into a beautifully decorated restaurant. It was well lit for a restaurant, which Amanda greatly appreciated.

The hostess walked over and smiled immediately. "June? Hi! Oh my gosh, how are you? It's so nice to see you."

"Hi, Marybeth, I'm very well. It's wonderful to see you, too. How is your little one?"

"She's amazing. And she's a big sister."

June's face lit up. So many people seemed to have programmed responses to the usual fare when it came to small talk. June, on the other hand, had an authentic reaction to the hostess's comment about having a second child.

"A big sister? How wonderful!" She put one hand over her heart and grabbed the hostess's hand with the other. "I guess I haven't seen you in quite some time." June spun to face Amanda and then looked back at Marybeth. "Oh, my manners. Where are my manners? Amanda, this is Marybeth. Marybeth, this is my friend Amanda." Amanda and Marybeth exchanged hellos as they followed Marybeth to a table. As they walked, Amanda noticed beautiful paintings on the wall and perfectly folded napkins set out on the unoccupied tables.

"Is this okay, ladies?" Marybeth stopped and motioned to a round table in the corner that was neatly set with two place settings. June looked at Amanda as if to silently ask her approval.

Amanda nodded. "Looks great, thank you."

"Thank you, Marybeth. Give those little ones a hug for me," June added as she pulled out her chair.

"Will do. Enjoy your meal."

Amanda put her napkin in her lap and looked around at the ceiling and walls, then at the people around her. She had subtly moved herself to the seat closest to the wall when they had walked over. Having her back to the wall gave her some small reassurance about being in a public place with so many other people.

"This place is beautiful," Amanda started. "What do you recommend? I know I had said pizza, but everything on the menu sounds so amazing."

"Up to you, dear. We can get pizza if you'd like. They make a delicious chicken and bacon pizza. Or if you're not in the mood for pizza, the chicken arancia and the shrimp and scallops ala vodka are both perfection on a plate." Amanda considered her options. It had been so long since she had actually had food from a restaurant that wasn't slightly soggy from the Styrofoam containers on the defroster in the delivery car.

"June, is it okay if I don't get pizza? All these things sound so good."

"Of course, honey. Get whatever you'd like. They'll bring bread first. It's to die for."

Amanda's ability to speak easily to June helped push away the feeling of uneasy nervousness that she couldn't help but have in a public place.

"Amanda," June started as she took a sip of her ginger ale, "can I ask you a question? Please, tell me if it's none of my business."

Amanda paused. She was happy to talk to June about just about anything at this point.

"I'm ready," she said.

June smiled back. "It's not a very exciting question at all. I was just wondering if you had been looking for a new job or if you were comfortable with the way things are."

"You have great timing. I actually picked up a bunch of applications today while I was out, right before I came over to your house. I was going to get them filled out and mailed out as soon as I could."

"Oh, wonderful. Is there anything specific you were looking to do, or were you keeping your options open?"

"At this point I'm open to pretty much anything. Except..." Amanda paused, raised her eyebrows, and made a half-smile, half-grimace face. "Maybe no bartending jobs ever, ever again." Amanda was proud of herself for being able to make somewhat light of a difficult topic.

June nodded slowly. "That's probably a pretty good plan."

"I thought so." Amanda continued, "But in all honesty, I'm just looking for some steady employment with decent co-workers. I was a communications major in college, but I didn't have much luck finding anything related to that field in my travels today."

June took a thoughtful bite of her chicken. She chewed slowly for a moment and then took another sip of ginger ale. "I may have a job that I could help you apply for, if you were interested. I can't promise anything, but I can do all I can to help you."

"Really? That would be wonderful, thank you. Where is the job, and what would I be doing?"

"I have a very close friend who works at Claiborne Area Dispatch, the place that answers emergency calls and dispatches the police department, fire department, and the ambulance services. I don't know if that is something you would be interested in. They say it can be stressful at times, but it can also be very rewarding."

Amanda twirled a bite of food on her fork. She imagined it could be very stressful. People calling on their worst day, asking for help when they feel helpless. Amanda thought of how badly she wished she or someone else could have called 911 the night she was attacked. Perhaps it could have been prevented. Or at least stopped before she was beaten almost to death. Amanda wanted to do it. She wanted to be there to help. She wanted the chance to be that one glimmer of hope, the link that brings the helpers to the helpless. Before she realized she was even answering, Amanda practically yelled, "Yes!"

June blinked quickly in midchew. She put her hand in front of her mouth as a sign to Amanda that she was about to answer but needed a moment to finish chewing her food.

"Are you sure? I would love to introduce you to my contact that works there if you are interested."

"Yes, please, June. That would be wonderful. The thought of being able to help someone—or help them be helped, I guess—sounds so rewarding."

"Wonderful. You let me know when you're available to go, and we'll find a day to go over and meet some people and pick up an application."

"Well, I'm done with my food, so whenever the waitress brings the check, I'll be ready to go," Amanda kidded.

The waitress brought the check a little later, and June quickly took it from her.

"Hey!" Amanda reached for the check. "I said it was my treat."

June moved her chair back and gave Amanda a coy smirk. "I'll tell you what. I'll get it this time, and if the job works out, you can thank me by paying next time. Maybe."

Amanda tilted her head slightly. "Should I even bother arguing with you about this?"

June smirked. "Nope. Not worth it." Her smirk turned to a smile as she slid her credit card into the plastic sleeve.

"Fiiiinnne." Amanda exhaled and tried to sound exasperated. "If you insist. Thank you very much," she said sincerely.

"You're welcome, honey."

"I'm going to use the ladies' room. I'll be right back."

"Okay, dear, I'll sign my receipt and meet you right back here."

Amanda pushed back from the table and headed to the corner of the restaurant. She was just about to the hallway where the ladies' room was when she heard a voice behind her.

"Excuse me...Amanda?"

Amanda froze. It wasn't June's voice, and she didn't know any other people in the area well enough to talk to randomly on a trip to the ladies' room. She turned slowly to see a middle-aged woman with long brown hair wearing black pants and a flower-print top. Tall and in good shape, Amanda guessed that she was around her father's age. She had crow's feet at the corners of her eyes, and there were small creases at the corners of her mouth, but she was still very pretty. She was standing behind Amanda with a credit card in her hand. Before Amanda could say anything, the woman began to speak.

"I'm sorry if I startled you, but you dropped this back there." She reached her arm out and handed Amanda the credit card. Amanda looked down and saw her name in embossed letters on the card.

"You stood up from the table, and when you started to walk, I saw it hit the floor."

"Oh." Amanda paused to let herself calm down a bit. She had been startled and had went on the defensive while wondering what this woman wanted. She took a breath and, as she exhaled, said, "Thank you. I must have forgotten to put it in my purse before I left the table."

"You're welcome. Hope you enjoyed your food." Amanda felt bad ignoring the woman's comment about the food.

"It was very, very good," Amanda said as she started to turn back toward the ladies' room.

"Good. We restaurant owners hate when people don't enjoy the food."

Owner. Amanda repeated the word in her head. Now she felt badly about trying to ignore the woman. She turned to face her again.

"It was delicious. Thank you so much. I'll definitely be back."

"Wonderful." The woman smiled and disappeared through a door to what Amanda assumed was the kitchen. As Amanda walked into the ladies' room, the woman looked back through the glass window in the door she had walked through seconds before. She took out her phone and typed a quick text message.

"Just met Amanda Killingly. The bartender. She likes the food. I'm sure she'll be back."

Amanda was washing her hands in the beautiful marble sink in the ladies' room when she heard the door open. She paused briefly and realized this was the first time she had used a public restroom since her attack. She wasn't quite sure what made her leave June at the table and head to the bathroom like it was no big deal, but she tried to push past the thought of being in a room with one door and no windows. She turned to face the door and saw a girl a bit older than her enter with a small child in tow. Amanda smiled at the girl as she passed.

"Excuse us," the woman offered. "We're learning to use the potty, and apparently it is very urgent."

Amanda felt a bit calmer. "Good luck," she said as she dried her hands. She pulled open the door and headed back to her table. As she approached the table, she saw June with her phone to her ear.

"Okay, great, we may see you soon." June set her phone on the table and looked up at Amanda. "Would you like to continue our date?" she said as she stood up.

Amanda raised her eyes and smiled. "Ice cream?" she asked. June smiled.

"Well, we can certainly get ice cream," June responded, "but I just spoke to my contact at the Dispatch Center, and she said she'd love to meet you if you're up for it."

Amanda thought for a second and decided to take June up on her offer. Part of her wanted to go home to relax and unwind, to just be home before it got too late or too dark. She was having a great time with June, though, and she decided it was a sign she should go with her now.

"No time like the present," Amanda said happily.

"Really? Are you sure?" June answered. "I think you'll really like her."

"Sounds wonderful. Am I dressed okay? June, I'm wearing jeans. Is this an interview? Do I need to change?

Maybe stop and grab an evening gown or throw on a quick three-piece suit?"

June laughed. "You're fine, dear. It's not really an interview, just a casual conversation."

Amanda followed June to the door of the restaurant. She looked around cautiously as they walked to the parking lot. She couldn't help but search the parking lot for other people, look for strange men, and notice the dark corners. She hadn't been out this late since her attack. She was very glad she had June with her. They passed a man in the middle of the parking lot.

"Hello," June offered as they kept walking.

"Hi, ladies. Enjoy your night."

Amanda looked over quickly at her. Her eyes and facial expression must have been relaying her message of *what the hell are you doing* quite well, because June's expression quickly changed from a quiet smile to an understanding, slightly embarrassed look. When they reached Amanda's car and were safely inside, Amanda locked the door and looked over at June. Not wanting June to feel bad, Amanda spoke up first.

"Did ya have to talk to the strange man? I mean, what if he was an ax murderer. Or worse, a door-to-door salesman. Or a vampire." Amanda did her best to smile and be just melodramatic enough that, she hoped, June would know she wasn't upset with her.

"Well, honey, if he is a vampire, I'm pretty sure I ate enough garlic tonight to keep him far away." June managed a shy smile before she offered, "I'm sorry. I wasn't thinking."

"It's okay." Amanda nodded her head. "I'm the one who isn't quite normal yet. Most people would have said hello out of politeness."

"Okay, dear. Slowly and surely, you'll get there," June said, patting her arm. "Okay, so," she continued in an effort to keep the evening happy and help Amanda feel at ease, "left out of the parking lot, right at the light, and left at the first stop sign."

"Left, right, left. Yes, ma'am." Amanda playfully saluted June.

"A salute? Very official."

"Well, if I'm going to work in the world of public safety, don't I have to learn to salute? Maybe wear a uniform? Play a bugle at dawn?"

June laughed out loud. "Oh, you remind me so much of your mother. She'd be so happy and proud that you got her energy and sense of humor."

"I'd like to think she knows. Maybe looks down on me from time to time."

"I'm sure she does, honey. And I bet she is just as happy and proud as can be of the woman you turned out to be."

Amanda glanced at June and smiled. "Thanks. Okay, we've turned left and right, and here is our next left."

June pointed out the windshield. "Straight ahead. Turn right into the parking lot by the big overhead light."

"Isn't that the fire station?"

"Yes, it is. The dispatch center is in the fire department headquarters."

As Amanda turned into the parking lot, she very quickly found herself wondering if she would see Lieutenant Whiting. She glanced in her mirror at her hair and ran her fingers through it. Apparently, she wasn't very subtle.

"You look beautiful, dear."

Amanda pressed her lips together and looked at June out of the corner of her eye. "Thanks."

"I told you, though, that it's not an interview; it's just a conversation. And, Amanda, if it helps, my contact is a female. I'm not sure if I said that."

As she and June got out of her car, she heard a truck start and saw the doors of the firehouse opening. She could see flashing lights bouncing off the buildings across the street. She heard a second and third truck start and the low wail of a siren starting. She and June stood back as the trucks pulled to the end of the parking lot. The first truck blew a very loud horn before turning onto the street. The second truck followed. The third was a giant truck with a huge ladder on top that appeared to actually be part of the truck itself. Amanda watched as the person in the passenger seat rolled down the window and leaned out.

"You gotta stop following me. I mean, this is getting ridiculous."

Amanda recognized him immediately. She smiled, just a little. "Good luck with your giraffe hunt," she called back. Whiting smiled and yanked on a cord hanging from the ceiling of the truck cab. The air horn sounded, and the truck roared onto the street.

"Ahem," June said aloud and quite deliberately.

Amanda turned and raised her eyebrows. "Hi."

"Hi," June called back. "So, I guess all that hair fixing and lip gloss wasn't because we were meeting a friend of mine to talk about a job."

"Oh, it totally was. It just... yeah... should we go inside now?" Amanda grabbed June by the arm and began walking quickly and dramatically to the door.

"He's very handsome," June offered, hoping Amanda would play along.

"Who is?" Amanda looked at her with her best *I don't know what you're talking about* expression.

"Mmmhmm." June laughed as they walked toward the door. "Now we can go in through the fire station since the overhead doors are still open, but I'm guessing you don't have much interest in the fire station. Not since the fire trucks left, anyway." June smirked at Amanda.

"Whichever door you'd like, ma'am."

June led Amanda to a side door and up a few steps. She picked up a phone receiver hanging next to the door, and Amanda heard it start ringing immediately. She heard a murmur on the other end, and then June said, "Hi, we're here to see Kelly Montgomery."

Amanda heard a loud buzz and a click. June pulled on the door handle and opened the door.

"This is very CIA-ish and exciting," Amanda kidded.

"Well, I'm pretty bad ass," June said casually, making Amanda giggle.

June smiled as she pulled open a second door in the hallway they had walked into. They walked only a few feet to the bottom of a staircase and came to a third door. June knocked and waved at a small camera hanging on the wall. Another buzz and click. June pulled the door open. Amanda walked through the door and stopped almost immediately to look around. She was somewhat in awe of what she saw. High up on the wall there were flat screen TVs in every corner, evenly spaced around the room. Several desks filled the room, each with three computer monitors, two phones, and a space-aged-looking office chair on wheels. One TV screen was playing a constant radar loop of the local weather. Another had a list of streets in the city, listing things like "closed" and "one-way traffic only." She was still taking in everything around her when she heard June's voice.

"Hi, Kelly."

She turned to see a tall brunette in a gray pantsuit walking toward June. Her energy was palpable, even halfway across the room. Her thick hair fell to well below her shoulders, and she was fit, lean, and had brilliant blue eyes. Kelly could be intimidating with her sharp features and power suit, but her eyes were kind, and so was the smile that broke out on her face when she saw June.

"Hi, Mom," the woman answered as she leaned in to hug June.

"Honey, this is my friend Amanda. She is John Killingly's daughter."

The woman reached out her hand. Amanda shook her hand and looked up at her.

"Very nice to meet you, Amanda. I've heard lots of stories about your parents."

Amanda smiled quietly. "Thanks to your mom and our dinner date tonight, so have I."

Kelly smiled. "Let's go for a walk, and I'll show you around. My mom said you may be interested in working for us?"

"Yes, I'm job searching now, and when your mom talked about what you all do here, it sounded very fulfilling. A bit nerve racking, but satisfying."

Kelly turned to face Amanda. "A bit, yes. But it's a great job." She had walked Amanda to the front of the room and turned to face all of the desks in the room. "So this is a regional dispatch center for the area. We dispatch the Claiborne fire department and police department, along with about forty volunteer fire departments and ambulance services. Claiborne is about forty square miles, with a population of about thirty-six thousand people, so that alone keeps us fairly busy. In addition to that, however, we also work with other towns in the region, some with just a few thousand people. We are staffed twenty-four hours a day, and each dispatcher works a twelve-hour shift. We field emergency calls and send the appropriate units to each incident. Some days are rather quiet, but other days are very busy and the communicators and dispatchers have a lot going on. The way the system works is like this." Kelly shifted her weight and pointed to a phone on the desk. "An emergency call comes in through one of these phones. One of the communicators answers it and starts to gather all the necessary information. They enter it into the computer system, which is then sent to the dispatcher. The dispatcher utilizes the computer system as well as maps, our smart boards, and TV screens to dispatch the correct department or departments, which then helps get units to the scene quickly and safely."

104

Amanda was looking around the room, trying to take in everything Kelly was saying. The more Kelly spoke, the more interested Amanda was in the job. "Once the units are on scene, our communication with them continues. We are the link to anything they need. We talk to them until the emergency is over and they are back to their fire station, ambulance station, or safely in their police cruiser." She touched the shoulder of a girl sitting next to her and said, "Turn the com volume up, Carrie. Please, and thank you." The girl moved her computer mouse over and increased the volume of the speakers set throughout the room. Amanda hadn't noticed, but there had been people talking and dispatchers responding to them the entire time Kelly had been talking. Amanda turned slightly and looked at June.

"This is so cool," she mouthed without actually speaking. June smiled.

"So right now the firefighters that are stationed here at headquarters are at a motor vehicle accident. They were leaving about the time you guys got here, I think."

"Oh, yes, they were, dear," June said to Kelly as she smiled quickly at Amanda. Suddenly, Amanda realized that maybe she'd be able to hear Lieutenant Whiting on the radio, although she doubted she'd be able to distinguish his voice from the other firefighters.

"Am I allowed to ask what happened?" Amanda spoke up.

"Oh, of course. Privacy laws cover what happens at the scene between the firefighters, ambulance personnel, and the patients or victims, but any Joe Somebody with a scanner from the electronics store can listen to our radio traffic." Kelly walked over to one of the TV screens on the wall in the front of the room. She motioned to Amanda to come closer. She began pointing to the words on the screen. "Okay, so the units listed in green are the ones that are at the emergency scene. When they are driving to the scene, they are yellow, and when they are in the firehouse or available for a call, they are white." Amanda looked at the TV screen. Any blue text you see means the unit is on the road and not in the firehouse but is still available for a call."

Engine six and TAC ten were written in white. Engine two, ladder four, and rescue seven were written in green. Battalion one was in blue.

"Okay, so when we got here, some of the trucks were leaving. Engine two, ladder four, and rescue seven are in green, so I'm guessing they are the ones that we saw drive out of here?" Amanda offered.

"Correct. They responded to the motor vehicle accident." Kelly turned to one of the dispatchers. "Anthony, can you share your screen to monitor four, please?"

The dispatcher clicked some keys on his keyboard, and one of the flat screen TVs at the front of the room changed to mirror the computer monitor at the dispatcher's station. Kelly began pointing as she spoke. "Okay, so this is the time they were dispatched, this is the time they started responding, and this is the time they arrived on scene. This number in the corner is a timer since the last radio transmission. It isn't all that crucial on a call like this one, but it helps when there is a building fire. It allows us to know how long it has been since we've had an update about what's going on at the scene."

Amanda was fascinated. She had always been a little bit of a tech nerd and had done some cool stuff with computers in one of her communications classes in college. This was far more advanced, however, and she found herself quite enthralled with the entire dispatch center. She began glancing from screen to screen and listening to the radio traffic in the background all at the same time. She looked at the TV screens, read the road closures, and watched the radar loop on one of the TVs for a handful of seconds. As she continued looking around, her gaze met June's. Amanda looked back and forth quickly and gave June a shy smile. "Did I miss something? Why are you staring at me?"

"Just watching you look around. You seemed like you wanted a minute to take everything in."

"Oh, sorry. It's just so cool to see what happens at a place like this."

"I'm glad you think it is interesting," Kelly offered. "Did you want to stop in my office quickly and get an application?"

"Yes. Oh my gosh, yes, please."

They walked to Kelly's office, where Kelly motioned for Amanda to sit as she sat in her own desk chair.

Kelly set a packet of papers on the desk. "This is the application for employment and the overview of the test and the test instructions.

"So fill out the application, mail it back here, and then I get a date for the test if they like me?"

"Actually," Kelly said as she handed Amanda one more piece of paper, "here is the time, date, and location of the test. It is at our administrative office a few towns over. Directions are on the back."

Amanda turned the piece of paper over and found the date. She glanced back up at Kelly. "Tomorrow?" Amanda asked, probably a bit louder than she should have.

"The test is on cognitive skills and computer ability," Kelly started. "It isn't something you can really study for, so don't worry about it being tomorrow. You will be seated at a computer and given a pair of headphones. You'll be asked to use the computer while also being given verbal information through the headphones. Sounds a lot more complicated than it is. You'll be fine."

She drew in a deep breath and held it for a second, then let it out slowly in a dramatic sigh. "Okay," she started. "But for the record, I've never been a good test taker. I get nervous, and I start to doubt myself if the question seems too easy, or I feel stupid if it seems too hard. Then I get upset because I read it again and decide it should be easy, but it's not to me. Sometimes I even get writer's cramp, and my eyes water." Amanda looked up at June, who was smirking as she listened to Amanda's dramatic list of test-day ailments. "And sometimes I get tennis elbow, and..." June cocked her head to the side and raised her eyebrows. "Fine." Amanda conceded. "But you're coming with me."

June smiled. "Kelly, honey, is it okay if I go with Amanda tomorrow?"

"Of course, Mom. You can't be in the testing room with her, but you can go with her and wait in my other office while she takes the test."

"Your other office?" Amanda looked over at Kelly.

"Yes, I have one here at the dispatch center and one in our administrative building." Kelly smiled. "If you want to use my computer quickly right now, you can register for the test tomorrow."

Amanda stood and moved to the other side of the desk. Kelly pointed to her computer screen and walked Amanda through the registration process. When she was finished, Amanda thanked Kelly, and she and June headed to the parking lot. As soon as they got to the last door, Amanda took a quick breath. She still didn't like parking lots much. June heard the breath and took Amanda by the arm playfully in an attempt to ease her tension.

"I'd like an escort to my vehicle, please," June said in a terribly overdone British accent.

Amanda smiled and played along. As they entered the night air, Amanda was very thankful that the parking lot was so well lit. There were no dark corners. Giant flood lights washed the entire parking lot in a bright, bluish light. They got in Amanda's car and headed for home. She dropped June off at her door and drove across the street to her own house. She had left her porch light and her kitchen light on, like she always did. She got out of her car quickly, key in hand, and headed for her door. Once she was inside, she checked to make sure all her doors and windows were locked, turned off the kitchen light, and headed upstairs to get a good night's sleep before the test.

Chapter 10

Amanda woke to her cell phone alarm and looked at her bedroom window. She could see brightness through the blinds already and hoped that meant a nice day ahead for the test she still couldn't believe she had agreed to take. She walked to the bathroom and turned on the shower. She brushed her teeth while she waited for the water to heat up. As she stepped into the shower, she tried to think about what the test might entail. Kelly said she'd be asked to use the computer while also listening to verbal information through the headset. Her best guess was that she would be listening to fake emergency calls and using the computer to document the information, then passing it along to the police or fire department. It sounded quite straightforward, and Amanda really hoped it was as simple as it sounded. After her shower, Amanda realized she had another problem. She had absolutely no idea what she was supposed to wear. Her thought was something semi-formal and business appropriate, but not overdressed in a suit or nice dress. She opened her closet door and stared into it as if the racks of clothes had all the answers to life's most difficult questions. She pulled out a few outfits and set them on her bed. After a minute or two of staring at them, she decided she needed a second opinion. She picked up her cell phone and took a picture of the clothes on her bed. She composed a text message to June that said *HELP. Don't know what to wear.* She attached the picture and sent it off to June.

What seemed like only seconds later, she heard a knock on her front door. Apparently, June understood the urgency of Amanda's wardrobe debacle and was there to help pick out an outfit. Amanda trotted down the stairs and pulled her robe belt to make sure her robe was securely closed. She was almost to the front door when she froze. She all at once realized that she was walking full speed to her front door and was about to open it without even knowing who was on the other side. She looked at her phone, but there was no response from June. She decided that June would have responded and said she was coming over to help pick out clothes before just knocking on her door. Amanda walked to a different room and carefully peered through the blinds. On her front step stood a man about her age. He was wearing a T-shirt and jeans. Medium build, clean shaven, dark brown hair. Amanda took her cell phone out and took a picture of him through the window. She wasn't sure if she should call the police, answer the door, or just pretend she wasn't home.

She was standing with her back to the wall, staring at the closet where she still kept her father's shotgun. Amanda almost jumped when she felt her phone vibrate. It was a text message from June. *Got your message. Bringing you coffee and fashion advice. Be there in a flash.* Before Amanda could reply, she heard another knock. She looked out the window again to see June on her front step, but the man who had been standing there was gone. Amanda carefully walked to the door and opened it a crack. June's smiling face was quite a relief.

"Good morning, honey," June said excitedly. "Today is going to be a great day." Amanda opened the door to let her in and looked out into her yard and the street. Amanda's face must have looked as panicked and confused as she felt.

"Something wrong, dear?" June said as she set two cups of coffee on a table in the foyer. Amanda scanned the street and then her front porch. She held her breath as she saw a small box with a silver bow on top. It wasn't wrapped, but it had no writing on it, either.

"June?" Amanda said, barely breathing.

"What, honey? What is it?"

Amanda was still staring at the box. "Did you see a man on my front porch?"

"A man?" June walked up next to her. "At this hour? No, honey, I didn't see anyone. Why?"

She reached out a slightly trembling finger and pointed at the box. Amanda explained the series of events to June. How she almost opened the door, thinking it was her, but looked out to see the man on her porch. June walked past Amanda and picked up the box. "Can I open it?"

"Yes. Please." Amanda was still barely breathing.

June pulled the top of the box open and took out a small card. She showed it to Amanda. All it said in very neat, all capital letters was *FOUND HIM*. June looked quizzically at Amanda. She pulled something else out of the box. "Something you lost?" Amanda let out a long breath and looked up at June. She was holding a small stuffed giraffe. Amanda hesitated for a second and then let out another breath. She took the giraffe and looked it over. On the tag, in black marker, were the letters CFD. Claiborne Fire Department. She let out a long sigh.

"Lieutenant Whiting has a sense of humor," Amanda said out loud.

June paused. After a moment, she looked down at the box in her hand and then back at Amanda. "Huh," June said knowingly as a slight smirk broke out across her face. "The firefighter from the night we visited Kelly. Hanging out the window. All but holding up a sign that says *I Love You, Amanda Killingly?* That him?"

"June, he was not hanging out the window. He was just saying hello."

"Right." June rolled her eyes and smiled.

Amanda found herself staring a little too much at the giraffe. She was a little concerned about who had actually left the box on her porch. It wasn't Lieutenant Whiting; she would have recognized him. As uneasy as a strange man on her front porch had made her, her panic was fading, and a warm smile that she felt all the way across her face was slowly spreading. His gesture made her feel like all the goodness in the world wasn't dead and gone. The little stuffed animal made her quite happy. It was a small glimmer of happiness in her otherwise gray and icy view of the world. She looked up at June and hoped she wasn't blushing. June stood patiently waiting for more information, her eyes staring at Amanda and her mouth slightly smirking. She was fairly certain Amanda wasn't going to offer any more information, so after another minute of waiting, she poked Amanda's forearm with a single finger and said, "Let me guess." Amanda felt her cheeks get warm, and she tried to think of some way, any way, to avoid the conversation that was about to happen.

"Okay, okay. He's just a firefighter I've talked to a few times."

"Oh, good. You talked to him a few times, and he sent you an adorable stuffed animal. So after your first date, is he going to buy you a house?" June kidded.

"One could only hope." Amanda smiled and said, "He's just being friendly."

"Oh, honey, friendly is holding a door for you when you walk into the coffee shop in the morning. Friendly is picking up your keys if you drop them in the grocery store. Friendly is—"

Amanda cut June off quickly. "Are ya done?"

June laughed. "Hardly."

She smiled at June and glanced at the clock on her kitchen wall. "June. The test!"

"Oh, goodness, yes. Let's get going."

They both ran up the stairs like school kids happy to be home on a Friday afternoon. June threw in a couple more, *Ooh-la-la, he likes you* comments that made Amanda laugh. Amanda put her arm around her in a sideways hug and said, "I'm so glad we've become friends."

114

"Me, too, honey. So very glad."

June had the outfit picked out before Amanda was even done showing them all to her. A blue collared shirt that Amanda had always loved, light khaki pants, and a pair of black shoes with just the slightest bit of a heel. June opened a jewelry box on Amanda's dresser and handed her a sterling silver necklace with a hibiscus flower pendant, along with a silver bangle bracelet. While Amanda got dressed, June gathered her keys and her purse for her and waited on the stairs. Amanda came hurrying out of her room and stopped to look at June.

"Well?" Amanda cocked her head to one side.

"You look absolutely wonderful, honey. Now let's get going."

As they were pulling out of her driveway, Amanda took a deep breath and let it out slowly. "I'm nervous," she offered.

"Don't be nervous. You'll be fine," June said. "Besides, you can keep your mind off the test by telling me about this Mr. Firefighter who sent you an adorable stuffed animal."

Amanda glanced over at June as they pulled up to a stop sign. "Mr. Firefighter? Do we really have to discuss this now?"

June glanced out the windshield and back at Amanda. "Well," she started, "we can either talk about Mr. Firefighter, or we can discuss Mr. Police Officer, who desperately wants your attention."

"Huh?" Amanda furrowed her brow. June pointed out the windshield to a police cruiser at the left-hand side of the four-way intersection. Matt was sitting in the driver's seat and was waving out the window. Amanda waved back. He pulled up alongside her as she rolled down her window.

"Hey, Amanda," he said with a smile.

"Hey, how are you, Matt?"

"I'm good. I hear you have a big day ahead of you."

"Um," Amanda started. "Yeah, I guess you could say that. How have you been?"

"Good. Please don't be upset. A very good friend of mine works for the city. She told me she had seen your name on an application to work at the dispatch center, and I know the test is today. I figured that was where you were headed."

"Yes. I guess news travels fast, no matter how big or small the neighborhood." Amanda smiled.

"So true." Matt shifted his weight and leaned out the window, his arm extended. He was holding a piece of paper. "I'll let you get to the test, but I wanted to give you this."

Amanda reached out and took the piece of paper.

"I hope it isn't test answers. Aren't you police officers supposed to be super honest and trustworthy?" Amanda kidded.

"I'm as trustworthy as they come. Not test answers. Just some information I thought you might find helpful and interesting. Just...one thing."

"What's that?"

"This is unofficial and off the record, okay? Just a conversation between two old friends."

Amanda hesitated and then nodded. "Okay. Got it. Thank you."

"You're welcome. Drive safely, and good luck today." Matt leaned down so he could make eye contact with June. "And I wasn't being rude, ma'am. I'm Matt."

June leaned toward Amanda. "Very nice to meet you, Matt."

"Yes, ma'am. You, too. Have a safe day."

Matt pulled away, and Amanda looked over at June. She knew what was coming.

"I don't suppose there is any chance we can *not* talk about this."

"No chance whatsoever," June said excitedly. "Okay, so we have Mr. Firefighter, who sends you adorable little stuffed animals and unsigned love letters."

"Love letters?" Amanda interrupted with a surprised laugh. "It was a blank card with two words on it."

"Tomato. Ta-motto," June said as she waved a playful hand at Amanda. "And then we have bachelor number two, the very handsome Mr. Police Officer, who just happens to drive to your neighborhood to bring you—look at that— another love letter. This could be a soap opera."

"June, that isn't a love letter, either."

"Mmmhmm. You haven't even looked at it, so how would you know?"

"Because I know," Amanda said, smiling. "I'm not looking at it until after the test. I don't want whatever is on that piece of paper to change my mood or mindset."

"Fine." June sat back in her seat. "Once the test is over, we're opening up the love note from Mr. Police Officer."

"He has a name, ya know."

"Oh, right." June batted her eye lashes. "Officer Mmmmmmmmmatt," she said as she closed her eyes.

"Funny. Can we talk about something else, please?"

"Sure." June rested her chin on the back of her interlaced fingers and looked up at Amanda. "Who is taller, the cop or the fireman?"

"You are incessant."

"One of my best qualities."

They laughed as Amanda drove the rest of the way to the test center. She eventually got June to stop asking about Matt and Lieutenant Whiting by telling her that Matt was just a friend from high school who she had reconnected with during her trips to the police station, and that Lieutenant Whiting's first name was Brian. She parked, took a deep breath, and looked at June.

"You'll be fine, honey. Let's go find Kelly."

Amanda was glad that she had June and that, by proxy, she kind of had Kelly, too. She felt a little guilty about having met Kelly ahead of time and having had a conversation with her about the job and the test. The chance of a new and exciting job, though, helped her guilt subside. Kelly met them at the front door. Something else Amanda was grateful for, as she had no idea where, in the building, she was going.

"Good morning," Kelly said with a bright smile.

"Hi, honey," June said as she hugged her.

Amanda looked at her. "Simple and straightforward, right?"

"You've got it," Kelly answered. "Nothing is meant to trick you. Just follow the instructions and the prompts, and you'll be just fine."

"Let's hope so."

Kelly showed Amanda to the testing room. Several computer monitors sat at individual stations made to look very much like the desks and computers at the dispatch center. She sat at station number eight. A number she had always admired because of its balance and symmetry. She hoped it would bring her luck. Others filtered in, until all the stations were full. Amanda hadn't really thought about how many people would be taking the test. With a quick check around the room, her best guess was that there were twenty-two stations or so, and Kelly had said there were multiple groups testing each day. She scanned the others in the room, looking for details about them and trying to remember what they looked like. A habit she still hadn't gotten out of since after her attack. No one looked threatening. Everyone in the room had somewhat of a nervous expression. At least she wasn't the only one. The murmur of conversation in the room slowly faded as she saw someone walk to the front of the room.

"Good morning," she called out.

The crowd returned, "Good morning," in a low tone.

The proctor explained the rules of the test and informed everyone where the restroom and the emergency exits were. She gave basic instructions on how the test would work and when to expect the test results. After she had explained everything, she looked at the clock and said, "You may begin." Amanda clicked the blue "Start" button on her computer screen and hoped for the best.

She had lost track of time and the number of calls she had taken. She was about to pick up her flashing phone when her computer flashed *TEST COMPLETED*. Amanda looked up from the computer screen and glanced around the room. It was hard to get a feel for how other people thought the test went just by looking around, but she hoped she had done okay, at least.

"You can leave any notes you've written on the desks," Amanda heard Kelly say. "Computers stations can be left on. This is the end of your test. Thank you all very much for coming. Test results will be in before the end of next week. The scores will be reviewed, and we will be calling those who qualify for interviews in the next week or so. Thank you again for coming, and enjoy the rest of your day."

Amanda stood up and stretched. She turned to leave and met Kelly halfway to the door.

"Thank, Kelly. That was actually kind of fun."

"You're welcome. I'll be in touch soon. I've got some things to do this afternoon, but," Kelly said, pointing through the door to June, "I heard she has a surprise for you."

"Oh boy. A June surprise? I can only imagine."

Kelly laughed. "Talk to you soon. And good luck."

Amanda glanced at June and then back at Kelly. "With the test results or your mother?"

Kelly raised her eyebrows and smirked. "Definitely Mom."

Amanda took a dramatic deep breath. "Here goes nothing." With that, she waved to Kelly and headed in June's direction.

She was almost to her when she turned. "What's up, Buttercup?"

"Hi, lady." Amanda instinctively hugged her.

"A hug. What was that for?" June asked happily.

"Just because." Amanda smiled. "Now what have you been doing all this time that I've been focused on the test?"

June looked up at the ceiling. "I don't know what you're talking about."

"Well, thankfully for me, Kelly seems to be on my side. Spill it. What is this surprise you've supposedly been working on?"

"Oh, nothing, really. Just something that I thought might make you smile."

"Well, what is it?"

"You don't really know how surprises work, do you, honey? If I tell you, it's no longer a surprise."

"Yes, I'm aware of how surprises work, but have you met me? I'm the overly anxious and slightly emotionally-damaged girl that you've befriended and now are stuck with forever."

Amanda's dramatics made June laugh out loud. "Honey, you're the best thing to happen to me in a long time. We're headed to a restaurant. I'll let you in on the surprise once we get there. Is that okay?"

Amanda threw her head back and sighed dramatically. "Fiiinnne."

"You know, your father never mentioned how melodramatic you were. You should have been a stage actress," June kidded.

Amanda turned up her nose in faux scorn. "I'm not melodramatic. I'm just very passionate about my expressions."

June rolled her eyes playfully. "Okay then, passionate one, let's get going."

"Where are we going?" Amanda asked as June took her by the arm and hurried her to her car.

"You ask far too many questions."

"I drove us here. I kind of need to know where I'm driving us now."

"Same place we had our first date," June said as they reached Amanda's car.

"So, this surprise... We have to go to the restaurant to get it?"

"How did the test go?" Amanda glanced at June and rolled her eyes. "If you're looking for clues or hints, I'm just going to keep changing the subject."

"Come on. One hint."

"Fine. It's a speed boat. No, it's a new car. It's a pony." June put on her best Cheshire cat grin.

Amanda glanced at her again. "Do I look amused?"

"Kind of. Okay, fine. It's something from your childhood that you really liked."

"My childhood? Now I'm really lost."

"No, you aren't." June added quickly, "Take a right at that traffic light, and the restaurant will be ahead on the left."

Amanda smiled and sighed. "Not what I meant."

June just grinned. As she turned into the parking lot, Amanda looked for any kind of clue as to what the heck could be going on. She looked over at June, who was still smiling and humming to herself.

"Ready?" June asked

"Do I get to know what the surprise is?"

"Let's get inside, grab a table, and then we will chat about the surprise." June opened her door and waited for Amanda at the front of the car. She offered up her arm and smiled. "Shall we?"

"We shall," Amanda said happily. She was a little nervous about whatever June was planning, but she was also quite flattered that June was so good to her. Two months ago, Amanda had simply been the daughter of someone June was friends with years ago. Now she treated her like a longtime friend, or even her own daughter.

As they reached the door, June looked at Amanda. "Deep breath, okay? You know I wouldn't plan something that was going to make you uncomfortable."

"I know, June. Thank you."

Amanda opened the door, and she and June walked to the hostess station. The girl that June had chatted with the first time she and Amanda visited Antonio's met them with a smile.

"Hi, ladies," she said brightly.

"Good afternoon," June began. "We're a party of three today."

Amanda gave her a quizzical look.

"Okay, so are we waiting for the third person, or did—"

Before she could finish, a deep voice answered from the end of the bar that was adjacent to the hostess station.

"I'm already here."

Amanda looked over and saw her father sitting and smiling back at her.

"Dad?" Amanda felt her nose start to tingle, and her eyes began to tear up.

"Hey, kiddo," her father replied as he stood from the chair at the bar. He took a few steps toward her as she just about ran to him. He picked her up in a big bear hug. She wrapped her arms around his neck and kissed his cheek. He set her down and took her by the hands.

"You look well."

"Thanks, Dad. So do you. Are you the surprise June has been telling me about?"

"I think so. Disappointed?" John smiled.

"No way. This is amazing."

"I know it's been a while since I've been able to visit." John started.

"Eleven months and sixteen days." Amanda said, slightly embarrassed that she had been keeping track.

"Well, I guess it's been much longer than I thought. I'm sorry, honey."

"It's okay, Dad. I'm very glad you're here now."

"Come on, you two," June said as she waved her hand at them. "Our table is waiting."

Amanda walked next to her father and chatted about how he had been and what she had been up to. To some

124

people, not seeing their parent for eleven months wouldn't have been a big deal. But having lost her mother so many years ago, and having been through the hell that was her kidnap, beating, and rape, eleven months without her Dad seemed like a lifetime. They got to their table and sat down. Amanda felt bad; she had almost forgotten June was there.

"Thank you for arranging this, June."

"You're welcome, honey."

"It has been too long," John spoke up. "I'm sorry I haven't been out to visit lately, honey. I have been trying to—"

"Dad." Amanda reached out and touched her father's forearm. "This is your busiest time of year. Don't apologize. The phone works both ways. I could have called you, too. I never so much as sent you a Snapchat video or anything."

"Snap-what?" June asked quizzically.

Amanda laughed a little. "I forget that your generation doesn't do well with technology."

"Hey!" June pointed a playful finger at Amanda. "Our generation? I'm pretty..." June searched for some things to prove she was in tune with Amanda's generation. "I'm... hip with the times and know what's cookin' and am down with that, and I know how to... hang." Amanda laughed out loud as June ended her speech with a hand gesture that was somewhat of a thumbs-up and somewhat of a wave.

All three of them laughed, until they noticed the waitress standing patiently at the side of the table. They gave her their orders and went back to happy conversation.

Amanda was enjoying listening and had hoped that June and her father wouldn't notice her sitting quietly and taking everything in. As she sat listening, she looked around the restaurant. As Amanda scanned the back wall of the restaurant, her eyes stopped abruptly when they got to a woman who was looking right at her. Amanda glanced away for a moment and then looked back, only to find her still staring. This time, when Amanda's eyes met hers, the woman looked away casually. She was on the opposite end of the restaurant, in a dim corner, but Amanda was almost certain it was the same woman who had handed her back her credit card the first time she visited the restaurant with June. She looked back at her, trying to catch her eye. The woman lingered for a minute, shuffling some napkins and silverware on a tray, and then disappeared through a door at the back of the room.

"Amanda? Are you okay?"

Amanda's eyes focused on her father, who was sitting across the table, waving at her.

"Sorry, I'm fine. There was a woman staring at me from the back of the restaurant. As soon as I made eye contact with her, she looked away and walked through a door."

"Maybe she was just looking around, honey. Sometimes it just seems like people are staring when you happen to look at each other at the same time. I'm sure it's nothing." John reached across the table and rested his hand on Amanda's arm.

"That's not all, though." Amanda looked around the restaurant for the woman in an effort to point out who she was. "Last time I was here, when June and I came for dinner one night, that woman stopped me on my way to the ladies' room and handed me back a credit card she said I dropped. She said she was the owner of the restaurant."

126

June looked slightly relieved. "Amanda, honey, unless something has changed, this place is owned by a police officer. He tries not to make it too public since he has a full-time job working for the city, but everyone knows he's the owner. I know his wife is here a lot, though. She is a nice lady. She and I have talked before."

John looked at June and started to say something. June glanced at him and shook her head quickly and subtly. Amanda was still looking around the restaurant, searching for the woman, when June spoke up again.

"Honey? Did you want me to have her come over, and I'll introduce you? If she was the one looking at you, I'm sure it's nothing. Maybe she recognized me. I haven't seen her in quite a while, but she may have just been trying to get my attention."

Amanda looked at June, pressed her lips together, and drew in a long, deliberate breath through her nose.

"Okay," Amanda said. "I'd like to at least meet her and see why she's been staring at me. Creeper."

"Hey, hey, hey, feisty girl. Deep breath." June stood up from the table. "I'll be right back."

Before Amanda had fully calmed herself, she saw June approaching with the woman who had been looking at Amanda.

"Amanda, is this the woman you were talking about?"

Amanda felt slightly embarrassed and wondered if there was any way the conversation would be anything but awkward. Not having much choice at this point, she stood and took a step toward the woman.

"Hi, I noticed you looking back this way and was hoping everything was okay. I'm not sure if you remember me, but last time I was here—"

"You dropped your credit card," the woman said.

"Yes. You were nice enough to hand it back to me. I just wasn't sure if everything was okay tonight. I saw you looking this way."

"Oh, I'm sorry. I thought I recognized you, and I thought it was June sitting with you, but I hadn't seen her in quite some time. Last time I saw you here, you said you loved the food. Did we do okay again tonight?"

Amanda felt slightly like she was trying to change the subject, but she followed the conversation anyway.

"It was delicious, thank you."

"I'm glad. I'll be sure to tell my husband. June told me that she helped reassure you that I was married to the owner, that I'm not some—how did you put it, June—creeper?"

Amanda smirked and glanced at June. "Yes, she did."

"Well, I'm glad you liked the food, and if you need anything, feel free to let me know."

"Thank you," Amanda said.

"You're welcome." She turned to leave but stopped and faced them again. Amanda looked up as she heard the woman speak again.

"I'm so sorry. I never actually introduced myself."

"Oh, it's okay," Amanda said.

"I feel awful. I know your name is Amanda Killingly from the credit card you dropped. My name is Darcy Harding. I think you've met my husband, Sergeant Bill Harding." Amanda felt herself flinch as she wondered how much this strange woman had heard about her from Sergeant Harding. She hoped no one else had noticed.

"Very nice to meet you, and yes, I have met Sergeant Harding. He's very nice."

"Don't let him fool you," Darcy started. "He's old and crabby and needs to retire," she said, smiling.

Amanda did her best to smile back at her.

"I'll leave you folks to enjoy your food."

"Take care."

Darcy turned and smiled at Amanda before walking back across the restaurant and though the door she and June had walked out of a few minutes before.

Chapter 11

Lieutenant Brian Whiting was just about to take his first bite of a delicious-looking club sandwich when the bell in the firehouse sounded. He set his sandwich down and waited to hear which units from his firehouse were being dispatched.

"Ladder four, rescue seven, and battalion one, respond to the vicinity of ninety-two Cornwall Avenue for a motor vehicle accident, motorcycle versus tractor trailer. Repeating, ladder four, rescue seven, and battalion one, respond to ninety-two Cornwall Avenue. A motorcycle struck a tractor trailer. Rider is now underneath the truck."

Whiting abandoned his sandwich and stood up from the table.

"Let's go," he called to the others sitting in the kitchen of Firehouse 21. He and the other firefighters walked briskly to their respective fire apparatus, pulled on their gear, and climbed into the seats. There was a hum of diesel engines mixed with short bursts of conversation and the voice of the dispatcher on the radio as the trucks rolled into the street. Lt. Whiting turned over his shoulder and talked into his headset. "When we get there, stabilize that truck and let the rescue guys get in there with the extrication tools." His two firefighters in the back nodded. The ride there wasn't very long, but still Whiting had hundreds of scenarios playing out in his head to try to prepare himself to take the right action when he got to the scene. As they approached, Whiting saw a tractor trailer, jack-knifed, smoking, with a trailer that looked ready to tip over. The ladder truck came to a halt, and all four firefighters climbed out quickly and went straight to work.

"Nelson, webbing and chains. Griswold, get the cutoff saw and a halligan bar. Carlson, back the rig up and get in position alongside the trailer. We're gonna dead-man it to the truck so it can't roll over." Brian Whiting was walking, pointing, and giving orders to his crew when he heard someone call his name. He turned to see the battalion chief quickly approaching.

"Chief?"

"We are gonna lose that rider under the truck and trailer if we don't get it stabilized."

"Copy that, Chief. Carlson is gonna move the rig so we can dead-man the trailer to it, so then it can't roll."

"Good. While your men get situated, I need you with the patient. Ambulance is four minutes out, and you're the only other person I have with advanced medical training."

"Ladder four, get that trailer rigged and hooked to the front of the truck. Once it's stabilized, help the rescue with the extrication."

Whiting heard a chorus of *yes, sirs* as he quickly walked to the other side of the trailer. He lay on the asphalt and looked under the truck. He saw a younger guy who was pretty beat up and definitely stuck under the truck. As he was about to stand up, he noticed something else. On the man's left calf, there was a tattoo. An ivy vine wrapped around what looked like a gun, or maybe a cross. Whiting called to the police officer standing at the end of the tractor trailer. "Hey, McWilliams, come here."

"What's up?"

Whiting motioned under the trailer. "That the same tattoo that the chief told us all to keep an eye out for a handful of months ago?"

McWilliams crouched and looked under the truck. He leaned up and looked at Whiting.

"It sure the hell is. That ambulance doesn't leave without me either in it or behind it."

Whiting nodded. "Copy that. Now get outta my way and let us work."

McWilliams smirked and nodded. "Okay, tough guy, make it quick."

Whiting lay on the asphalt again and reached for the man's neck to check his pulse.

"Sir, if you can hear me, my name is Brian, and I'm with the fire department. I'm here to help."

He didn't hear a response from the man pinned under the truck. His fingers found the man's pulse. It was weak and thready, but at least he had one. He started to see if he could reach and pull the man out from underneath the trailer. As soon as he started to pull, the man let out a loud groan. Whiting stopped pulling and stood up. He looked at the surrounding scene and nodded to the chief.

"He's alive, Chief. He's got a weak pulse and isn't bleeding too badly, but I can't do anything until we get him unstuck. How far out is that ambulance?"

"I don't know, but I'll find out. In the meantime, help the rescue any way you can. Your crew has the truck stabilized. It's time to lift and cut and get that rider out from underneath."

"Yes, sir. Keep me posted about that ambulance."

The chief nodded and walked to the other end of the trailer. Whiting headed toward the crew from the rescue truck, which was beginning the extrication process. They lifted with large Kevlar and rubber air bags that lifted the truck slowly. As they lifted, they placed large blocks of wooden cribbing under the truck to keep it stabilized. Once the truck was high enough, they went to work cutting and removing pieces of the truck to get the rider out from underneath it. Whiting kept checking the man's pulse and talking to him as they worked to free him. He was mostly removed from the wreckage when Whiting heard the ambulance pull up to the scene. The two paramedics from Ambulance 81 rushed over, each carrying a large bag of medical gear. Whiting was glad to see them. Kelly Jankowski and Tamara Bouchez were some of the best medics in the city.

"Whatta we got?" Tamara asked as she pulled on a pair of purple medical gloves.

"Motorcycle rider. Only responding to painful stimuli.

He's got a pulse, but it's thready and weak. No verbal communication yet, other than a few groans when I first tried to pull him out."

"Okay. He almost free from the wreck?"

"Yeah, one more cut to get that last piece of the trailer away from his leg and he'll be out."

"All right." She turned to her partner. "KJ, long board and collar, and then straight to the rig. We gotta get this guy to Claiborne Central Medical as soon as we can before we lose him."

"Coming out," one of the firefighters yelled.

Whiting turned and helped them get the rider up and away from the wreckage. They put him on the backboard, and KJ and Tamara went to work getting him secured and stable. As they were rolling the stretcher to the ambulance, Whiting motioned to Officer McWilliams.

"Tamara," Whiting called to her. "McWilliams is gonna go with you. Patient might be someone he needs to talk to when he wakes up. *If* he wakes up."

Whiting watched them load the stretcher into the ambulance and drive off. He headed back to the scene to help his crew clean up. After the vehicles were cleared, they packed up each firetruck, returned tools to the correct compartments, and headed back to the firehouse.

Whiting climbed down out of the officer's seat of ladder 4 and headed to his office. He scrolled through his email inbox, looking for the email from the chief about the ivy vine tattoo. He found it and began to read.

All department personnel: Be on the lookout for the following tattoos or markings. Individuals with similar tattoos, logos, or other markings similar to those pictured below may have important information regarding an open and ongoing investigation by the Claiborne Police Department.

Below the first paragraph were a few pictures of tattoos. He had remembered the tattoo and that the police department had flagged it, but he couldn't remember which case it was linked to, or if there were any details given. Whiting continued reading.

The individual with the tattoo or other marking similar to those pictured above may be armed and potentially dangerous. Notify Claiborne Police if an individual bearing any similar marking is involved in an incident you are at, working on, or have previously responded to.

Whiting finished the final sentence and realized there were no details about which case it might be linked to. With good reason, he supposed. Nonetheless, he was quite curious as to what an ivy tattoo had to do with a criminal investigation. He reached for his office phone, picked it up, and dialed a number quickly. He listened intently as the phone on the other end rang.

"Claiborne Police. How may I direct your call?"

"Bill Harding, please."

"May I ask who is calling?

"Lieutenant Brian Whiting from Claiborne Fire."

"One moment, please."

After a brief pause, Whiting heard Harding's somewhat gruff voice.

"Hal-low."

"Bill."

"Yeah."

"Brian Whiting from over at Firehouse 21."

"Oh, hey, kid. What's up?"

"We sent McWilliams with a patient in the rig today. Motorcycle rider wrecked and ended up under an 18-wheeler. I noticed an ivy vine tattoo on his leg. McWilliams was hoping he would wake up so he could ask him some questions."

"McWilliams just called. Nothing yet. But good eyes. Thanks for getting McWilliams in the rig with him."

"Happy to help. Out of curiosity, what are the ivy vine tattoos all about anyway? Gang membership?"

"Not quite. More like a band of middle-aged douche bags who think they can buy their way out of any situation their stupid asses land in."

"Got it. There one case in particular that is still open, or you just want any of them you can find so you can question them? Or should I stop asking questions and stick to fighting fires?"

Harding chuckled. "Well, usually I'd tell you ax jockeys to mind your business, but considering I knew your old man before you were born, I'm okay with you asking the questions. A group of these idiots kidnapped and raped a young girl. Left her for dead. And even though she came forward and gave us a positive I.D. on one of them, we can't touch him. He's got better lawyers than OJ and seems to have more money behind him than all of Hollywood

Boulevard combined. We tried to hold him, but they tied up a trial with legal bullshit, and the case is standing stagnant. Bugs the hell outta me, too. So I appreciate you getting McWilliams into the back of that ambulance more than you know."

"Happy to help. Sounds like an awful situation for everyone involved. I'll keep an eye out for more tattoos."

"Thanks, Brian. And hey—"

Whiting cut in before Harding could finish. "Tell everyone I know, make flyers, and hang them up at the firehouse so everyone knows you told me about all of this, right? I'm on it."

Harding grinned into the phone receiver. "You always were a smart ass. Stay safe, kid. See ya."

Whiting hung up the phone and took out his cell phone. He opened the camera and took pictures of his computer screen. After a story like that, he wasn't going to let any ivy vine tattoo go unnoticed. He opened a new email message and started typing. He addressed it to the lieutenants of the other shifts. His message was brief and to the point. He wanted everyone to be on the lookout for ivy tattoos now that he had heard Harding's story.

Hey All,

Had an MVA today with extrication involved. Patient had an ivy vine tattoo on his leg. Sent McWilliams from CPD in the rig with him. Please keep an eye out. An earlier email from the Chief outlines what I'm talking about. Thanks.

-Whiting

Whiting locked his computer and headed out of his office. He was headed out to make sure the trucks were back in order and all tools and equipment were ready for the next call. One of the girls from the office stopped him in the hallway.

"Lieutenant? I just wanted to tell you that dispatch has been trying to raise Ambulance eighty-one on the radio for quite a while and hasn't gotten a response. They called here to see if there were any problems with their radio that we knew of."

Whiting shifted his weight. "Not that I know of. Did anyone try their cell phones?"

"I called. Straight to voicemail, both of them."

Whiting was about to ask if they had called the hospital to see when the ambulance arrived when he heard the bell in the station ring and the loud speaker click on.

"Engine twenty-one and ladder four, respond to the parking lot of Claiborne Central Medical for a vehicle fire. Reported to be an ambulance parked close to the building."

Whiting's eyes widened. He ran down the hallway and burst through the door and onto the apparatus floor.

"Let's go, let's go, let's go. That's our ambulance. Move!" He shouted loudly enough for the whole firehouse to hear.

The trucks left the firehouse in a blur of lights and sirens. As they pulled up to the hospital, Whiting saw an ambulance fully engulfed in flames. It was parked under the roof of the emergency department sliding doors. Whiting jumped out of the truck before it even rolled to a stop.

Whiting saw KJ and Tamara standing with a group of hospital staff at the doorway to the emergency room.

"Where the hell is McWilliams? Where's the patient?" he said, with emphasis on the last word.

"They took the patient. Lit the rig on fire and sped off. McWilliams tried to follow them, but he didn't have a cruiser, because he was with us in the ambulance."

Whiting walked back toward ladder four.

"Set up the truck and swing the ladder up to the side of the hospital. Check the temperatures and make sure we don't have any extension into the structure."

Whiting's crew went to work setting up the ladder truck while the firefighters from the engine stretched a hose line and put the fire out. Whiting walked over to the hospital doorway to talk to KJ and Tamara.

"What the hell happened? Someone lit the rig on fire?"

"We were almost here. Guy cut us off and got out of the car with a gun." KJ started. "I panicked, floored it, and drove around him, then pulled up here. They followed us. Before we had time to do anything, one climbed in the back of the rig with Tamara and McWilliams. I jumped out but didn't get far. The guy in the back told McWilliams to throw his gun on the floor of the rig and get out. As he was climbing out, another guy got out and shoved McWilliams toward me. He pointed a gun in my face. Told us not to move or they'd kill us. A third guy got out and ran to the door of the emergency department. A nurse came out, and he grabbed her and pointed a gun at her. Told everyone to stay inside and not call anyone. The guy in the back told Tamara to fix up his friend and keep her hands where he could see them. They walked me over to the side of the parking lot and held me at gunpoint. Tamara tried to explain that the guy needed surgery, but they didn't care. She worked on him for a while. He was pretty banged up. She kept telling the other guy that he needed a hospital and that she wasn't a doctor. He kept screaming at her to just fix him. She did all she could and then wrapped him with some dressings. They threw her out of the back of the rig. Two guys dragged the rider into the back seat of their car while the other kept the gun on us. Once they had him in the car, one guy got out, opened the hood of the rig, and stuffed a rag down inside the motor. He lit it and stood there, watching it until it got burning well enough for us to not be able to do much. Once it was burning pretty good, they drove off."

Whiting put his hands on his head and sighed.

"So much for figuring out who that guy was and if the cops could get any information."

"Oh, I know who he is." Tamara smirked. "I have his wallet. McWilliams grabbed it to get the guy's name for his incident report, and I pocketed it when they threw me out of the rig."

"You're the best, Tamara. You two sure you're okay?"

"We're good. Just need a new ambulance."

Whiting turned to see Officer McWilliams jogging out of the emergency department door.

"We got his address. Harding is gonna pick me up, and we're headed to the guy's house. I'll keep you updated."

Whiting nodded. Before he could say anything, McWilliams jogged to the parking lot and got into a police cruiser that was just pulling up. Whiting turned and reassessed the scene. Tamara and KJ were safe, the fire was out, and McWilliams and Harding were headed to figure out what the hell was going on. Things weren't great, but they were starting to calm down a little, at least. He turned to KJ and Tamara and motioned for them to come over to where he was standing.

"The guy say anything?" he asked.

"He was in and out of consciousness the entire time. We didn't really hear anything from him," Tamara said.

"Okay. Well, since your ambulance is junk, why don't you ride back to the station with us."

"Can I drive?" KJ asked, smiling excitedly.

Whiting chuckled. "Not a chance."

Chapter 12

Amanda smiled as she thought about the day's events. She didn't want to get her hopes up, but she felt the most at ease and focused that she had in a very long time while she was taking the test. The scenarios had been challenging, but she felt no hesitation as she worked through each one. Her good vibes from the test were complemented by a delicious lunch, and seeing her father made her heart incredibly happy. All in all, she had had the best day she could remember in a very long time.

"Hey, Dad?" she called as he walked down the stairs.

"In here, honey," John called from the living room. "What's up?"

"Wanna make popcorn and watch a movie like old times? Or are you going to get going soon? I know it's a long drive back to the farm."

"I think I'll start the drive around three o'clock."

Amanda glanced at the clock and frowned. "It's three forty-six."

John smiled. "Three o'clock tomorrow. If that's okay with you."

Amanda's face lit up. "Of course! I mean, I'll see what I have going on and do my best to pencil you in, but I think it will be just fine." Amanda smirked and gave him a sideways glance before her smirk broke into a smile.

"Oh, honey, I've missed you. I'm so glad June called me. I had been trying to plan a visit but couldn't figure out when a good time was. When June called and said you were taking a test for the dispatch center, I decided now was a good time."

"I'm glad she called. She's an amazing lady, Dad."

"She is. Your mother loved her so much. They were the best of friends."

"She has some awesome stories about you and Mom and the things all of you did when you were younger."

"Let's hope she didn't tell you everything." John grinned.

"Why not? What else is there to tell? Are you a secret agent?"

"Nothing that exciting. I was just a boring old accountant, who has turned into a boring old farmer, who has the greatest daughter on earth."

"Thanks, Daddy. You're not so bad yourself." Amanda smiled and kissed his cheek.

"Amanda?" John started and then paused. Amanda looked at him. "How is the progress with your case? We've been having such a great time that I didn't want to change the mood and ask, but I'm your father, and I am curious."

"I've resigned myself to the fact that I need to become comfortable with the old adage that no news is good news."

Lines appeared between his eyes, and he frowned. "Why is that?"

"It's been quite a while. I used to call and ask if there had been any progress, and they always told me they were working on it. I don't want to *not* believe them, but it has been frustrating, to say the least. I promised myself I wouldn't let it keep me down and that I would keep living my life, even if I didn't hear anything else."

"That's an incredible attitude, honey. I'm proud of you."

"Thanks. I'm trying."

"When was the last time you talked to anyone at the police station?"

"Well, I ran out on June one afternoon because I felt like I had to get the details of what I remembered on paper before I forgot."

"You remembered something new?"

"I remembered a gun in the seat of the truck. It was decorative and flashy, like it was custom-made. It had an eagle carved into the handle. It seemed unique. I thought maybe that would help."

John caught himself before the flash of recognition could show on his face.

"How long ago did you tell the police about it?"

"Not long ago, so I'm still cautiously optimistic that it will help them find something."

"That's good, honey. I hope they do find the bastards. Actually, I'd like to find them first so I can—"

"Dad." Amanda cut in before John could finish his sentence. "I know you would." She looked up at him for a moment, until his expression had softened. "Love you."

John let out a breath he had been holding since he had cut his sentence short. "I love you, too."

Amanda smiled and patted his arm. "Okay, so. Movie genre?"

He playfully stroked an imaginary beard and tapped his finger on his lips. "Hmmmm. I choose...suspense."

"Overruled," Amanda said playfully as she clapped her hands together.

"I wasn't aware I was making a motion to the grand jury."

"I vote comedy."

"We each have one vote, and they're conflicting. Now what? We need to have a tie breaker vote to honor true democratic process. Or whatever the hell we're doing."

Both of them laughed. Amanda took out four movies and set them on the arm of the couch. Two comedies and two suspenseful movies.

"Now what?" John asked.

"Now we call someone to help us decide. We should call June."

Amanda and her father looked at each other and simultaneously called out, "Ohhhhh, Juuuuunnnne." They both laughed out loud. It had been something her Dad always teased her about when she was younger. In high school, if she had said, "I want to call Stacey," her father used to cup his hand to the side of his mouth and yell,

"Ohhhhh, Staaaaceeeeyy," and then cup his hand to his ear in a dramatic listening gesture and say, "Huh. Not home."

She grinned at the memory. "How about we try again using a real phone?"

"Good idea. You call her, and I'll make the popcorn," John said as he stood and walked to the kitchen.

He opened the cupboard door and found a box of popcorn. He opened a bag and put it in the microwave to pop. While he was waiting, he perused the menus Amanda had neatly put in a folder next to the refrigerator. The microwave beeped. He took out the popcorn, opened the bag, and shook it into a large bowl. He walked back to the living room to find June and Amanda sitting on the couch, staring at him.

"That was quick. How long was I gone, three minutes?"

They bantered good-naturedly for a few minutes, finally decided on one, and settled in with their popcorn. Amanda was so happy to have her father visit that she didn't want him to leave. Her friendship with June was still somewhat of a surprise to her when she thought about how quickly they had become so close, but she certainly wasn't complaining. After what she had been through, it was nice to have June in her life. They sat and quietly enjoyed the movie. When it was almost over, her father stood up.

"Where are you going, Dad? The movie is almost over."

"I'm going to grab menus from the kitchen so you ladies can decide what I'm buying you for dinner."

June sat, staring intently at the screen, raised her hand slightly, and extended her index finger. Without ever looking away from the TV screen, she said, "Lobster, extra

146

butter, crab cakes as an appetizer, and maybe a small center-cut filet mignon."

"Peanut butter, extra jelly, on wheat. Got it." John smirked and disappeared into the kitchen.

He returned a handful of seconds later with the folder of menus. He sat back on the couch and started to flip through one as the movie finished. As soon as the credits started, he started passing out menus to Amanda and June. He pointed his index fingers at each of them and said, "Okay. Before anyone tries to argue, this is my treat. I don't get to visit very often. Lunch was so much fun, and I'm buying dinner. Got it?"

Amanda and June spoke quickly and simultaneously in a furious blast of words.

"Yup."

"You got it."

"Thanks."

"Sounds good."

"You're the best, Dad."

"Thanks, Johnny."

John tilted his head in playful frustration. "That was the part where you're supposed to argue, at least a little, and offer to pay."

"Guess that backfired, didn't it?" June laughed. "We'll split it. How's that?"

John shook his head. "Nice try, but it's my treat. What sounds good?"

"Thanks, Dad," Amanda said as she leaned over and kissed his cheek. "I vote either Chinese or sandwiches from Rizzo's."

"Oooh, I haven't had Chinese takeout in *years*," June said.

"Years?" John raised his eyebrows.

"I like to cook. Until a short time ago, I had no one to enjoy takeout with, and I typically didn't feel like having a date with myself just to order Chinese food," June said as she flipped through a menu.

"Fair enough. So it sounds like you two ladies are both okay with Chinese food?"

Amanda and June both nodded, saying, "Yes, please."

John stood and gathered the menus. He put them all back in the folder except the Chinese food menu. He looked at it briefly and then handed it to Amanda and said, "You two ladies pick out what you'd like and call it in. I'd like a C-nine, please. I'll put the menus back and grab my keys."

"I can pick it up, John," June added.

"That's okay. I'm going to call and check on the farm, then grab a few supplies while I'm out. I have a delivery scheduled for tomorrow, and I want to make sure my guys didn't forget. You order, and I'll make my call and then head out to get the food and the stuff I need for the farm."

June and Amanda perused the pages for another minute and then called in the order. When she hung up, June called out, "Number twenty-eight, ready in about thirty minutes."

A moment later, John appeared in the doorway. "Okay, girls, I'll be back with the food in a bit."

Amanda glanced at him. "Okay, Dad. Drive safe."

Amanda was just about to lock the door, a habit she hadn't grown out of since her attack, when she heard her father calling through the door.

"Just me, honey. I forgot my wallet." She opened the door for her father, and he disappeared into the kitchen. He returned a few seconds later, wallet in hand. "For real this time, be back soon." As John opened the door, there was a deafening sound of screeching tires, colliding metal, and breaking glass. Amanda looked out the door just in time to see two cars sliding down the street, entangled and smoking. As they slid, one car hit the curb line, and the sudden stop forced the car on its side. The inertia from the other car and the collision kept both vehicles rolling, and one flipped over violently a few times before it finally came to rest on its roof near the end of the street. Before Amanda could even say anything, her father was halfway out the door.

"One of you should call nine-one-one. The other needs to get me the fire extinguisher from the basement stairway."

June took out her cell phone and dialed 911. Amanda ran to the basement stairway and grabbed the fire extinguisher, then ran back to the door.

"Dad, here." She met him on the steps and handed him the extinguisher. She looked back to see June in the doorway, talking on the phone. She followed her father and ran to the mangled cars. She watched her father go to work, helping the people get out of one car. She was amazed at how fluid and seamless his actions were. He opened a passenger side door and started to pull a teenager out of the car as it began to smoke from under the hood.

"Dad, move. The engine is smoking."

"Amanda, back up, honey. I don't want you to get hurt."

"Dad, you need to move.

"Amanda, back up. He's almost out. I've got him."

Amanda picked up the fire extinguisher next to her father and ran to the front of the car. The hood was smashed, and there was a spot where it was peeled up and dented. She stuck the fire extinguisher nozzle into the opening and squeezed the lever. As the dry chemical from the fire extinguisher hit the fire, Amanda gasped and held her breath as best she could. John saw her and yelled, "Amanda! What are you doing?"

"I've got it, Dad. Just get him out."

When the fire extinguisher stopped spraying, Amanda dropped it and ran to help her father. He had freed the teenager from the passenger seat and was now attempting to get to the driver. Amanda heard sirens in the distance and was relieved to hear that help was close. She and her father tried to open the driver side door of the car but couldn't get it to budge. She looked up and saw three firefighters walking briskly toward them. She and her father instinctively backed up and moved to the side to let them get to work. She watched as the firefighters put blocks of wood under the car and began cutting and prying apart the jagged and crumpled cars, piece by piece. She was watching them pull the driver out of the mangled mess and put him on a stretcher when she heard one of the firefighters call out.

"Hey, Lieutenant. We've got a little bit of a problem over here."

Amanda turned to see two firefighters standing at the other car.

"What's up?" the lieutenant asked.

"Two car seats, one kid. The driver conscious enough to answer any questions?"

The lieutenant started talking, then turned and pointed at Amanda and her father. One of the firefighters came rushing over.

"Excuse me, did you folks see any little kids when you first got here to help?"

Amanda felt her stomach drop. She hadn't even looked in the back seat. She felt so terrible. She stared at her feet, and the rest of the world started to fade away. What if there had been children who were hurt or trapped, and she had done nothing to even look for them, let alone help? She was brought out of her trance by her father's deep voice.

"No kids that we saw outside of the cars. I did see one in his car seat. but he was awake and didn't look hurt, so I didn't really think to look for a second kid."

"Okay, thanks." The firefighter turned and hurried back to the car.

"Dad, what if there is another little kid somewhere? We didn't even look."

"Amanda, honey, we looked. You just didn't realize it. Your adrenaline was pretty high." Amanda leaned in and hugged her father. "I saw you looking in the windows of the cars. You made sure June was calling nine-one-one without even realizing it. You moved quickly and decisively. I'm very proud of you. And you did great with the fire extinguisher."

"Yes, you did," a voice said from behind Amanda.

Amanda lifted her head off her father's shoulder and tuned slowly to address the mystery voice that had complimented her fire extinguisher skills. Lieutenant Brian Whiting stood behind her. She knew by the quiet smile on his face that he knew who she was before she had even turned to face him. He had on what Amanda only knew to call bunker pants because of a Halloween costume a friend in college had worn. He was wearing a coat of the same color, with reflective stripes on the sleeves, and a helmet. Amanda felt her face flush and hoped Whiting and her father hadn't noticed. Her mind raced to think of something charming or funny to say. She was just standing there. It felt like hours. Finally, she took a quick breath and said, "Cute costume, but you kind of missed the mark for Halloween. Wrong month."

Whiting's smile instantly grew despite his best attempt to hide it. Amanda felt a little excited and a little nervous, hoping she still remembered how to joke around and actually have a conversation.

"Oh, these? I put them on for Halloween, too, but I can't get people to take me seriously when I ride around in that giant firetruck unless I have *something* to make me look credible."

"Ohhh, I see." Amanda turned and looked toward the firetrucks parked on her street. "So which one is yours, the little red and white SUV with the flashy lights?" She smirked as she pointed up the street. She turned to say something else and caught a look at her father's face. He was doing his best not to say anything but was wearing a look that screamed, "Did I miss something?"

Before she could say anything, Whiting spoke up. "My apologies for not introducing myself, sir." Whiting stuck his hand out to John Killingly. "Lieutenant Brian Whiting, Claiborne Fire Department. I just wanted to tell you and Amanda that you did a great job helping those folks before we got here, and the other child is accounted for. He was not in the car when the accident happened."

John grabbed his hand and shook firmly. "That's good news. Glad we were able to help. I take it you've met my daughter before?" John Killingly kept a firm grip on Whiting's hand while he waited for an answer. Before Whiting could respond, June came walking briskly toward them.

"Hi there," June said brightly. "June Robertson. Thank you so much for all your help. Did I hear you say you're Lieutenant Whiting?"

Amanda shot June a look in an attempt to quiet her enthusiastic greeting and obvious excitement to meet Whiting.

June stuck her hand out to him. John let go of his hand so he could shake June's.

"Very nice to meet you, Ms. Robertson."

"Oh, the pleasure is all mine, Lieutenant." While she was still looking, perhaps a little too intently, at Whiting, she said, "Johnny, I need your help in the house with something." She turned and grabbed John by the arm. "You two kids chat as long as you'd like. Come on, Johnathan."

With that, June just about dragged John up the steps and disappeared into the house.

"Thanks for all your help. You and your Dad helped us out a lot by starting the rescue process."

"You're welcome. I don't feel like I did much, but I'm glad I was able to do *something*."

"You did a lot. If you hadn't grabbed that fire extinguisher, we would have had a much bigger fire to put out before we could help the people in the vehicles. You are a hero, Amanda Killingly."

"Okay, okay, I wouldn't go *that* far." Amanda looked up at him from her slightly bowed head. She was hoping he didn't notice her blushing. She was about to say something when a booming voice cut through the air.

"Hey, Lieu. Tools are packed up. You getting a ride home later, or should Mom and Dad wait for you to be done chatting?"

Whiting glanced over his shoulder. "Subtlety is not their strong suit."

"I see that." Amanda smiled. "Well, don't keep Mom and Dad waiting. I wouldn't want you to break your curfew."

"How about you tell me when your curfew is, and I'll make sure to make an early enough dinner reservation," Whiting said as he started walking backwards toward the firetruck.

Amanda's stomach lurched. She still reacted negatively to being asked on a date despite how long it had been. She swallowed and quelled her stomach before answering.

"My dad is in the house. Should I go get him and ask when my curfew is? Maybe you guys can shake hands again." She raised her eyebrows and smirked.

"No handshake needed. I'll shake it when I pick you up tomorrow night. Dinner at six-thirty, just in case you turn into a pumpkin at nine."

Amanda blinked and answered, even though she still felt uneasy.

"Cinderella got until midnight."

"Cinderella *wanted* to go out and have fun."

"Where are we going?"

Whiting smirked. "Some place you've never been but will always remember."

"If I were to go, what should I wear?"

"Whatever you'd like, but bring something warm just in case. See you at six-fifteen, Amanda."

"Maybe." She smiled and shrugged.

"I'll take a maybe." With that, Whiting turned and jogged back to the group of men standing around the firetruck. They clapped and offered overly dramatic bows and salutes as he walked between them. Amanda watched the truck head up the street and make a left turn. Once it was out of sight, she turned to walk up her steps and was startled by June's face in her window.

Amanda walked up the steps and said, "What's up, nosey?"

"Who, me?" June shrugged and looked around. "I was just checking your screen. It felt like there were bugs in here, and I figured maybe the screen was loose."

"Mmmhmm." Amanda opened the door and walked into the house. Her father met her in the kitchen doorway.

"Well, June thinks he's all kinds of cute," John Killingly said as he walked toward the front door.

"Handsome." June corrected. "Okay, well, maybe striking is better. Dreamy? How about delicious?"

"June!" Amanda called out, trying not to laugh.

"Okay, okay, just plain old hot it is," she said as she pretended to fan herself.

"I'm going to get the food that's probably very cold by now," John said as he pulled his keys out of his pocket.

"Okay, Dad, be safe."

"I will. Try not to let June get *too* excited about Fireboy."

"Man," June corrected. "Fire. Mmmmman."

"Goodbye," John called out as June laughed and hurried him out the door. He was barely to his truck when June sat down on the couch and grabbed Amanda's arm.

"Let's hear it. Where are you going and when? Don't starve an old woman of what may very well be the most exciting details of her life in a decade."

"I didn't even really say yes yet."

"Why not? Honey, he is tall, dark, handsome, witty, charming, and he drives a damn fire truck. If you don't want to go, I will."

Amanda laughed. "Well, he said we were going somewhere I've never been but will always remember. And he told me to bring something warm."

"Warm? Like a sweater, or a casserole?"

"I'm going to guess sweater." Amanda laughed. "Am I going? I don't know what to do. I'm not ready for this."

"Amanda," June said gently. "He wants to buy you dinner, not walk down the aisle. And besides, if he's a terrible date, he works for the city and is easy to hunt...I mean, track down."

"June Robertson." Amanda playfully swatted at June's hand.

"Honey, are you comfortable with a date?"

Amanda thought for a moment. She took a deep breath and let it out through her nose. "I think..." she started. "I'm ready. I can handle a dinner date. I can't hide behind my own shadow forever."

"That's my girl. Now, before your father gets home, let's talk about what you're going to wear."

They headed to Amanda's bedroom to look for an appropriate outfit for her first date. They pulled out all sorts of combinations of dresses, pants, shirts, and sweaters, and even an argyle sweater vest that she had left over from college, which June loved but Amanda very quickly threw in the "no" pile. They were in the midst of a shoe debate when they heard John call up the stairs.

"You two fall asleep?"

Amanda glanced at her watch and let out a somewhat startled gasp. "June, it's been an hour."

"An *hour*?" June called back as if she and Amanda were fifty feet apart. "What? Did ya get lost, Johnny?" she called down the stairs as she handed Amanda a pair of shoes to put in her closet. As they walked down the stairs, Amanda looked into the kitchen to see her father dishing food from takeout containers onto plates. Steam was billowing from the container with each scoop of his spoon.

"How on earth is the food still that hot?" Amanda asked.

"Your boyfriend had the restaurant make us new food so it was hot," John said without looking up from his spooning efforts.

"My what?" Amanda asked, slightly surprised but mostly confused.

"Brian. He's a good kid. He was at the restaurant with another guy from the firehouse when I went to pick up the food."

"Okay, so, he's not my boyfriend. And how on earth did he convince the restaurant to make you an entire new order?"

"Well, I guess that's for me to know and you two to discuss on your date tomorrow night."

Amanda felt her face flush. "My what?"

"You seem awfully confused about this date. Especially since you're the one going out to dinner," John said as he poured himself a glass of iced tea.

Amanda looked to June for some kind of help from her father's razzing, but June put up her hands in a *don't look at me* gesture.

"Dad," Amanda said as she walked over and stood next to him. She put her hand on his arm to stop him from scooping food and said, "Are you mad, or are you teasing me?"

John stopped what he was doing. Amanda leaned down and tried to look up at him and make eye contact.

"Honey." John set the spoon down and wiped his hands on a towel. He lifted her chin up with his index finger. "When I'm upset, what do I do?"

June's voice chimed in from the other side of the kitchen. "You tell people. With blinding and brutal honesty."

"Thank you, June," John called back, still looking at Amanda.

"You're welcome, Johnny."

158

Amanda looked at her father.

"She's right, Amanda. If I was upset, I would tell you. If you are comfortable and ready for a date, I'm happy for you. As your father, I never really *like* the idea of you going on a date, but it's one of those things we fathers have to deal with." John kissed Amanda's forehead. "Besides, I like the guy. Granted, we only had a fifteen-minute chat in the lobby of a restaurant, but for a first date, I think he'll be okay. Don't forget. He's easy to find if I need to chat with him." John smiled.

Amanda looked at June. "Did you two rehearse this?" she asked with a half-smile.

"Nope," June said as she crossed the kitchen and reached for a drinking glass. "Just a case of great minds thinking alike."

The three of them grabbed plates of food and sat together at the table. Amanda felt excited for the first time in quite a while. She was happy to have her father visiting and happy to have June as her mentor and sidekick of sorts. And for the first time in a long time, she was excited about going on a date. They sat and ate and laughed together for a long while. Amanda wasn't sure what time it was when they all stood up and stretched.

"Are you sure you have to go home tomorrow? I've loved having you here, Dad. I'm going to be so sad when you leave."

"Well, I figured I should at least stay until Fireboy picks you up for your date. Maybe scare him a little."

Amanda smiled. "Scare him, huh?"

"Well, I mean, he's gotta know whose little girl he's taking on a date. I don't need him thinking you're just another girl he can brag about at the firehouse."

"Dad." Amanda pulled away from the hug. "He asked me to dinner, not to the French Riviera."

"Okay, okay. We'll see how he does with dinner."

"Okay, Dad. Night."

"Goodnight, honey. See you for breakfast."

Amanda ascended the stairs and walked into her bedroom. She sat on her bed and unlocked her phone. She wasn't sure what she expected to be there, but she opened her social media apps and checked her messages anyway. The only ones who ever sent her messages were June and her father. But June had just left, and her father was in the guest bedroom.

"One day," she said aloud. One day she would have messages and people to chat with. Perhaps a message about a group of friends going to dinner, or maybe a message from Brian about dinner and a movie. Whatever the case, there was part of her that hoped very much to continue on her path to normalcy. She had come leaps and bounds from where she was immediately following her attack. She had befriended June, and she could grocery shop and go out in public with minimal anxiety. It was her hope that this path would continue and that things would keep getting better. She set her phone on her night stand and pulled a pair of shorts and a tank top out of her drawer. She changed into her bed clothes, washed her face and hands, brushed her teeth, and climbed into bed. As she lay quietly, reflecting on the events of the day, she was overcome with a feeling of appreciation for her father and June. Without them, she would be a shell of her former self. Or perhaps more of a shell than she already was. She closed her eyes, and for the first time in a long time, she hoped that she would dream. After all, her date tomorrow was with someone quite handsome.

Chapter 13

Whiting pulled the compartment door closed on ladder four in the firehouse. He set his gear back on the floor, where it lived during his work shift, waiting for another call. He had just returned from a vehicle fire, and he was looking forward to a shower and some sleep before either his shift ended or the alarm went off again. He was passing the overhead doors when a vehicle pulled up. A man about Whiting's age, wearing a black-hooded sweatshirt, got out and started to approach the firehouse. Whiting watched as he walked into the side door of the firehouse and made eye contact with Whiting.

"You Brian Whiting?"

Whiting knew there was no sense in lying, as his last name was on his uniform shirt.

"Yeah. Who wants to know?"

"There cameras in this firehouse?"

"Not on the apparatus floor. Cameras make you nervous?"

"Not necessarily. Just don't need any record of what's about to happen."

Whiting tensed slightly.

"I should let you know I'm pretty good with an ax."

"Easy. I'm not looking for a fight." The man looked over his shoulder and then around the room quickly. When he was certain no one was around, he took another half step toward Whiting. He didn't move, but Whiting was ready to react.

"You know that ivy vine tattoo you spotted on that crash victim a little while ago?"

Whiting took a quick breath before answering. "Yeah, what about it?"

"We've got reason to believe that someone in this firehouse has a connection to that group of assholes."

Whiting felt some of the tension leave his face and chest. He let out the breath that he had apparently been holding. "Who?"

"I don't know. But we need you to find out, if you're up to it."

"Who is *we*?"

"Let's just say I belong to a..." The man paused. "A concerned group of citizens who all happen to wear the same color shirt Bill Harding knows how to reach me."

Whiting felt the tension leave his clenched fists. Bill Harding was a friend of his, and apparently, the hooded man whom Brian presumed was an undercover detective was a friend of Harding's. He took a quick breath and said, "Okay, got it."

"Help us if you can, Lieutenant." With that, the man turned to leave, but before he could get far, Whiting called out to him, and he stopped.

"I'll keep an eye out. But who are these idiots with the tattoos? They a gang?"

The man in the hoodie looked around quickly. "Not a gang. But they are pretty untouchable. We've questioned a few of them who we believe have a connection to a rape and attempted murder case, but they're like ghosts with good lawyers.

"Untouchable how?" Whiting asked, his interest growing.

"We had one kid dead to rights for being part of the attack. We went to serve him a warrant to search his apartment, and quite conveniently, he didn't live there anymore. He didn't seem to live anywhere."

"So am I looking for someone with money? Multiple houses?"

"Maybe. But maybe not. Their connection could be by association. Keep an eye out."

With that, the man pulled his hood over his head and disappeared out the door. Whiting was watching him drive away when he heard KJ's voice behind him.

"Who was that?"

Whiting turned. "Oh, just a guy looking for directions. Couldn't find Memorial Street."

"Oh, okay. I'm headed to bed. Night, Lieutenant."

"Goodnight," Whiting said as he turned and walked down the hallway to the locker room.

While he showered, he couldn't help but wonder who on earth had some connection to the group with the ivy vine tattoos. He had some guys in the firehouse with rough pasts, but they were all good guys now. He trusted every one of them with his life. As he headed for his sleeping quarters, he decided to focus on something happy. He started to think about his date with Amanda. It had been a long time since he had been on an actual date, and he was looking forward to it. He fully intended to plan out the date in his head, but he was exhausted, and before he knew it, he was sound asleep. By some stroke of luck, there were no calls the rest of the night, and Whiting managed to get a handful of hours of pretty good sleep. He woke, looked at his watch, and decided that even though his alarm hadn't gone off, he was ready to get up. He walked into the locker room, showered, brushed his teeth, grabbed his duffle bag from his locker, and headed to get a cup of coffee from the kitchen. He drank his coffee on the apparatus floor and checked the truck to make sure it was ready for the oncoming shift. After a little while, he headed for the briefing room to talk to the officers of the oncoming shift. He wanted to tell them to keep an eye out for anything that resembled a connection with the ivy group, but he just wasn't sure what to tell them or how to make it seem subtle.

He found the officers and passed along the information in as casual a manner as he could. Once the briefing was over, Whiting headed to his truck. He usually went straight home and saved his errands for the afternoon, but he had a stop to make outside the city. He needed to make his date with Amanda something she would enjoy and never forget, and he had a feeling he needed something more than a nice bouquet of flowers. He parked in front of a beautifully decorated restaurant. Tall stone columns supported the arch in the front, and giant glass windows ringed all sides of the building. Whiting walked in, dressed completely inappropriately for the setting. An older man in a suit and tie met him at the front of the restaurant. He was dressed neatly, not one hair out of place, his shoes shiny enough to see yourself in. He wore a small silk handkerchief, folded perfectly, sticking just slightly out of his pocket.

"Welcome to The Scarlett Rose, sir," he said in a crisp and proper British accent. "We are not open yet. Can I help you? Would you like a table later on, perhaps something out back, out of sight?"

"Sir? And out back? Your tie on too tight?"

The man in the suit shifted his weight and looked around. He stared at Whiting for a brief moment before a broad smile broke out across his face. "Hello, young man. Wonderful to see you."

Whiting reached out and hugged the man in the suit. "Hi, Robert. Good to see you, too. Is my brother here?"

"Yes, he's in the kitchen, I'm sure, micromanaging as he does so well. If he's not there, best to try his office. We get a new delivery of plates and glasses today, and you and I both know that means he'll need to inspect every one of them."

"Oh boy. Thanks, Robert."

"You're welcome. Don't be such a stranger. We haven't seen you in months," Robert called after him.

Whiting smiled. "Will do." He walked through a stone archway and onto the main floor of the restaurant. He crossed over to the bar and walked to the far end of the room and into the kitchen. He spotted his brother talking to one of the sous chefs. He looked new, as he wasn't anyone Brian recognized. Since that was the case, he decided it was time to have a little fun. Whiting grabbed a sheet of paper from a nearby counter and took a pen out of a drawer below. "Health Inspector," he called out. "We got reports of a sous chef mishandling food."

A brief silence filled the kitchen. When most of them saw Whiting, they smiled quietly and went back to what they were doing. The young man talking to his brother froze. Brian walked over to him briskly.

"Good morning. I work for the city. We got reports of a sous chef mishandling food. What's your name, son?"

Whiting's brother rolled his eyes and smiled. "He's not mishandling anything. Put down your pad and pen and go back where you came from. Or start washing dishes. We all know you can't cook."

The young sous chef stood between Whiting and his brother, frozen and barely breathing. Finally, Whiting's brother broke the tension. "It's okay. He's my brother, and he may work for the city, but he certainly doesn't know the first thing about cleanliness of a kitchen. Go head back to work. Thank you."

The young man quickly disappeared to the far end of the kitchen. Whiting leaned in and hugged his brother.

"Hi, little brother. Long time, no see," he said as Whiting set down the pad and pen.

"Hi, Dean. Place looks amazing. Smells pretty good, too."

"Thanks. We're back in the full swing of things now that the upgrades to the kitchen are done and the rooftop dining area is finished. And we're flat-out busy, which is great." Dean started walking toward his office door, and Whiting followed. "I'm guessing you're not here because you want breakfast before we open?"

"Well, I'm not going to turn down breakfast if you're offering."

Dean laughed. As they walked, he stopped briefly at one of the food-preparation stations. A girl about Whiting's age turned and smiled. "Hi, Brian. Yes, I'll make him breakfast," she said to Dean and laughed. "I'll have one of the servers bring it to your office."

"Thanks, Jennifer," Dean said as they kept walking. "She would date you in a heartbeat, you know," he said to Brian.

"Yes, I'm aware. You tell me that every time I'm here."

"Well, kid, you've gotta do something. Your first real relationship was long, and we all thought that it was going to end in marriage. We were all surprised when Kelsey packed up her dolls and dishes and moved to another country on a whim."

"Yeah, well, she was a free spirit. What can I say?" Whiting said, desperately hoping his brother would change the subject.

"Brian." His brother stopped walking and looked at him. "I know you think what you had with Kelsey was perfect and irreplaceable."

"It was perfect," Whiting shot back sharply. He took a long breath and let it out slowly before calmly repeating, "It was perfect, Dean."

168

"Okay, it was perfect," Dean agreed. "But she's been gone four years. I loved her like a sister, but she's not coming back. You deserve to be happy. And Jennifer, well," Dean started in an attempt to lighten the mood, "she might not be marriage material, but I'm sure she'd love to ask you what it is that makes you..." He paused briefly and smirked. "Happy."

This got a small smile from Brian. Although he still felt bad for upsetting his brother, Dean knew him well enough to know that while what he said upset him, Brian was mad about the situation and not mad at him.

"And she is adorable and a great cook," Brian responded. "But I happen to have a date with someone else."

"A date? You?" Dean gasped.

"Ha-ha, funny guy. That's kind of why I'm here."

"You need a table? Of course, kid. Whatever table you want."

"Actually..." Brian paused. "I'd like to eat in the garden if that's okay." Dean stopped and turned to his brother with his eyebrows raised.

"You must really want to impress this girl. Of course it's okay. Let me know when, and it's no problem at all."

Brian smirked. "Well, it's kind of short notice, but—"

Dean interrupted before he could finish. "You've been my brother my whole life thus far. I'm fully aware that the reason you're here today is because your date is tonight. So yes, tonight is fine. What time?"

Brian smiled. "Six-thirty, please and thank you." He was about to continue, but Jennifer knocked on the door to Dean's office.

She walked over and set a plate on the table in front of Brian. "Here you are, handsome. If you're still…" She paused and looked at him for a moment. A broad smile danced across her lips as she continued. "…hungry when you finish, let me know." She turned and walked away slowly, glancing over her shoulder at Brian when she reached the door.

"Tell me you're not that oblivious." Dean chuckled once Jennifer was out of sight.

"What?" Brian said as he smirked. "I'm sure she meant if I was still hungry for food."

"Mmmhmm. I'm sure that's what she meant." Dean laughed and sat next to him. "So all dates aside, how the hell are you, bud?"

Brian took a sip of juice. "I'm good. Firehouse has been busy, but I've got a great bunch on my truck. My whole firehouse, actually, is filled with awesome people. House is good. Renovations are mostly done."

"Good. I'm happy that you're happy and doing well. You still talk to Mom and Dad pretty often?"

"Oh yeah. I call Mom a few times a week, and Dad sends me more text messages than most of the guys at the firehouse now that he knows how."

They both laughed. "Good," Dean said. "They're going to come out and see the restaurant now that it's done. You're gonna be here to have dinner with them. Just telling you now. Don't be working on the twenty-second."

"Not a problem. I'm off that day. It'll be good to see them. I wish they lived just a little closer so visits were easier."

"They live close enough for frequent visits. I've just always been their favorite, so they come to see me more often."

Brian laughed out loud. "You just keep telling yourself that." He was about to start telling his brother why he was actually the favorite child when a young waiter knocked on Dean's open door.

"Mr. Whiting? The shipment of glassware is here. I know you said you wanted to look at it."

"Thank you," Dean said as he started to stand. "And, Alex, sleeves down before we open, please."

Brian glanced at the young man's arms. His sleeves were rolled up to reveal a tattoo of an American flag on his forearm.

"Yes, sir. Sorry."

"No need to apologize. I've got two tattoos myself. Just have your sleeves down when we open. Thank you."

As soon as Brian heard the word tattoo, he started to speak. He managed to stop himself so he didn't interrupt his brother. As soon as the waiter was out of earshot, however, Brian turned to Dean.

"I know you want to go check on your shipment of glassware, but before you go, I have a question and may need a favor." There must have been a sense of urgency in his tone, because Dean put his hand on his brother's shoulder.

"Okay, bud. What is it? You okay?"

"Yeah, I'm okay. You see a lot of affluent people given the caliber of your restaurants. You ever come across anyone with an ivy vine tattoo?"

Dean thought for a moment. "I own four restaurants. They're not all as nice as this one, and I see a lot of people. Nothing sticks in my mind about an ivy vine, but I'll keep my eyes open. What's so special about an ivy vine?"

Brian took a step closer. "We've had some calls lately that involved some real assholes. One of them torched our ambulance after throwing the paramedics out of it. One of the city detectives stopped at the firehouse and told me to keep my head up and eyes open. Apparently, the ivy vine tattoo is the mark of some group that has been acting like they own the city."

"Good to know. I'll keep my eyes open, and I'll ask the guy who does my ink about the ivy vine."

"Thanks, bud. And, hey, Dean? Just make sure your"— Brian paused and made air quotes with his fingers—"'ink guy' doesn't *have* an ivy vine tattoo before you ask him."

Dean rolled his eyes and smirked. "Thanks for the tip."

"Anytime. Go inspect your cups and saucers, and be nice to the people you bought them from."

"I'm always nice. Ish," Dean said as he smiled and hugged him. "I'll see you tonight. Six-thirty."

"Thanks, kid," Brian said as he turned and walked back out through the kitchen. He said goodbye to Robert at the front door and headed for his truck.

He drove home with mixed emotions. He was excited for his date, and he was very happy he got to chat with his brother, but he was also somewhat distracted by what the detective had told him the night before. He managed to shake off his negative thoughts and replace them with excitement about his date. He turned his radio up and sang along as he drove. It was a beautiful morning, and he had a date later on with a beautiful girl. He stopped on his way home and bought flowers. It was something he could have done right before he picked Amanda up, but he knew the owners of a small Mom-and-Pop florist that he liked very much. They had always treated him well, and over the years, he had developed somewhat of a friendship with them. The owner asked him questions about his date and incessantly asked for details until her husband finally told her to stop with the third degree. Whiting left the flower shop with one more stop to make before he went home. It would only take a few minutes. He had only one item on his list. A stuffed giraffe.

Chapter 14

Whiting was walking back to his truck, giraffe in hand, when his cell phone rang. He glanced at the screen and saw it was his brother calling.

"Hey, kid, what's up?"

"Hey. That delivery I just took in of plates and glasses, right as you left..."

"Yeah? What about it?"

"The rep from the company was a really nice guy. Even threw in an extra sixty wine glasses because three of the plates were broken. Anyway, he had a tattoo on his leg. I never would have seen it, but he pulled his pant leg up to tie his boot. It was an ivy vine. Plain as day. And well done, too. Not some quick sketch that someone threw together. It was done by someone who really knows what they're doing."

"You know his name?"

"Yeah, of course. It's on the invoice as the contact person for any problems. I'll text it to you."

"Perfect. Thanks, bud."

"You got it. See you tonight."

Whiting hung up and put his phone back in his pocket, then continued his walk to his vehicle. He hadn't noticed, but when Dean called, he had stopped walking all together. He found his truck, jumped in, and his phone vibrated. The text from Dean had come through. He decided that he wanted to focus on his date with Amanda, but he knew that if he didn't follow through with the information Dean had sent him, he'd be preoccupied all night. He opened his phone and dialed the police department. A young girl answered, and he asked to speak to Sergeant Harding. She put him on hold for a brief second, and then the phone rang again. After two short rings, a deep voice was on the other end of the line.

"Bill Harding."

"Bill, it's Brian Whiting. How are ya?"

"What's up, kid?"

"I've got another person with an ivy vine tattoo. I just wanted to pass along the information."

"Oh, good. Let me get a pen. Another one of them end up as part of a call you guys went on?"

"No, I'm actually off shift right now. I went to see my brother this morning and asked him to keep his eyes open. I didn't give him many details, but Dean knows a lot of people since he has restaurants all over Claiborne, you know?"

"Sure, that's a good thought."

"Well, I had only been gone about a half hour, and he called me. The sales rep from the company he buys glassware from has an ivy vine tattooed on his leg. Dean saw it by chance when the kid rolled up his pant leg to tie his boot."

"Really? You have any info on him?"

"Yeah, I have his name and cell number whenever you're ready."

"I'm ready. Go ahead."

Whiting read him the name and number that Dean had passed along. After he finished, he added, "I know there are a lot of companies out there, but maybe your wife knows a little bit about the company or has ordered from them before?"

"We have ordered from them before. All the time, actually. Thanks, Brian. This is a great piece of information."

"You're welcome. Happy to help. I figured maybe you could pass along the information to a friend of yours who happened to stop by the firehouse the other night. Hooded sweatshirt, doesn't say much, no badge, and no uniform. Sound familiar?"

"Yeah, I think I might know a guy who fits that description. I'll let him know. How's everything else?"

"Good. I actually have a date tonight, which is hopefully a good thing." Whiting chuckled.

"Good for you. Are you bringing her to our place to eat?"

"You were second on the list, but I figured I should patronize one of my brother's restaurants for the first date. If there's a second, I'll be sure to head to your place."

"There will be a second. And a third. You're a good kid, Brian. I'm sure she'll have a great time."

"Thanks, Bill. We'll talk to ya."

"You got it. See ya."

Whiting hung up the phone and felt relieved and excited. He had passed along the information and felt like he could focus on his date and not be distracted. He drove home happily, singing along with the radio, excited and a bit nervous for his date. He showered and did a load of laundry, and while he was waiting for it to dry, he cleaned up his kitchen and tried to pick out clothes for dinner. For the most part, he was a calm and level-headed person. He could walk into a burning building and stay focused and composed. Car accidents, natural disasters, high angle rescues, and crawling into a confined space were all things he didn't even think twice about anymore. This date, however, had him feeling nervous and sideways. He put on at least four pairs of pants before he decided on one. Every shirt he tried was either not the right color, too short, tight in the sleeves, or didn't match any of the pants that he had left sprawled across his bed. He decided to take a break from his self-inflicted fashion war with the hope that if he left his bedroom for a while, he could walk in again and know immediately what to wear.

He headed outside and into his yard. He had mowed his lawn the day before, so he didn't need to do that. He found ways to keep busy for a while. Simply being outside had always helped him stay calm and relaxed. Most of the people he worked with lived in the city or just on the outskirts. He had a bit longer of a drive, but to him it was well worth it. He needed a yard, and grass, and a garden and quiet. His house was older, but a few years of hard work and a little overtime money had allowed him to turn it into a truly beautiful home. He had taken the time to make a beautiful front lawn with flower gardens and a stone walkway, and he had even built himself a small barn in the backyard. Trees lined one side of his house, while the other bordered a field with a small pond in the center. On the edge of the yard closest to the field was a small vegetable garden. Dean said he was crazy to live away from the city. He told him he would miss being close to the pulse of the city. Brian disagreed. He needed space. He wanted the pulse of the city to be too far away to hear or feel. His neighbors were great people, but they lived far enough away that he couldn't see their houses unless he went out of his way to. That was the way he liked it.

He pulled a few weeds in his garden, tidied up the barn, swept his garage, and washed his truck. He glanced at his watch as he dried off his truck and realized more time had passed than he thought. Hopefully, it was enough time that his fashion debacle could quickly come to an end, and he could decide what to wear. He headed inside and walked straight into his bedroom. As soon as he was through the doorway, he grabbed a pair of gray dress pants, a teal button-down shirt, and a silk tie with diagonal stipes that were navy blue, royal blue, and teal. He decided he wasn't changing his mind again, that this would work. Or so he hoped.

After his time outside, he decided he needed another shower. He showered and shaved, and during one of his final strokes of his razor, he cut the top of his upper lip. Nothing major, but he was quite aggravated about having a small cut on his lip during a first date. He pressed a tissue against it to stop the bleeding and began to get dressed. He peeled the small wad of tissue off his lip as he began to tie his tie. The bleeding had stopped, thankfully, but to him the cut looked enormous, and he felt as if that's all Amanda would be able to see. Finally pulling himself away from the mirror and trying to convince himself that maybe she wouldn't notice, he grabbed his keys, his wallet, and Amanda's flowers.

As he drove, he rehearsed what he was going to say. He repeated lines over and over in his rear-view mirror. He felt somewhat ridiculous. He'd been in front of news cameras and massive crowds of people before for press conferences for the fire department, and was even interviewed by a national news outlet during fire prevention week after saving a teacher from a fire at a school. He was comfortable talking to the press and to large groups of people. The girl he bought the stuffed giraffe for, however, had him feeling like he didn't speak English anymore. He repeated every form of *Hi* and *Hey* that he could think of. He checked his breath, checked his hair, checked to see if his tie knot was straight. He was in the middle of practicing his best *nice to see you* line at a red light when he glanced over and saw a young girl, about four years old, looking at him quizzically. He pressed his lips together in an embarrassed smile and managed a small wave. He saw her say something to the driver, and in a brief moment, her window was down. Whiting rolled his window down and smiled at her. She smiled back and said, "You're the fireman that came to my school. You look very nice, even without your fireman suit."

Whiting felt all the tension leave his body, and a warmth spread across his face as he felt himself smile. The power of a child. A compliment wrapped in childish innocence. Still smiling, he said, "Thanks, kiddo. You look very nice, too." The little girl waved as her window went up and the car pulled away. Whiting felt such a sense of relief, and he was hopeful that his nerves would stay calm for the duration of his date. His calmness ended slightly sooner than he had hoped, however, and he felt his hands start to sweat as he remembered that he was meeting Amanda's father again, or so he assumed. He parked his truck in front of her house and took a deep breath. He always told his firefighters that if they felt nervous, scared, or overwhelmed when they got out of the fire truck, to take a deep breath and count to five. It sounded strange to them at first, but they had all admitted to him that it helped a great deal. Whiting took another breath and counted to five. He exhaled slowly and got out of his truck. He slowly grabbed the flowers from his front passenger seat and headed to the door.

"He's here!" June yelled as she scrambled away from the front door and into the kitchen. "Amandaaaa. Get your butt down here. He's here."

John shook his head and smiled as he walked into the living room and headed toward the front door. "You two are acting like you're still in high school."

"Have you *seen* this man?" June said as she fixed her own hair in the reflection of the microwave. "You're a handsome man, Johnny, but this boy is half a step away from being a Greek God."

"June," Amanda called in a hoarse whisper as she hurried down the stairs, putting her earrings in. "Stop yelling. He's going to hear you. And are you two *sure* you don't have something else to do right now?"

June crossed into the living room. "No, no, honey, we're ready. I mean, we're here for you and will just say hello to Lieutenant Fine-As—"

"June!" Amanda interrupted her before she could finish her sentence.

Her father and June turned to face Amanda. John stopped walking all together. "Honey, you look beautiful."

Amanda looked down. "Thanks, Daddy. It's been a long time since I've worn a dress. Do I look okay?"

"You look breathtaking," John said.

"Oh, honey, yes you do," June said as she met her at the bottom of the stairs. She hugged her and kissed her cheek lightly. "He's not even going to know what to say. You're exquisite."

"Thanks, guys. Were you planning on standing right here as I opened the door, or do you maybe have something to do in the kitchen?"

"Just let me see him one more time. Let an old woman be happy," June said as she smirked.

Her father crossed the room and gave her a hug and a kiss. "I'm proud of you. I know it wasn't easy to say yes to a first date. But I'm very proud of you."

"Thanks, Daddy. Love you."

"Love you, too, honey."

Before anyone could say anything else, the doorbell rang. June took a position standing next to John, trying to act normal. Amanda opened the door slowly.

As it opened, Whiting took a deep breath.

"Hi," Amanda said quietly.

He stared at her through the open door. She was breathtaking. He didn't know what to say, especially since there was a small audience behind her. "Hi," Whiting managed. After a brief moment of somewhat awkward silence, Whiting spoke up. "You look incredible," he said as he looked down quickly and then back up at her.

Amanda was certainly flattered, but she was determined not to show it. She didn't want him to think she would turn to mush at the first compliment he threw her way. Although she *was* pretty flattered and excited to hear him say something so sweet. She glanced up at his eyes and stared for a second, then did her best to break the tension.

"Any emergencies involving zoo animals today?"

"Nope, thankfully not," Whiting said, happy that Amanda had broken the tension and calmed his nerves a little.

"Would you like to come in?"

"Sure. We should probably find these some water," Whiting said as he held up the bouquet he had been holding down to his side.

"What beautiful flowers," June shrieked as she walked hurriedly over toward Whiting and Amanda.

"You must be Amanda's sister," Whiting said as he extended his hand.

"Oh, I like him," June said to Amanda as she shook Whiting's hand. "Charming older sister, yes. It's very nice to meet you," she continued as she stared at him.

"Water, June?" John spoke up from behind her.

"Oh, no, Johnny. I'm fine, thanks."

"I meant for the flowers."

"Oh, right. The flowers. These are so lovely. Thank you. Well, I mean, Amanda thanks you. They're obviously for her and not for me, so I'll just head on into the kitchen and... well, I'll have to find a vase and—"

"Okay, okay, Audrey Hepburn, let's go," John said as he took June by the arm. As she started walking toward the kitchen, John turned back to face Whiting. He extended his hand. "Good to see you again. Thanks again for the Chinese food. This is the part where I'm supposed to say 'don't have her home too late,' right?" John smiled a little.

Whiting grabbed his hand and shook firmly. "Good to see you again, too. You're very welcome. And I figured you were coming on the date with us," Whiting said as he smiled.

"Confidence and jokes under pressure. I like this kid." John laughed. "No specific time. Just please be safe, you two."

"Will do," Whiting answered.

John and June walked into the kitchen with the flowers. Amanda could hear June talking quietly under her breath and her father laughing at what Amanda could only imagine was June continuing to profess her newly found love for her date.

"Sorry about them," Amanda said as she turned to face him. "They mean well. They just..."

"They just want to make sure that I treat you the way a beautiful young woman should be treated."

Amanda smiled and felt her face get hot. "Maybe." She spread her hands. "Or they're just out to embarrass me as much as they can."

"Either way, I'm very happy you're letting me take you out. You look wonderful."

"Thank you," Amanda said.

"Ready?" Whiting asked as he extended his arm for her to hold.

"Yes, I am," Amanda said happily as she linked her arm with his.

As they walked to the truck, Amanda had so many thoughts running through her mind. She was doing her best to let Brian's charm and her excitement mask her nervousness. She told herself that now that the date had started, things would be just fine, or so she hoped. Whiting opened his truck door for her and helped her into the seat. He closed the door gently and rushed to his own side to get in.

"Nice truck," Amanda said, looking around the interior.

"Should I wait for a joke before I say thank you?" He smiled.

"No, I mean it. It's very nice. And I'm sure it's nicer to drive than the firehouse tricycle you usually pedal," Amanda said with a smirk.

"I figured an actual compliment was too good to be true. And hey, my tricycle is awesome. They let me put a bell on it."

Amanda laughed. She was getting less and less nervous with each passing minute. Being in a pickup truck brought back a minor flood of raw emotion, but she managed to suppress it by keeping up their conversation. It was refreshing to be able to talk to him like a normal person without any hesitation or fear that she was going to offend him.

"So where are we headed?" Amanda asked

"I figured we could grab a burger and fries at the drive-thru. My treat. You can even get extra fries if you're feeling crazy."

"Oooh, instead of extra fries, can I get a second sandwich? I didn't have lunch, and I'm so hungry."

"Sure. I might live on the wild side and get a milkshake with mine."

"Now you're talking," Amanda said, smiling.

Whiting smiled back. "I'm kidding," Whiting started. "There is a pretty nice restaurant on the other side of town. Just on the outskirts. It's got amazing food, tremendous scenery, and a great atmosphere."

"Sounds like you went to a lot of trouble to get a reservation at this place."

"Well, it's not every day that someone as pretty as you agrees to have dinner with me."

That was the third time he had complimented her looks. She was going to tell him he didn't need to continue with the incessant flattery, but it was nice to be complimented. They drove for a short time, conversation flowing fairly well for a first date. She asked about the firehouse, and he asked how she knew June. She was about to make a joke about him being lost when she noticed the truck stop. She looked out her window and saw where they were.

"The only restaurant down past this section of town is The Scarlett Rose. And unless you had a reservation before you even met me, I'm pretty sure we're not getting in. I've heard they have a six-month waiting list for reservations."

"Oh, so they don't take walk-ins? I haven't been on a date in a while. People still call and make reservations?"

Amanda could tell by the giant grin on his face that he was kidding. She hoped. Although she was feeling like he had a reservation with someone else, and they cancelled on him. Doing her best not to feel like a stand-in date, she joked a little more.

"You can try to walk in. I'll wait in the truck, and you let me know how it goes."

Whiting put a contemplative index finger over his lips. "Hmmm. What about bribery? Does that still work? If I slip the maître d' some cash, will they let us in? I'm thinking maybe a five-spot? Maybe ten. I hear it's a nice place. I don't want to seem cheap."

Amanda smiled at Whiting and decided his grin was a good sign that he had some sort of plan. After a few more minutes of driving and small talk, he pulled up in front of The Scarlett Rose. Amanda was still confused as to how he managed to get a reservation in such a short time. She started to ask a question but was startled into silence when her door was pulled open.

Chapter 15

“Good evening, ma'am.” She turned to see an older man in a suit and tie offer his hand to help her out of the truck. She glanced at Brian, slightly unsure of what to do.

“It's okay. He's being serious. He'll be offended if you don't let him help.”

She turned back to see the man smiling and waiting patiently. She took his hand and stepped out of the truck and onto the sidewalk. She looked over and saw a man about her age talking to Brian. He heard them laugh and heard him say, “Fuel it up after you're done joy riding.”

He walked over to her and extended his arm once again. She took his arm, and the man who had helped her out of the truck walked to the door and opened it for them. Amanda was in shock. She had heard about The Scarlett Rose but had never actually been inside the front door. It was breathtakingly beautiful. She looked at him. “How?

How on earth?" she said as she looked around, trying to take in everything she was seeing. A few steps inside the door, Brian started talking to someone. She turned and saw a perfectly dressed man in a suit and tie standing across from Brian. He was handsome for someone of his age, with a full head of white hair that was combed neatly. His face was lean but kind looking, with bright blue eyes and a sharply angled jaw line and cheekbones. Crisp folds in his shirt collar and a perfect tie knot descended down to pants with absolutely no wrinkles and leather shoes that were pristine and clean. They were laughing, and the older gentleman was holding Whiting's arm in a prolonged handshake that he seemed to not want to let go of.

"Amanda, this is Robert. The Scarlett Rose is incredibly lucky to have him. He keeps this place up and running, isn't that right, Robert?"

"Well, I certainly like to think so," he said in his distinguished British accent. "Although I still can't seem to get Dean to share the same opinion."

"It's very nice to meet you, Robert," she said as she extended her hand.

The older man took her hand gently and lowered his head and kissed it. "My pleasure to meet you, my dear. Let's get to your table, shall we?" Robert extended his arm, and Amanda took it, somewhat hesitant to walk through a gorgeous restaurant full of people who she guessed were much wealthier than anyone she knew. She kept looking over her shoulder to make sure Brian was still following them.

"Oh, don't worry, dear. He's like a piece of bubble gum that you've stepped in. Takes a lot of time and effort to make him go away," Robert said as he smiled.

"I heard that," Brian called out.

Amanda smiled. She glanced at her surroundings and realized they were headed for a door in the back of the restaurant. She started to feel uneasy and was about to ask what was going on when Robert opened the door to reveal a beautiful marble staircase with polished railings. She could see her reflection in the glossy, polished marble, and the vast open space with sky-high ceilings created a faint echo of footsteps as they walked.

"Is this how you got a reservation?" she managed to say through her nervousness. "We're sitting up in the attic?" Amanda joked as they climbed the stairs.

He shrugged. "Hey, it was the best I could do on short notice."

Once at the top, Robert opened a giant door. "Welcome to The Scarlett Rose's best kept secret."

Amanda stopped walking and, for a moment, could only stand and blink. She was standing at the opening to a room bigger than any space she had ever been in save for a grocery store or shopping center. The polished floor reflected crimson and orange hues from dozens of lights scattered across the vast ceiling and wall. Beautiful flowers grew in large planter vases as well as inside a stone wall that ringed the room on all sides. At the corners of the stone wall were tall stone pillars, ornately decorated with climbing stems of brilliant flora. Across the top of one section of the stone wall was a cascading stone waterfall, dotted with more bright orange, yellow, and crimson flowers. Behind the waterfall, on the far back wall, was a table, nestled gently between flowering trees and bushes. The wall that the table sat closest to was glass from floor to ceiling, and it overlooked a rolling hill that seemed like it should be hundreds of miles from any place that resembled a city instead of just a few miles outside Claiborne. Amanda stood quietly and tried to form a sentence. She was impressed, flattered, excited, and awestruck. She wasn't quite sure what to say. It must have been apparent that she was frozen in place because Robert spoke up.

"This way, my dear," he said as he extended his arm again. Amanda took his arm slowly and walked toward the table. Robert pulled out Whiting's chair while he pulled out the chair for Amanda. She sat, still looking around and trying to take in the sight of what was absolutely one of the most beautiful places she had ever been.

"Dean will be your server this evening," Robert said as he turned to leave. Whiting's voice stopped him.

"Dean? Dean will be our server? Robert, come here, please."

Robert tuned to face Brian and smiled. "Yes, sir. Dean. He's very curious as to who gets the honor of dining in the rooftop garden this evening. And by that, I simply mean he's being nosey." Robert turned slowly and grinned as he walked away.

"Who is Dean?" Amanda asked. "And why is it bad that he is our server?"

"It's not bad that he's our server. It's just a little strange seeing as he owns The Scarlett Rose. And three other restaurants throughout the city."

190

"Owns?" Amanda took a sip from the water glass that was in front of her. "You're making the *owner* wait on us?"

"Oh, I'm not making him. Apparently, he chose to."

"Do you know the owner, at least?" Amanda asked as she sipped her water again?

"I do, yes. He and I have a lot in common., most specifically our last name. We even shared a room for a few years when I was eight."

"Your brother owns this place?" she asked, her eyes still carefully wandering around the beautiful room.

"He does. He's taken a liking to the restaurant industry. Just strange that he's decided to wait on us."

She wasn't sure if she should be nervous or not. This had turned from what she thought was a simple dinner date to dining in the most beautiful place she had ever seen, and now meeting some of Brian's family. They sat happily, talking and laughing. Amanda couldn't remember the last person she was so comfortable talking to. Perhaps no one. That thought excited her and terrified her all at once. She was loving the conversation and had been smiling more tonight than she had in a very long time. She was doing her best not to be apprehensive about letting someone learn so much about her. They talked about where she went to college, Brian being in the fire academy, where they grew up, what their parents were like. He told her about the fire department, and, oddly enough, she had so many questions. She had never considered herself a question asker, but she felt like she was asking him questions without a chance for him to take a breath between answers.

She took another sip of water to slow down her endless inquiries. "I'm asking too many questions," Amanda said as she lowered her eyes and stared at her napkin in her lap.

"No way. I love it. No one ever asks me about my job. I spend most of my time with people who are in the same line of work, so they don't want to hear about it. Ask me anything. I haven't enjoyed a conversation this much in a very long time."

Amanda brushed her hair behind her ear. She was about to ask him another question when a man appeared at the top of the stairs and began walking their way.

"Our waiter is here," Brian said as he stood up to greet Dean.

"Hi, little brother," he said as they shook hands. Dean pulled Brian in for a hug. "So glad you came to see us."

"Me too," he said as he turned to face Amanda. "Dean Whiting, Amanda Killingly. Amanda, this is my brother Dean. He owns this beautiful restaurant, and apparently" —Whiting paused and smirked at Dean—"he's also our waiter for the evening."

Dean smiled. "I will certainly go get one of the wait staff and have them take care of you. I just wanted to meet the lovely lady who was gracious enough to go on a date with you," Dean said as he turned to face Amanda. He continued in a tone that reassured Amanda he had no interest in flirting but was simply extending a compliment as part of his introduction to her. "You look beautiful. It's wonderful to meet you. If there is anything you need tonight, let me know. And if he gets out of line, let me know that, too, and I'll take care of him," Dean said as he winked and smiled at Amanda.

"Will do. And thank you," Amanda said, trying to take the compliment in stride. Two very polite and well-mannered men had called her beautiful in the same night. Her happiness with the compliments was mixed with a slight tinge of nervousness about being in a room alone with two other men she barely knew. She swallowed her anxiety as best she could and took a breath. She wasn't even sure how to respond to the compliments. Her father had always called her beautiful, and the regulars at the bar had always said she was gorgeous, but they were typically very intoxicated. All of a sudden, she started to feel hot as she remembered one of her attackers using the word beautiful to describe some very specific parts of her. She drew in a quick breath and tried to push the thoughts out of her head. She didn't want to shut down in front of Brian and his brother. She was starting to feel nauseous, and before it got any worse, she managed to speak up. "Could you point me to the ladies' room, please?" she said quietly.

"Of course. There is a private bathroom up here. Top of the stairs, on the right. Would you like me to walk you?" Dean asked.

"Oh, no, I'm okay. Thank you. I'll be right back."

"Of course," Dean said. "We'll be here."

Amanda walked as quickly as she could without giving off the impression that something was wrong. Once she was out of earshot, Dean looked at Brian.

"She's beautiful, Brian."

"I know," he said, still watching Amanda walk away. "I could barely talk when I saw her wearing that. She's just...I don't know. She is so pretty, and talking to her is just so easy. I don't know that I've ever enjoyed anyone's company this much before besides..."

Dean smiled and spoke up quickly to stop Brian from digging up a memory of his lost love and ruining the cheerful mood. "That's a good thing, kid. She seems like a sweet girl."

"I know, but what if she doesn't like me? I'm so taken with her. But I can't just blurt that out. I'll scare her away."

"You don't need to blurt anything out. But tell her how you feel. I know subtlety is not your strong suit, but give it a shot. You don't want to scare her off by getting down on one knee, but you also don't want her to wonder if you like her, either. Tell her you love talking to her. Compliment how great she is at conversation *and* how nice she looks. Don't drool too much when you tell her the second part." Dean chuckled

"I'll do my best not to. Bring me a bib maybe, smart ass?" Brian said, smiling.

"I'll have one of the servers come up and wait on you guys. I'm sure Amanda was nervous enough about a first date without it feeling like she was being set up to meet your family. I'll check in with you before you leave."

"Thanks, bud," Brian said as he watched Dean walk to the stairs.

Amanda splashed cold water on her cheeks in an effort to keep her makeup mostly intact. She had managed to calm herself down, and the nausea had faded. She stood and stared in the mirror. "You're safe, you're strong, and you're in control," she said out loud. It was a line from one of the self-help books she had read. It had always sounded so strange when she practiced saying it in the mirror at home, but it actually seemed to help. She repeated the phrase a few more times and dabbed her forehead with a little more water. As she walked back to the table, she noticed all the beautiful things around her. The space she was in was even more stunning than she had previously noticed when they walked up the stairs a short time ago. Glass butterflies and hummingbirds spotted the beautiful flowers that were flowing down across the tops of the stone pillars. Blue and turquoise lights danced beneath the surface of the running water. The space was truly incredible. As she approached the table, she noticed Dean was gone.

"Our waiter up and left? Just when I thought this was the nicest restaurant I'd ever been to."

He smiled. "He's going to have one of the servers come up and take care of us. He figured a first date with me was painful enough without him kicking around."

Amanda smiled back. "He wasn't bothering me, and..." She paused to take a breath and let it out slowly. "This is the most wonderful date I've ever been on. So please believe me when I say it's not painful."

His eyes met hers, and they smiled and stared at each other for a brief moment. Amanda felt like her entire body was staring at him. He was incredibly handsome, and she was enjoying his company so much. As she started to feel like she was staring too long, she made herself speak up.

"So more questions are okay? I know I asked a lot already."

"More questions are absolutely okay. Ask me anything you'd like," Whiting answered. "I'm your open book tonight. Work, home, family, favorite color. I'm all ears."

"Well," Amanda started. "First thing's first. Are you a vegetarian?"

He paused. That wasn't quite the type of question he expected. He was hoping this wasn't leading up to her saying that she was one. Not that it would make him like her any less, but his brother's restaurant had so much good food that he was excited to order, but nothing on his mind was vegetarian.

Whiting looked at her and tried to gauge if she was hiding a smile. "I'm actually not a vegetarian."

"You didn't seem like the type," Amanda said, one corner of her mouth tugging up into a grin. "Next question."

"Yes?"

"How on earth do you decide what to order here? I want to order the entire left side of the menu."

Whiting felt a giant sense of relief. "Well, let's go over it together." He slid his chair over next to hers and pointed to the menu. She smelled amazing. She turned and looked at him. When she did, he was suddenly aware of how close he had moved to her.

"Is this okay?" he asked.

She hesitated briefly, unsure if it was too close, but then took a small breath and said, "This is perfect," then turned slightly in her chair. Her face was so close to his. She had been worried about being close to him on the date, about feeling overwhelmed and uncomfortable given her past. In this moment, however, she felt absolutely at ease and was hoping he wouldn't move away anytime soon.

"So," she continued, "I'm okay with suggestions. As long as you don't tell me to order a salad." They both laughed as they turned back to look at the menu. Whiting was so drawn to her. He didn't want to move. He suggested a few things to her and watched her eyes glance back and forth across the pages of the menu. Every once in a –while, she would glance at him out of the corner of her eye, and his entire body would tingle.

"I know you've probably almost decided," he offered, "but we never looked at the specials menu."

"What were we thinking?" Amanda said playfully.

Whiting picked up a small tri-fold menu on the corner of the table. He opened it, set it on the table in front of her, and leaned toward her to point.

"This," he said as he tapped the glossy menu. "Look no further. I'm getting this. It's my favorite thing they make."

"Is that a recommendation, or is it just you telling me that you love steak and lobster?"

"Well, if you love steak and lobster, this is what you want. If you don't, salads are on the second page of the regular menu."

She smiled and grabbed his arm. She tilted her head down slightly and then raised her eyes to look at him. She crinkled her nose as she spoke. "I said no salads. That special sounds amazing."

Her touch was electrifying. He thought about pulling away from her warm, inviting hand that lay gently on his forearm. He did his best to remember what Dean had said about Kelsey. He stayed put and gave in to the feeling. It gave him goosebumps and made him feel like it was ninety degrees inside. She slid her hands down his arm to let go, and as their hands met, she paused for a second to look at him and smile. While Whiting was enjoying every single second of her hand slowly dancing its way off of his arm, he heard a voice behind them.

"Have you two decided, or do you need a few more minutes?"

Whiting turned to see a familiar waitress. She turned to address Amanda and introduced herself.

"Hi, my name is Whitney, and I'll be taking care of you two all night. I'll be back and forth between floors to give you guys a nice, quiet dinner space, but I'll also check on you to make sure you have everything you need. Can I get you guys started with a drink or an appetizer?"

"I think we are ready to order," Whiting said as he glanced at Amanda, making sure he wasn't ordering too soon.

"Yes, we are," Amanda said.

Whitney turned to face Amanda. "Excellent. What can I get for you?"

"Could I have the Scarlett Filet please?"

"Of course, wonderful choice. How would you like that cooked?"

"Medium, please."

"Medium...you've got it. Anything to drink?"

"I'm fine with water, thank you."

"Of course, you're welcome." She turned to face Whiting.

"And for you, Mr. Whiting?"

"I'll have the same, please and thank you, Whitney."

"Excellent choice. Anything else I can get you to eat or drink?"

"Water is fine for me also, but can we have the fried calamari appetizer also?"

"Of course."

"Thank you, Whitney."

"You're very welcome. Be back soon with your appetizer."

As she walked away, Whiting turned to Amanda.

"So I was just kinda hoping that you liked calamari, even though we never really talked about an appetizer. If you don't like it, I guess I'll have to eat it all myself."

Amanda acted surprised. "Calamari? Is that the Italian bread with pepperoni and stuff inside?" she asked plainly.

Whiting didn't know if she was kidding or serious and was too flustered to answer because she had grabbed his arm again. After a brief pause, she let him off the hook by saying, "I'm kidding." Whiting let out a deep breath. Amanda was a little impressed with herself that she could make him so flustered and unable to respond quickly to her jokes. She smiled to herself as she started one more to keep the joke rolling.

"So calamari is okay, but I only eat the wild stuff because I think it's inhumane to have them raised in captivity and forced to lay eggs just so they can sell them."

Whiting looked at her and smiled. He was slowly regaining his ability to speak and act like a normal human being.

"Well, rest assured; this is one hundred percent wild calamari. And they collect the eggs in little foam-lined baskets so they don't crack them or damage them."

"Wow. That is *so* reassuring. I didn't know you had such extensive knowledge of marine life and how it is harvested. I mean, giraffes are one thing, but sea life, too? You're pretty impressive."

His sides jostled, trying to hold in a laugh. He found her so refreshing and wonderful to talk to, and he adored her sense of humor. He felt like they could talk for hours, about anything and everything. Amanda smiled. "Okay, okay. Yes, calamari is fine. Yes, I know its squid. No, I don't care where the heck they caught it. As long as it's crispy and delicious, I'm good."

"It is amazing. The kitchen staff here are some of the best in the country. My brother is a firm believer in good food, good fun, and correct compensation, as he calls it. So many people have told him they're astonished that he pays his kitchen staff so well and still manages to make the menu prices reasonable. But he expects a lot. If you're hired as a sous chef, he assumes you need no training, only familiarization with the kitchen and other kitchen staff. He has had people from all over the world come and ask to work for him. When you have that kind of candidate pool to choose from, you get to boast that your food is top notch. He's just a great guy and a really smart businessman." Whiting paused. "Sorry, I'll stop rambling about my brother."

"Don't stop," Amanda said. "It is wonderful how much you love and respect your brother. I love hearing you talk about him like that. You never need to stop talking about your family, let alone apologize for it. I always wanted a sibling, so I love hearing you talk about yours."

"Okay. Sometimes I start to ramble and don't know enough to shut up."

"No need to stop. I haven't had this much fun talking to someone in, well, ever."

A broad smile spread across his face, and he didn't bother hiding it. "Me, either. But I've talked a lot. Tell me about yourself, please."

As comfortable as she was talking to Brian, she wasn't sure what to say about herself. She didn't have much to tell. She wasn't going to share stories from high school, she was certain he didn't care about her college years, and her attack wasn't exactly good dinner conversation. She was stuck and didn't know where to begin.

"I'm very boring," she said as she sipped her water.

"Boring? You are the best conversationalist I know. You are far from boring," Whiting replied.

"I get that from my Dad. He likes to talk. But typically, he has very wise things to say. I don't."

"Hey now. That's enough being so hard on yourself. I haven't had a conversation this good, and that has felt so natural, in a long time. And on top of all that, I've never been on a date with someone as beautiful as you."

As soon as he said it, he felt himself flush. He hoped he wasn't overdoing it with the compliments, but he did think she was just so, so pretty. Amanda couldn't help but smile.

"Thank you. Likewise with the conversation. But I am not beautiful."

"We'll have to agree to disagree on that one. Tell me more about your dad and the wise things he says."

"Well, typically, he saves his best quotes and philosophy lessons for the cows. They get to hear John Killingly, Philanthropist Extraordinaire, at his finest," Amanda said, smiling.

"Cows?" Whiting began. Amanda was a bit nervous he was going to be less interested now that he knew she was technically a "Farmer's Daughter."

"Yes, cows." She looked at him nervously.

"Beef or dairy?" Whiting asked quickly.

"Um," Amanda started, not sure where this was going. "Both, actually."

"Holstein dairy cows?" Whiting said with the slightest hint of a smile.

"Yes."

"And beef cows, Black Angus or the white-faced ones that are kind of brown?"

"White-faced Hereford."

"Those are the ones!"

"How did you know? Did my dad give you a quick lesson when you saw him at the restaurant the other night?"

Whiting rolled up his sleeve and held his arm out in front of Amanda. She wasn't sure what he was doing, but she played along.

"Is this the part where girls usually see your big, strong fireman arm and swoon?"

Whiting laughed. "They don't need to see my arms to swoon. It usually happens when I walk into a room."

Amanda smiled at his blatant narcissistic comment. "Mmmhmm."

"Forget the swooning ladies, though. You asked how I knew all those breeds of cows. See this?" Whiting said as he pointed to a long U-shaped scar on his forearm.

"The scar? Yes, I see it."

"Shorthorn bull named Frankie. His horns weren't so short."

"You poor thing," Amanda said, rubbing his arm gently, mocking him just a little. "Were you a rough and rugged farmhand before you were a firefighter?" she asked as she patted his arm gently.

He grinned, and it faded into a smirk. "I tried riding a bull once. A very small but very, very powerful one. It was a charity event at a county festival. The story made it to the firehouse, and I referred to the bull as a long-horned bull. One of the guys from the firehouse has cows. He made sure to correct me and say that it was a short-horned bull. He then proceeded to give me a complete history of raising beef cattle, starting in seventeen eighty-nine, when his great-great-great grandfather's second cousin's mother, or whoever it was, started a herd from two cows and one bull and went on to have the second largest beef herd in the Midwest. Or maybe it was Canada. Could have been New Mexico. I wasn't really paying attention. Utah?" He shrugged and smirked as he took a sip of water.

"Oh, well, I feel bad for mocking a scar you got at a charity event," she said in a mostly sincere tone.

"That's okay," he said, his voice even. "He never stops talking about them. We give him a hard time about it, but in all honesty, I always love going to help him do things there. It's honest work that has an old-soul feel to it. So as much as I bust his chops about it, I don't mind one bit."

She glanced at him and smiled, happy to have discovered a common thread that helped them connect.

"Old-soul feel is so true. That's a perfect way to put it. My dad still rides horses out to the fields and pastures in the spirit of keeping things the way they used to be."

"Very cool. Your dad seems like a good man."

"He's one of the best there is." She smiled proudly. "But I'm probably a little biased." Before Amanda could continue, they heard a voice behind them, and they both turned.

"Okay, you two, here is your calamari, and, Brian, this is for you." Whitney set a glass on the table full of dark brown liquid.

"Oh, Whitney, I didn't order a drink. I'm fine with water."

"Your brother said that you've ordered a Roy Rogers every time you've been here, so today will be no different."

Whiting pressed his lips together and sucked in a breath through his nose. Whitney set the food down and asked if they needed anything else before heading back down the stairs. He looked up at Amanda, who was smiling and waiting to make eye contact.

"Roy Rogers, huh?" she said as her smile grew from ear to ear.

Whiting didn't know what to say. It was a silly drink for an adult to order. Typically, kids at weddings ordered them so they could feel like they ordered a mixed drink even though they weren't old enough to have alcohol.

"I…" Whiting started and trailed off.

"You." Amanda said, leading him along in his statement.

"Do you know what a Roy Rogers is?"

Amanda smiled. "I was a bartender. Yes, I know what it is. I never actually made one for an adult…" She stopped herself and smiled.

Whiting looked down sheepishly. "The Roy Rogers is because that's what I always order here. My brother made me one when he opened his very first restaurant to celebrate. He was waiting for his liquor license to arrive and couldn't really serve alcohol yet. He did a soft opening for close friends and family. So I asked him to make me a Roy Rogers so he could go behind the bar and mix a drink in his new restaurant. After that, it just kind of became tradition. Sounds kind of stupid when I say it out loud."

Amanda tilted her head slightly. "Not stupid at all," she said, smiling. "I always wished I had a sibling to share traditions with. Someone to share little things with, things that start out as innocent, childhood games but soon become lasting memories and family traditions as adults. My dad is my rock. He's one of the most incredible men in the world, in my opinion. But a sister or brother would have been really great. Someone else my own age to grow up with."

She started thinking of her mother and how much she missed having a mom when she was growing up. Her stomach lurched a bit with emotion. She took a breath and calmed herself, taking a sip of water. He was in love with listening to her talk. They had been chatting for a while now, but it was a lot of question and answer and joking around, and she hadn't talked at length since the date started. Her voice was beautiful, and she was so well spoken. He was trying to hide the fact that he was staring at her while she spoke, but then he remembered what Dean had said about telling her how he felt. Before he knew it, a comment stumbled out of his mouth.

"I could listen to you talk for hours," he said.

"What?" she said, surprised, as her face turned a bright shade of pink. "I'm sure talking to me is the same as talking to anyone else."

"Not at all. I hear lots of people talk every day. Between the people I work with and the people who visit the firehouse. People that call the firehouse. Even people in line at the grocery store. I talk to a lot of people in the course of a week, and I can't think of anyone I like talking to and listening to as much as you."

She was struggling with the decision of whether to tell him she loved talking to him, too, or whether she should make a joke to change the subject so she could avoid a panic attack in such a nice restaurant. Thankfully, her decision was interrupted by Whiting as he held a fork up with a piece of calamari on it. She looked at him and smiled.

"Ladies first," he said, waiting patiently.

"No sauce? I thought you were trying to impress me."

Whiting laughed. "What was I thinking? Cocktail sauce or marinara?"

"Cocktail sauce all the way. Marinara is for pasta."

Whiting dabbed a little bit of cocktail sauce on the calamari ring and held it back up toward her. She leaned in slowly and took the bite off the fork. She couldn't help but let out an audible *mmm* as the flavors flooded her taste buds. The tang of the cocktail sauce mixed perfectly with the savory flavor of the golden-brown ring that she had bitten into. It was the perfect consistency, with no hint of being chewy or rubbery. The warm breading seemed to dissolve as she chewed, and she was doing her best to eat slowly despite being eager for another bite.

"Oh my God, that is good," she said once she was done chewing. She sat with her hands folded and made a dramatic show of pretending to wait for another bite. He looked at her, a warm grin gliding across his lips.

"Do I have to do this all night, or could I have some, too?"

"Well, fine. I suppose they gave me a fork, too," Amanda said, her voice playfully dramatic.

They ate and talked some more about anything and everything. He loved when she asked him questions, and he loved it even more when she talked to him about the things he could tell she was passionate about. After a handful of minutes, and as the calamari plate grew emptier, he asked a question Amanda wasn't expecting.

"Your dad seems like a great guy," he offered. "What is your Mom like? She must be beautiful and have an amazing personality, just like you."

Amanda finished chewing and took a contemplative breath before she spoke. "My mom passed away a long time ago."

Whiting winced at his own question.

"I'm so sorry. I didn't—"

Amanda stopped him. "It's okay. You had no way to know. She died when I was a little kid. But I've heard so many stories about her. My dad and his friend Dave have told me stories for years. And my friend June, who you met at my house... she has told me so many wonderful things, too. Everyone said she was one of those people who was just so full of life. She greeted every day as an opportunity for success, happiness, and the chance to meet someone new or change someone's life. I wish I got to know her better, especially now that I'm older. But I'll have to live with the stories and hang on to my memories. That's all I can do."

"Well, I obviously didn't know your mom," he began, trying not to push any more of his foot into his mouth, "but I bet she's proud of the incredible person you've become."

A sense of pride filled her, mixed with a sort of quiet sadness. She let out a small puff of a sigh through her nose and smiled as she thought of her mother.

"I'm not incredible. But thank you for the compliment."

"You are. And you're welcome. You said your dad's friend Dave told you stories. Do you see him often?"

Amanda's thoughts began to jumble. She hadn't seen Dave since just after the attack. She remembered that she didn't need to elaborate, just answer the question.

"I used to work at the bar that he owns. I haven't seen him since I stopped working there, though." Amanda finished her sentence and looked down at her water glass, hoping he wouldn't ask anything else about Dave. Her facial expression and body language were quite telling, and he took the hint. He asked another question that he figured would break the tension.

"Your friend June. Is she a friend, relative, neighbor? She has quite the personality."

Amanda looked up, relieved he had changed the subject.

"Oh, June." Amanda laughed a little. "She is a neighbor and a long-time friend of my Dad's. She knew my mom, too. She does have quite the personality. I'm sorry for all her, well, blatant flirting and unexpected comments."

"It's okay," he said, his words mixing with a quiet chuckle. "She seems like a very nice person. Genuine, I mean. Good-hearted but says what's on her mind."

"That's June," Amanda said brightly. "And it's incredible, but we really haven't been friends that long. I walked across the street one day to introduce myself. I knew she was a long-time friend of my parents, and she's known me for a very long time, but I didn't really even know her to talk to. I'm so glad I went over that night. She's been such an amazing friend and sounding board, and she's really helped me get back to being a normal person after my being attacked."

As soon as the words left her mouth, she regretted them. She hadn't meant to tell him that she was attacked, but she was rambling on about June, and it just happened. She looked across the table at Whiting, fully expecting him to be staring blankly. Before she could start to explain or change the subject, he spoke up with a comment that was as refreshing as it was surprising.

"Well, thank goodness for good friends. And it's great that she lives so close and has known your family a long time. Growing up, and as a teenager, I was close with our neighbor like you are with June. He was a little older than my dad, and he had so much knowledge about everything. He knew about carpentry, mechanical stuff, farming and raising animals, cooking, cars, gardening, and just about life in general. He was also a volunteer firefighter, which is how I got started in the fire service."

Amanda let out a sigh of relief. She didn't know if she should thank him or explain her comment. She looked at him and smiled.

"Am I rambling again?" he asked. "Want me to stuff a dinner roll in my mouth?"

"Thank you," she said warmly.

"Thank you?" he said in mock surprise. "Does that mean you do want me to stuff a roll in my mouth? I mean, I can, but this is my brother's restaurant, and I don't want him to scold me for being childish and inappropriate."

Amanda laughed a little. "I mean thank you for not asking me to elaborate about what I said. Most people wouldn't have been able to let that comment go without more details."

"I'm not most people. And I figured that it wasn't a story that you really wanted to tell on a first date. So, if you'd like, you can tell me on our fourth or fifth date." Whiting winked at her, hoping she'd think he was still a little cute and charming.

"Fourth and fifth dates? You're giving yourself a lot of credit. Are you sure this won't be the only one? What if you get really grossed out by the way I eat steak?"

"Thankfully for you, I eat three meals a day with a group of guys who act like they've never seen hot food every time they eat. I think you're good."

A quiet smile was making its way back across her face. "Well, I guess that's true. So maybe I'll let you take me on a second date."

"I'll take maybe," he said, sipping his Roy Rogers through a broad smile.

Just then, a voice called to them from the top of the stairs. "How's everything, guys?"

Whiting turned to see Whitney walking toward them with two salad plates in her hands.

"Things are wonderful," Amanda said, looking directly at Whiting.

"Good," Whitney said. "They're about to get even better. Salads are here, and when you're done with those, I'll get your dinners right out." She set salads in front of each of them. "Finished with the calamari?" she asked as she gestured to the empty plate in front of Amanda.

"Yes, thank you," Brian said.

"Anything else you need? Need another Roy Rogers?"

He pressed his lips together and raised his eyebrows a bit, still slightly embarrassed by his drink of choice and that his brother insisted on sending one up without him asking for it.

"No, thank you, Whitney. I'm fine."

"Okay, you guys enjoy. If you need anything, let me know. Otherwise, I'll be up shortly."

He and Amanda thanked Whitney. As she walked away, Amanda turned to her plate. They ate their salads and talked more. The food was delicious, and the conversation was seamless. After a short while, Whitney returned with their dinners. She set a plate in front of each of them, filled their water glasses, took the empty salad plates, and left them to eat.

Amanda looked down at her plate and then back up at Whiting.

"This is like a work of art. It's almost too pretty to eat."

"Well, if you want to just look at it, you can, but I'm eating mine."

"I said *almost* too pretty to eat. Let's not be silly."

They both laughed together as they started in on their food. Again, Amanda marveled at the perfect flavors of the food. The tender bites seemed to melt in her mouth, and the flavors of each ingredient melded together into an exceptional bouquet of flavors on every forkful. Amanda had never had food this good. She was just so happy to be having amazing food and great company, and to be out in public. This was the most normal she had felt in a long time. They talked and laughed as they ate. The food filled her stomach, and the conversation helped fill in a few more spots of her missing self. For the first time in a long time, Amanda was happy, truly happy, and she certainly didn't want the date to end.

Chapter 16

John set his water glass on the counter and put his plate in the sink. He stared out the window contemplatively, his mind pulling itself in several directions.

"Johnny," June called out as she walked over. "How many times do I have to tell you? Use. The. Dishwasher." She paused after each word for emphasis.

"It's two plates and two glasses. I'm not running the dishwasher for that. I know it uses less water, but it's silly to run it for these few things."

John turned on the kitchen sink and began washing the dishes he and June had used for dinner. He kept staring out the window above the sink, like the sky outside was going to give him some secret answer he'd been looking for.

"Oh, I forgot water is free out in the country." June chuckled.

"Sure is," John said in a low, distracted tone. His gaze remained fixed out the window. "Dishwasher is more efficient, I know, but just two plates and two glasses. It'll go quick."

"You said that already," June said, glancing up at his eyes. They were still focused out the window. "We'll hand wash them if you want to, but there are fourteen more plates in the cupboard. It should be okay for those to be in the dishwasher."

"Yeah."

June turned to face him and put her hand on his shoulder in an effort to break his mindless staring off into space. "You okay, John? Worried about Amanda? She'll be okay."

"Yeah. I'm fine. Just thinking about something Amanda had said. That gun she mentioned. It had an eagle on the handle, right?"

"I think so. Why?"

John shrugged one shoulder. "No reason. Just tough to hear my little girl talk about that night again." He took a deep breath and let it out through pursed lips. "June? How about I go get us some ice cream?"

"That sounds delicious. Let me get my shoes."

"No, no, I'll go. You can stay here. I'm sure there is some sleazy romance movie you'd love to watch while I'm gone."

She tilted her head and studied him. "I'm sure there is."

"Enjoy it while it lasts, because when I get back, we're watching something else. What kind of ice cream? Sundae, chocolate ice cream, hot fudge, whipped cream, and Reese's Pieces on top?"

"That a boy," she said, her voice sincere. "You've got a good memory."

"Well, I am younger than you."

She rolled her eyes at him and said, "Hurry back."

He grabbed his coat and his keys and headed for the door. His mind hadn't been able to settle since he had heard Amanda talking about that gun. He was certain he knew what kind of gun she meant, and, unfortunately, he was fairly certain he knew who owned it.

He drove across town, constantly looking out the window at everything and everyone, as if his thoughts about the gun were pubic knowledge and everyone was out to get him. He pulled into a familiar parking lot and put his truck in park. He figured he shouldn't hesitate too much, or he may change his mind about what he was about to do. He reached under his front seat and took out a small metal box. He touched his thumb to it, and the lid popped open. He reached inside and took out a black handgun in a nylon holster. He pulled back the slide just far enough to see the silver casing of the copper-plated, hollow-point round waiting patiently in the chamber. He clipped the holster to his jeans and pulled his shirt down over it. He took a deep breath and climbed out of his truck. He got to the door of the building and was about to open it when he heard a voice behind him.

"Got a light?"

John tensed slightly but turned slowly and saw a young man about Amanda's age standing behind him.

"No, sorry," he said slowly. "I don't smoke."

"No worries, bro," he said as he wandered toward a group of men standing outside another door.

John pulled on the door handle and slowly opened the door. Once inside, he made his way through a handful of people and to a small office in the back of the room. He watched every move that the people around him made, not knowing if any of them could have something to do with the night his daughter was attacked. He got to the door of the office, looked through a small window, and saw who he was looking for sitting at a desk with a phone up to his ear. John didn't bother knocking. He opened the door, stepped inside quickly, and closed the door behind him. The man on the phone paused as he looked at John.

"Let me call you back," he said into the phone receiver. He hung up the phone and stood to face John. "Long time, no see, stranger."

"Yeah," John said plainly.

"How's things? How's Amanda?"

John took a few steps and sat in a chair in front of the desk. "Got a minute?"

"Of course. Hell, I haven't seen you in what seems like years. Of course I've got a minute. What's up?"

"I'm not really in the mood for idle small talk, so I'm just gonna get to the point."

"Okay?"

"The Golden Eagle forty-five you got as a gift all those years ago. Still have it?"

There was a miniscule hesitation before he spoke that most people wouldn't have noticed, but John did. "Yeah, of course I do. Why? You need a gun? Is everything okay?"

"No, I don't need a gun," John said as he sat back in his chair. "Just glad to hear you still have it. It's a nice gun. It'd be a shame to sell it."

"Yeah, of course. Why do you ask? You sure you're okay?"

John ignored the question and said, "Can I see it?"

Again, the slight pause that, to most people, would have been barely noticeable. But John had known him long enough to know that any hesitation meant he was looking for an answer.

"It's at home. It isn't here. I have pictures of it, I think. You want to have one customized in a similar way? I mean, pictures could help do that. I think I even have the specs written down somewhere. Eagle on the grips, custom trigger, all chrome plating on the—"

"Shut up, Dave," John said with an exasperated sigh. "I've known you long enough to know when you're lying. That gun. *Your* gun. Amanda had a memory come to her the other night about the night she was attacked."

"John, hey. Okay, I can explain."

"Explain?" John Killingly stood. "Did you rape my daughter, Dave? Hmm?"

"No!" Dave said loudly. Before he could say anything else, John continued.

"That why you up and vanished after you stopped in that one time to see us, after she stumbled home, bruised, beaten, and left for dead? The flowers make a lot of sense now, too. All that guilt for doing something so disgusting and so vile to a girl you've known since she was born.

Imagine my surprise when I heard my little girl relive the night she was raped and describe a gun that I know belongs to a man I've considered my best friend for thirty years."

Dave sat motionless in the chair, a look of sheer terror and panic on his face.

"Stand up, you son of a bitch," he said sharply.

Dave's eyes briefly rose to meet John's.

"I said stand up!" His voice boomed as he slammed his hand on the heavy wooden desk.

The murmur outside the office quieted slightly. Dave stayed sitting. A tear rolled down his cheek as he looked up at John. His eyes stayed raised this time.

"Eighty-thousand."

John was surprised by the comment, and it interrupted the tension in the room. His body relaxed, but only slightly. "What?"

"Eighty-thousand," Dave repeated. "It's what I owed. They took the gun because I didn't have any more cash to give them. They took my Corvette, the gun, my father's watch collection, and all my mother's jewelry. They said they'd kill me if I reported any of them stolen."

John had known Dave long enough to know when he was lying. He wasn't anymore. His body relaxed a little more, and he sat down and leaned forward toward Dave's desk. "Okay, listen," he said, the anger now gone from his voice. It was replaced with a quiet understanding. Dave started to cry harder. He put his head in his hands to try to control his sobs, but it wasn't very effective. John stood and closed the shade on the office door.

"I'm so sorry, John," Dave said, sobbing. He took a few deep breaths so he could keep talking. "They thought she was my daughter. I told them she wasn't, and to leave her out of this, and that I'd kill them if they ever did anything to hurt her. And they…" He trailed off as he started to cry harder again.

John sat back and ran his fingers through his hair. He blew out a long breath. "Okay. Take a breath. I believe that you didn't kidnap Amanda. But you know who did. And I need to know."

Dave took a handful of deep breaths and wiped his face with his hands. "They'll kill me."

"Kill you? Three minutes ago, when I walked in here, I had planned to kill you. Who are they?"

"I can't," Dave tried. John interrupted.

"You can't what? Tell your best friend who kidnapped and repeatedly beat and raped his daughter, then left her for dead?"

"You don't understand. These guys are ruthless."

"Don't understand? I had to listen to my little girl's story of what they did to her. I had to help her change bandages all over her body from teeth marks, cuts from knives, and places where she'd been whipped with pieces of rope. I helped her hold ice packs on her back where they had kicked her, over and over again. I sat with her as she got a haircut and tried to laugh off what happened when the hairdresser asked her how chunks of her hair had been ripped out. I waited next to her while she answered phone calls from doctors, hoping and praying that she hadn't been given any diseases by those useless fucking *pigs* that you have decided to befriend."

The anger in John's voice rose, and the increasing decibels shook the small office. He didn't care who heard him.

Dave looked at John. He was trying to say something, but he was just staring at him silently, tears rolling down his cheeks.

"I'm pretty sure I understand how ruthless these guys are. What I don't understand is why you didn't tell the police what you know. Or, for Christ's sake, tell me, at least."

"So you could do what, John? Confront them and get yourself killed?"

"So I could do something." John's voice echoed loudly in the small room. "Instead of spending more than a year sitting idly by, hoping the cops would find these assholes."

"The cops can't touch them. They've got connections in the police department, City Hall, even the Mayor's office. Nothing ever happens to them."

"Yeah, well, someone needs to do something, and if it's not going to be police justice, maybe it needs to be some other kind."

He scoffed. "This isn't the wild west, John."

"Shut the fuck up, Dave. You've been my best friend a long, long time. But you've also been a cowardly gambler who relies on other people to get you out of trouble. I love you like a brother, but it has been thirty years of close calls, and tight spots, and selling stuff to find money to pay off your debts. And now it's gotten my little girl involved in something that she will never forget. The same little girl you helped me raise when my wife died. You saw her first steps, heard her first words, pushed her stroller, and then when the wheel broke on the stroller, you carried her on your shoulders all day at the amusement park because my shoulder was in a sling. She wrapped her arms around your neck and hugged you when you bought her that bright pink bike with the streamers when she turned eight. You remember who she is now, Dave?"

Tears rolled slowly down John's face.

"Amanda. Your best friend's little girl. Amanda Killingly. Because of you, she almost died before she turned twenty-two. Because of you, a group of strangers raped her. Held her down and raped her. Tied her arms and legs down and raped her. One after another. Sometimes all three at once. And when they had all finished, and she was covered in their filth, they beat her until she passed out and left her tied to a bed to die. And these are the people you're going to protect?" John's body shook as he took a slow, deliberate breath in through his nose and let it out the same way.

"If they don't kill you for telling me who they are, I'll kill you for keeping it from me. So now you tell me, you cowardly, spineless son of a bitch. Who are they?"

Dave was trembling. His teeth were clenched, and he could barely speak without crying harder than he already was. He took a short breath and said, "Buchoff. Bartholomew Buchoff. He goes by Bart. He's the only one I know. He comes in here to drink every once in a while. He's the one who collects the money. But he's not in charge."

"How much do you owe them?"

"Eighteen thousand left."

"Set up a time to meet him. I wanna talk to this asshole."

"John, you don't understand."

He slammed his fist down so hard the phone receiver rattled.

"Say that again, Dave. Please say I don't understand again. If you ever had to look into your daughter's eyes and see what I saw, and hear what I heard, you'd know that I don't care who they are or how connected they are or how many Goddamned guns they own."

Before Dave could answer, there was a knock on the office door. A young girl opened the door and stood in the doorway. Dave and John looked up at her. The girl looked quickly back and forth between Dave and John.

"What is it?" Dave asked in a clipped tone.

She hesitated a moment, staring at Dave's red eyes and tear-stained cheeks. She quietly said, "Mr. Buchoff is here to see you."

Dave did his best to act normally. "Okay, thank you. Tell him I'll be right out."

The girl disappeared back through the door. John walked slowly toward a small window that faced the bar. He stood to the side of the window and peered out. "Which one is he?" he asked.

Dave stood slowly, wiping his face with his sleeve. He walked up behind John and looked out.

"Third stool in from the right. Black shirt. John. Please. You can't go out there."

"I'm not going to. He's going to come back here."

"John, please."

"Shut up, Dave. Take a deep breath and tell the bartender to send him back here. We're just going to talk. Don't you dare tell him who I am."

Dave walked over and picked up a phone on his desk. He punched in a few numbers, and John heard the sound of a distant phone ringing. He walked back to the window and looked out to see the bartender pick up a phone at the far end of the bar. She looked around hesitantly as Dave was speaking. After a few seconds, she hung up and walked toward Buchoff. She said something to him, and he stood, left cash on the bar, and began walking toward the door to the back room. John moved slowly back toward the door to the office. He stood with his back to the wall, leaning on the door casing.

"Stay calm, Dave. I'm just an old friend who stopped by to visit."

Dave nodded nervously.

"You remember that time we got a flat tire on the way to the concert and we had no spare?"

Dave looked up nervously.

"Come on, Dave. It's gonna look a little strange if we're sitting here in silence when he walks back here."

Dave took a quick breath. "How could I forget? We moved the spare so we could have room for beer and lawn chairs."

The door to the back room began to open.

"Well, we couldn't put it in the back seat. They were checking inside cars for that kind of thing," John continued. "And besides, a beer was like three bucks back then."

"I wish they were three bucks now." Dave played along as Buchoff walked toward the office door.

"Me, too. Christ, now you can't buy a coffee for three dollars," John said. As he finished his sentence, he turned and looked at Buchoff.

"How ya doin?"

"I'm good, man. How are you?" he said, his tone almost jovial.

"Good, thanks. John," he said as he extended his hand. Buchoff was much better dressed than John would have thought. Dark colored jeans, a black button-down shirt with a crisply folded collar, leather shoes, a bracelet on one wrist, and a much nicer watch than John had ever owned on the other.

The man took John's hand and shook it like he was actually glad to meet him.

"Good to meet you, John. I'm Bart. I didn't mean to interrupt."

"Oh, no problem. We were just telling stories. I've known this guy for a hundred years. I'm only in town for a few days, so I wanted to stop by. I'll let you two chat. Good to meet you, Bart."

"Yeah, you, too. Take it easy."

John turned toward the door he had come through. He walked at a normal pace in an effort to make sure Bart didn't think anything strange was happening. He got in his truck and tuned the key. His hands began to tremble. He had wanted to kill Buchoff right then and there, but he needed information. At least now he knew what he looked like, what he sounded like, and that he ended up in Dave's bar every so often. He took a giant breath and let it out slowly. He put his truck in gear, put his seatbelt on, and headed to get June's ice cream.

He drove for a few minutes and arrived at the ice cream shop. He ordered a chocolate milkshake for himself and ordered June's, then asked for it to go. He drove home in a haze, unsure what to do with the new information he had gotten when he went to Dave's. Visions of running Buchoff over with his truck flashed through his mind every time he accelerated or turned a corner. He arrived back at Amanda's house and parked his truck. He needed a minute before he went inside. He drew in several deep breaths and let them out slowly. He decided no one else could know what just happened or that he went to see Dave at all.

He walked in the door and found June still on the couch. He had just turned to set his keys on the table by the door when he noticed a police cruiser approaching the house. On any other day, he would have just figured the cop was doing a roaming patrol and wouldn't have thought twice about it. He was still so on edge, however, that he rushed out the front door before he could think better of it. He walked swiftly toward the police cruiser. As he approached, the officer inside rolled the driver's side window down.

"How are you tonight, sir?"

"I'm fine. Is everything okay, officer? I noticed you outside the house and was worried something was wrong."

"Everything is fine. Is this your house, sir?"

"It's my house, yes, but I don't live here. My daughter, Amanda, does. I'm just visiting."

"Oh, okay. I hate to ask, sir, but do you have an I.D. I could see?"

John almost felt offended until he remembered that, despite not having apprehended Amanda's attackers, they probably drove by the house every so often just to check in.

"Of course, yes," John said as he pulled out his wallet. He handed the officer his driver's license.

"I thought you looked familiar, John. I'm Matt McPherson. I went to high school with Amanda. Sorry for asking for identification, but I know this is where Amanda lives, and well, quite frankly, you're not Amanda." They both smiled. "Sorry for asking, but I had to check."

John leaned a little lower to see in the window better. "Not a problem at all. Thank you for checking. How are ya? I didn't even recognize you with the badge and a gun."

"I'm good, thanks. Busy, but I love the job. How is Amanda?"

"She's good. She's quite the girl. She is just about back to normal, and given the circumstances, that's pretty amazing in my book."

"It absolutely is. Tell her I stopped by, if you would."

"I'll do that. Have a good night."

"You, too."

John stood and began to walk away. He was almost to the house when Matt called to him. He stopped and turned.

"We're still looking for them. Tell Amanda we haven't given up. I won't give up."

"Thank you. That means a lot."

"You're welcome. Have a good night."

"You, too." John walked back into the house, unsure of what to do next. He walked into the living room and sat down. June looked over at him and did him the favor of pretending nothing was wrong.

"I think it's a good night for a comedy, Johnny. So I found us a good one."

"Thanks," John said quietly. "I could use a laugh." He sat, not saying much, laughing occasionally. His mind was still so occupied with the thought of meeting Buchoff. He needed to do something.

When the movie was over, John walked with June across the street to her house. He said goodnight and headed back home. Once inside, he tidied up the living room and headed to bed. It was still early, but he was tired, more mentally and emotionally than physically. He figured Amanda would be home soon, but he left lights on for her anyway. He crawled into bed and stared at the ceiling, hoping he would fall asleep quickly. He did.

A dream crept in, the beginning of it blurry and without focus. After a brief moment, a form began to take shape. John's subconscious had produced a perfect replica of his late wife. She looked so vivid and so clear. She was standing in a long, yellow and white sundress. Although it was a dream, she looked so real. John moved closer to her, and she began to speak. "Our daughter is beautiful. You did an amazing job raising her." John tried to speak, but his dream-self just stood silently. The voice of his wife continued. "The police need to know what you know, John. Amanda needs you to tell them."

He tossed in his sleep in an effort to reach out to her. His thoughts seemed to move as if they were coated in a thick, sticky tar. He tried to reach for her, but his arms felt empty and void of the ability to move. As he struggled to do *something*, he watched the apparition. As quickly as it had come, the image of his wife began to fade. He finally managed some words in his dream.

"Don't go. Please don't go."

His beautiful wife blew him a kiss and started slowly drifting off into the blank nothingness of his subconscious. He reached for her in his sleep, finding nothing but an empty bed and a bare pillow next to him. He called out for her in his sleep. He called out again and again and begged her not to go. He let out one more lonesome call, and as he was desperately trying to keep the image of his wife alive and talking to him, he lunged for her.

He woke, damp with sweat, his arms wrapped around a pillow and a pile of sheets on the bed. He looked at the clock. It had only been an hour since he went to bed. Without hesitation, he climbed quickly out of bed, put on the clothes that were still setting on a chair, picked up his keys and his cell phone, and headed to his truck. His wife had never come to him in a dream before. He hadn't seen her in a very long time. He wasn't about to ignore her, dream or no dream. He scribbled a quick note to Amanda and left it on the kitchen island.

Hey, honey, ran out for a few. Don't wait up. Love you a lot. Dad.

He set the pen down and headed for the door. He jumped in his truck and took off, headed for the police station. After a brief drive, he parked and walked through the front door and approached a window with a small microphone stuck to the glass. He glanced around the room but saw no one. He was about to say something when a voice from behind the glass spoke up.

"John?"

Somewhat startled, John looked through the large window. It wasn't quite one-way glass, but it was difficult to see the person on the other side.

"Uh, yes, John Killingly." He squinted, trying to see the figure behind the glass.

Before he could say any more, the door next to the window opened, and Matt McPherson stepped into the room.

"I thought that was you. Everything okay?"

"I was wondering if I could talk to the person in charge of Amanda's case. I don't even know if it's her case anymore. I know it's been a long time. I just need to talk to someone that's involved with it."

"Well, I can certainly take some information for you," Matt said. "Let me get a pad."

He disappeared through the door he had walked through just a moment before. When the door opened again, a large, stocky man in uniform stood in the doorway.

"John?"

"Yes. John Killingly," he said as he extended his hand.

The man grabbed his hand and shook firmly. "Sergeant Bill Harding. Good to meet you. I overheard you telling Matt you had some information about Amanda's case."

"Yes, I do."

"Okay," Harding said. "Let's go find a place we can talk in private."

He led John through another door and down a hallway. He opened the door to a small conference room and gestured for John to go in. Once inside, Harding told John he could have a seat at the table. Harding sat across from him and took out a pen.

"John, is this an on-the-record statement? Or is it an off-the-record one?"

"I'm not quite sure."

"Well, you tell me what's on your mind, and we can decide together if it's on the record or not."

"Okay." John took a deep breath. "I'm not sure where to start. I'll give you a little background, if that's okay?"

"Absolutely."

"The bar Amanda was working at the night she was kidnapped is owned by a long-time friend of mine. David Barlow. The other day... or yesterday... I can't remember which. But Amanda was talking to another good friend of mine, and she mentioned that on the night she was attacked she saw a gun on the seat of the truck."

"Yes," Harding said. "She actually came down here and gave us a description of it. We did the best we could with only a physical description to go off of, and we had an idea of who owned the gun she described."

"Dave owned it," John said. "My long-time friend. He owned the gun that was on the seat of the truck that my daughter was assaulted in."

"Yes, we checked with Dave. He said he had the gun out that night at the bar and that he showed it to Amanda and told her it was there if she ever needed to protect herself. He figured maybe she remembered it from earlier that night.

"Dave has been an excellent bullshit-artist his entire life. But I've known him long enough to know when he is lying. Anyway, when I heard Amanda describe the gun, I went to see Dave. I asked him to see it, and he said it was at home. I told him he was a liar. I told him I knew that he has been chasing gambling debts his entire life and asked where the gun was. He told me it was taken from him as collateral for a debt he owed someone. Like I said, he's been my friend a long time, but he's been begging and borrowing money from anywhere he can since he was sixteen. Anyway, he told me the guy who took the gun was named Buchoff. Bartholomew Buchoff. He goes—" Before John could finish the sentence, Harding did.

"He goes by Bart. He is the one who took the gun?"

"That's what Dave said. He said they took it because he owed them money. Buchoff is apparently the guy they send out in public. Dave said that they thought Amanda was his daughter. And so, to collect on their debt and show him they were serious, they…"

"Okay," Harding said. "You don't have to finish that part. I get it."

"Okay. Thank you. And what's worse is that I met the son of a bitch. He stopped by to see Dave while I was there. I looked right at him. And I won't lie. I wanted to take matters into my own hands, but I thought better of it.

"Good idea. Keep talking," Harding said as he took out a pen. "This part is going on the record. We're gonna find these animals and nail them to the wall."

Chapter 17

Amanda took Whiting's arm as they descended the staircase of The Scarlett Rose. She was very full for sure, but she was also the happiest she had been in quite some time. The sweet swirls of perfectly matched dinner ingredients and delectable desserts still danced happily in her mouth. The company she had was even better than the food. About halfway down the stairs, she turned to face Whiting.

"Thank you."

"For what?" Whiting smiled.

"For..." She took breath as she looked around. "For bringing me to a stunning restaurant, for buying me the most delicious meal I've ever had, and for making me laugh so hard my cheeks hurt."

"You're very welcome," he said, desperately trying to hide his excitement. "I had a lot of fun."

"Me, too." She smiled and began walking again.

They reached the bottom of the stairs, and Amanda noticed tables still dotted with people. Some couples and some tables of four or five, a happy murmur still swirling around the room.

"What time is it?" she said, her eyes still scanning the room.

"Ten..." Whiting glanced at his watch and blew out his breath in a whistle. "Forty-six. Hopefully, your dad was kidding about your curfew."

"Oh, he'll be fine," Amanda said. "Just be prepared for June to be watching us from her window when we get home. She'll probably be spying on us, hoping for a goodnight k..." Amanda trailed off and started to blush.

Without hesitation, Whiting kept the conversation moving so Amanda wouldn't be embarrassed.

"Well, hopefully, my bringing you home goes well. I don't want this to be the only date I get with you."

"You'd like a second date?"

"And a third."

"I don't know, maybe." Her smile was a fairly good giveaway that she would love a second date. "You'd have to call me for that to be the case, though."

"I think I can handle that." His teeth broke through his lips as his smile broadened.

Amanda suddenly realized how close they were standing. Her face was only about a foot from his. His eyes were locked with hers. She felt herself leaning toward him. Their faces grew closer and closer. She wasn't sure if she was ready for a kiss, but she couldn't stop herself from leaning toward him. She started to close her eyes, his face only inches away, when suddenly a voice broke in.

"Here is you're truck, Mr. Whiting."

Amanda opened her eyes and took a half step back. She looked at Whiting and smiled as he let out a small sigh and, in a tone that was polite but frustrated, managed to say, "Thank you."

He opened the door to the truck for her, and she climbed up into the passenger seat. He walked around the front of the truck and watched her through the windshield. He got in the driver's seat and said, "Well, he is my least favorite valet ever."

Amanda laughed and said, "Why is that? He seemed very nice."

"Uh-huh. So, so nice," Whiting said, rolling his eyes and smirking.

They drove home surrounded by cool night air and happy conversation. He parked in front of her house, quickly got out and walked to her side, and opened the door for her. As she climbed out, Whiting offered her his hand. She was standing on the step of his truck, so they were about the same height. Their eyes met again. She wasn't sure what to do. She hadn't kissed anyone in a very long time. Even before her attack, it had been a while since she had been on a date. She felt strangely comfortable save for the butterflies in her stomach. She had wondered if this would happen and if her mind would get the best of her and ruin the moment. She tried to relax, quiet her mind, and just do what felt natural. She leaned toward him and was about to close her eyes when she heard the sound of a vehicle coming down her street. Whiting turned his head quickly at the sound of screeching tires. They both watched as John's truck came roaring down the street and came to an abrupt stop in front of the house. John climbed out quickly and was starting to walk to the house when he noticed the two of them standing on the edge of the lawn near Whiting's truck.

"Dad? Are you okay?" Amanda said, walking toward him.

"Yeah, honey, I'm fine. I, um... I was just driving like a fool. Late at night, music up. My long-gone youth was trying to make an appearance."

"Dad."

John wiped his forehead. He had hoped they hadn't noticed he was sweating.

"Really, honey, I'm fine. Just a little case of road rage. There are idiots all over the place at this hour."

Amanda gave him a scrupulous look. "Okay, Dad."

At that moment, John noticed Whiting standing next to his truck. "Hey, Brian. Sorry for the, uh, interruption."

"Not a problem, John. We had just pulled up when we heard you coming around the corner. You sure you're okay?"

"Yeah, I'm good, thanks."

Amanda looked at Whiting and shook her head very slightly as if to say He's *lying*.

"Okay, well, you have your dad as an escort to the door, so you are in good hands. It was a pleasure having dinner with you."

Amanda suddenly realized that her chance to make plans for another date had now drifted away, at least for the moment. Whiting was too much of a gentleman to stick around and make the situation more awkward than it already was.

"I—" Amanda started.

"The number at the firehouse is easy to find. Just in case you need to report a lost giraffe," Whiting said, smiling.

Amanda smiled back.

"I'll be on the lookout. Thank you for dinner."

"You're very welcome. Goodnight, Amanda."

"Night, Brian. Sorry for…" John trailed off.

"Nothing to be sorry for. You two take care."

With that, Whiting got in his truck and started it. As he fastened his seatbelt, he watched Amanda and her father walk up toward the house. She was leaned close to him, talking, trying to get answers, he imagined. He wasn't sure what had happened with John Killingly, but he was certainly sad that his date with Amanda was over.

Amanda put her key in the door and unlocked it. "Dad, what's going on? Why were you driving like you were being chased?"

"It's fine, honey. Really. I was just fooling around and driving like a fool."

Amanda set her purse on the counter and saw the note her father had left. "Dad, where on earth were you this late at night?"

"Honey?" John began in somewhat of a pleading tone.

"Yes, Dad?"

"It's not important where I was. I just had to run out and do something."

"What did you do? Dad, it's late at night, and you came flying down the street like you were in a car chase. What's going on?"

John took a deep breath and let it out slowly. "You are your mother's child when it comes to being stubborn and persistent."

"Thank you," Amanda said, smiling. "Now tell me what happened."

Her father sat on the edge of a kitchen chair and pulled off his shoes. After a brief moment, he spoke up and said, "I was just trying to beat you and Brian home, that's all. I wanted to be here when you got back, and I wanted to be inside the house so you two would have a chance to talk when he dropped you off. And I wanted to see if he would walk you to the door. But I messed all that up because I came home and interrupted the chance for you two to talk."

"Great story, Dad. But where were you to begin with?"

"I went to see Dave."

"Oh." Amanda frowned. "Just because?"

"Well, I've been in town a little while and haven't seen him, and I haven't talked to him in a long time, either. I figured I'd just go say hello and see how things are with him."

Amanda narrowed her eyes and looked at her father, trying to read his face. "Okay. Going to see Dave, I believe. But why this late at night? And what's with the drive-it-like-you-stole-it ride home?"

"Like I said, desperate to relive my youth. It won't happen again, Mom," he said with a smirk.

"Mmmhmm," she said as she pointed to the guest room door. "Off to bed with you."

"Yes, ma'am," he said quietly. He kissed her forehead and gave her a hug. "Goodnight, honey."

"Goodnight, Dad. See you tomorrow."

Amanda ascended the stairs as John walked into the downstairs bathroom. He ran cold water for a few seconds and then took a handful and splashed it on his face. He splashed a second handful on his face and looked in the mirror. He stood up slowly and dried his face with a towel. He took three deep breaths and looked back in the mirror. He wasn't sure who owned the black pickup truck that tried to run him off the road and follow him home, but he certainly needed to find out. He walked into the guest room, threw his jeans and shirt on the chair next to the dresser, and fell into bed. He had thought his mind would go a thousand different directions and prevent him from sleeping, but before he knew it, he was sound asleep.

Chapter 18

H e woke to a beautiful breeze coming in through the bedroom window and the faint sound of someone in the next room. He pulled his clothes on and walked into the kitchen.

"Hey, sleepy," Amanda said.

"Hi, honey. Sorry I slept in. I haven't slept this long in years." He looked at the clock on the microwave. "Is it really seven forty-five AM?"

"Yes, it is. Breakfast is almost ready. Coffee is in the pot. Cream and sugar are on the island."

"I should visit more often," he said, thumbing the handle of a coffee mug.

Amanda was taking pancakes out of the pan when her cell phone rang.

"Who the heck is calling me this early?" she said aloud.

"Maybe June smells the pancakes and wants some."

"Oh, I already talked to her. She'll be here in a minute," Amanda said as she picked up her phone.

"Hello?"

"Hi, Amanda, its Kelly. I'm sorry to call so early, especially on a Sunday."

"It's okay. How are you?"

"I'm good, thanks. I wanted to call and offer you a job. Again, I'm sorry for the Sunday call, but you can start this week if you'd like to."

"Really?" Amanda said vibrantly. Her words were quick and excited. "Okay. I mean, yes, I accept."

"Great." Kelly said. You'll have some paperwork to do first thing, so can you meet me at my office at eight on Wednesday morning?"

"Yes, absolutely."

"The actual dispatcher shifts start at six in the morning, but you can meet me at eight to start your paperwork."

"Yes, I absolutely will. Thank you so much."

"You're welcome. Enjoy the rest of your day."

"Thanks, you, too."

Amanda set her cell phone on the counter and ran across the kitchen to her father. She just about knocked him over with a hug.

"I got the job."

John's face lit up. "Good for you, honey. I never doubted you for a second."

Amanda had just let go of her father when she heard the front door open. She ran out of the kitchen and into the living room. "June!" she called out as she ran.

"Yes, honey? What is it?"

"Kelly called. I got the job," she said as she hit June with a tackle-hug much like the one she gave her father.

"Oh, that's wonderful news, Amanda. I knew you would, and I am so very proud of you. When do you start?"

"Wednesday."

"Well, that is even better news. Congratulations, honey."

"Thank you. I don't know why I'm so excited, but I just am. I feel like I'm going to be a normal person again. A job and somewhat of a social life," she said as she and June walked into the kitchen.

"Hi, Johnny," June called out as she walked to the coffee pot.

"Morning. Judging by the squeals of delight and the laughter, I'm guessing she told you about her phone call."

"She did indeed, and I couldn't be happier. I'm so proud of you, honey," she said as she poured a cup of coffee.

"Okay, okay, I am forgetting my hostess duties. Time to serve breakfast."

Amanda passed out pancakes and sausage to her father and June and then made herself a plate. They sat together in the kitchen, talking about the job that Amanda would start in a few days. She was excited but also a little nervous. She had felt okay the day of the test, but she was about to be dealing with actual emergencies sooner than she thought. The three of them ate and talked for a while, laughing together, as they seemed to always do. Once they had eaten and the breakfast dishes were cleaned up, June headed home, and John started to get his things together for his drive back to the farm.

Amanda spent the day picking out the things she thought she might need for her first day of work. She packed a small work bag, something she hadn't done in quite some time. She packed her day planner and a light sweater. She remembered it being a little cold in the dispatch center the day of her test. She threw in a cell phone charger, her wallet, sunglasses, and a hair brush. All the things she figured she'd pack but never use. She was hanging up shirts in her closet when she heard her cell phone. She walked over, picked it up, and looked at the screen. A text message had come through.

I hear you're going to tell me where to go and what to do starting this week.

Amanda paused. She hadn't gotten a text message from anyone besides June and her father in quite some time. She thought for a moment and realized it was from Brian. Her face broke into a giant smile. She didn't want to seem too eager to respond, so she went back to hanging up shirts and decided she'd make him wait for a response. Before the third shirt was even on a hanger, she found herself, phone in hand, trying to decide what to type. She didn't want to make it easy on him, so she responded with three simple words.

Who is this?

After a very brief instant, another message arrived.

Sorry, I thought this was the number of the strikingly beautiful girl I took on a date the other night.

Amanda smiled. He obviously knew it was her, and she didn't want to avoid the chance to have actual conversation with him, so she gave up on her game of cat and mouse and decided to respond normally.

Thank you again for dinner last night. And yes, as of Wednesday, I'll be learning how to tell you what to do.

She spent far too long debating which emoji, if any, she should send with the message. She decided on the common smiley face, inserted it, and sent the message. She finished hanging up her shirts and tidied up her room and closet. She was about to head downstairs when her cell phone rang. She looked at the screen and recognized it as the number that had just texted her. She answered, smiling.

"Hello, Lieutenant."

"Lieutenant? So formal."

"Well, I mean, super-cool fireman sounded a bit over the top."

"That's what my mom writes on my t-shirts. Well, firefighter. Have to be politically correct, you know."

Amanda smiled into the phone. "How are you?"

"I'm good. I'm very glad you answered."

"I'm glad you called."

"I called because I wanted to see what time they had you starting on Wednesday."

"I'm starting at eight AM. Is that good or bad?"

"Eight is fine. Your shift will typically start at six, I'm guessing. So maybe I can buy you breakfast one day before your shift, unless you don't want to eat that early."

"Time makes no difference when it comes to food," Amanda said, laughing a little.

"Good. There is this awesome little place that makes the best breakfast. You wouldn't even know it was a restaurant by looking at it."

"How about Wednesday? I don't have to be to work until eight. We could eat a lot of breakfast with that much time."

Whiting smiled. "Wednesday it is. Do you want to meet me at the restaurant? I'd love to pick you up, but you're going to CAD afterward, right?"

"CAD?" Amanda asked.

"Sorry, Claiborne Area Dispatch. We call it CAD for short."

"Oh, yes, I am. I can meet you at the restaurant if you want."

"How about I meet you at the dispatch center? I'll meet you there, and I'll drive to the restaurant. It isn't far, but it's a little hard to find."

"Okay, that works. What time?"

"Well, did you want a certain amount of time to eat, or..." Whiting laughed a little.

"What time do they open? I mean, can we get a two-hour breakfast in?"

"Absolutely. See you at four AM."

Amanda laughed into the phone. "I'm kidding. If we meet at a little before seven, does that give me time to be at work by eight?"

"Yes. They're quick with orders, and it really is close to work."

"Okay, good. I'll see you Wednesday morning, then."

"Can't wait. Bye, Amanda."

"See you."

Amanda slid her phone into her back pocket and headed downstairs. She didn't want to see him go, but her father would have to leave this afternoon, and she wanted to spend as much time with him as she could before he left. He was in the living room, setting his duffle bag by the front door and making sure he had everything else picked up.

"Do you have to go?" Amanda asked.

"Unfortunately, I do," he said.

"Okay. Thanks for staying as long as you did, Dad. I loved having you here."

"I love being here, honey. These past few days have been wonderful. And I'm going to make sure I visit more often. I know I don't visit enough. I've always worked too much. You got the short end of the stick having to grow up with just me as a parent."

"Dad," Amanda said, giving him a reassuring look.

"I'm so sorry that you had to grow up without Mom, honey. And worse than that, you had to grow up with a workaholic Dad." John looked up at her, eyes filled with tears.

"Dad. Never. Not once in my life have I ever been sorry or upset that you are my father. You raised me while working full-time, transitioning to becoming the owner of the farm, being involved in the town, bringing me to school events, watching my soccer games, cooking me dinner, and making sure I had nice clothes, hot food, a roof over my head, and, most importantly, your love."

John looked up with tears sliding slowly down his cheeks. "Thank you, honey."

"I meant every word," Amanda said as she hugged him. "June tells me I'm a lot like Mom, so you must have done a pretty good job raising me, because everyone says she was a wonderful woman."

"She was the most wonderful woman on this earth. And they tell me everything happens for a reason, but between your Mom dying and you going through what you went through, that's a real hard pill for me to swallow."

"I know, Dad. Me, too."

She hugged him tightly and walked back to the kitchen with him. She had called June a bit earlier and invited her to have lunch with them before her dad went home. She arrived with lunch in tow, and they ate together amidst the familiar hum of good conversation.

"Thanks for your hospitality, honey," John said as he walked to the door. "And thank you, June, for keeping an eye on my little girl."

"Anytime, Johnny," June said as she hugged him. "She's my favorite part of the day."

John hugged June and then hugged Amanda.

"I'll be back as soon as I can," he said.

"Maybe I'll take a trip to see you, Dad. Would that be okay?"

"That would make me extremely happy, honey. You let me know when, and I'll be ready."

"Bring hot-stuff, the fireman," June said with a wink.

"We've only been on one date."

"Oh, but there are going to be lots more. Just trust me on this one."

Amada rolled her eyes at June and laughed. "Whatever you say."

The three of them hugged again, and John walked to his truck. Amanda and June waved from the front steps. When he got is his truck and started to drive away, Amanda felt her nose start to tingle. June looked over, saw her eyes glistening, and pulled her in for a sideways hug.

"He'll be back soon, honey, or you can go see him soon. It'll be okay."

"I know. It was just so nice having him here. Made me feel safe."

"He may not live as close as you'd like, but he's always there for you. You're everything to him."

"Thanks, June."

"You're welcome, honey. Now." She settled her gaze on Amanda and raised her eyebrows. "Let's hear about the dinner date with that delicious helping of man candy."

Amanda grinned. June could always make her smile. The pair walked up the steps and into the house.

"Did he kiss you goodnight? Where did he take you? Was the food good?"

"Listen, nosey, if you want details, you're gonna have to listen to the whole story."

"Fine," June said as they both sat down on the couch. "Let's hear it."

Chapter 19

J ohn was stopped at a red light, thinking about when he could visit again. He was quietly singing to the radio when he noticed a black pickup truck in his rear-view mirror. It was slowly pulling up a few cars behind him. He couldn't be sure, but it looked like the truck that had tried to run him off the road the day before. The light turned green, and John pulled away. As he was getting farther out of the city, traffic was getting lighter. Despite the decreasing traffic, the black truck stayed behind him. It was just far enough back that he couldn't get a license plate or see who was driving, but it was close enough that he knew it wasn't a coincidence. He turned left down a road he didn't need to be on, just to see if the truck followed. It did. Trying not to think too much of it, John calmly drove to the end of the street and took a right. He continued down a few side streets, doing his best not to panic about the truck behind him. When he got far enough around the corner that the truck was out of sight for a minute, he stopped at a stop sign, quickly dialed 911, put his phone on speaker mode, and set it on the seat next to him.

"Nine-one-one. What's the address of your emergency?"

"Hi, I'm on, uh, Winthrop Court, off of Central Avenue."

"Okay, sir, what is your name, and what is your emergency?"

"I'm being followed by a black pickup truck. I had the same truck follow me home the other night and try to run me off the road. My name is John Killingly. I just left my daughter's house on Wentworth."

There was a brief pause and then, "Okay, sir, please stay on the line with me and stay calm. There is an officer near your location who is heading your way."

John looked in his mirror for the truck. There was no one behind him. He pulled away from the stop sign and continued down the street. When he got to the next intersection, he stopped at the stop sign, put his signal on, and began to turn right, back onto Central Avenue. He looked left and right, and as he began to pull away, something caught his eye. He turned his head just in time to see the black pickup truck come speeding through the intersection and smash into the side of his truck. He closed his eyes just before the impact.

As the trucks collided, his body lurched sideways, and there was a cacophony of squealing tires, breaking glass, and hot metal screeching and smashing. When he opened his eyes, he saw that the airbags in his truck had gone off. The windshield was cracked, his driver's side window was smashed out, and the door was pressed tightly against his left leg. All the sounds were muffled, and hot blood poured from a gash on his forehead, running down his nose and across one eye. He wiped the blood from his face with his sleeve, only to have it instantly replaced with more blood. As fast as he could wipe it away, more of the hot liquid poured from the wound on his head and clouded his vision. He pressed his sleeve against his forehead and managed to focus enough to see two men climbing out of the black pickup truck. He had no idea how they were up and walking so quickly, but they were headed right for him.

John pushed the accelerator pedal to the floor. His truck was smashed, but it was still running and still in gear. He drove past the two men and pulled hard on the steering wheel, only to find it wouldn't turn. He kept trying, but his wheels were locked straight by gnarled metal. The truck roared and coughed as it dragged its way down the road, tires rubbing on the bent fenders, smoke starting to rise from under the hood. He managed to get himself across part of Central Avenue and kept driving as fast as his mangled truck would go. His head was pounding, and his mind was a mess of clouded thoughts that he kept trying desperately to clear up. Every time he moved his hand from his forehead, he was met with a blinding pain in his left eye as more hot blood rushed down his face, dripping off his eyebrow and into his eye. He had to stop the bleeding, but he couldn't do that while he was being chased. His truck started to slow, and John figured it was finally starting to give up after being smashed by an equally-large vehicle.

He pressed his hand and sleeve back against his forehead and kept driving, his truck slowly lessening its getaway speed. He glanced in his rear-view mirror, which, amazingly, was still intact despite the large cracks in his windshield. He saw the two men following on foot, running across Central Avenue. He knew his truck was slowing greatly if the men were keeping up simply by jogging. He squinted his one open eye and quickly looked left and then right in an effort to form some kind of plan. There was no place to pull over and run for cover, and soon his truck would provide only limited shelter as the motor slowly gave up. He glanced in the mirror again, only to see the men running with their hands raised. Before he could react, gun shots snapped and echoed behind him. He heard loud thuds as the rounds slammed into his already-dying truck. He was approaching an intersection and was quite certain his truck would stop long before he could get through it. He pressed the accelerator to the floor once more, but the truck didn't move any faster. He slapped the dash board in a futile attempt to coax a little more life out of the machine, but it was of no use. He looked out the mangled windshield and saw two police cruisers driving straight toward him.

He pulled over and jumped out, the final rattling cough of his truck dying off behind him as he ran toward the oncoming cars. He waved his free hand wildly as he ran, the other still pressed tightly against his forehead in an effort to keep his vision somewhat clear, and to hopefully keep enough blood in his system to keep him from passing out. The cruisers sped down the street, flew past him in a blur of blue, white, and flashing lights, and stopped just past where John was standing. The doors opened, and three officers jumped out, crouched behind their cars, and opened fire on the two men from the truck. John ran toward the cruisers to take cover behind them. As he was running, he felt a searing pain run through his entire body. Still running, but starting to fumble and fall, John Killingly looked down to see blood pouring out of his abdomen. He instinctively pressed his free hand against the throbbing pain in the side of his stomach and felt sick when he felt a hole that literally went all the way through him.

He stumbled and crashed onto the pavement before he could get to the police cruisers. Matt McPherson ran to him, gun raised and firing, his knees bent in a fast-moving crouch. He dragged John's limp and bleeding body back toward the cruisers. He slid him behind the back tire of the car and turned to return to his position behind the driver's side door. As he took the first step, he opened fire and tried to duck behind his police cruiser. After he fired the second round, he felt a blinding, numbing pain in his neck. Before he could take another step, he fell to the ground. John looked over and saw his body lying in the road, blood escaping from his neck at an alarming rate. The two men retreated toward their pickup truck. One officer ran to McPherson and John while the other got in his police cruiser and pursued the men running back toward the black pickup truck. John tried to open his mouth to speak, but nothing came out. He was trying to move toward the officer to help with McPherson, but his body wouldn't budge. He tried to lean forward and crawl to him, but it was no use. He was trying everything he could to make his bleeding body move. Before he moved an inch, he felt himself getting lightheaded. Everything got blurry, and suddenly, everything went black.

Chapter 20

S ergeant Harding stood in a room full of police officers. Most of them dressed in plain clothes, some in suits, and a handful in uniform. All wore guns, and most of them had visible badges.

"Okay, listen up," he barked. "The group with the ivy vine tattoos has just made themselves the number one enemy of this police department. A few hours ago, they opened fire on a man driving home from his daughter's house after smashing into his truck with theirs. They also opened fire on three of our own. Officer Matt McPherson and the driver, John Killingly, were both shot during the incident. Whatever cases you're working on, stop right now until we find these low-life pieces of shit and put an end to their bullshit. Do you understand me?"

"Yes, sir!" the group echoed loudly and forcefully.

"They are not a gang by standard definition, but we are going to treat them like one. They're not into selling drugs or illegal guns, and they don't have any rival groups in the area that they've engaged in a turf war with. However, we are dealing with a large group of people, with their own hierarchy of membership. From what we know, the man at the top, or closest to it, is named Benjamin Rudley. He's a real estate tycoon and the owner of BR Enterprises, which is a very large construction company. Rudley seems to have a bottomless bank roll and a taste for good food, expensive cars, and revenge."

He crossed the room and pointed to a series of pictures posted on a dry-erase board.

"His group members all have ivy vine tattoos. They're smart enough to not use the same tattoo parlor, but the design is always the same. Location of the tattoos are all over the place. Some on the leg, some on the forearm, others on the shoulder. Typically, with gangs, we're dealing with kids who dropped out of school or never even bothered going in the first place. These guys are intelligent, well spoken, and some of them are highly educated. Benjamin Rudley has a degree in finance and business management. One of the other players is a graduate of Mandrake Law School just on the other side of the city. They know the laws, and they know how to keep themselves out of prison while running around and ruining our city."

Sergeant Harding looked around, seeing nods of understanding and hearing a low murmur from the group.

He raised his voice and continued, "But they shot one of our cops. They also shot the father of a girl who they kidnapped, raped, severely beat, and left for dead. It ends here. It ends now. We need to start getting an idea of where these guys work, where they live, and who they deal with on a day-to-day basis. We've had several cases involving their members, and now we have two of them in custody."

The murmur in the room grew to a low and constant hum of conversation.

He pressed on as he felt the energy in the room rising; he wanted it to be put to good use as they all went to work.

"We had one of the suspects from the rape and assault of the guy's daughter in custody not long ago. We brought him in and questioned him, but we couldn't hold him. He had the best three attorneys money can buy before we were even done reading him his rights."

"Can we pick him up for anything else?" one of the detectives in plain clothes asked. "Possession? Dealing? Unregistered firearms?"

"We've tried. We had an undercover unit follow him for an entire week. He never put one foot out of line. Not as much as a cigarette butt on the sidewalk."

"Sarge?"

"Yeah?"

"We have addresses for any of them? Maybe send a car to watch them for a few days?"

"We tried that, too. These guys, in some ways, are just normal people. They have jobs, they have regular bank accounts and bills, and some of them even have families. They have perfected the art of hiding in plain sight."

Another officer spoke up from the back corner of the room. "Sergeant?"

"Go ahead."

"How many of them are there?"

Harding took a deep breath and glanced around the room.

"We can only guess at this point, but our best estimate? Almost a hundred."

More murmurs and whispers darted through the crowd despite Harding's best attempts to stop them.

"Okay, let's focus," he said just loud enough to get his point across. "We are still gathering information. But these guys are out there, and we need to learn everything we can about them. Eyes open, shoulders back, guns ready. Ten-four?"

"Yes, sir," the crowd said in unison.

"Rutledge, you're with me. We're gonna question these two assholes."

The room emptied quickly as Rutledge met Harding in the front of the room.

"What's our play? Good cop, bad cop?"

Harding thought for a minute and said, "How about bad cop and worse cop?"

"Sounds good to me."

The two of them walked down the hallway to an interrogation room. They met another officer standing inside the observation room.

"Okay, Charlotte, what do we know about them?"

"Daniel Snyder and Alexander Hotchkinson. Both twenty-six years old. Snyder did a short stint at a medium-security prison in Waveton. Hotchkinson is clean as a whistle. Not even a parking ticket. I'm thinking he might be a lot newer to the game than Snyder."

"Okay, then he'll crack first if that's the case," Harding said, looking at a folder of papers that Charlotte had handed him. "Either one have a family? These guys are looking at life as far as I'm concerned. Let's remind them that their family time is gonna be through a glass wall."

"Snyder has a wife and an eight-year-old son. Hotchkinson isn't married. Looks like he may have a girlfriend, but his mother is elderly and ill. She lives with him; he's her full-time caregiver."

"So we play nice with him, tell him we want to make sure his mom is looked after? Get him to flip?" Rutledge asked.

"The opposite. Tell him Mom's going to die a cold and lonely death on his kitchen floor because he's not going home to see her ever again. Squeeze him. He shot a cop. Keep the pressure on him. I picked you, Rutledge, because you know how to do this better than anyone else. If you have to resort back to your interrogation habits from when you were in the Special Forces, I'm okay with that."

"Ten-four."

Rutledge walked through a door and closed it behind him. Harding took a few steps down the hallway and entered a second room. He closed the door and threw the folder he was holding on the table.

"You did something very stupid today."

"Oh, yeah? What's that, officer?"

"It's Sergeant," Harding said sternly. "I'm gonna guess you did a whole lot of stupid things today. But we're going to focus on how you just ended your son's life."

Snyder stood up quickly and opened his mouth to say something. Before he could make a sound, Harding yelled, "Sit down," and pushed him down into his chair by the shoulders.

"You stay away from my son."

"Me? You really are stupid, aren't you?" Harding said as he crossed behind him. "I serve and protect people. I don't hurt them. That seems to be your job. But I read your file there. It says your son, Cameron...it says that he's a great student. You hire private tutors to make sure he excels in school, buy him only the best sports equipment, and a private car brings him to a private school every day. And seeing as your wife doesn't have a job, I'm going to guess that once you're rotting in prison, the money stops coming in. Well, I bet that Emily finds someone else for Cameron to call Daddy."

Snyder grit his teeth and glared at Harding.

"If she doesn't, no more private car for rides to school, no more tutors, no more private school, and no more perfect life for Cameron. He'll be a regular kid at a regular school. And his father will be doing life in prison. You know what kind of kids he'll start hanging around with?"

Harding crossed and stood behind him, where he was only visible as a reflection in the one-way glass of the interrogation room.

"The kind of kids whose fathers are also in prison. First, it'll be bad grades and booze, then maybe a little coke or heroin. And pretty soon, little Cameron will be right in prison with you for stealing purses for money to buy more shit to shoot up his arm or snort up his nose. That'll make his mother so sad and depressed that she'll probably turn to booze, too, and try to drown all those problems that you created by being a useless piece of trash. You see, Daniel. No one has to do anything to your family. You're destroying them all by yourself."

"Fuck you," he said sharply.

Harding continued as if Snyder hadn't said a word.

"Your only hope is that someone beats you to death your first day in the joint, and you'll never live to see your wife and kid become bottom-feeding shit-bags like you."

Snyder glared at Harding, his eyes glistening. Harding could see that he had gotten to him, but he didn't think he was going to crack that easily.

"I want a deal," he blurted out.

"A deal? I've got a deal for you. Life in prison with no chance for parole. You plead guilty, and I'll make sure your buddy in the other room shares a cell with you. That way you two can become lovers before anyone else claims you."

Snyder shifted in his chair. "Fuck you, Sergeant," he said slowly and deliberately.

"You know, we've been doing a lot of looking into these friends of yours. The ones with the ivy vine tattoos. And we realized that they are everywhere. I know they're even in this police department."

Snyder smirked. "Oh yeah?"

"Oh yeah, they are. But see, that's a good thing for me. And a bad thing for you. Because when I walk out that door, I'm going to tell everyone that we have a great lead because you flipped and told us whatever we wanted to know. See, that way," Harding said as he leaned in close to his ear, "even if you somehow don't go to prison for life, your ivy vine buddies will gut you like a fish and pay your wife a little visit to deliver the news of your death. So, either way, prison or your own friends. You're going to die a slow and miserable death. Your choice."

Harding crossed the room and headed for the door. He had his hand on the door handle and began to push it down. Just as the door cracked open, Snyder yelled.

"Wait. Let's talk." Harding paused. "I can give you details. Locations of stash houses. There are four of them. All on the west side. And we've got one other place. It's in Forest View. I'm just a mid-ranking guy. I can give you names. Where they keep their cash, how they stay protected. Let's talk."

"We will," Harding said. "We certainly will."

With that, Harding opened the door and walked out.

"Hey!" Snyder called. "Hey. Get back here. You said we'd talk," he screamed as the door closed behind Harding.

Harding walked down the hall to the observation room. Rutledge was walking out of the interrogation room.

"How'd it go?" Harding asked.

"The tough guy act ended when we started talking about Mom. He's ready to talk. I told him I was getting him a cup of water."

"I'm gonna go in for a minute."

"Have at it. I'll grab a coffee."

Harding opened the door to the room and walked in slowly. He sat down at the table and looked at Hotchkinson.

"You comfortable, Alex?"

Hotchkinson looked around the room, slightly puzzled.

"I'm okay," he said, his anxiety bleeding through every word. "You the good cop?"

"Me? No, I'm the realistic cop. I'm the guy who tells you that no matter how tough you think you are, or how many people you know, you're going down for shooting a cop and an unarmed citizen. Your trial won't last long. Judges hate cop killers. Your sentencing will be over before the court even breaks for lunch. And your life, well, your life will be over the day you walk into that cold, dark prison cell. You see, Alex, I've been a cop a long time. And I've come to learn there isn't much use in the what-ifs and the hopeful plea deals. All that matters is that your friend in the other room gave you up and told us all he did was drive the truck."

Hotchkinson turned slightly in his chair in what seemed like an attempt to hide his face from Harding.

"Anything you want to say to help us sort out the details, Alex? They say there are always two sides to every story. So far, we've only got one of them. And your friend's version of how things went down doesn't look too good for you."

Hotchkinson turned to face Harding. "No way he gave me up. We don't do that. We've got more honor than you could ever hope to have."

"Honor?" Harding said as he leaned in close to him. "You wanna talk about honor? How honorable is it that you shot a cop in cold blood? A cop with a family, who never did anything to you except try to stop you from being the bottom-feeding shit-bag that you are. How honorable is it when you kidnap and rape young girls, or when you get a teenager hooked on heroin? No, Alex, you're mistaken about knowing what honor is. Maybe you're mistaking it with the word horror. And no matter what happens," Harding said, his voice falling to a raspy whisper, "...no matter how smart or connected you think you are, you will know horror. I'm gonna cut your trigger finger off and put in your mother's tea cup. You see, Alex, I knew Detective Rutledge would get to you. And I knew that your friend would give you up as soon as we asked him what happened. But what I didn't know was that your poor mother has no one else but you. And when you're rotting in prison or, better yet, in a cold, bloody heap in the prison laundry room, Mommy dearest is going to starve to death right there in your kitchen as she claws at the empty cans and food boxes. So after all is said and done, even if you could live with being a criminal and a cop killer, I bet that you won't ever get over killing your own mother slowly and painfully."

Harding turned and walked toward the door.

"Wait," Hotchkinson said. "I want to tell my side of the story."

"You will," Harding said as he opened the door and left.

Hotchkinson slammed his fist on the table. Harding left the room and crossed over to Rutledge, who was sipping his coffee.

"Reel him in. He's panicked and paranoid now. Get his side of the story. I'm going back to talk to the other one." As he started to walk away, his cell phone rang.

"This is Harding. Okay? What time? Yeah. No, I'll... Yes, sir I'll handle it. Yes. I'll do it."

262

Harding pushed his phone back into his pocket. He took a deep breath and held it. After a moment, he blew it out in a quiet sigh. He frowned at Rutledge. "That was the hospital. McPherson didn't make it."

Detective Rutledge ran his hands through his hair and sighed heavily.

"This would be easier if we could just kill 'em."

"Deep breath," Harding said as he took one himself.

"Sarge? Let's hang these bastards for the whole world to see. Make an example of them."

"We will. We'll find more of them, these ivy tattoo pricks. And we'll end them."

Chapter 21

Amanda woke to the sound of her phone ringing. She rubbed her eyes in an attempt to see her screen clearly. She looked at the clock and noticed the time. She figured it must be a wrong number at this hour, so she hit the silence button and rolled over. She was dreamily on her way back to deep sleep when she heard her phone beep once, the alert for a voicemail. Her head lifted from the pillow, and struck with curiosity about why a wrong number would leave a voicemail in the middle of the night. She sat up and picked up her phone, and suddenly, she became very awake. She sat motionless as she listened to the message. Tears began to stream down her cheeks as she listened to Sergeant Harding's voice tell her that her father had been shot. She didn't know what to do. She felt like she wasn't breathing deep enough to get any oxygen. She gulped at the air and tried to take deep breaths, but it still felt like there was a truck resting on her chest. She pulled on sweatpants and a sweatshirt and ran into the hallway. She fumbled down the stairs haphazardly, barely able to see through the tears in her eyes. She wasn't thinking clearly enough to make a phone call, so she burst through her front door and out onto the steps. She walked across the street and began pounding on June's door.

"Juuuuune! Please come here. Juuuune," she sobbed as she collapsed against June's door. A light turned on in the living room, and she heard June call out.

"Amanda, honey, I'm coming."

June opened the door, and Amanda fell against her. She helped her to the couch and tried to get her calm enough to tell her what was wrong. It wasn't working. Amanda could barely put two words together, let alone explain the voicemail. Amanda opened the voicemail message and handed her phone to June. She sat motionless, just as Amanda had, listening to the message. After a moment, she set the phone down and hugged Amanda tightly. She was crying herself but knew she needed to be strong for Amanda's sake. After a few minutes of silence, June lifted her head and peered up at Amanda, raising her head with one finger lightly on her chin.

"It's going to be okay, honey. Deep breath. It's going to be okay."

"Okay?" Amanda said, trying to breathe normally. "They shot my father, June."

"I know, honey. Deep breath. We're going to figure this out. One thing at a time. Let's go over to your house and get you dressed a little differently, or at least get you some shoes and your purse. I'll drive you to go see Sergeant Harding."

"Okay." She sniffed.

They crossed the street to Amanda's house. She changed her clothes, washed the tears from her eyes, and got her purse and shoes. They drove in silence, Amanda staring out the window. As they walked in, Amanda was looking down and doing her best not to cry. She turned to say something to June, and before she could get a word out, she ran into something and knocked herself to the floor. Already upset and incredibly embarrassed, Amanda felt tears welling up in her eyes. She slowly pulled herself together and was beginning to stand up when she felt two arms embrace her and lift her to her feet. She looked up and saw Brian standing in front of her, his hands on her shoulders as he asked if she was okay. She didn't say a word but leaned into his chest. He was a little caught off guard but didn't want to upset her, so he hugged her and didn't say a word. She slowly pulled her head away from his chest, wiping the tears from her eyes. His hands still on her shoulders, he looked at her.

"Are you okay?"

Amanda nodded yes. She took a deep breath and ran her fingers through her hair.

"My dad was shot," she managed.

Whiting's eyes widened. "What? When?"

"Earlier tonight, on his way home." Amanda couldn't stop the sobs.

Whiting looked at June, who nodded, and he pulled Amanda back in to hug her.

"It's okay, love," he said as he held her. "It's okay to cry." After a moment, she looked up and took a deep breath.

"What are you doing here?" she asked.

"One of my guys got a little hurt, so I had to come here and get some paperwork."

"Oh, is he okay?" She sniffed as she wiped away more tears.

"You are the most amazing human being I know. You just told me your father was shot, and you're asking if my firefighter is okay. He's fine."

"That's good." She sniffed. "Can we postpone breakfast tomorrow morning?"

"Amanda, of course we can," he said. "You have more important things to worry about than breakfast with me."

"Amanda?" she heard a deep voice call out. It was Sergeant Harding, and he was headed down the hallway in her direction.

"Sergeant Harding," Amanda said as he drew closer. "Tell me you have the person who did this."

"We do. They're in custody, and we're interrogating them now."

"Who did this?" Amanda asked.

"We have the men in custody. They have a connection to…" Harding trailed off as if he had just noticed Whiting for the first time. "Hey, kid. You two know each other?" He gestured to Amanda and Whiting.

"Yes, we do. Who are they connected to, Bill?"

Harding sighed and looked around. "They're part of the group with the ivy vine tattoos."

Whiting shook his head in a mixture of frustration and disgust. "Just like the guys who torched the ambulance."

"Yeah. And the same group that…" Harding stopped when his eyes met Amanda's.

"The same group that kidnapped and attacked me," Amanda said.

June's eyes filled with tears. Amanda stood, staring at Harding, glancing every once in a while at Whiting.

There was a long pause of deep silence. After it had lasted long enough, Amanda spoke up.

"I know no one wants to talk about it, so I will. It's okay to say it. It was a long time ago. The men who attacked me are tied to the men who shot Dad?" As soon as she said the words *shot Dad*, her eyes filled up with tears.

"Yes, Amanda, they are all part of one very large group," Harding said.

"The same group that torched our ambulance and that worked for the glassware company," Whiting said, still stunned by the news and the connection.

"Excuse me, Sergeant Harding?" a voice called from behind them. Harding spun around quickly to face the doctor. He glanced at Amanda and June. "Are you all family?"

"I'm his daughter," Amanda said, expecting him to say she needed to identify the body.

"The surgery went well. He's not out of the woods yet, but—"

"Surgery?" Amanda interrupted.

"Yes, ma'am. We had to do emergency surgery to remove the bullet. He's not out of the woods, but he should be fine with a few days here for observation, and then he will need a lot of rest at home. You can see him now, but family only, please."

Amanda was trying to find words to put into a sentence. She had thought her father was dead.

"He's alive?" Amanda said, her eyes filling with tears.

"Yes, Amanda," said Sergeant Harding. "I'm sorry. I thought I said that in my voicemail."

"I just heard that he had been shot, and I stopped listening. I assumed he was..." She stopped herself.

"He's alive. And you can see him now." The doctor smiled quietly and excused himself.

Amanda didn't know where he had been shot or how extensive the surgery had been. She prepared herself for the worst and kept walking toward his room. Standing at the door, she turned to see Harding and Whiting standing right where she had left them. She took a deep breath and walked into the room. She crossed to her father's bed. When he saw her, he did his best to smile through the pain. "There is the most beautiful girl I know."

With that, tears streamed down her cheeks. She walked to him and hesitated before she hugged him. She didn't want to hurt him. He could sense her holding back. "Get over here and hug me."

She hugged him slowly but tightly. She sobbed into his shoulder, and he stroked her hair and kissed her cheek.

"Shhhhh. It's okay, honey. I'm fine. It's gonna be okay. Deep breaths."

She continued to sob and hug her father until she felt like she was about to hyperventilate. She pulled away and wiped her face with her hands, then took a deep breath. She stood, looking at her father, who was doing his best to act like he wasn't in pain and everything was okay.

"Daddy," she said and started sobbing again.

"Shhhh. I know, honey. I know. It's okay."

After a minute or so of tears and trying to breathe, Amanda was finally able to stop crying. She took four long, deep breaths, sat in the chair next to her father's bed, took his hand, and squeezed it gently. Harding must have been watching, because soon after she sat down, he entered the room.

"Hey, John," he said as quietly as his deep, raspy voice could manage.

John nodded upward. "Hey."

Harding crossed to the other chair in the room and sat down, seemingly to say that he was in no hurry to leave, that he was there for whatever they needed.

"If you're up to it, I've got a few questions," Harding said.

"Yeah, I'm okay. Fire away. No pun intended," he said, smiling.

Amanda was amazed. Her father had just been through emergency surgery after being shot, and he was still smiling and making jokes.

Harding grinned at him. "Okay. So what happened before the shoot-out? We have you calling nine-one-one to report the truck following you, and McPherson and Schaffer were to your location pretty quick. What happened to get where we are now?"

"I reported the truck following me. After I hung up, I thought I had lost them. I took a few side streets and made a few double-back loops to see if I could keep them gone. I thought I had. I got to the stop sign, looked left and then right, and started to pull away. As I started into the intersection, I looked left again, and before I could react, there was the truck. It slammed into me, going what felt like eighty miles per hour. I managed to open my eyes and see that they were pretty banged up and had started to get out of the truck. I looked down and noticed my truck was still running. I took a chance that it would still move and floored it. She moved all right, but the wheels were smashed, and I couldn't really turn. I got a little way down the road, and your guys showed up. I jumped out into a hail of gunfire as your guys shot back at them. I got hit and figured I was all done. Your guy, McPherson, he dragged me behind the cruiser. I owe him a beer."

Harding looked at the floor and pinched his lips together. He looked back up and said heavily, "McPherson didn't make it. He was hit twice in the vest, twice in the leg, and once in the neck."

Amanda's eyes filled with tears. "Matt McPherson?" she said, inhaling sharply.

"Yeah. He was one of the officers who responded to help your dad. He was fatally wounded in the shoot-out."

John looked at Harding. His eyes glistening, he inhaled with a quick sniff. "He have family?"

"No wife or kids, thankfully, but his sister and mother live close by. They're on their way here."

Amanda cried quietly while she listened to her father talk to Harding. She wasn't close with Matt, but since her attack, he had helped her on more than one occasion. She always felt safe knowing that he knew the details of her case, and she was always glad to see him driving by in his cruiser during his shifts.

"John," Harding started. "I don't mean anything by this next question. I know you're not the kind of person to be mixed up in this sort of thing, but why did they target you?"

"Dave," he said. "I'm guessing he couldn't keep his mouth shut and ended up saying things he shouldn't have said."

"Dave? The guy who owns the bar where..." He glanced at Amanda, and his voice trailed off.

"It's okay, Sergeant," she said. "I'm okay."

"Okay," Harding said with a nod that said *I'm sorry* and thank you all at once. "Dave is the guy who owns the bar where Amanda was kidnapped?"

"Yeah," said John. "I went to see him the other day. I told you about the gun, right?" Harding nodded. "Well, I went to see him and ask about it. One of the guys he's mixed up with showed up while I was there. I'm sure he started asking who I was after I left. Dave told me about them and what he was mixed up in, so I'm guessing they were trying to keep me from telling anyone."

"We got the two low-life idiots from the shoot-out. Despite their best attempts to be tough and keep their mouths shut, they already started to crack. When I leave here, I'll head back to the station and see how much we got out of them."

"Thanks," John said.

"You're welcome. If you guys need anything, you call me anytime, day or night." He handed a business card to Amanda and John. "My cell is on the back. Anytime. You call me anytime."

"Thank you," Amanda said as Harding walked out.

"Dad," Amanda said, her eyes filling with tears. "You went to see Dave, and you ended up getting *shot*? What the hell is this?"

"It's okay, honey," John offered.

"Okay? What if the police had gotten there two minutes later, Dad? You'd be dead. All because Dave is some low-life gambler who is in debt to *what*? A gang? This needs to stop. And they said it's the same group that kidnapped and raped me? Beat me over and over and left me for fucking dead? And you're telling me it's okay?" Her voice raised half an octave as she continued. "It's not okay. And the police just keep turning them all loose, even after they've been arrested. Something needs to happen to them. Someone needs to do something. They all deserve to fucking die." All her life she had been quiet and reserved, never raised her voice for much of anything. The death of her mother had left her without a female role model, and so she simply tried to go unnoticed. Her years of quiet and calm were boiling over now. She had no more room for cool and collected, and in that instant, her quiet grace was replaced with rage. Amanda reached her foot out and kicked the arm chair with searing intensity. It made a loud cracking sound as it slid across the floor and stopped abruptly when it slammed into the wall. She collapsed in a crying heap into it. She was not a violent person, but she had reached her breaking point.

"Shhhh, honey. Deep breath," her father said softly. "Come on, honey, deep breath."

She sat up slowly and looked toward her father, then down at the floor. She was looking past him, seeing only the visions in her head. Her mind slowed enough for her to see things fall into place, and her thoughts got more organized for the first time since she had gotten Harding's voicemail. She seemed to have been momentarily transformed, her thoughts getting clearer.

"Amanda, honey, are you okay?" She slowly lifted her gaze from the floor tiles to her father.

Her eyes met his and she said, "You okay, Dad?"

"I'm okay, honey. Are you okay?"

"Yes. I am. Once they say you can leave here, we'll get you home and get you better."

"Sounds good to me. Are you sure you're okay? You kind of zoned out for a minute while we were talking."

"Yeah, I'm good. I was having a moment of true clarity for the first time in a long time."

"Is that a good thing or a bad thing?" John raised his eyebrows at her a little.

She tilted her head and paused. "Depends on who you ask."

Chapter 22

June pointed a slowly-rotating finger at John. "If you get up out of that chair one more time, Johnathan Killingly, so help me."

"Okay, you two," Amanda called from the kitchen. "You behave while I'm gone."

"Are you sure you're ready for this, honey?" June asked. "I can call Kelly and tell her that you want to postpone your first day of work. She certainly won't mind given the circumstances."

"Dad made me promise I'd go to work. Isn't that right?"

"That's right. The doctor said they removed all of the bullet fragments, and there was no organ damage. My only restrictions are no heavy lifting and minimal leaning and bending. I'm not planning on doing yoga anytime soon, or ever, so I'm fine."

Amanda kissed John on the cheek and hugged June. "Here goes nothing," she said, her eyebrows raised in a slight smile. She walked to her car and took a deep breath. The air was warm but not humid, and it felt refreshing as she inhaled deeply. She was trying to calm her nerves when she noticed a black mark on the pavement. It was a skid mark from where the car had crashed that day. She and her father had jumped in to help without a second thought. She remembered the events of that day well, and they helped reassure her that she had the capacity, and the ability, to be good at her new job. She made the short drive to the dispatch center in silence. Her radio off and her window down slightly to let the delicious air in to swirl around her seats. She pulled into the dispatch center and parked. She closed her window, turned off the ignition, and took several deep breaths. She hadn't noticed the distance from parking lots to buildings in quite some time after her attack. Today, however, she took a deep breath and let it out slowly as she noticed giant overhead lights that ringed the parking lot as well as light posts along the walkway to the door. It was light outside now, but with her normal hours of six AM until six PM, she imagined that in some months, her trip to and from the building would be in the dark. She opened her car door and grabbed her bag. She closed the door, looked around to survey her surroundings, and headed toward the building. Before she was halfway to the steps when she heard a voice call out to her.

"You are one determined woman," Kelly said from the steps. "My mother told me what happened. Are you sure you want to start today?"

Amanda waited until she was just about to the steps to answer. "I'm sure. Dad is in good hands with June watching over him. And I need a sense of normalcy to my life."

"Ohhh, your poor father. He's with Mom today? Probably better you're here, then," she said, smiling. "Come on in."

The dispatch center—or CAD, as Brian had called it—was just as impressive as Amanda remembered. TV screens lined the walls, and computer monitors wrapped around the desks of each dispatcher station. The walls were bright, the carpet was clean, and it smelled like a brand-new TV or computer inside. A smell that was hard to describe, but one Amanda had always enjoyed. She followed Kelly to her office and sat in one of the comfortable chairs in front of her desk.

"Okay," Kelly said as she pulled a pen from her drawer. "You did most of your paperwork the day of your interview, so there are really just a few forms to do today. After that, we'll get your fingerprint scanned into the system, activate your badge, get you a head-set, and have you get familiar with one of the dispatch stations. After that, I'm buying you lunch."

"Oh, you don't have to buy me lunch," Amanda said. Before she could say anything else, Kelly cut in.

"I know I don't have to, but I want to. And after lunch, we'll come back and take a tour of the center, and you can go home early your first day. Not a bad deal, right?"

Amanda smiled. "Sounds good to me."

She filled out forms as Kelly passed them to her. A few needed a signature. Most were information packets on policies and procedures, privacy statements, forms on dealing with stressful phone calls, and things like that. The time passed easily as Amanda and Kelly chatted about the forms and the job. She outlined a typical day for Amanda and told her that some days they had time to watch the news and weather on one of the TVs in the center, and other days they barely had time to take a sip of water in-between phone calls.

"It's stressful at times, but it's so rewarding," Kelly said. "We've had people stop by and say thank you. People we've helped along the way. That is really rewarding. When they come in and tell us that the police got there in time to stop the person who broke into their house, or that the CPR instructions the dispatcher gave brought a family member back to life...those are the awesome days."

"I'm guessing there are not-so-awesome days, too?" Amanda said, signing her last form.

"Yes. That comes with the territory. But on the not-so-awesome days, we remember to talk to each other and rely on each other as a support system. We've got a really great group at this point. All of our dispatchers are highly skilled and great at what they do, and they are also like a family. They're excited to have you on the team."

Amanda smiled and nodded. "I'm excited, too."

Kelly organized the forms on her desk and looked up at Amanda. "Okay, paperwork is done. Let's head over to our Network Administrator, and he'll get you into the system and activate your badge."

As they walked through CAD, Amanda noticed the dispatchers smiling and talking happily. She took comfort in knowing that they could still have fun, and have good days, despite being the people who answered the calls from people having their worst day.

"Knock-knock," Kelly said aloud. A dark-haired man in a polo shirt motioned for her to come in.

"Come on in," he said, glancing up from his computer screen.

"Spencer Abbot, meet Amanda Killingly."

He looked up from his monitor and extended his hand. "Welcome," he said enthusiastically.

"What are you working on, Spencer?"

"The new app for responding officers and apparatus. I've given it to a few officers and one of the fire officers to try out. I need real time data to finish the tests. I gave them a demo version so I can see how it works." His voice was excited.

"You're a geek." Kelly laughed.

"Since the first grade and proud of it," Spencer answered, smiling.

"Which officers have it?"

"I emailed you the list, but since you're here, Davis has it, and so does Finch. I also gave one to Zoe at headquarters. I was going to give one to McPherson..." He trailed off and stopped himself before saying anything more. "Well, anyway, I gave it to Adams instead," he said reverently. "On the fire side, I gave one to McKenna and one to Whiting. They're supposed to stop by in a few days and let me know how they like it, and I'll make any adjustments we need to before we let it go live."

Amanda was excited and nervous that Brian may stop by on a day she was working. They hadn't given themselves a title, but she liked him a lot and wasn't sure how to act around him near other people.

"You've been busy," Kelly said, bringing Amanda's focus back to the current conversation.

"Well, I also watched a lot of daytime TV while I was here. That's okay, too, right?" Spencer smiled.

It was both upsetting and comforting to Amanda that Matt's name could be used, a slight pause taken, and then conversation resumed as usual with the same happy tone it had started with.

"You can get back to your soap operas in a few minutes," Kelly joked. "But first I need you to activate Amanda's badge and get her prints into the system."

"Of course," Spencer said excitedly. "Right this way, Miss Killingly. This will only take a minute, and it only hurts a little bit."

"He's kidding," Kelly called after them as they walked down a short hallway and into another office. Spencer put Amanda's hand on a glass screen and took several scans. She wasn't paying much attention. Instead, she was staring at a large, flat-screen TV on the wall. It had a list of addresses and a list of roads. Some were written in orange text, others in red, and others in a light blue color.

"What are those?" Amanda asked, motioning to the TV.

"Ahh, that's my ELSA. She's another one of my projects," he said happily.

"Elsa?" Amanda said, raising her eyebrows. "Like the princess?"

"Huh?" Spencer said, looking back at her.

"Never mind." Amanda smiled.

"She's my princess for sure, but it's E.L.S.A. It's an acronym for Emergency Location Safety Assessment. It lists the addresses of vacant houses that the fire department may choose not to enter because there is no immediate threat to life. Or at least there shouldn't be. Sometimes homeless people break in and sleep there, which is tough to prevent, but the city started marking them in an effort to keep the firefighters safe. They're trained to put life safety first, and so, quite often, they'd be running into a burning building looking for someone when, in reality, the building was completely vacant. The others are high-risk addresses, and some are addresses of high-occupancy buildings that the fire department and police department pre-plan in the event of an emergency. All the fire trucks have a tablet in them. When they respond to an address, it tells them what the status of the building is. If they find an address to add to the list, they can log in and enter the information into a form. I programmed the system to update in real time, so if a lieutenant enters information at four in the morning and a different fire truck responds to the address at eight in the morning, they already have the current data they need for that address."

"Wow," Amanda said, raising her eyebrows. "That's really impressive. You designed all of that?"

"Yeah. Tech has always been easy for me. Girlfriends, high school, sports, large gatherings...not my thing. But technology and I have always gotten along very well. Okay. You're all set. I'll get your information processed, and your badge should work for building access as of right now."

"Oh, okay. Thank you," Amanda said.

Amanda turned and looked at the TV once more. "Spencer?" she said.

"Yeah?"

"Is it, like, top secret information what all the colors and addresses mean?" she said, smirking.

"Oh gosh, no. So the orange ones are what we call O.O.S. It stands for Occasionally Occupied Structure. When it is occupied, it's orange to represent a high-life hazard. For example, the elementary school has the potential to be a very large problem if something goes wrong at ten in the morning during a school day. But if it's two in the morning, the life safety issue diminishes. At two in the morning, there typically isn't anyone there, except maybe a cleaning person or two."

"So how does..." Amanda paused. "How does ELSA know when to change the color?"

"Well, the schools are a little different because their status really does change a lot. The principal has the ability to access the system and can mark the school as occupied or not. So as a default, it typically turns from orange to light blue after six in the evening, when most of the entire staff has gone home. However, if there is an event at the school at night, say a sports event or something, the principal can mark the school as occupied, and it will stay orange. Every orange location up there isn't as detailed as the school. Most places just remain orange to let the responding units know that there is a potential that it will be empty."

"Got it," Amanda said, still looking at the TV screen. "I'm guessing red is the places they don't even go into?"

"Correct. Those have been marked unoccupied and have the potential to be very hazardous in that they may not be structurally sound anymore. They also have a sign on them from the Fire Marshal's office so the firefighters know not to go inside."

Amanda studied the screen. This was all fascinating to her, and she was truly impressed that she was talking to the person who designed and implemented it all. "Okay, one more question, and then I'll leave you alone."

"It's no trouble. I don't get many visitors."

Amanda smiled, feeling a bit sad for him. She knew what it was like to feel closed off and secluded from the rest of the world. She had felt that way for a long time.

"The maroon addresses. I only see a few of them. What are those?"

"Those are what we call an R.O.S., or Rarely Occupied Structure. They're places that seldom have visitors or occupants. For example, that one there." He pointed to an address on the board. "From the outside, it appears to be a normal house, and I can say it's a very nice house since I live nearby. However, it is a model home for a construction company. There aren't many people building houses now, so ninety percent of the time, no one is there."

Amanda paused. She opened her mouth to say something but closed it again and said nothing. She opened it again and said, "Thanks for the information, Spencer. It was nice to meet you."

"You, too. Have a great day, and if you ever need anything, let me know. I'm here Monday through Friday from eight until four-thirty. Or sometimes until midnight if there is a server problem."

"Good to know," she said with a small smile.

Amanda headed back down the hallway to meet Kelly and finish up her day. They walked around the center, had lunch, and finished Amanda's day a little early, just like Kelly had said. On her way home, Amanda decided to drive past 63 Rudley Street. She was interested in the system Spencer had designed and wanted to see if she could if tell the house was seldom occupied, or if it looked like any other house. Amanda took a few lefts and a few rights and pulled onto a quiet street. She scanned mailboxes until she saw the number that had been on the board in the dispatch center. The number was written in gold letters on the side of a mailbox, in front of a large house at the end of the street. She pulled over and put her car in park. She turned to look out her window and get a better look at the house. Before she could even finish turning her head, her heart started to pound. The stone steps, the maroon front door, the perfectly manicured front lawn with a statue of a lion on the front step. Details came flooding back to her. She knew the house. She knew the steps. She had walked down them, broken, bruised, and barely breathing, what seemed like a lifetime ago. Amanda had just parked in front of the house where she was raped and left for dead.

She put her hands to her face, index fingers against her lips and thumbs under her chin. She exhaled slowly and felt the breath fall through her fingers. She wasn't sure if she wanted to get out and look around, check inside for other bruised and battered women, or just go tell the police. She took another deep breath. She opened her car door and stepped onto the asphalt. She had just started toward the house when a car approached. It slowed down, and she looked out of the corner of her eyes to try and get a look at the driver. It was a middle-aged woman. She continued a moment and then turned her car into a driveway nearby. She exited the vehicle and took a grocery bag out of the front seat. Her other door opened, and a child about eleven years old got out and grabbed a second bag. This was a normal neighborhood. The men who did this to her were literally hiding in plain sight.

The house where Amanda was beaten and raped sat perched atop of beautiful front lawn with a stone wall and beautiful stone steps. It had a decent-sized yard on one side. The other side was a smaller lawn that ended at a well-made wooden fence that divided it from the neighbor's yard. Amanda's stomach turned. A girl who appeared to be about eleven, and her parents, lived just a few hundred feet from where Amanda was held captive for two days. She turned to get back into her car, hoping she wouldn't throw up, as the details of her attack began coming back. She pulled her door open quickly and fell into her seat.

Safely in her car, she locked the doors and turned the key. As she was about to drive away, she saw a car pulling into the driveway of the house. She watched as a girl who looked to be about her age climbed out with cleaning supplies in hand. She carried a small tray with spray bottles in it, along with a steam mop, up the front stairs. A cleaning lady. The pieces of garbage who did this to her had a cleaning service for the house they used to rape and torture women. Amanda wanted to throw up again, but she also wanted to go inside the house. She was incredibly torn, but she had to make sure there wasn't someone inside, left the way she was. She shut off her car and climbed out. She locked the door and held her keys tightly in her hand. As she got closer to the house, she walked slowly and carefully. Doing her best to act naturally, she walked up the stairs and stopped at the front door. She rang the doorbell as if she were visiting a friend on a Sunday afternoon. After a few seconds, the door opened, and she found herself staring at a familiar face.

Chapter 23

Frozen in place, and trying to act normally, Amanda opened her mouth to speak. Before she could say anything, the girl spoke up in a cheerful voice.

"Hi, Amanda. I don't know if you remember me. Samantha, or Sam. I work at the police station."

"I remember," Amanda said. "Do you work here, too?"

"Oh, no," she said casually. "My sister owns the cleaning company, but one of her girls called out sick, so she asked me if I could come clean this place. She said it's an easy clean because no one really lives here. Hopefully, it doesn't take too long."

"Yeah," Amanda said. "I was actually wondering if anyone else was here."

"Just me, well, us now. My sister told me where to find a key and said no one would be here."

Amanda's thoughts raced. Samantha was a young, very pretty girl. And her sister had sent her to clean a house that was used by a group of men who kidnapped and raped young girls. She didn't know how to get her to leave, but she wanted nothing more than to blurt out how much danger she might be in. Unsure if she knew anything about the house or the group of men who owned it, Amanda treaded lightly.

"Come on in," Sam said. "I'm just getting set up and organized."

"How long has your sister been cleaning this place? I don't live very far from here, and I never knew it was here. Seems like a really nice house for no one to live in."

"I guess it's a model house, one that the company shows to people who want to hire them to build them a house. It's supposed to showcase how nice of a house they can build you."

"It is a nice place," Amanda said, trying to sound convincing.

"They pay my sister a ridiculous amount of money to clean it. The guy always tells her she does a great job and that if she ever needs more money, to let him know."

"Is she friends with the guy, or does she only know him from cleaning the house?"

"Just because she cleans," Sam said as she started to spray and wipe down the countertops. "She said she thinks they throw some wild parties here, though. She's come to clean before and found beer bottles, wine glasses, and random clothes on the couches and counters."

Amanda's stomach screwed itself into a ball. Her clothes were scattered across the bedroom in the basement of this house once. She took a breath and tried to keep the conversation going normally.

"Clothes and beer bottles? Sounds like quite the party."

Sam laughed a little. "Right? My sister doesn't ask any questions. She figures what they do here is their business. And the guy who she deals with scares her a little. She says he's almost too nice. Like, creepy nice. But the checks always clear, and he's never been rude or gross with her. He shook her hand once when they met, and she said he's never touched her since. He's always very polite."

Amanda's interest peaked. Sam's sister had met someone who was either directly involved in her attack or who possibly knew someone who was. She took another deep breath. She didn't want to let the conversation stop. She wanted more information.

"So the guy obviously doesn't live here, but your sister has met him? I bet his real house is bigger than this one."

"She met him at a restaurant. Some really nice place. I don't remember the name. Something flower-related."

Amanda's breath stopped short. "The Scarlett Rose?" Amanda offered.

"That's it. She said it was really nice and had amazing food. He bought her dinner when they first talked about her cleaning here."

Amanda's heart raced. The Scarlett Rose. Brian's brother's restaurant. Before she got too upset, the rational and logical side of her seemed to still be present, and she reminded herself that hundreds of people go to the Scarlett Rose, and Dean doesn't necessarily know all of them. She was fighting an internal battle, trying to decide if she wanted to stay here with Sam and look around the house, or if she wanted to go to the police station and tell Sergeant Harding that she knew the address of the house where she was attacked. She was still trying to decide how much she would tell them about what Sam said. She wanted so badly for the police to stop the men who did this to her. But a small, determined flame burned in the bottom corner of her heart that was constantly telling her that she should be the one to bring justice to the men who did this. She had never been a violent person; she didn't even like to watch violent movies. Somehow, however, the flame that had been ignited would seemingly never go away.

"Can you do me a favor?" Sam called out from a downstairs bathroom. Amanda was so deep in thought that she hadn't even noticed her walk away.

"I can. What's up?"

"On the counter is the key. Can you put it back in the lock box out front for me? Otherwise, I'll keep cleaning and lose it. The code is four-eight-nine-four." Sam caught herself too late. "I'm not sure I should have told you that, so, um, keep it a secret, please."

"I will." Amanda picked up the key and walked to the front door. Outside, tucked behind the stone lion, was a little lock box attached to the wall. She pushed the numbers 4-8-9-4. The door sprung open with a click to reveal a small space behind it. As she was about to put the key back, she noticed an engraving on the base of the stone lion. The letters *N.J.R.* were neatly engraved in the rectangular base that surrounded the lion's paws. She wasn't sure what it meant, but she would add it to her list of mental notes. She set the key inside and pushed the door closed. She would bid farewell to Sam. Now that she knew how to get the key, she would come back and have a look around when no one was there. She walked back into the house and found Sam vacuuming the first floor. She waved to get her attention so she wouldn't startle her. Sam shut the vacuum off.

"I'm going to head out. Nice to see you again. Sorry to bother you while you cleaned."

"Not a bother at all. It was nice to have someone to chat with."

"Nice chatting." Amanda smiled.

"Hey, one minute," Sam called out. She walked over to Amanda with her phone in hand. She held the screen up for Amanda to see. "That's my number. Put it in your phone, and maybe next time we hang out, it doesn't have to be with cleaning supplies in tow."

Amanda smiled again. "I'd like that."

She put the number in her phone and bid farewell to Sam again. She was happy to have made another connection. She was feeling more like a normal person every day. Even though her new normal had a small fire growing inside her that wanted to find the men who attacked her and bury them alive.

Chapter 24

The keypad seemed to make a deafening "click" when it sprung open at this hour. When she had put the key back for Sam, it seemed to make no sound at all. Now, however, it sounded like two old, rusty train cars coupling together, or so it seemed. Amanda took the key and slowly walked to the door. She checked to see if it was locked, just in case. There were no vehicles anywhere around and no lights on, so as best she could tell, no one was home. She inserted the key into the lock and turned the handle slowly. The door opened quietly. She had made sure to look for an alarm panel while she had talked to Sam. There wasn't one. She stepped up onto the floor, and it made a slight creak. She slowly shut the door behind her and locked it, then turned on a small flashlight. Walking slowly from room to room, Amanda looked at the entire house. She found herself exploring four bedrooms, three bathrooms, a kitchen, a dining room, an office, and a library/den type of room. All of them looked as she supposed they should, like a museum or showcase. The beds were neatly made; the counters were cleaned and not cluttered. The bathrooms had cool tile floors and glass-door showers. She had been around the entire house, except the basement. Amanda walked to the basement door and opened it slowly.

She started to feel a tightness in her chest as she stood at the top of the stairs she had once walked up, barely alive. Taking slow and quiet breaths, she descended the stairs. She got to the bottom and turned left. She stood face to face with the door that she had once been locked behind. She tried the knob. It was locked. She still held the key to the front door and wondered if it was the same. She inserted the key and tried to turn it. Nothing. She removed the key and turned around. There was another door to the right. A sign on the door said *Office.* She grabbed the knob and turned slowly. It was unlocked. She entered the room and shone the flashlight around. She looked for windows and didn't see any, so she looked for a light switch. Her fingers found one and flipped it up. The room brightened. The newly cast light revealed two desks with computers at each one. Leather rolling chairs sat neatly in front of each desk. A few filing cabinets dotted the room, and a small table sat close to the corner, with two chairs tucked underneath. The carpet was a light blue color and quite comfortable. The walls were a slightly darker shade of blue, and the room smelled like warm honey and brown sugar. She was standing in a beautiful room in the basement of a gorgeous house, and right across the hall was a room where unthinkably brutal and ugly things happened. She shook her head and tried to stay focused.

She crossed to one desk and opened a few drawers. There was nothing very interesting inside. Pens and pencils, a ruler, some small note pads. Typical office stuff. She continued her search with the next desk. This time she found something slightly more interesting: a bottle of scotch and a pair of decorative high-ball glasses. She was careful not to touch the bottle or the glasses with her bare hands. They were neatly wiped clean, and she didn't want to leave a fingerprint or smudge that could be easily noticed. She moved on to the filing cabinet. Amanda pulled open the top drawer and looked inside.

In the very back of the drawer was a large envelope tucked inside a black folder. She carefully took the envelope out and unwound the string that held it closed. She carefully pulled out the contents, making sure she kept them in the same order she had found them. The first page was a handwritten note that said something nonsensical. *Follow ups, lunch orders, and bills to pay. One at a time. Thanks, Ben.* She set the first page on the table, face down. The second page was a picture of a sign from what seemed to be a restaurant called Marty's. The next page stopped Amanda's page turning and made her heart race. It was a picture of Dave. Across the front, in large, black letters, it said, "WEEKLY-$2,000." Amanda set it aside. The next page was even worse, and as Amanda focused on it, she felt her stomach heave and her spine tingle. It was a picture of a woman, naked and lying on a bed. A man was kneeling in front of her. The large black letters cut across her face. "MONTHLY-DON'T GET GREEDY."

Amanda turned another page. There were pictures and documents, all seeming to be about people and money.

Restaurant names that she recognized and pictures taken in familiar places around the city. Amanda was flipping through pages, being careful to keep them in the correct order. She was just about finished with the stack when she came to a page that stole the air from the middle of her breath. It was a picture of her. A picture that was from what seemed like a lifetime ago. It was a picture of her leaving Dave's bar after work one night. Amanda's stomach turned again. She was studying the picture, trying to figure out if it was taken the night she was attacked or not. She scanned the picture for details. It was a few nights before her attack. She had bought a new purse the day she was attacked, but she was carrying her old one in the picture. She continued to scan, her eyes feverishly searching for clues. Large black letters again cut across the top of the picture. One word written in big block letters. "DAUGHTER."

Amanda tried to gather her thoughts. Her heart was racing as it was, but now the confusion of the two pictures had made it worse. The picture of Dave had a monetary amount across the top. Her picture was labeled daughter, presumably because they thought she was Dave's daughter. She presumed she was attacked because Dave owed someone money. Her heart pounded in her chest, and her eyes stung with the beginnings of tears. They collected two thousand dollars a week from him, or tried. She assumed that when he couldn't pay, they resorted to making him suffer in other ways by taking who they thought was his daughter.

"You son of a bitch," she whispered to herself. "You useless son of a bitch," she said again, staring at the picture of Dave. She set out the picture of herself and the picture of him, being careful not to lose their place in the stack. She took a picture of each one with her cell phone and put them neatly back where she found them within the rest of the documents and pictures.

As she tuned to leave, she caught her shoe on something. It was a small metal ring, recessed into the floor. One of the screws on the plate that held it to the floor was partially out, and her foot had caught it. She reached down and touched the ring. It raised easily out of its recess in the floor. Amanda pulled on it and felt it move slightly. She pulled a few more times but to no avail. She tried pulling again. Nothing. She could now see the outline of the panel, though, and she knew something was below her. She grabbed the ring and tried to twist it. After a few seconds, and a lot of effort, there was a loud click. Amanda pulled gently, and the panel in the floor now moved. She stood to the side and pulled the panel up slowly.

Underneath was a vault of some sort. It was rectangular in shape and about six feet deep, and from the best Amanda could tell, it was maybe ten feet wide. She turned on her flashlight and peered into the hole in the floor. Inside the vault, beneath the floor of the house where she was raped, were three things. A stack of guns, four pairs of women's underwear set neatly on a small crate, and a pile of money that would fill a hot tub. Amanda closed the hatch and turned the metal ring. She made sure the room was as she had found it and left. She climbed the stairs slowly, determined more than ever to find who did this to her. She had felt herself change over that course of rebuilding her life. She was a little harder than before, but she supposed that was to be expected. But she also kept feeding that small fire inside her that was burning to get revenge on the people responsible for her attack.

She opened the door slowly and clicked on her flashlight. The house was still quiet. She walked slowly to the door, peered out the glass side-light window briefly, and opened it once she knew there was no danger lurking outside. She locked the door behind her, placed the key back in the lock box, and hurried to her car. Her hands were sweating, and her heart hadn't stopped pounding since she had gotten there. Safely in her car, she started the engine, took two deep breaths, and drove home. On the ride, she remembered her father had gone to see Dave. He has said it was just to visit him, but then he had ended up being chased and shot soon after. Her father knew. He must have found out something and then convinced Dave to tell him. Amanda was headed home to a very uncomfortable but very necessary conversation with her father. She parked in front of her house, headed inside, and told her father to get comfortable, as they had a lot to talk about.

John had never had a more difficult conversation. He had no earthly idea how or where to begin. Telling Amanda that her mother had died had been the hardest conversation he had ever had to have with her. Until now, that is. He drew in a deep breath and let it out as slowly as possible, seemingly trying to delay the dialogue as much as he could. He knew it was inevitable, and he also knew that after all Amanda had been through, she deserved the truth.

"Okay, honey," he began, rubbing his face slowly with both hands. "Where do you want me to start?"

"How long has Dave been mixed up with…" She paused, unsure of how to describe them. "With people like that," she said, not finding a better word to use.

"A long time, unfortunately. I always hoped that he'd grow out of it, but he never did."

"When you went to see him, you knew something, didn't you?"

"Yes," he said slowly, drawing in another long breath. He explained Dave's past a little more and then told her what had happened when he went to visit.

"When I heard you telling June about the gun, I knew. It was a perfect description of a gun I knew he had and would never part with willingly. My mind raced for an explanation, desperately hoping I was wrong. I wasn't."

"Did he tell you that he owes people money?"

"Yes, not that he needed to. He's owed people money since we were younger than you. I wasn't surprised, but I was angry that he never told me. I figured that's where the gun came into play. He's owed people for so long that he's lost countless possessions over the years to the debt collectors. Guns, watches and jewelry, drugs, booze, and he even had a car taken."

John recalled his most recent conversation with Dave, when Dave had told him they had taken his Corvette. He shook his head and sighed.

"Two cars, actually. We may be a lot older now, but the story with Dave will always be the same. He's owed before, he owes now, and, sadly, he'll owe again."

"Did he say who it was?"

John Killingly pondered the question. He didn't want to tell her that he had looked straight at one of the men connected to her attack. He was worried she'd do something foolish that would land her in a situation just as bad as the one she was still recovering from. He didn't want to tell her, but he didn't want to lie to her, either. He nodded slowly and said, "He did. One of them came to the bar while I was there."

Amanda's expression fell blank for a moment. She opened her mouth, but no sound came out. She opened it again and managed to blow out a long breath. After her initial shock had somewhat subsided, she asked, "Came for what?"

John continued and told her what had happened at the bar. It was a long conversation for sure, but one that gave Amanda a small sense of relief. It certainly didn't change the fact that she hated Dave, especially since now she had determined he was responsible for her kidnap and rape as well as her father being run off the road and shot. John looked at the floor when Amanda talked about the night she was raped. It was impossible to hear, even after this much time had passed. She was his little girl and would be forever. Hearing such brutal details about what had happened to her made his eyes fill with tears and his stomach churn. But Amanda needed to talk about it and help herself process through what had happened the night John went to visit Dave. A man who was supposed to be her father's closest friend had let something so awful happen to her. The more Amanda uncovered, the more it seemed that he not only let it happen to her, but he was also partly responsible for her attack. Their conversation took hours, and by the end, they had both cried, punched a pillow on the couch, hugged each other tightly, and even laughed a little during their last hug, when John made a joke about Amanda getting snot on his clean shirt.

"That's the whole story?" Amanda asked.

"That's it," John said. "That's the whole story."

Amanda sighed. "Okay, Dad. Thanks for telling me, and sorry about the snot on your shirt." John smiled. She was thankful he hadn't asked what sparked her inquiry about the night he visited Dave.

"You're welcome, honey. Just promise me you won't do something crazy?"

"Dad, I'm not an action hero. I'm me. Your little Amanda."

"That's not really a promise," John said, smirking. "But I guess it will have to do. Goodnight, honey."

"Goodnight, Dad. I love you very much."

Chapter 25

The second most difficult conversation of Amanda's life kind of brought itself up one night after an incredibly romantic dinner date and a movie back at Brian's house. They had become distracted from the movie with something far more fun and exciting. As things progressed, she started to feel anxious and pulled away in the middle of a kiss. She wanted desperately to be intimate with him, but as awkward and uncomfortable as it was, sex was going to have to be preceded by a lengthy and difficult conversation.

She knew it would ruin the mood, but she needed to explain why she had just shown all the signs of being interested in taking him to bed and then, in an instant, gone completely cold as small snippets of the night she was attacked flashed through her mind. Instead of being mad, he put his shirt back on and walked her to the couch in the living room. He sat next to her and told her she was safe and could tell him anything. Her story started slowly, and she tried to limit some of the details. After a few minutes, though, the details couldn't be stopped. If he was upset, he never showed it. He sat silently, looking at her and listening intently. When tears started to form in her eyes and gently slide down her cheeks, he silently dabbed them with a tissue that he seemingly produced out of thin air. She stopped briefly a few times to take deep breaths and another handful of times to quietly cry. He never interrupted her, and the only words he spoke were to tell her that she didn't need to continue if it was too difficult. She pressed on and finished the story, ending it with being dropped off at home by the woman she didn't know but took a chance on and asked for a ride. When she was done speaking, she collapsed in a sobbing heap against him. He wrapped two strong arms around her, pulled her close, and let her cry. It had been ages since she had thought of so many details of that night, and to say it was an emotional story to tell was an understatement. After what seemed like an hour of trying to pull herself together, she leaned back from his embrace and looked at him.

"Still want to be my boyfriend?"

"More than words can even say. I just wish I could do something to help take away the pain and the memories of that night for you."

"Thanks," she managed. "I'm okay. I promise. It's been a very long time since I relived all those details at once. I'll never forget what happened, but I had managed to keep the memories to small flashes here and there on occasion. Telling the whole story was tough."

He started to apologize, but she interrupted.

302

"And don't apologize. I know you're about to. It was my choice to tell you, and I knew that it would be difficult. But I needed you to know." She took in a long breath and held it briefly. She let it out in a long sigh and managed a small laugh as she said, "Do I know how to ruin the mood or what? Still like me?"

"I love you," he said meaningfully.

The words washed over her like a warm shower on a frigid afternoon. She lifted her eyes to meet his and stared at him, her eyes glistening.

"I love you, Amanda." He repeated the phrase and took her hands in his.

Her heart leapt into her throat. She was caught off guard by the comment, but in the same instant, she was the happiest she had ever been. She had incredibly deep feelings for him but had been worried that one day she'd have to tell him her story, and he'd turn tail and run in the opposite direction. For that reason, she hadn't let on how strong her feelings were. The day had come, and she had revealed her darkest secret from the past. She was ready for him to find a reason to break things off and run away from the broken and jaded girl she had revealed. Instead, however, he listened to every word of her story and responded not by running but by saying those three wonderful words. As he said them, she was overwhelmed with the feeling that there was nothing he wouldn't do to protect her and make her feel safe, no matter the risk or consequence. She composed her thoughts, took one more deep breath, and leaned in to kiss him deeply. After a moment, she pulled away slightly, took his face in her hands, and softly said, "I love you, too."

She stayed with him that night, but he jokingly told her he was going to lay down some very strict rules. He did it in a jovial and slightly melodramatic manner as not to make her upset, but he needed her to know what the last thing he wanted was her to think that he said he loved her in an effort to get her to have sex with him.

"Okay now," he started, holding up both hands and cocking his head slightly. "I had a lovely time tonight, but don't go thinking I'm one of those guys who gets all mushy after a great night and can be taken advantage of. I'm a nice boy with high morals, and I live to make my mother proud. We can share a bed, but any attempts at funny business, and I'll be sleeping on the floor."

His smile shone through his weak attempt at formality. She smiled back, loving him even more for finding a lighthearted way to make sure she knew that he had no expectations of what had become the societal norm when two young people that were dating shared a bed. After that night, Amanda felt free to express herself with him and allowed herself to fall deeply in love. She felt safe, loved, trusted, and free to be herself with him. The feeling was absolutely freeing. Her emotions had been a twisted and mangled mess for so long. Her relationship with Brian had allowed the tangled knot of feelings to slowly unwind, and she felt as if he had breathed new life into her.

Sometimes Amanda had to take a step back and convince herself that this was actually her life. Not so long ago, she had felt like a fragile shell of her former self, ready to break at any minute. With time and the support of good family and friends, though, she had grown into a renewed version of herself. A version that she was very happy with. She was dating the most wonderful man she had ever known, working full-time, and loving her job. She still had dinner every week with June, and she had dinner with her father (and usually June, too) at least once a month. Occasionally, she had to give herself a reality check, just to make sure she wasn't dreaming.

As good as things were, there was just one small piece of the puzzle that was missing. So much time had passed, and the men who attacked and raped her had still never been brought to justice. The two men that Sergeant Harding arrested for shooting her father were in jail, which was a good thing, but Harding had said that they didn't give up much information in regard to the other members of the ivy vine group. Amanda, however, had not forgotten about the information she found that night in the house on Rudley Street. As a matter of fact, she had been gaining information little-by-little as time had gone on. If her father taught her anything, it was that patience was as valuable as it was necessary. She remembered him telling her that you don't pull on the fishing pole as soon as you see it wobble. You give it a minute, have patience, and then set the hook. So Amanda had been patient. She had gathered small pieces of information here and there. She had linked the pieces of a very large and intricate puzzle together and started to form what she had once thought was only an idea for revenge.

She called Sam on a somewhat regular basis, and they went out for lunches and dinners and caught each other up on whatever gossip and news they had to share. Through her friendship with Sam, she had managed to have her invite her sister along to a dinner one night. This afforded Amanda the opportunity to ask her questions about her cleaning business and very subtly get the name of the man who owned the house she cleaned, where Amanda was attacked. She had been back to Antonio's several times with June and got Darcy to chat a little bit here and there about the folk who visited her restaurant, and what her husband, Sergeant Harding, was working on at the police station. Her trips to The Scarlett Rose afforded her the opportunity to speak with Dean about customers he may know who had a lot of power or influence in the community. They say knowledge is power. Slowly, and consistently, Amanda's power was growing.

Chapter 26

Amanda opened the windows, infusing the living room with clean and beautiful air. Hoping to clear her mind, she had busied herself all morning with cleaning the house. As she was vacuuming, she knocked a book off the bookshelf in the hallway. As she reached down to pick it up, she froze. She bent slowly and gently picked the book up off the floor, transfixed on the front cover. An ivy vine wrapped around the spine, winding its way up the cover. Inside the first page was an inscription:

Best of luck, you two. Love, Nel.

She read the title, looked at the author's name, and, in that instant, she felt as if the floor had fallen out from beneath her. Rudley. The words seemed to take forever to read aloud to herself. She reread them slowly and deliberately. Nelson. James. Rudley. N. J. R. The house where she was attacked was on Rudley Street, and the base of the lion was engraved with what she now knew to be the initials N.J.R. She pulled her phone out as quickly as she could. She searched for Nelson James Rudley, a well-known author from years ago. He was from an in-between generation, as she thought of it. Older than her parents but younger than her grandparents. He had written dozens of books, all of which did quite well and made him a hefty sum of money. He had three children, two girls and a boy. It was amazing what you could find online with a simple search. His wife passed away when she was very young and left his children to be raised by the dedicated but somewhat eccentric writer. Amanda kept reading. His daughters had also become quite well known in the world of literature. The oldest owned a publishing company, and she and her younger sister published textbooks for high school- and college-level subjects.

When Nelson was middle-aged, friends of his had him committed, as they said his writing had become his reality and he was slowly losing his mind. His youngest child, a boy, seemed to have suffered the most from his father's committal. Younger than his sisters by a handful of years, he was left behind when they got older and moved on to college. He was in and out of trouble, or so the article said, and he barely finished high school and never went to college, until much later in his life. Amanda was starting to feel bad for him, the outcast child whose family left him behind. Her empathy disappeared as she read the next few sentences. His son was Benjamin Rudley. He owned a construction company and the house where Amanda was raped.

She took the book and clung to it. She needed to know who it had been signed for. If it was a book her father had found at a tag sale...fine, just a random coincidence. But if her mother and father had known him, that added a whole new dynamic to her pursuit for answers. She dialed her father and anxiously awaited his answer.

"Hey, honey, what's up?"

"Hi, Dad. Quick question." Before he could answer, she continued. "There is a book on the downstairs book case, with a big ivy vine on the front. There is a note inside the front cover from someone named Nel. Is that note to you and Mom, or did you buy the book at a tag sale or something?"

"It was a gift from a friend of ours. His name is Michael. He gave it to us as a wedding present. He was friends with the author and his family. He had it signed for us."

"Michael what?" she asked pointedly.

"Michael Flaherty. Why, honey? What's wrong?"

Amanda needed to cover herself. Her father had no idea she had been to the house and knew so much about the men behind her attack.

"Oh, I just knocked it off the shelf while I was vacuuming, and I saw it was signed. I guess I had just never seen it before."

"Oh, okay."

"Thanks, Dad."

"You're welcome, honey. Bye."

"Bye, Dad."

Her head was swirling. She took to her phone again to search. She typed in *Michael Flaherty, Claiborne.*

There were a lot of Michael Flaherty's in Claiborne, but one in particular stood out. He was about the same age as her father, and there was a picture of him with Nelson Rudley.

She couldn't help but think Michael looked familiar. She figured she just wanted him to look familiar so she could have a connection and help herself feel better about things. She kept reading article after article on Michael Flaherty. He seemed to be very involved in the community still, and she wondered if he would be as easy to find in person as he was to find online. She was reading an article about the construction of a new playground for one of the schools in the city when she froze. Her hands instantly felt cold, and her mouth suddenly felt as if she had tried to swallow an entire mouthful of stale cereal. Halfway through the article, there was a picture, set alone in the center of the page. It stood out glaringly, like fresh blood on a crisp, white pillow case. She felt her stomach lurch, and then she found herself not breathing and gasped violently. In the background of the picture, standing quiet and stoic, was a fire truck. Claiborne ladder four. In the foreground, standing next to Michael Flaherty was Brian Whiting.

Chapter 27

During dinner at The Scarlett Rose that night, Amanda realized she had her father, June, and Brian all in the same spot. She needed them to tell her more about Michael Flaherty, somewhere they couldn't change their story. She wasn't worried about Brian's story, but her father and June seemed to have a way to only share details they thought were safe for Amanda to know. And she wanted answers.

"Dad?" Amanda said when there was a lull in the conversation. "After I found that book today, I looked up Michael Flaherty."

She glanced around to see if anyone's facial expression shifted to one of slight discomfort or nervousness. Everyone seemed fairly normal.

"Oh yeah? What's Michael up to these days?"

Before Amanda could continue, Brian spoke up.

"Michael Flaherty? Any chance it's the same one who helped build the school playground a handful of years ago?"

"That's him," Amanda said, watching Brian's facial expression closely.

"I didn't realize you knew him. Small world," Brian said casually.

"Small world for sure," John said. "Michael was at our wedding. He's a great man. I'm sure June remembers him."

"Of course, I remember him well. He spent most of the night of your wedding helping all the drunken fools either find a cab or another ride. I think he even brought some of them home himself and then came back to the wedding."

"Yes, he did."

"Have you talked to him lately?" June asked.

"Oh, Jesus, it's been years. I couldn't even tell you the last time I talked to him. I don't even know if I owned the farm then."

"I saw him two weeks ago," Whiting interjected. "He's doing well."

Amanda felt her face getting hot.

"How do you know him?" Amanda asked.

"He's the Chaplin at the firehouse. We see him every few months or when, God forbid, we have an accident and one of our people gets hurt, or worse."

"Dad?" Amanda posed another question to keep the information coming.

"Yeah, honey?" he said, chewing happily.

"How did you meet him, and how did he know the author of that book he gave you?"

312

Amanda was mad at herself as soon as the question left her mouth. Brian was going to ask about the book, and once he saw the picture on the cover, she imagined he would put things together and figure out that she knows more than everyone thinks.

"Mason's Bridge," June said. "That was the first time we met him, right, John?"

"Oh yeah." John took a breath. He swallowed a bite of food and casually said, "Yes, it is."

"What happened on Mason's Bridge?" Amanda asked as calmly as she could manage.

"There was a young girl who was going to jump," June started. She stared off toward the corner of the room as if replaying the scene in her head. "We were behind her in traffic. She was going a little slow over the bridge, and all of a sudden, she stopped. We just figured she was stopping to take a picture. The water looked nice in the setting sun."

She looked to John, who nodded in agreement while happily chewing another bite of food.

"She got out of her car, stepped onto the curb, and climbed over the railing. The car behind us was Michael. He came running. He was to her before the rest of us could even get out of our cars. He ran to the girl and tried talking to her. We couldn't hear what he was saying because of the wind and the traffic noise on the bridge. She was holding onto something, a piece of paper or a picture, maybe. Michael tried talking to her and reached his hand out for her, but before you know it, she disappeared over the side. Michael leaned over the railing to look, but it was too late. He came walking back toward us and asked if we were okay, and if we knew who the girl was. We said we didn't and just happened to be behind her in traffic. He asked if we saw what she was holding."

Amanda found it all too coincidental that a young girl had jumped to her death, and Michael had been the last one to talk to her. She was also suspicious of how interested he seemed to be in whether or not her father and June had heard their conversation or seen what she was holding.

The dinner conversation continued, but Amanda stopped participating around the time she started to mentally build a chart of names and relationships in her head. She climbed into Brian's truck after hugging her father and June goodbye. As he drove home, he asked, "Are you okay, babe?"

"Hmm?" Amanda said, distracted.

"Are you okay? You got quiet halfway through dinner."

"Oh, yeah, I'm fine. Just missing my mom after talking about her. I'll be okay."

"Okay," he said, grabbing her hand with his. She looked at him, smiled, and went back to staring out the window. She had indeed been missing her mother. However, more importantly, she was contemplating how she would discreetly get answers from a man who happened to visit the firehouse on a regular basis.

Chapter 28

Amanda dialed a number she had found on the city of Claiborne's website. She was going to be direct and to the point.

"Hello?" a pleasant voice said on the other end of the phone.

"Could I speak with Michael Flaherty, please," Amanda said plainly.

"This is Michael."

"Hi, Michael, I'm the daughter of an old friend of yours, and I was wondering if you could answer a few questions for me?"

"Well, I can certainly try," he said happily. "Ask away."

"Actually, I was hoping we could talk in person."

"Oh, okay. Did you have a place and time in mind?"

"How about right now?"

There was a pregnant pause before he continued. "Oh, um, I think I can do that. Let me look at a calendar. Now should work. Where would you like to meet me?" he asked pleasantly.

"How about the café next to the train station?"

"Sounds great. I'm only about ten minutes from there, so I'll see you shortly. By the way, could I know whom I'm meeting?"

"The daughter of an old friend. Let's leave it at that."

"So mysterious." His quiet chuckle did well to mask the fact that he knew exactly who he was speaking to.

"See you soon, Michael."

Amanda hung up the phone. Her hands were shaking. She took a knife from the drawer next to the bed. She was going to be in a café and in plain sight, so she hoped she wouldn't need it. She figured that she was going to feel silly when she walked in and saw this kind old man sitting and waiting for her. Nonetheless, she kept her guard up and reminded herself that, friend of her father's or not, he was still connected to the Rudley family in some way.

She turned her car off and checked her back pocket. The knife was still there. She got out of her car, focused on the doorway, and wondered if Michael was inside yet. Before she was ten steps from her car, a kind yet untrustworthy-sounding voice stopped her where she stood.

"Hello, Amanda." His voice dripped with eagerness for her to turn around and be surprised. And she certainly was. She tuned slowly and found herself staring at a man standing at about five-foot-ten, with a medium build. His eyes were a happy blue color but seemed so cold and

316

distant when she looked into them. He wore a black shirt and khaki pants. He was very neatly dressed, and his thick, silver hair was combed in a precise line, sweeping across his forehead. Amanda had no idea how he knew her name. She had never given it over the phone, and she had blocked her number when she called.

"Amanda?" she said, testing whether he was bluffing.

"It's been quite a long time," he said, taking a step toward her from behind a row of parked cars.

"Do I know you?" Amanda asked.

"You don't remember me?"

Remembering the knife in her pocket and the fact that there were dozens of people in the parking lot, she stood her ground.

"Why would I remember you?"

"I used to visit you at the bar. Every so often, I'd sit on the stools and pretend to be drunk and lonely. Part of it was true. I was lonely. I've been lonely since the love of my life died."

Amanda swallowed a gasp. That's why he had looked familiar in the pictures online. His hair was gray now and his skin more weathered and worn than it was in the long-ago pictures, but it was definitely him. He used to come into the bar. Amanda's head was reeling.

"Oh yes, I remember now," she said, trying to stay calm.

"I suppose we don't need any introductions, but I'm going to stand on principle. I'm Michael Flaherty."

"Charmed," Amanda said coldly. "You visited the bar quite a bit."

"At my house, there is no pretty bartender to look at. And you see, Amanda..." He paused, looking at the ground for a brief moment before continuing. "When the person you love most dies, it's very painful. But even more painful was watching her marry someone else when she was still young, vibrant, and alive."

Amanda wanted to tell him to shut up and get over it. "So that's the reason you came to the bar? Because I'm pretty and you were upset that you loved someone who married someone else? Sounds rough," she said unsympathetically.

He took a step toward her again. His voice was calm but brimmed with emotion. His eyes glistened as he spoke, yet he still seemed cold and disconnected. He spoke as though he didn't require another person present to have a conversation. Almost as if she wasn't there, he would still carry on with his monologue.

"That's not the only reason. You see, Amanda, more important than beauty is your unbelievable resemblance to the woman I loved."

"I see," Amanda said. "Maybe you just hoped I looked like her since I was the one listening to your sad stories behind the bar."

A hint of annoyance crept into his voice. "Oh, no, my dear. You look just like her. You could pass for her younger sister. And rightfully so. She did give birth to you, after all."

The comment hit Amanda like a backhand slap to the cheek bone. She heard her heart pounding in her ears. She glanced around quickly to make sure there were still people around.

"That's right," he said slowly, an eager satisfaction rising in his voice. "It's all coming together now, isn't it? Your mother was the most beautiful woman who ever lived. I loved her with all my heart. I told her time and time again, but still she married your father. Tall and strong, but an intellectual midget compared to myself. What she saw in plain old John Killingly, I'll never know."

Amanda was desperately struggling with whether to leave or keep listening. She needed the information, but she was starting to get the feeling that Michael Flaherty wasn't concerned with being reported or turned in. After all, he hadn't done anything wrong yet.

"So you loved my mom. Me, too. And it sucks that she died. I get that, too. But maybe it's time to move on."

"Move on?" His voice raised slightly for the first time in a cagey annoyance. "Just up and forget about the woman of my dreams?" His eyes glistened, and his voice shook as he continued. "Forget her angelic face and full, pink lips. And how I longed to feel her touch and taste her kiss. To feel her naked body pressed against mine. But never did. And I never will."

Amanda shifted her weight. She was slightly worried about her well-being, but she was also not about to stand there silently while he fantasized about her mother that way.

"Okay, enough. I'm sure there are lots of nice ladies that you can..." She stopped and chose her words carefully. "Be with."

"Oh, I've tried. Believe me, dear. I've tried. No woman I've found compares to what I imagined your mother would be. I've spent years trying. So many women. Dozens. So many disappointments. Some were willing to be with me. Some not so willing. But the not-so-willing ones just needed a little convincing. You took a lot of convincing. You kicked, screamed, and fought so hard. You have your mother's spirit."

The words seemed to suck the air out of her lungs. Amanda felt like she was going to throw up all over the parking lot as what he was saying sunk in.

"Judging by the pale look on your face, you're putting this all together very quickly. You see, there was only one problem with the night we were together."

"One problem?" Amanda started. "You kidnapped, beat, and raped me, you sick fuck."

He snapped back at her. "That's enough name calling, Amanda." His voice was cool but still speckled with annoyance. "See, the problem was that after I had you, after I held onto your breasts firmly and pushed every inch of myself inside you, I wanted to be the last one who would ever do that to you."

His face turned to a half grin, and he closed his eyes as if he were reliving the moment. He continued talking, his eyes still closed.

"I told Benjamin to make sure you were dead after I was done. That way I would be the last one to ever be inside you. The one you would remember forever."

He opened his eyes. His smile vanished. "But apparently, Benjamin and the poor pathetic losers who work for him just don't have the stomach for killing. Kidnapping and beating you, they handled well enough. And they managed to get it up long enough to rape you, too. But they just couldn't bring themselves to kill you. So they left you there and told me you were dead. Yet here you are!" His voice grew louder with the same annoyed tone, now pulsing with frustration. "In all your beautiful glory."

Amanda took a step back toward her car. She needed to leave before he came any closer, but she had changed from scared and disgusted to outraged and hungry for vengeance.

"Leaving so soon?" Michael said, smiling.

"Get the fuck away from me," she said, loud enough to attract just enough attention.

"Shhh, Amanda. Don't raise your voice. People might get the wrong idea and think that you and I are fighting."

Amanda opened her car door. "You put me through hell, you self-righteous piece of shit. Be prepared to go even deeper into hell than you dragged me."

"I'll look forward to it. I'd go anywhere with you."

He turned slowly and began to walk away, calling over his shoulder, "See you soon, my love." After a few steps, he stopped. "Oh, Amanda? One more thing. I know where you live, and where June lives, and where Brian lives. So maybe you should think of which one of them to warn first. Just in case I come knocking."

Amanda started her car and closed and locked the doors. She put the car in gear, stomped the accelerator into the floor mat, and headed out of the parking lot. Her choices now were no good no matter which way she looked at it. She called June first. Brian was at work, so he was safe for the time being. A firehouse full of people who were all like family to Brian was as safe a place to be as any.

"Hey, honey," June answered happily.

"June. You need to go to Dad's house. The farm, June. Go to the farm right now, please."

"Amanda, what's wrong?"

"June, please. Get your keys, pack a bag quickly, and just leave. Michael Flaherty is connected to the people who kidnapped me."

"Oh, Amanda, I'm sure things are just out of sorts and seem strange because of all the random connections between Michael and the book and your parent's wedding. Michael is a good man."

"June!" she hollered, unable to keep the anger out of her voice. "For God's sake, listen to me. Michael raped me. And just told me that he did. Face to face. Get to my father's house, please. Now, June."

"Amanda. There is no way that Michael—"

Amanda cut her off. "Damnit, June!" She didn't want to yell at her, as she was the closest thing Amanda had to a mother, but she was growing tired of no one believing her. "He just confessed that he was in love with my mother. And that she married Dad, and so he hated Dad. He told me that I looked just like Mom, and since he couldn't have her, he had me instead. He raped me, June. If you value our friendship at all, please trust me and get to my father's house. As far as I know, Michael doesn't know where Dad lives. But he knows where I live, and where you live, and where Brian lives."

"Okay, honey," June stammered in disbelief. The severity of the situation was finally sinking in, and she began to walk briskly from room to room, gathering things and throwing them in a bag. "Okay, honey, I'm going."

"Thank you. I'll call Dad and tell him you're on your way. Please call me so I know you're there safely."

"Okay, honey. But, Amanda, where are you going?"

"I'm going to meet Brian at the firehouse and tell him."

"Okay. Are you two coming, too?"

"I hope Brian will listen and go to the farm."

"Okay, honey, be careful."

Amanda hung up the phone and took a deep breath. She was almost to the firehouse. She checked her rear-view mirror. No one seemed to be following her, which was a good thing. She turned into the firehouse, parked haphazardly between two lines, and jumped out of her car. The overhead door to the firehouse was open, and she walked in quickly. A few familiar faces greeted her.

"Hey, guys, is Brian around?"

"Yeah, he's in with the chief, but they're just talking about call volume and maybe replacing a truck. You can knock."

"You okay, sweetie?" one of the female firefighters asked as she put her hand on Amanda's shoulder.

"Yeah, I'm okay. Just a bad day."

"I'll knock for you. Wait here."

The girl crossed over to a wooden door with frosted glass on top. She knocked twice, waited a brief moment, and then entered. She said something Amanda couldn't hear, and a few seconds later, Brian appeared.

"Hey, babe. What's up?"

"You need to come with me to the farm," she said in a low murmur.

"Why? What happened? Is Dad okay?"

"Yes, he's fine, but someone threatened me, you, and June. As far as I know, he doesn't know where Dad lives. Please. Tell your chief you have to go. Use a vacation day. Something."

"Whoa, deep breath. We are in a very safe place right now. And who threatened you?"

"That's not important. Please. Just come with me."

"Not important? Amanda, please tell me what is going on."

Amanda pulled him aside and moved between two of the trucks to gain a little extra privacy. "Brian. Please," she pleaded.

Whiting took a deep breath. "Okay. We'll go to your Dad's. But if, and only if, you tell me what is going on so we can call the police."

"Fine. I'll tell you on the way. Please, Brian, we're wasting time."

Whiting sighed heavily. "Wait here."

He crossed back over and walked into the chief's office. After a moment, he appeared at the doorway.

"Thanks, Chief," he called as he started walking toward Amanda.

She grabbed his arm and pulled him toward the door.

"Whoa, hang on, Amanda. I need to tell the guys I'm leaving and grab my keys and stuff from my locker."

"Okay, sorry," she said, doing her best not to sound frantic, annoyed, or to scream at him that his locker could wait.

Whiting talked to the other officers on shift for a minute and headed to his locker to get his keys and his bag. As he was walking out of the locker room, Amanda's phone beeped. She quickly pulled it out of her pocket and typed feverishly, her thumbs punching her phone screen. "Okay, June is safe," she said aloud.

"Amanda, you've got to start explaining. You're starting to worry me."

"I will. Just...please, let's get going first."

"Are we taking my truck, your car, or both?"

"Both, I think. I was going to leave my car here, but I don't want them to do anything to it while I'm gone."

"Who? Amanda, you need to start explaining."

"I will. I promise. Both vehicles for now. Let's go, straight to my Dad's, no stopping, okay?"

"Okay." Brian sighed, trying to be patient.

They each got into their vehicles and headed toward the farm. Once they were all there and all together, she would explain. The drive was a blur to Amanda. Typically, she loved looking at the houses, the open fields, and the beautifully upkept barns as they got closer to her father's house. Today, however, after meeting the man who planned her kidnap, rape, and attempted murder, the ride seemed to all fade together. Before she knew it, she was pulling into her father's driveway.

She found June and her father sitting on the front porch when she and Brian pulled in. She got out of her car, looked around suspiciously, and crossed over to the porch. She didn't even wait for Brian.

"Hey, kiddo," John said, standing to give her a hug. "You okay? Have a seat, and let's all hear what's going on and why we are all here, sitting on my front porch. Not that I'm not excited for the company, but you've got me a little worried."

"I don't even know where to start," Amanda said, somewhat thinking aloud. She didn't want to tell them everything. She needed to keep the house a secret, and the fact that she knew where the key was, and the pictures in the basement office. She'd start with Michael.

"I made a phone call to meet up with someone because I had a few questions about how he might fit into our lives."

"You called Michael," John said plainly.

"Yes. I did. And I made arrangements to meet him at a café."

"Amanda, you could have talked to him at the firehouse anytime. All you had to do was ask," Brian said.

"Yeah, I figured you'd say that. But I wanted him to be himself and not feel like he had to tailor his answers given his surroundings."

"Okay, so you met Michael at a café, and I'm guessing he bought you coffee and talked about how he knew Mom and I, right?" John asked.

"Oh, he talked about you and Mom, all right," she said sarcastically. "And he never bought me coffee. We never made it inside the café. He was waiting in the parking lot and stopped me before I was fifteen feet from my car."

"He probably just wanted to walk you to the door, babe. He's just that kind of a guy. He always walks the female firefighters and paramedics out to their cars if he's at the firehouse at the end of a shift." Brian said.

"And if he said something that sounded strange, honey, it's probably just his sense of humor," June added.

They weren't getting it. Amada could feel her frustration building. They all thought he was this great guy. No one knew what he had done or what he was capable of. Her father, Brian, and June kept talking at her. Telling her that Michael was a great guy and how he is always helping people. She felt the anger rising inside her. It was the feeling of being forever isolated in the world. She couldn't stop it. She breathed deeply but knew it wasn't going to help.

"He fucking raped me!" she screamed, her voice echoing across acres of open space.

There was silence from the group. Amanda wasn't sure if they were awestruck by what she said or by the fact that screaming and cursing was very out of character for her.

"He raped me," she repeated, her voice slightly calmer. "He orchestrated my kidnapping, and I'm sure the other pigs raped me, too, but it was his idea, his plan, his goal to rape me. And he succeeded. And the best part is, he told the men who kidnapped me to kill me after he was done raping me. But by some stroke of luck, or maybe my misfortune, they didn't. They left me there and told him I would die." Amanda looked at all of their faces as they stood there, silent and shocked. She drew in a breath and let it out in a sigh. "But I didn't die, at least not in the physical sense, so here we are. And don't any of you dare try to explain this away or defend him."

John, Brian, and June stood there, dumfounded, silent, and still. None of them had made a sound since Amanda broke through their attempts at reassuring her with a palpable scream.

"Now, if you're interested in what Michael Flaherty actually said to me as opposed to all the excuses you created for him, I'll tell you."

"Tell us, please. Please," John whispered, still shocked.

"He met me in the parking lot. He knew who I was right away. He looked very familiar, but I couldn't figure out why until he told me that he used to visit me at the bar. He would come in and give me a sob story about how lonely he was. I never paid much attention to him. Typically, lots of lonely people sit on bar stools, hoping the alcohol will make them less lonely. But he would come in at least two or three times a week." She paused and scanned their faces, waiting for someone to interrupt her with another comment about Michael being a great guy. None of them dared to say a word. Hearing nothing but their careful breathing, she continued. "Today, he told me the reason he was lonely was because the woman he loved was dead. He then continued to tell me I looked just like her. He got a sneering grin on his face when he assured me that I looked just like the woman he loved because I was her daughter."

Again, Amanda scanned the group for a reaction. They were all sitting across from her, dumfounded, but no one looked like they had anything to say, so she continued.

"He told me that he loved Mom, and he wanted to marry her and make love to her. And then he told me how angry he was when she married you, Dad. And then...this is the disgusting and psychotic part. He told me he raped me because he couldn't have Mom. That since I looked just like her, and I was her blood relative, he had me kidnapped so he could rape me and be, as he put it, the last one to ever be inside me."

John let out something that sounded like a grunt and a muffled scream. June put her hands over her mouth, her eyes filling with tears. Amanda looked at Brian, who was on his feet and headed toward his truck.

"Where are you going?" Amanda asked.

"I'm going to see Michael," he said, not looking back.

"Brian, stop," she called. He didn't. "Stop!" she called again, this time in a forceful tone. He stopped walking and tuned to look at her.

"What happened to me is over. We can't take that back. But for now, we need to stay here and get on the same page. Michael is connected to some very bad people. And he has a lot of money, guns, and other resources because of it. So before we get ourselves hurt or killed, remember we are safe here. He knows where I live, he knows where you live, and he knows where June lives. As far as I could tell, he doesn't know where Dad lives."

"I'm calling Harding," John said as he stood and headed for the door.

"Right behind you," Brian said, jogging to join him.

Amanda hadn't accounted for this part. Naturally, they would want to call the police. But she wanted her own justice. They say street justice never works, but after what she went through, she was going to give it a try anyway.

"Dad. Brian." Her tone was enough to stop their forward motion.

"What?" John replied, fighting back the urge to raise his voice, as he remembered that none of this was Amanda's fault.

"I understand you want to call the police."

"Actually, I want to go to Michael's house and beat him until he can't walk."

As soon as she heard the word house, Amanda got an idea. She figured Michael would prepare for her to call the police and would not be home. He would expect her to let John and Brian go to his house, or have the police go. Amanda knew Michael wouldn't be home. She called them back to the circle of chairs on the porch, and they formulated a plan.

June would stay at the farm for a few days, John was going to call Sergeant Harding and help him in any way he could, and Brian was going to go back to the firehouse to tell the chief about Michael. He was going to stay on for a few shifts in case Michael went to Brian's house. As for Amanda, she was supposed to stay with June. But that wasn't what was going to happen. In some ways, Amanda thought June knew that as soon as it was said. They stayed at the farm for a few hours, making sure they were all on the same page and knew what was going on. John and Brian thought they would handle the situation with the help of the police and the fire chief, and that was just fine with Amanda. She had her own plan in mind.

She waited for Brian and John to leave, and then she spent some time talking with June. June said she was going to start dinner so she could at least be helpful while she was at John's house. Amanda said she was tired and was going to rest. Except she didn't rest at all. She went upstairs to her father's bedroom and unlocked the gun safe. She took out a hand gun that her father had taught her to use when she was a teenager. A .357 magnum that held seven rounds. She didn't plan on using it; she hoped she wouldn't have to. But she was certain that she would need it to convince Michael to stay where she wanted him to. She opened the cylinder and carefully loaded the gun before putting it in the waistband of her jeans. It was awkward and bulky against her slender waist, but she could put it in her purse when she got to her car. She quietly walked out the back door, started her car, and left as quickly and quietly as she could. When she got out of the long driveway, she drove for a few minutes and pulled over. She picked up her phone and sent a text to Michael that said *I want more answers.* A moment later, her phone beeped and she read his response. *Can't wait. When and where? Love, Michael.* She told him to meet her in the parking lot of the grocery store. She knew it would be too crowded and difficult, although not impossible, for him to do something to her. She was about to pull away when her phone rang. It was Sam.

"Hey, Sam," Amanda said as cheerfully as she could.

No response.

"Sam?" she said again.

This time she heard sighing and heavy breathing. Then she heard a thud.

"Amanda, help me!" Sam called out.

"Sam, what's wrong? Where are you?"

"She's fine," Amanda heard a voice say.

"Who is this?"

"I'm hurt that you don't recognize my voice, Amanda. It's me, Michael. Forget the grocery store. If you want to help Sam, you'll meet me at one-twelve Knox Street. And you should probably hurry. I am a very patient man, and I have no real interest in forcing myself inside your little friend Samantha. The other boys, however...they've been licking their lips in anticipation ever since we tied her up and got her halfway undressed. See you soon, love. Oh, and Amanda? We have friends who work at the police department and will tell us if you call the police. If you do, we'll all have some quick and rough fun with Sam and then leave her dead body for the police. So make sure no one does anything stupid."

Amanda hung up the phone and started to feel like she was going to throw up. She took a few deep breaths and put her car in gear. If she thought about it too much, she wouldn't be able to do anything, but if she just rushed there to meet Michael and didn't make any kind of plan, it would be a disaster. She had an idea, and no idea if it would work, but she needed to act quickly and save Sam from the hell that they were about to put her through. She took out her phone and searched for 112 Knox Street. It was a laundromat not far from Rudley Street, where she had been held captive. She called Brian.

"Hey, honey, you okay?"

"Listen to me. You need to get Sergeant Harding and some other cops to one-twelve Knox Street, I think it's a laundromat. Samantha, who works at the police station, is being held captive there. Call Sergeant Harding and have him bring a bunch of other officers. But you can't let dispatch know. The people there have access to scanners and can hear you. Besides that, Michael has people inside the police department as well. So just take the guys for a ride. Can you do that? It needs to be Harding and people he trusts only. And tell him they can't look like they're going on a call. Have them say they're running to get coffee or something. Please. These guys all have that ivy vine tattoo."

"Okay, but where are you?"

"I'm safe, still out near Dad's farm. Please call Harding now, Brian. And be careful, please. Let the cops go first. Sam says they have guns."

"Okay, stay put, and, Amanda—"

"Brian, *please*. Just call," she interrupted.

"Okay, I love you."

"I love you, too."

Amanda hung up the phone.

She prayed that Harding would listen to Brian and would get there in time. Brian had told her to stay put but she had no intention of doing anything of the sort. She put her car in gear and headed for the laundromat.

Chapter 29

"Listen up." Harding spoke into the headset of Claiborne ladder four.

"We'll go first. These guys are armed to the teeth, if I had to guess. No firefighters go inside the building until we clear it."

"You got it, Sergeant," Whiting said, looking into the back seat.

"And remember, they've got Samantha. She gets out alive, and so do we. What happens to the idiots inside, I don't care, but let's keep it by the book. Ten-four?"

"Yes, sir," the others said in unison.

Whiting's ladder truck carried his usual crew, a driver, him, and two firefighters. In the other four seats were police officers. Their uniforms were covered by fire gear. In the pockets of their coats were their sidearms and extra ammunition.

"Sergeant, when you knock on the door, they're going to ask you why you're there. Tell them you received a still alarm for this location and just need to check it out."

"What the hell is a still alarm?" one of the officers asked.

"Exactly," Brian said. "I'm hoping they don't know and won't question it. Tell them you need to check the circuit breaker if you need to get farther into the building."

"Sounds good," said Harding.

The ladder truck pulled up in front of 112 Knox Street. Four officers clad in fire gear climbed out of the truck. Four more climbed out of the engine that parked right behind the ladder truck.

"Slow and easy, guys," Harding said. "Brian, who would you typically send where. This needs to look legit."

"Three guys to the front door, two others to the back, and three standing by outside the front door. Take this meter, this thermal imaging camera, and one of you take an ax." Whiting handed them the tools. They nodded and headed toward the house. Harding and two officers approached the front door. A young guy met them before they could even knock.

"Can I help you guys?"

"How ya doing? We received a still alarm for this location and need to check the building," Harding said as casually as he could manage.

"A what?" he asked.

"Still alarm. Doesn't look like there is any problem, but we just need to check your circuit breaker and alarm panel if you have one."

The man looked hesitant and unsure, and he turned to walk away and said, "Wait here."

As soon as he was out of the doorway, Harding stepped in.

"Hey," the man called out, his face a mix of confusion and concern.

"We just need to check it out. I'd hate for there to be a fire in the wall and you burn up after we leave," Harding said as he entered the laundromat.

The young man looked nervous. Harding wasn't sure if he was scared of what the others would do to him or scared that there might actually be a fire. But scared was good in this case. It would make him drop his guard.

Harding saw a door swing closed out of the corner of his eye. It was the entrance to a separate room behind all the washers and dryers.

"Hey, bring your meter over to that row of dryers and make sure you don't get any readings. And check it out with the camera to make sure nothing is hot."

Harding's men did as they were told. They were spreading out and making it harder for the guy inside to keep track of them, a plan they had rehearsed before leaving the firehouse. Brian had briefed them on the terminology and equipment they'd be bringing in, and Harding walked them through the plan to clear the building.

"Are there phones and appliances in that office?" Harding asked, motioning to the door that he had seen close.

"Oh, there isn't really anything back there. Storage mostly."

"That's the most dangerous place," Harding said. "The places that don't get used very often get forgotten about and could cause a real hazard." Harding crossed toward the door.

"You can't go back there," the man insisted.

Harding ignored him and kept walking. "Anything on the camera or the meter, guys?"

"Seems all clear over here, boss."

Without any word from Harding, they began to cross the room to join him. Harding looked toward the door and saw that the other three officers had silently entered the building. Once they were inside and close enough to him, Harding picked up his pace. He tried the door and found it locked. He spoke one word to the rest of his men, and what happened next happened with military precision and speed. One of the officers who had just entered grabbed the young man standing in the room. He covered his mouth with a gloved hand and threw him to the ground quickly and quietly. Another officer grabbed a gun out of the man's waistband and checked both ankles for a second gun. As soon as Harding saw his officer had taken the now restrained man's weapon, he drew his own sidearm, yelled out, and threw his shoulder into the old wooden door.

"Claiborne PD!" he yelled as he shoulder-checked the door just about off the hinges. Inside, men scrambled toward doors and windows. Harding and his men entered quickly and smoothly, guns firing at them as soon as they entered. They returned fire. It was a furious and loud storm of angry shouts and the cracks and snaps of bullets ripping through the walls of the small room.

"Drop your weapons!" Harding yelled over the cacophony of gunfire.

One by one, the offenders dropped to the ground after being shot by Harding's officers. Some ran for the back door. Two officers at the back door grabbed most of them as they tried to run by. They stopped all but two of them. The two that took off ran in separate directions. One officer tried to chase them on foot but lost sight of them by the time he got himself untangled from the heap of people that piled out the back door. Once the gunfire had stopped and things had calmed down, Harding walked over to the far corner of the room. Sitting behind a desk, half dressed and tied to a chair, was a young girl with brown hair, but it wasn't Samantha. They untied her and helped her to her feet. One of the officers took off his fire coat and put it around her shoulders. They helped her outside to an ambulance that was waiting by the fire truck.

"Hey, Bill?" Brian said. Harding looked at him. "That's not Samantha."

"I know," Harding answered. "Which means I now need to find out where they are keeping her."

Brian took out his cell phone and sent Amanda a text message.

They got the girl, but it's not Sam. They're still looking. Love you.

"I'll see if she's made contact with Amanda again."

As Whiting finished his sentence, one of the officers came running over. He had shed his fire gear and was in a hurry to tell Harding something.

"Sarge," he said, slightly out of breath. Harding turned.

338

"Traffic camera picked up the two that ran. They were heading west past Clairmont. Your car is here. Mine, too. I had Jesse and Will bring them over since we came here in the fire truck."

"All right, let's go," Harding barked as the officers began shedding their fire gear.

"Lieutenant Whiting?" a voice called behind him.

"Yeah?" he said, turning. His eyes landed on a young boy on a bicycle.

"Some guy paid me fifty bucks to give you this." He extended his hand to Whiting. He handed him a piece of paper. Whiting unfolded it and read.

Old Father John, he had a farm,

E-I-E-I-Uh-Oh...

There was a pencil sketch of a small ivy vine on the bottom of the page.

Whiting's eyes darted back and forth as he read and reread. It only took him a moment to decipher the blatantly obvious rhyme. They knew where John Killingly lived. Someone must be headed there.

"Bill!" Brian yelled.

Harding stopped and turned.

Whiting ran over and handed him the paper. As he read, Whiting began talking rapidly.

"They know where John lives. John and Amanda and June are all there."

Harding paused for a very brief second and then shouted.

"Barrett, McDermott, Murray, Ohlson, get a vehicle and follow those two offenders. Split up if you have to. The rest of you, with me." The four officers took off as the others ran to Harding.

"Listen up. We may have some of these idiots headed to John Killingly's house. Brian's girlfriend, Amanda, is there with her father and their friend June. We need to get there before they do. These guys are the ones..." Harding paused and glanced at Brian. "These ivy vine pricks are responsible for the kidnap, assault, and rape of Amanda. We move now. Let's go. And listen to me. Consider them armed and dangerous. We do this by the book, but use any means necessary to make sure they do not get away. Let's go."

They all ran toward a group of cruisers parked close to the laundromat.

"Where are you going?" Harding asked Whiting as he ran next to him.

"Don't even think you can try to stop me. I'm coming with you."

Harding didn't argue. He knew it wouldn't do him much good. They jumped in a dark gray SUV and took off toward the farm. Brian called Amanda and got no answer. He tried the house to tell June to lock the doors and windows. No answer. He called again and again to no avail. He tried John's cell phone and June's. He tried the house phone again. No answer on any line. Brian prayed they weren't too late.

Chapter 30

Amanda looked at her caller ID when she saw Brian calling. She wanted to answer, but she was focused on the shadows moving inside 63 Rudley Street. She had gone there after getting Brian's text that said Sam wasn't the girl they found at the laundromat. She parked far enough away not to be seen and was watching the shadows in the windows. She saw only one car in the driveway but had no idea how many people were inside. She needed a plan. The animal that raped her was in that house, or at least she was fairly certain he was, and Amanda wanted revenge. And after her conversation with Michael, she couldn't suppress the feeling of rage that tried to climb up out of her every time she thought about him. On top of that, they shot her father, killed a man she had known since high school, and now they had kidnapped one of her only friends. Amanda's phone beeped again. It was another text message from Brian.

They know where your dad lives. They are going there. Lock the doors. On my way with Harding and his team. Please call me.

Amanda's heart started to race. She picked up her phone to call Brian. She heard it ring once and then go silent. She looked at her phone screen. Dark. Her battery had died. She hadn't brought a charger. She didn't know what to do. She wanted to get to her father and June. She started to turn the key and stopped. Brian and Harding were headed to her father's house. They would get there first no matter how fast she drove. And Sam still needed help. She took her keys and climbed out of her car. She put her phone in her pocket, although it was nothing but a paper weight now, and climbed out of her car. She had a small flashlight, a knife in her back pocket, and not a clue how she was going to save Samantha. She took a long deep breath and closed her car door. She walked slowly and silently through the street and across back yards wherever she needed to. She stopped frequently and listened for something, anything, that might suggest someone was outside and going to see her. She began moving slower and slower as she got closer, and she kept her eyes focused on the shadows in the windows of the house on Rudley Street.

There were two people inside that she could see. She had no idea who else might be in there. She paused next to a car parked on the street near the house. It was Sam's. They either brought her here in her own car, or they lured her here. Amanda looked around and took a deep breath. She had absolutely no idea what she was going to do. She crept slowly toward the house, staying in the shadows. She slowly crossed the lawn, looking around for people. She saw no one. It had gotten darker since she started her slow stalk through the neighborhood, and every shadow in the moonlight made her eyes play tricks on her and think someone was there, hiding behind a car or standing behind a street light. Slowly, she made her way to the side lawn of the house. She knelt in the damp, dew-covered grass, next to the basement window of the room where she had been tied up and brutalized. The glass was painted black, save for a few flecks of paint that were missing. By some miracle, the window wasn't pressed tightly in the frame. The top corner was tilted forward slightly, just enough that she could partially see inside. She looked down and saw Samantha sitting on the bed, tied to the headboard. She was mostly dressed, and Amanda hoped that meant they hadn't tortured her yet. She peered in and looked around the room. The door was closed, and no one else was in the room. She leaned her head close to the window.

"Sam," she said in a loud whisper.

Samantha looked around, her makeup streaked down her cheeks, and her eyes still filled with tears.

"At the window," Amanda whispered.

Samantha turned and looked up at her. The light from inside the basement cast enough light for her to see it was Amanda. Sam started to cry harder.

"Shhhhh. It's okay. Shhhh, Sam. Don't make any noise," she said in a hoarse whisper.

Samantha stayed silent as the tears ran down her cheeks. Amanda took the knife out of her pocket and cut the screen from the window opening. She lay down on the grass and pried at the window from the top corner. She pulled and twisted, making her best effort to stay silent. After a moment, the window pulled free from the top of the frame. Amanda set it flat against the ground and put her body through the opening as far as she could without falling. She reached down and began sawing at the thick rope with the knife. Hurriedly, she pulled the knife back and forth. The rope started to fray and come apart. Samantha pulled against the rope to help break the strands. Finally, the rope cut in two, and Samantha pulled her hands down from where they had been tied above her head. Amanda pulled the loops from around her wrists and freed her hands.

She did her best to hide the anxiety in her voice and whispered, "Come on."

Amanda backed out on the window and left her hands inside. Sam stood on the headboard of the bed and stuck her arms and shoulders through the window. Amanda pulled on her, and Sam writhed and pulled on the window ledge until she was free. Crying, bruised, and thankful to be alive and free from her confines, Sam sobbed into Amanda's shoulder as she finished pulling her through the window and onto the grass.

"Shhhhh. I know, Sam, I know. Take a breath. Look at me."

Sam looked up, her sobs quieting a bit.

"Did they rape you?"

"No. They hit me, tied me up, spit on me, and grabbed me a little, but they never did anything else. One of them said he was waiting for you to get here, that he only wanted you. He told the other one he could..." She started crying harder.

"Shhh. Told him what, Sam?"

"He told him he could rape me to death for all he cared; he only wanted you. But he had to wait until you got here."

344

Amanda hugged her tightly. Her mind whirled as it started putting pieces together. Michael was here. He was the one who would have said he only wanted her. She wondered who the other man was.

"Shhhh. It's okay. I'm here, and they aren't going to hurt you anymore. Do you know their names? Is one of them Michael?"

Sam looked up, puzzled. "How did you know that?"

"It doesn't matter. Do you know the other one's name?"

"Benjamin. I heard the guy call him Benjamin."

"Okay. How many are here?"

"Just those two. Benjamin and the one you said is Michael."

"Okay. Listen to me. Where are your car keys?"

Sam looked up at her, trying to collect her thoughts.

"In my car. I left them in my car. They called and said my sister left something here and asked if I could come get it."

"Okay. We can't start your car right here, or they'll hear it. We have to push it to the end of the street."

"What?" Sam looked frazzled.

"It's okay. We can push it. Leave your lights off until you're at the end of the block."

"Um, okay." Sam said wearily.

"When you get to the end of the block, call the police. Tell them you are going to the hospital. They'll send someone to meet you there. Tell them your story. But, Sam. Do not tell them where you were."

"Why not?"

"There are men associated with the men who took you that work for the police department. They'll warn the others that you're telling your story. Ask to talk to Sergeant Harding. If he isn't available, ask to speak with the captain. Harding says the captain can be trusted."

"Okay," Sam said, nodding. "But how do you know all of this? Aren't you coming with me?"

"I need to make sure these two idiots stay put until you're gone."

"How do you know so much about them?"

"That's not a conversation we have time for right now. You need to get out of here."

"Okay," was all she could manage as a reply.

She knew Samantha would have dozens of questions, and she would have to find a way to deal with them eventually. Now, however, she needed Samantha to get somewhere safe. She put a reassuring hand on her shoulder. "You'll be okay, Sam. I promise. Deep breath. Get to the hospital." They pushed her car down the slight incline silently. Sam climbed in at the end of the street.

"One more thing." Amanda looked into Sam's open door. "Do you have a vehicle cell phone charger I could use?"

Sam didn't say a word. She looked at Amanda anxiously and silently handed her one that was on her passenger seat.

"Thanks," Amanda said. "Be safe."

Amanda crept back toward the house and glanced back inside, suddenly aware that she hadn't been paying attention to the men in the house while she was rolling Sam's car down the street. She looked to each window, searching for silhouettes inside. She saw one cross over to the far side of the kitchen. She waited and watched, hoping they hadn't heard her talking to Sam. She crouched down and listened for footsteps. It was eerily quiet. Finally, she saw the other shadow move across the kitchen and sit at the table. She crept closer to the window, to a spot where she could still see the silhouettes but could also see the basement window that she had pulled Sam out of. Amanda tried to calm her breathing. She had no idea what she was going to do or how she was going to do it.

Since her attack, she had played out hundreds of scenarios in her head about what she would do to her attackers if she was ever given the opportunity. Now two were inside, and she had no idea what to do. For a moment, she thought she should just call the police. Then she remembered what Michael had said. There had been dozens of women. Dozens of women whom he tied up, beat, and brutally raped over and over again, herself included. Amanda's blood boiled, and her nerves began to calm, and her mood took a vengeful turn. Michael didn't deserve the police. He deserved to be tortured the way he tortured her and so many other women.

Amanda took a deep breath and, as if someone flipped a switch, went to work, barely knowing what she was doing. She was moving across the lawn swiftly and carefully. She felt as if something inside her was driving her and making the decisions for her. She tried to understand it, tried to fight it, but she couldn't stop it. She gave into the feeling inside and followed her instincts. She crossed to the edge of the street and hid near a car that was parked beneath a tree. She bent down and picked up a large, dead tree branch that had fallen. It was in a small pile of other sticks and branches that someone had made at the base of the tree. Amanda swung the large branch she had selected onto the roof of the car. It hit with a loud thud, and instantly, the alarm in the car sounded. It was a combination of horn chirps and a loud, shrill alarm. She picked up another large stick, one that was easy to handle but large enough to hurt someone with, and ran back toward the house.

She knelt in the shadows, her eyes glued to the door. She watched as one of the men—Benjamin, she assumed—walked onto the porch. He looked around and walked slowly to the car. Amanda saw a light come on in the house next door, and a woman began to walk out into the street. They met in front of the car and began talking. Benjamin looked around suspiciously, but the woman kept talking at him, and he seemed to lose interest in scanning the area for other people. After a few minutes of chatting, he picked up the stick off the roof of the car. He looked up into the branches above his head.

"Must have fallen from the tree and hit the car just right."

"Oh geez, I guess so," said the woman. After a moment of small talk about the tree and the weather in general, the woman turned toward her house.

"I'm going to head inside. Sorry about your car," she said politely.

"It's okay. Have a good night."

"You, too."

The woman walked back into her house as Benjamin stood at the side of what Amanda now knew to be his car. He looked around once more but seemed to be observing the weather more than looking for anyone to be in his general area. Amanda felt a tightness in her chest, and her breathing began to become more rapid. She wished she had the .357 she had taken when she first went to meet Michael. She had foolishly left it in her purse hidden in her car. She hadn't been able to decide if it would be helpful or if it would cause more danger in the event that someone got the gun away from her and used it to shoot her. She shook her head to clear her thoughts as her subconscious took over again.

Clutching the tree branch in both hands, she slowly crawled to the side of the house, making sure to stay low and move painstakingly slow. Benjamin walked cautiously and took out a cigarette. He pulled a lighter out of his pocket. The top of the lighter made a distinctive metallic clink when he flipped it open. He spun the wheel, and a large flame danced in the darkness. He turned his back to Amanda, and before he could put the lighter in his pocket, Amanda charged.

She ran swiftly and silently. As she approached him, she raised the branch above her head. With all the strength she could muster, and the momentum of her at an all-out sprint, she hit Benjamin in the back of the head. He toppled like a day-old foal trying to take its first steps. His legs bent at the knees, and the weight of his body pushed his head and chest downward more quickly than the rest of him, and he smashed face-first into a heap on the lawn. Thankfully for Amanda, he didn't even have time to make a sound. She wasn't sure how long he would be knocked out for, so she reached down, grabbed the lighter and a set of keys that was hanging on his belt loop, and hurried to her next task.

She moved quickly and quietly onto the porch and peered through the door at Michael. He was sitting in the kitchen, sipping a drink. She didn't have the element of surprise, so she needed to gain an advantage somehow. She ran down the porch steps and over to the basement window. She grasped the stick she had used to disable Benjamin and swung it against the glass of the small window. There was a loud thud, but the glass stayed intact. She watched for Michael's silhouette to move. He was still sitting. She adjusted her grip on the stick and moved back slightly so the tip of the stick would impact the glass, not the side of it. She drew in a quick breath and swung hard as she blew the breath out hard and fast. The stick made a low humming sound as it careened through the air, and there was a loud pop as the sound of broken glass interrupted the otherwise still air. This time she saw Michael jump up from his chair. As he crossed the kitchen to the basement door, Amanda ran to the porch. She looked through the crack in the door and watched Michael open the door to the basement. As he walked down the stairs, she quietly crept into the house. She waited until she heard the door at the bottom of the stairs open. She followed him down the stairs as quietly as she could. She stepped on a stair in the middle of the staircase, and it made a loud creak. She heard Michael stop. She held her breath. Before she could move, she heard Michael's voice. It was calm and casual.

"Miss Samantha is making quite the racket down here. Perhaps it's time I let you break her spirit a little."

Amanda said nothing. She was worried her lack of response would prompt Michael to look up the stairway. So she did the most dangerous thing she could think of and continued down the stairs. She heard him unlocking the room where he thought Samantha was. Amanda stood, ready. He opened the door and looked around. When he saw the broken window, he yelled and slammed the door.

"My *God*, can't you seem to do anything right, Benjamin?" he hollered.

Amanda heard him hurrying toward the steps. She stood firmly planted on the third to last step. Michael rounded the corner and raised his foot to climb the stairs. Amanda swung her make-shift club as hard as she could. Michael looked up at the last instant and raised his arm to block the blow. He stumbled and staggered but didn't fall down. Amanda jumped off the stair she was standing on and collided with him. She swung the branch again but was too close to him to have much momentum. He grabbed her around the waist and pushed her through the door to the room where she was once held captive. He threw her on the bed and ran at her. She bent both knees, and as he got close to her, she kicked hard with both feet. They hit his chest with a crackling thud, and Michael reeled back and fell to his knees. Amanda jumped up and grabbed her branch. She swung it with all her might and hit the side of his head. He fell for a brief second and then grabbed Amanda by the legs.

"To think it's going to end where it all began, my love," he managed to say. He breathed heavily, grabbing at her thighs and crotch. She didn't have room to swing the branch, so she swung her fist down like a hammer on the top of his head. He released his grasp on her legs. She took a step backwards and raised the club above her head. He jumped up and crashed into her, his arms around her midsection. They crashed onto the bed, his weight pinning her down. She was struggling to breathe, as it felt like someone had parked a car on her as he knelt on her chest. He slapped her across the face. Her head snapped to the side, and her cheek burned from the hard, open-palm slap. She tried to face forward, but he slapped her again and again. He reached for the button of her jeans and pulled it open. He pushed her down and bit her breast through her shirt. He tried to get his hands down her panties, but she managed to get her elbow to smash into the side of his head. It was enough for him to stop trying and grab her hands. When he grabbed her hands, she rolled sideways enough for him to put a hand down to keep himself from being thrown off of her. As soon as he released his hand, she reached for the knife in her pocket. She pulled it out and managed to flip it open with her thumb. She swung the knife down hard and before it touched him, he hit her arm with his and knocked the knife free. He jumped off the bed and dove for the knife. She leapt off the bed, and both her feet hit Michael in the face. He fell to the ground. She kicked him as hard as she could in the side of the head. He went mostly limp. She hit him with the branch once more for good measure.

As he lay there motionless, breathing slowly, she found a roll of duct tape on the dresser. She quickly buttoned her pants and pulled her shirt down to cover her midsection. She took the roll of tape and wound several thick wraps around his wrists. She did the same to his ankles. She wound a piece around his entire head and over his mouth. She quickly got the piece of rope from the bed. She wove the rope through his arms and legs and around his neck. Using all her strength, she pushed and pulled, and soon Michael was tied up tightly, his bound hands tied up forcefully around his chest, as if he were in a straight-jacket. Amanda stood on the bed and fished the other end of the rope through a large eyelet in the ceiling. She imagined the eyelet was used to tie up the countless women they had raped and tortured in that room, and she took satisfaction in knowing it would help keep Michael contained this time. She pulled on the rope with all the strength she could muster, until she felt his body weight tugging at the eyelet. She tied the rope back to itself. Michael was wrapped up tightly, bound with duct tape, and partially suspended from the ceiling. Hopefully, that would keep him contained.

Amanda got off the bed and brushed the hair out of her face. She picked up the knife off the floor and closed the blade. As she was putting the knife in her pocket, she felt the lighter and remembered that Benjamin was still on the front lawn. Or so she hoped. She put the roll of duct tape around her wrist and headed for the stairs. She walked quickly but cautiously, all the while wondering if Benjamin had woken up. She was halfway up the stairs when she heard footsteps. Amanda froze. She wasn't sure which direction to go. Upstairs meant facing whoever was up there, but going back into the basement left her with no way out. She decided the other rooms in the basement at least helped her gain the element of surprise. She began backing down slowly when the door at the top of the stairs opened. Benjamin Rudley stood at the top of the stairs. A line of blood ran down the side of his head and was caked to his cheek. He looked at her and grinned.

"There you are, you little whore. It's time you and I got reacquainted."

She continued backing down the stairs as he started walking down, matching her step for step.

"The night we took you, the other guys had all the fun without me. And then once we got you here, all I got to do was rip your panties off and bite those hot little ass cheeks a few times. Michael insisted that you were his first, and last. He was very anxious to shove himself inside you. We barely had you tied up, and he had his cock in his hand."

Amanda kept stepping backwards and said nothing. The ugly grin Benjamin had given her made images from the night of her attack come flooding back.

"So what do ya say, sweetie? Want to just skip the tying up this time and bend over for me? It'll hurt less if you participate willingly."

"Go fuck yourself," Amanda said sternly.

"So much fight in you. I like that."

Amanda reached the last step and stood firmly on the floor. She looked out of the corner of her eye and saw Michael motionless. At least she only had Benjamin to deal with. She turned and ran to the room where she had found the pictures. She shut the door behind her and quickly turned the lock button. She ran to a corner where she thought she could hide. On the way by, she took out her knife and smashed the light bulb above her head. She kept running and made it to the corner, then crouched behind a pile of boxes. She heard Benjamin crashing down the stairs. He kicked the thin wooden door, and it burst open. He flipped the light switch and the broken bulb crackled but remained dark. He crossed the room, looking around.

"Don't hide, honey. The longer you make me wait, the more I'm gonna make it hurt."

Amanda took the knife out of her pocket and held it tightly in her hand. She could see Benjamin walking through a space in the pile of boxes that helped conceal her. All of a sudden, he froze. He cocked his head to the side, listening to something. Amanda heard a sound from the other room. Michael was waking up. She started to panic. Two of them meant she was outnumbered. But if Benjamin went to untie Michael, she may have time to run up the stairs. Her heart pounded. She watched as Benjamin took a step backwards and turned around. He glanced over his shoulder, looked around the room, and walked to the doorway. He took a step into the hallway and slowly pushed the partially-open door away from him, allowing him a clear view into the room where Michael was tied up. He left the door open and returned to the room where Amanda was hiding. He stood in the doorway and addressed Amanda by calling out over his shoulder with an amused chuckle.

"Good job, sweetie. You put quite the pile of hurt on this horny old bastard. You saved me a lot of trouble."

Michael groaned through the duct tape around his mouth.

"Shut up, Flaherty," Benjamin called out.

"See, I let Michael think he had this master plan all along. And that he was in charge. But really, he was so focused on your tight little ass that he lost sight of the world around him. Every dollar we gave him, every line of coke or bottle of booze, was never enough. We brought him girl after girl to fuck, and he still was so wrapped up in you, his little Amanda, that he lost sight of the overall mission. So thank you, my dear little Amanda." He put a mocking emphasis on the words *dear little Amanda* before continuing in a casual tone.

"Not only did you keep him so distracted that he couldn't see what was really going on, but you beat the living shit out of him tonight, so I don't have to use much effort to kill him. I can save all my energy for fucking you to death."

Michael yelled against the duct tape.

"Shup up," Benjamin said flatly. "You want to watch, Michael, or would you rather not see me rape the girl of your dreams?"

He walked over to Michael and ripped the duct tape off his head, uncovering his mouth.

"Leave her alone," Michael breathed.

"Leave her alone?" Benjamin mocked. "And let you have all the fun? I don't think so."

"Then just kill her like you were supposed to the first time. Don't hurt her."

"Hurt her?" Benjamin snorted. "You had us tie her up so you could rape and beat her, and now you're telling me not to hurt her? Kind of a conflicting message, don't you think?" He cocked his head to the side and nodded mockingly. "Oh, Michael. You really are a fucking idiot. So in love with your little Amanda. I don't want to kill her just yet. I want to thank her for helping us."

Michael struggled against the rope and duct tape. "What do you mean *helping you*?"

He shook his head and chortled. "See? Blind. In love with that hot little thing hiding next door. So focused on getting between her legs that you couldn't read between the lines and see what was happening to you. We didn't kill her the first time on purpose. We needed her. We needed her to keep you doing what you were doing, so you would stay blind to what I was doing."

Benjamin crossed to the doorway of Amanda's room again. He scanned the room to make sure Amanda didn't try to run.

"We have pictures, Michael. And videos. Of you raping all those girls. Of you torturing them, beating them, and raping them again while they were barely conscious. And tomorrow morning, when Sergeant Harding gets to the police station, he is going to have a USB drive with all those pictures and videos sitting quietly on his desk, waiting. And you can take the fall for all of this. Now, they won't be able to arrest you, because you'll be dead, but at least they'll stop looking for me. So your turn to decide Michael. You or her first? You wanna see me break her in half, or would you rather die first so you don't have to watch?"

"Leave her alone!" he shouted as he struggled against his restraints. "They'll know I wasn't behind all this. All the ivy vine tattoos will be connected to you. The crime, the collecting money from business owners, the drugs, the guns, your puny empire that you built to impress Daddy. They'll figure out that they are all a fleeting attempt to impress your eccentric fucking father. They'll know that I wasn't the one calling the shots."

Benjamin gritted his teeth and frowned. He turned to face the door of the room Michael was in and roared, "Don't you mention my father!"

"Oh, come now, Benjamin." Michael was now the mocking one. He took on a contentious, condescending tone despite being tied up. "You remember what dear –old Dad used to say, don't you? That ivy had the ability to grow and climb over anything it encountered. That it could overpower, encircle, and overtake anything it was able to cling to as it wound its way up, growing bigger and bigger vines. He used ivy as a metaphor for the powerful. And he got you for a son, Benjamin. The furthest thing from a winner he could have ever hoped for," Michael continued, his tone still scornful.

"I did rise to the top. I run this entire clan. They all listen to me," Benjamin said, his voice gruff and annoyed. "So shut your mouth, and don't you dare talk about my father anymore."

Michael's voice took on a tone of faux pity. "Ohhh, why not? Did you forget that he loved your sisters more than you? And that you were his biggest disappointment? He was a man driven by a passion for education and writing, and you could barely write your own name, let alone a book." Michael's voice was high and dripped with sarcastic scorn. "Your sisters are so beautiful and successful. Both of them are well rounded and well educated. They can write just as well as your father. They grew up to own successful businesses and have intelligent children and beautiful families. And then there is you." Michael glowered at him, his tone serving to add further shame to his harsh words. "The scroungy third born who refused to learn the Goddamned alphabet. Or maybe you didn't refuse; maybe you were just too stupid. Your father would be ashamed of you. More so than he already was, anyway. I should call your sisters once I get out of here. Maybe I'll take them to dinner and have a nice, long, intellectual conversation. That's something they couldn't get from you, either. Poor little Benjamin," he clucked and shook his head. "You will forever be the messy-haired little boy that no one loves. At least your father has two girls to be proud of. Even before he fell ill, he had come to terms with the fact that you were a giant loser."

Benjamin started walking toward Michael.

"That's a boy. Come untie me, and I'll help you get over the fact that you're a useless and unsuccessful—"

Michael's words were cut short as Benjamin grabbed his head and snapped it quickly to one side. Michael's body went limp, eyes open wide, and all of his weight now gently swung from the thick rope. Benjamin spit on the dangling corpse and turned and walked back into the room where Amanda was hiding without further regard to the now lifeless Michael. He had lost his patience for the cat and mouse game he had been playing. Michael had made him so furious that he was blindly walking and throwing things out of the way while looking for Amanda. He was at the opposite side of the room, and the door was open. She had a clear path to run.

She took off from where she was crouched behind the boxes. He turned immediately as she stood up and jumped over boxes and the clutter he had created. A blinding pain shot through her scalp as he grabbed her by the hair as she ran by. He threw her back onto the floor, and as she fell, the knife bounced out of her hand. He knelt over her and pulled the roll of duct tape off her wrist. He tore off a long piece. She struggled to get free, but his massive body weight was too much to let her move. He taped her wrists together and then unbuttoned her jeans. As he tried to slide them off, he felt the lighter in her pocket. He pulled it out, and it almost seemed as if he forgot what he was doing for a minute.

"My lighter," he said, his tone very calm and matter-of-fact given the circumstances. "I thought I lost it, but you took it from me. This was my father's. He's not disappointed in me, you know."

He lifted her shirt and exposed her stomach. He flicked the top of the lighter open and struck the wheel. A flame danced to life and flickered in his hand. He held it close to her stomach.

"My father always carried a lighter, but he never smoked. He always said it was a lesson in preparedness, a reminder to respect the power of fire."

Amanda winced and tried to move, but it was no use with him sitting on top of her. He ran the lighter across her waistband and burned her stomach. He held the flame close to her face and ran it down her arm. He lifted her shirt more and ran the flame against her side, pausing at the side of her breast and then moving slowly to her armpit.

"You see, fire can destroy anything if you give it enough time."

With the lighter still lit, he leaned in and started to put his face between her breasts.

"Even those fucking ivy vines," she said as she leaned back and headbutted him as hard as she could in the bridge of the nose. He howled in pain as his body tipped backwards, and the lighter went flying, still lit. She used Benjamin's backwards momentum to her advantage and sat up while he was still falling. She pushed against him and sat up in one swift motion. His body hit the floor with a cracking thud. She managed to get free from under him and run to the far corner of the room. She had wanted to run to the door, but he had fallen that way, and she didn't dare run past him. She ran to a set of metal shelves and sawed through the duct tape with a sharp edge on one of the bars. With her hands free, she crouched and picked up her knife. She saw Benjamin slowly getting to his feet, his nose and face streaked red with blood. She was slowly moving backwards against the wall, watching him, as her back touched something cold and metal. She glanced quickly and saw a fire extinguisher mounted on the wall. She took it down carefully and quietly. She watched him rip off a piece of his shirt and use it to wipe the blood off his face. She moved over slightly. She had one plan, not a very good one, but she hoped it would work. She kept moving as he wiped his face off. When she got to the spot she needed to be, she slowly leaned down and opened the hatch in the floor, which she had discovered the night she first explored the house. She left it open and quietly moved a box in front of it. She went back to the wall and slowly circled the room until she had somewhat of a path to the door. Benjamin finished wiping his face and threw the torn t-shirt fragment on the ground.

"You're gonna pay for that, you little whore," he said, starting to walk toward the direction Amanda had originally run. When he got to a spot where Amanda thought her plan might work, she stood up.

"Are you really your father's biggest disappointment?" she asked casually.

He huffed and snorted and then turned slightly and glared at her. "You're going to wish you didn't say that."

"I didn't mean to offend you. I was just trying to make conversation," she said indignantly.

He stared at her as he walked slowly toward her.

"I'm sorry about your nose. But I guess it's only fair. You burned my underwear, jeans, and favorite bra, and you tried to burn my boob." She lifted her shirt slightly and exposed her stomach and the bottom of her bra on one side.

"See? You burned me."

His eyes widened as he stared at the bright pink fabric covering her breasts. "And you burned my stomach and jeans, too." She pulled her still-unbuttoned waist band down just enough to expose the top of her pink underwear. He continued his advance, with his eyes glued to her bra and skin.

"You must really like pink," she said as she walked slightly to the side. He kept walking toward her, slowly, his eyes locked on her body. She held the fire extinguisher to the side, hoping he wouldn't see it. She was suddenly aware of a haze in the room. She looked past him and saw a pile of papers smoldering in the corner. When he fell, his lighter had landed in the corner of the room. It must have caught a pile of papers on fire. Benjamin was so focused on her exposed skin, bra, and underwear that he didn't notice the fire at all. She stopped walking and smiled. She was about ten feet from him, still out of reach if he tried to grab her, but the open hatch was right at his feet. She hoped he was so fixated on her that he didn't notice. She reached down and tugged on the other corner of her shirt. She lifted it slightly and then let it fall. She hooked her thumb under the waistband of her underwear and pulled it up slightly, exposing the top of her thigh, where the waistband met the cut-out in the pink lace for her leg.

"So now what do we do, Benjamin?" Her voice was quiet and almost seductive. She had to sound convincing if her plan had any hope of working. "You hit me, and I head-butted you. Should we call it even and maybe do something that's a little more fun than fighting?" she said, tilting her head to the side.

"No matter what you want to call it, you're going to hurt when I do it to you," he growled.

She needed him to step into the hatch, and she needed him to do it quickly, before he noticed where he was standing.

"Well, how about I play hard to get?" she said, taking three quick steps backwards and turning as if she were going to run.

That was enough. Benjamin lurched forward and fumbled into the open hole in the floor. His back leg bent up behind him as he fell, and his face hit the edge of the opening. Amanda rushed over and tried to close the hatch. She had it lifted slightly when his hand grabbed her ankle and started pulling. She struggled to get free, but when she lifted her foot, he pulled harder, and she fell into a sitting position. He reached for her, trying to regain his footing. He could barely reach out of the hole and seemed to be hanging by his stomach on the edge of the opening. He pulled at Amanda and punched anything his hands could find. She reached back and grabbed the hose of the fire extinguisher. A hot flash of pain surged through her leg as he sank his teeth into it. She screamed and kicked at him with her other foot. His hands pawed at her, and he managed to get his grimy fingers into the top of her jeans. He was pulling her across the floor, and she was just about to the leading edge of the opening. Her grip on the fire extinguisher slipped. He pulled harder, and she slid closer. She was coughing from the smoke that had now filled the room as the paper and boxes continued to smolder. With all the strength she could muster, she kicked hard with both feet. They both hit his chest, and it was enough leverage to slide her back closer to the fire extinguisher.

She pulled the pin and spun it around, blindly spraying the yellowish-white chemical in his direction. Some hit the floor in front of the hatch and then his chest. Finally, she managed to spray it in his face and eyes. He howled in pain and released his grasp on her, clawing at his eyes and face. He started to slip into the opening in the floor. She hit him with the blunt end of the extinguisher, and he fell down. The momentum of her swing made her drop the heavy can, now only partially full of the yellow powder. It hit the floor hard and bounced into the hole on top of him. She scrambled to close the hatch. She pulled so hard her muscles burned, but she finally got it moving and swung it down. As soon as it hit the floor, she jumped on it, and it made a loud click. She was breathing hard from the struggle, and each breath she took burned as she inhaled more and more of the growing cloud of yellowish-gray smoke. Her instincts took over again, and she ran toward the stairs, as she wanted to shut the door to each room. One room held a tied-up Michael Flaherty, who was lifelessly hanging against the rope he was wrapped in. She paused briefly and looked into the room at him. She had never really thought about what she would feel if she saw a dead body, but the fact that it was the man who brutally raped her for two days and left her to die made it easy enough to process. She unceremoniously pulled the door shut. She turned and looked into the room where Benjamin was trapped beneath the floor. A small box in the corner was quickly giving off more and more of the pungent, yellowish-gray smoke. She didn't see any flames yet but knew it was just a matter of time. She briefly started to scan the room for another fire extinguisher. She made it part of the way around the room with her gaze when she saw the large envelope on the desk.

She hurried over carefully, keeping an eye on the hatch the entire time. She would give the envelope to Harding, and that should be all the proof he needs. She grabbed the envelope and ran back to the door. In it was the pile of pictures she had found when she searched the house some time ago. Her picture was in there, along with picture after picture of Benjamin Rudley and Michael Flaherty doing God-awful things to women. Rope, chains, whips, belts, guns, knives, candles, lighters, and crow bars. Some women were covered in blood. Others were bound. She remembered a picture of a woman with all her hair cut off, Benjamin Rudley standing proudly with her hair in one hand and a pair of crude scissors in the other. The next picture was Benjamin laughing as he shoved himself inside the helpless woman with no hair, and the scissors were stabbed into her side, just above her hip. Faces of dozens of women with terrified grimaces as they endured the same hell Amanda had went through. She clutched the envelope tightly and made her way to the door.

In the short amount of time it took to retrieve the envelope, the once small fire had grown dramatically in size. Around it were piles of cardboard boxes and papers, lying on the floor, vulnerable to the hungry mouth of the flames. The once smoldering box was now a bright ball of orange fire that radiated so much heat that it forced Amanda to put her arm in front of her face, even from partially across the room. As she looked around, trying desperately to figure out something to do, the fire crackled and roared as it consumed more and more of the flammable contents scattered about the floor. She thought about trying to put out the fire, but she hadn't seen another extinguisher. She took a few steps toward the flames, seemingly with the thought that being closer to the fire would help her better solve the problem. It didn't.

Physically pushed back by the immense heat, she quickly retreated to the door, covering her face and coughing as she went. The flames had now engulfed several boxes and the contents of one of the shelves, and it was starting to leave black marks up the concrete wall. She had to leave, as staying would certainly mean death. As she turned toward the door, she hesitated, turned back, and looked at the hatch in the floor that held her rapist captive. She theorized that leaving a person in there with the fire growing would undoubtedly result in death, but her sense of self-preservation took over, and she ran toward the stairs. She knew she wouldn't easily forget possibly killing another human being, but in many ways, Benjamin didn't qualify as human.

She rushed to the door and put it back in place as best she could. She ran up the stairs and into the kitchen. She shut the door to the basement and headed for the front door. She walked out of the house, shut the door behind her, and ran down the front steps. She ran to her car and quickly looked around. She didn't see anyone. She started the car and took off, her mind racing. She dug her phone out of her pocket and fumbled with the charger Sam had given her. She was happy enough to cry when it fit her phone. She plugged it in and was relieved to see the white battery icon with a lightning bolt flashing in the center. She turned it on and kept driving toward home.

She had no idea what to do. She needed to talk to Brian and her father and June to make sure they were okay. She still had no plan. She was almost home when her phone beeped with notification after notification. She pulled into her driveway and ran to the door, opened it and then locked it behind her again, and headed straight for the shower. She looked at her phone. She had messages from Brian frantically asking where she was. His texts said that he and June and John were safe and that Harding had arrested four men who came to the farm looking for them. She wrote back quickly and told Brian that she had come home to shower and was headed to work. She said she was safe and would be safe at work and that she would call him soon. She wasn't sure if he would believe her and was sure he'd call as soon as he saw the message. She also wasn't sure what her story was going to be, but she would have to tell him soon enough.

Chapter 31

Amanda was halfway across the parking lot when her phone rang. It was Brian. She took a deep breath and answered it.

"Hi, babe."

"Oh my God, Amanda, where have you been?" His voice was a mixture of relief and suppressed anger.

"I'm sorry. I'm okay. I promise. Take a deep breath."

"Where are you?" He huffed, ignoring the deep breath comment.

"I'm at CAD. Sam is safe. She managed to get away and went to the hospital. My phone died, and I had to find a charger so I could tell you I was safe and heading to work. Please, no lecture. I know it was dangerous to leave, but I'm fine."

Amanda kept walking as she talked. She managed to keep him calm and agreed to fill him in on everything.

He said that Harding and his officers had arrested four men, and they were fairly certain they were going to give them information about Michael and where he might be. Amanda listened intently but offered very little in the way of response to this, as she knew exactly where Michael was.

"I'm on my way there now," Brian said, his voice still pulsing with adrenaline. "Harding is in front of me. We will be there as soon as we can. I love you."

"I love you, too."

She walked to the back door, glanced at the camera that sat only inches from the keypad, raised her I.D. badge, and waited for the whine, whir, and click of the steel door. Once inside, she walked through the front hallway, past a handful of small offices, and into the dispatch room. Amanda greeted the other dispatchers. They looked at the clock and made jokes about her needing to get a life if she was this early for work. Amanda laughed and asked how the night had been.

"It's been crazy," one of them said. "And I hate to ask, but I haven't eaten in hours. Can you sit at my station for five minutes while I heat up some food from the fridge?"

"Of course," Amanda said.

She made small talk with the other dispatchers, glanced at the constant stream of news and weather that cascaded across the wall of large TV's in the front of the room, and leaned back in her chair.

"Any good calls come in last night or this morning?" she asked, adjusting the headset.

"You missed a good one just a little while ago. House fire. They got it out and then asked for the PD Major Crimes Unit and the arson investigators."

"Major Crimes? Did they say why?"

"Dead guy in the basement. Maybe two dead guys. One of them called us, but we lost the call. Not sure if he made it."

As Amanda listened to the last words of the sentence, she could hear what had become the familiar sound of her heart in her ears, and her stomach lurched. Benjamin had somehow managed to call for help. Amanda's mind went into overdrive.

She did her best to act unphased by the information about the call. She continued her small talk the best she could and focused on taking easy breaths as to not appear anxious. What happened now would have to be left up to fate. She couldn't prevent the fire department from doing their job. Whether Benjamin lived or died was out of her control.

She felt a small sense of relief, even if only for a moment. Benjamin being alive meant she couldn't be convicted of murder. She didn't intentionally set the fire, but she also knew it was burning when she locked him in a hole in the floor and left the building. She took one more deep breath and let it out slowly.

Chapter 32

At the end of her shift, she went home and felt like she could sleep for a month. As she climbed into bed, after a very hot and long overdue shower, she asked Brian the question she'd been wanting to ask all day.

"Was he alive?"

Knowing the reason she was asking, and still struggling with the *we really shouldn't talk about this* kind of feeling in his gut, he answered but never turned to face her.

"Yeah. He was alive."

"Is he still alive?" She emphasized the word *still* and put a hand on his shoulder in an attempt to get him to look at her.

"So far. He's in the burn unit. He was pretty overcome from smoke inhalation, but his burns were manageable."

"Okay." She sighed and stared at the ceiling.

Finally looking at her, he gave her a kiss and said, "It's over, Amanda. Once he's out of the burn unit, he'll be arrested and sent to prison for the rest of his life. Harding will make sure of that."

"Okay," she repeated. "I'm sorry for the one-word answers, honey. I'm exhausted."

"I know. Get some sleep. He's alive but contained to a hospital. As soon as he is well enough to move, Harding will put him exactly where he belongs. No matter how much you may think you wanted him to die so you could have revenge, it wouldn't have made things better or easier."

"You're right. I love you very much."

"I love you, too."

Amanda closed her eyes and fell asleep in minutes. Tomorrow she would give Harding her statement. Benjamin Rudley would stay in the hospital and then be arrested, tried, and sent to prison. She had found a way to have justice served. It was one hell of a long road to get there, but it was over. Sleep came quickly, and for the first time in a very long time, it was a deep and peaceful sleep.

Chapter 33

D octor Linda Fairchild approached the sliding glass
door to the scrubbed and sterile hospital room. As she
got closer, she reached into the pocket of her lab coat and
pulled out a pen and a stethoscope. She wasn't going to use
them for anything, but she needed to look credible. She took
the chart from the small plastic bin outside the door and
started to read. As she read, she lightly brushed the shoulder
of the police officer standing guard outside his room with
her ample and drastically pushed up breasts. He took a step
back and excused himself. She put a warm hand on his chest
and told him he had nothing to be sorry for. He nodded
politely and took another step away. She suppressed the
urge to give up her act and simply walk away, as she knew
that would mean awful things awaited her in the future.
Instead, she smiled graciously, exposing immaculately
white teeth behind bright pink, glossy lips. She told him
she loved a man in uniform, gently patting his lower back
before moving her hand lower to give him a gentle squeeze.

He was obviously uncomfortable, as he side-stepped again and asked if she needed to see the patient. She said she was a hospital administrator, flashed her badge, and said she was just checking on some of their high-risk patients. He nodded politely again and stepped aside to let her into the room. Her seductive smile vanished as soon as she was out of his line of sight. She sighed to herself, and she crossed the room, hating the lustful and overbearing role she had just slipped into. She was unsure of why she was doing what she was about to do, but she continued toward the center of the room. She stopped and pulled the curtain closed and leaned in close to the man lying motionless on the bed.

"I need you to stay quiet. If you are awake and can hear me, tap your fingers on your chest."

The patient slowly brought his hand up and tapped three times with his thick, gauze-wrapped hand.

"Good. Don't say anything. Just listen. You need to stay here for a while to get to a point where you can be transported. There has been a heavily-armed police officer outside your room since you arrived, so I'm guessing you aren't going anywhere but prison once you're well enough to leave. When that time comes, I will make sure that you are nowhere to be found in this hospital." She sighed again, still questioning why she was actually doing this. She let what she had said sink in and hoped that he couldn't sense that she was still unsure if she could go through with it when the time came. "Tap your chest if you understand." Once again, Benjamin Rudley slowly raised his arm and tapped his gauze-wrapped hand on his chest. She stood without another word and exited silently, ignoring the guard completely on the way out the door.

374

Chapter 34

Amanda kept working at CAD and also took on a part-time role as a counselor at a women's shelter in the area. She held sessions where women could tell their stories in a safe and judgement-free environment. She served as a life coach to help women find a way to put their lives back on track, work she found incredibly fulfilling. At first, it was difficult to listen to the stories without remembering all the gruesome details of her own attack, but eventually, Amanda learned to focus on the woman telling the story and leave her own details in the far back corner of her mind. She had survived something that should have been unsurvivable, and she had endured more than any one person should ever have to. She had literally crawled out of a basement after being held captive and tortured. Not only had she survived, but she had found the courage to tell her story and not give up on finding out who was responsible for the unthinkable things that were done to her. She had scars on her wrists, her back, her neck, and even a small one on her lip. They were proof of what she had been through, reminders that would stay with her forever, but she learned to embrace and regard them with a sense of matter-of-fact dignity.

She didn't see the world the same way she once did. She was certainly different from the girl she was in what seemed like another lifetime. But what happened was out of her control, and Amanda knew that. Her short hair fell just below her shoulders now and was always impeccably neat. Her slender body was now lean and toned from several self-defense classes and regular trips to the gym. She had fully accepted the fact that she would have been an entirely different version of herself if she was never attacked. She accepted it but didn't dwell on it. She made a choice to see the good in every day despite the awful things that had happened to her. The young bartender who was quiet but always eager for male attention was long gone. It was partly a product of her growing up, literally, and maturing with age. Most of it, though, was her transition from a young, flirty bartender to a survivor.

She regarded herself with dignity and was proud of the woman she had become. Her journey was an absolutely gut-wrenching, long, and bloody trainwreck, but it was over. When the police reports were finally stapled and filed away, and the scars on her skin became less and less noticeable, it was clear that despite everything that had happened, she had a second chance to be the person she wanted to be.

In the months that followed, things returned back to what Amanda figured would be her new normal. June came to visit quite often. Her father was back at his farm, with a standing plan for dinner with her and Brian at least once a month. In addition to dinner, she visited him as often as she could. Long days spent in the rolling fields and majestic barns of her father's property were better than any therapy session she could pay for. She stood silent one afternoon, gazing across the wide expanse of one of her father's hay fields. The sun was settling itself slowly behind the edge of the field, and it cast a magnificent golden glow on the red barn behind her, along with the few golden-brown hay bales left outside the barn door after the day's harvest.

"Thanks for the help, honey," her father said as he walked over to stand beside her.

"You're welcome, Dad." She swept her gaze across the horizon, stopped to give him a smile, and returned to her position looking out across the length of the field. "It's so quiet here." She tipped her head back and inhaled, drinking in the sweet smell of breezy summer air and freshly-baled hay.

He watched her tip her head back and breathe deeply. He marveled at how much she looked like her mother. He wanted to tell her so, but he let the moment pass in silence. As she lowered her head and looked out across the field again, he followed her eyes and looked where she did. "It's quiet some days," he said with a soft chuckle. "Unless the cows are making a fuss, the chickens get loose, or there are tractors and harvesters running. That one little brown cow with the horns can be a right regular pain some days."

She smiled. "You know what I mean. It is so peaceful. I don't have any clouded thoughts while I'm here, no indecisive moments, just quiet clarity."

"Quiet clarity, huh?" he asked, smirking. "Apparently, I'm not working you hard enough when you come to visit."

She leaned against his shoulder and laughed quietly. "I don't mind the work, either. It feels good to work my hands and arms doing something besides answering the phone and typing on a computer."

"It feels good to have you helping. Some days I really have to make myself remember to not think about how close I came to losing you."

"It's okay, Dad. You don't have to not think about it. I used to feel the same way, that if I didn't remember, it would somehow make it seem like it never happened." She turned to look at him and found his eyes glistening. She continued in order to keep him from feeling like he needed to respond. "It's part of me, though. It's the reason I am who I am today, not some almost-thirty but stuck in her twenty's bartender, searching for the right guy to date. It's the reason I have June in my life, and Brian. It's the reason I have been able to help so many women through their own horrific events. As awful as what happened to me was, I wouldn't be this version of myself if it hadn't. Like it or not, it's part of what makes me *me*."

"You would have been fine, honey," he said, trying to keep his sentences short as he held back silent tears. "You're a smart girl."

"Well, that's very true," she said, smiling, nudging his side with her elbow. It was enough to get him to laugh a little. The two of them stood silent for a while, soaking up the last rays of warm sunshine, being truly grateful to be able to stand together in such a beautiful place. After a few moments, Amanda broke the silence.

"It has been a roller coaster, but I survived, and I'm here."

She patted his arm.

"And for that, I will be forever grateful," he said. He stretched his arm out and put it around her shoulder. She grabbed his hand with hers and squeezed it gently. The sun slowly disappeared behind the horizon, leaving a brilliant pink sky watching over them.

"Me, too, Dad. Me, too."

The End.